REVERIE

REVERIE

RYAN LA SALA

sourcebooks
fire

Copyright © 2020 by Ryan La Sala
Cover and internal design © 2020 by Sourcebooks
Cover design by Leo Nickolls
Cover image © alexey_boldin/Getty Images
Interior design by Danielle McNaughton/Sourcebooks
Internal images © Karlygash/Shutterstock

Published by Sourcebooks Fire, an imprint of Sourcebooks
P.O. Box 4410, Naperville, Illinois 60567-4410
(630) 961-3900
sourcebooks.com

Library of Congress Cataloging-in-Publication Data

Names: La Sala, Ryan, author.
Title: Reverie / Ryan La Sala.
Description: Naperville, Illinois : Sourcebooks Fire, [2019] | Summary: While recovering from an attack that leaves him without his memory, gay teenager Kane Montgomery stumbles into a world where dreams known as reveries take on a life of their own, and it is up to Kane and a few unlikely allies to stop them before they spillover into the waking world.
Identifiers: LCCN 2019023947 | (hardcover)
Subjects: CYAC: Fantasy. | Dreams--Fiction. | Gays--Fiction. | Connecticut--Fiction.
Classification: LCC PZ7.1.L14 Re 2020 | DDC [Fic]--dc23

LC record available at https://lccn.loc.gov/2019023947

Printed and bound in the United States of America.
MA 10 9 8 7 6 5 4 3 2 1

For my sister, Julia, who saw what the world could be
and fought to make it so.

A dream you dream alone is only a dream.
A dream you dream together is reality.

• YOKO ONO •

REVERIE

· ONE ·
SMITHEREENS

THIS IS WHERE IT HAPPENED. THIS IS WHERE THEY found Kane's body.

It was on the verge of September, and the Housatonic River was swollen with late summer's weeping. Kane stood among the bishop's-weed frothing at the bank, trying to imagine what it'd been like the night of the accident. In his mind, being pulled from the river would have been violent. Moonlight sliced to confetti on the black, broken water as paramedics wrenched him up. But this river, during the day, seemed incapable of violence. It was too slow. Just gold water marbled with pollen, kissing his bare legs, and a fleet of silvery fish slowly wreathing his ankles.

Kane wondered if the fish remembered that night. He had the urge to ask them. He remembered none of the accident himself.

All that Kane knew, he'd learned in the five days since waking up in the hospital.

Something struck his head. A pine cone. It bobbed into the water and the silvery fish vanished.

"Stop daydreaming and help me."

Kane blinked, turning to Sophia. She stood on the bank where the weeds pressed up through crumbling pavement. He considered ignoring her, but she had several more pine cones and was a good shot. Actually, Sophia was a good *everything*. Just one of those people. Kane normally resented people like that, but she *was* his younger sister. He adored her. And he was intimidated by her, just a little. Most people were. That's why he'd brought her along today.

"I wasn't daydreaming," Kane said. "I was thinking."

Sophia whipped another pine cone at him, and he batted it away. "I know that look. You were thinking sad and poetic thoughts about yourself."

Kane suppressed a smile. "I was not."

"You were. Remember anything?"

He shrugged. "Not really."

"Well, I hate to distract you from your moping, but you're in full sight of the bridge. Anyone driving by could see you." She was right. The bridge, huge and elegant, hung in the shimmering summer air like a spiderweb. "And we have to meet Mom and Dad at the police station in like…" She checked her phone. "Forty-eight minutes. *And* we're trespassing. *And* you're actually trespassing *again* if you count—"

"I know." Kane let irritation color his voice. "You didn't have to come. You know that, right?"

"Well excuse me for trying to help my brother in his time of crisis."

"I'm not in crisis. I'm just…"

"Confused?"

Kane winced. *Confused.* When he first woke up in the hospital after the accident, when he first realized he was in trouble, it seemed like a good idea to hide behind that word until he could figure out what was going on. The police were asking questions, and the few memories he had from the accident barely made sense. He *was* confused. But now the word felt like a friend he couldn't unmake, always popping up to embarrass him. Discredit him.

"I'm not confused," Kane said. "I'm just trying to clear my name."

Sophia rubbed a smudge of sap on her palm. "Well, you're doing a shitty job."

She was right. He had been acting pretty terrible since the accident. Avoidant. Gloomy. Brittle. But these were things Kane had always been. It was just that now people were looking to him for explanations. They wanted answers, or at least to see a brave survivor of something terrible. Instead they saw Kane: avoidant, gloomy, brittle. No one liked it.

"I heard Mom say that Detective Thistler is doing a psych evaluation with you today," said Sophia. "They're going to ask you a lot of questions, Kane."

"They've already asked me a lot of questions, *Sophia.*"

"You might consider attempting a few answers this time. For instance: Why?"

"Why what?"

Sophia glared at him. "*Why* did you drive a *car* into a *historical site?*"

Staring across the lot at the charred remains of the old mill, Kane's mind went blank. He'd spent every minute since waking up wondering the same thing.

Sophia went on. "Mom said the police won't press charges while you're being evaluated, but I heard that the county might prosecute."

The whole county? Everyone, all at once? Kane imagined the entire population of East Amity, Connecticut, piled into a jury box. It made him smile.

Another pine cone struck his shoulder. He trudged back to the bank, letting his feet dry on the baking pavement as Sophia took pictures of the bridge. Then his feet were dry, and he couldn't stall any longer.

"All right, let's make this quick," he said as pulled on his boots. "I just need to poke around the crash site. Keep taking pictures, okay?"

"Are you sure it's safe to go in there?"

They stared at the mill.

Kane shrugged. It definitely wasn't safe.

Half imploded, the mill sat quarantined behind a web of caution tape. Behind it, rising through the young birch forest, stood the rest of the old industrial complex: a maze of abandoned factories and warehouses that represented the height of East Amity's manufacturing era. They went on for miles, proud and forever, slowly decaying beneath neglect as the forest grew up under them. This place was called the Cobalt Complex. This building before them—the old mill that looked onto the river—was the crash site. The crime scene. The cherished bit of Connecticut history Kane had rammed a Volvo into, which then exploded, one week ago.

He didn't even think cars really exploded on impact. That was movie stuff. Yet the mill, and everything within fifty feet of it, was scorched.

Kane laced up his brown leather boots. The old mill was a symbol of East Amity, appearing in the watercolor postcards sold all around town. Kane imagined the watercolor version of his crash. The dotted glass on the pavement. The inferno rendered in pale, tasteful shades of apricot. Greasy smoke eddying upward in violent, lovely twists against the restrained lavender of sunrise. Very pretty. Very New England.

"Come on, Kane, focus," said Sophia as she dragged him under the tape.

No new memories came to him in the chilled shade of the mill. Instead came an itch, the sort that simmers through your veins. An instinct. It had been crawling beneath Kane's skin since they got here. It said: *You should not have come back.*

Kane stood his ground. He needed answers, and he needed them now.

"Remember anything?"

"No."

Sophia sighed. She prodded a blackened beam.

"Try harder," she suggested. "Use your imagination."

Kane willed himself calm. He tested his weight on the sloping staircase. The fifth step let out a groan, but it held. "I think that using my imagination is the opposite of what I should be doing."

"You make stuff up all the time."

"Yeah, but in this case it might be illegal."

Sophia drifted farther into the inky interior while Kane climbed to the second floor. From below she called, "You never know. Maybe you're suppressing your memories subconsciously."

Kane thought this was a very clever way of making him feel guilty for not being able to produce an explanation. Sophia continued: "Maybe it'll only manifest through, like, art or something. You should try drawing, or painting, or—"There was a small crash that awoke a brood of bats somewhere in the rafters. Sophia appeared at the top of the steps. The bats settled. "Maybe you should decoupage something. You used to decoupage a lot of things."

"You think delivering my testimony as a kitschy craft project is going to convince a judge that I'm not dangerous?"

"Maybe."

"Sophia, that is the gayest thing I have ever heard."

Like a sudden spark, the familiar joke flared between them. In unison, the siblings repeated their favorite refrain: "*Just gay enough to work!*"

They laughed, and for a second, Kane wasn't full of dread.

Sophia hopped over a mess of broken bottles to join Kane on a crumbling sill that overlooked the river. They sat in silence in the mill's stagnant air until Sophia hugged his shoulder. This surprised him; she hated hugs.

"Hey," Sophia murmured. "We're all glad that you're okay. That's what matters most. We should be grateful for just that."

A stitch of guilt pulled tighter in Kane's chest. He agreed that being okay was what mattered most. He just didn't agree that okay was what he was.

"Plus," Sophie said, "your scars are gonna look awesome."

Kane smiled. His fingers itched to feel the tidy network of burns that wrapped like a crown around the back of his head, from temple to temple. They perplexed the doctors. They were shallow and would heal quickly, but sometimes at night they prickled with heat, turning his dreams to smoke and ash.

A gust dragged across the river, hit the shore, and whipped against the hemlocks and birch.

"Have you talked to anyone from school?" Sophia asked.

"Homeroom sent a card. The librarians sent flowers."

"What about friends?"

"Lucia sent a note."

"Lucia is a lunch lady, Kane."

Kane chewed the soft flesh of his cheek. "I know that."

"I know you know that. But what about people in your grade?"

"Umm…" Kane felt her consideration as a physical thing. "Homeroom sent a card."

Sophia let this go, and he was thankful for it. In the past, Sophia had taken it upon herself to conjure him a social life, which she assured him would do wonders for his self-esteem. *Wonders!*

Always said with jazz hands. It was a well-intentioned hobby of Sophia's but had always deeply embarrassed Kane, who did not think he had low self-esteem to begin with. He just wasn't like Sophia, who needed to befriend everyone and everything. No, Kane liked to think of himself as *Discerning!* with jazz hands.

And besides, if he truly wanted to, Kane could talk to people. But why risk it? It felt unnatural. It was better to resign himself to safer companions: dogs, plants, books, and Lucia the lunch lady, who gave him extra fries on Pizza Tuesdays.

Something poked Kane's cheek. He swatted Sophia away. "What?"

"I said that I overheard Dad on the phone with the police today. They said that your accident...wasn't looking like an accident. That the whole thing seemed deliberate and thought out, and they wondered if maybe you were trying to..."

The cicadas simmered through the silence, an invisible crowd gossiping around them. Kane had to be careful with his words now. Sophia had asked a question without asking it.

"I wasn't trying to kill myself," he said.

"How can you know that if you say you can't remember that night, or the months leading up to it?"

Kane could feel each jagged edge of denial in his throat. He tried to force it up but it cut and clawed. He just *knew*.

"Kane, two days is a long time to go without calling. And stealing Dad's car? That's larceny. And I know you don't want to talk about it, but if you don't clear your psych evaluation, Mom says that you might have to go live—"

8

"Stop it," Kane said, harsh now. "Look, I'm sorry. I wish I could tell you more. I wish I knew where I was, or what I was doing."

In a small voice Sophia said, "Or who you were with."

"What?"

"Well, someone must have pulled you out of this burning building and then helped you to the river. They should have checked your body for fingerprints."

Of everything, this unsettled Kane the most, as though he could feel the grip of ghosts upon his flesh. He felt the way the mill looked: history, in smithereens, haunted with the sort of shadows that squirm.

"Not that you can leave prints on a body," Sophia said. "I checked."

A familiar sense bristled over Kane. Sophia had always thought of him as a bit of a project. Had she made investigating the accident her latest focus? Did she know more about this than she was letting on?

"What else do you know?"

Kane might have noticed Sophia look away too quickly if he wasn't watching a shadow behind her break away from the wall and scamper, huge and spider-like, across a doorway.

"Something's in here," he whispered.

"What?"

He pulled her beneath the sill and along the wall, his eyes never leaving the doorway. "Something's in here," he repeated. "I saw something move."

"Kane, relax, it's probably a bat."

Just then they both heard a creak on the stairs—the cry of the

9

fifth step. Whoever it was must have known they'd given up their position. The mill shook as something large and fast thundered up the stairs and burst onto the second floor.

Kane and Sophia dashed into the closest room—one with a vaulted ceiling blackened by soot, a floor rotted through, and a heavy metal door. Kane swung it shut and slammed down the latch a moment before something rammed into the other side. The hinges screamed, but the latch held. Again and again something tried to muscle through, the ceiling releasing clots of dust with each impact. Then came the awful sound of metal scraping metal. A key, maybe? Or claws?

"There!" Sophia pulled Kane toward a window leading onto a roof so badly damaged it looked ready to cave in. Together they picked across sagging, broken beams. Inside the building, the shadows boiled—unreal, massive shapes that scuttled through the darkness below, tracking them.

"Kane!"

He caught Sophia's wrist just as her leg plunged through a rotted portion of the roof, but their weight was too much. In a plume of dust and decay, the roof tilted beneath them, throwing them down so hard Kane's teeth snapped together.

They were...outside? They'd tumbled over the mill's back edge. Around them shivered desiccated ferns bathed in thick yellow light. Behind them the structure continued to shake ominously. Kane's hand found Sophia and they ran, crashing through the forest of scorched saplings as a portion of the mill collapsed completely. Splinters showered their backs.

Kane threw a glance over his shoulder and saw a towering shadow printed upon the rolling cloud of dust and ash, so tall it could have been a tree. But then it turned and, finding them, lunged forward.

Kane focused only on keeping up with Sophia as they shot into the Cobalt Complex's sprawling maze of ancient buildings, pitted roads, and equipment overgrown with ivy, to the edges where rotten fences held back the forest. They'd hidden Sophia's car in the neighborhood that backed up against the mill, behind a wall of mountain laurel.

"Well, shit," Sophia said as she flung herself into the driver's side. She gulped breaths. "That was—"

The sound of sirens cut into Kane with the finality of a guillotine as a police cruiser rolled out of the shade, stopping before their idling car. Sophia let loose an elaborate string of bad words.

"Mr. Montgomery, we thought it might be you," said one. Kane couldn't even look her in the eye. "Step out of the car, please."

Together, they scooted from the car. Sophia shook off her shock first. "You don't understand. We were just walking along the path when this *thing* came out of nowhere and chased us. This massive animal…"

Sophia's voice fizzled out, leaving Kane to wonder if she'd seen the shadow that chased them. One officer said something into their radio. The other turned to Kane. "The Cobalt Complex is a crime scene, Mr. Montgomery."

Kane's mouth was dry. He nodded.

"And private property."

Nod.

"That you've trespassed on once already."

The world went wobbly beneath him. He grabbed the car's hood to keep from falling. What the hell were those things? There was no way to describe them and no point in doing so. The police wouldn't believe any of it. They would think Kane had caused the damage to the mill himself. Again.

Holy shit.

"It was my idea," Sophia blurted. "It was, I swear. I asked to come here. I wanted to see...to see it all for myself. The mill. Kane didn't even want to come. I made him come back. Please don't get him in more trouble."

The officers eyed Sophia incredulously. Her hair, the color of cocoa powder, had come unbraided and floated around her jaw, a few strands caught in glistening spit at the edge of her frown. She had on her Pemberton uniform—the all-girls private school in town, which was an honorable and mysterious institution that gave all the locals a superstitious pause—but it was a mess from their run. Still, the cops paused.

One nodded toward Kane. "Detective Thistler let us know you've got an appointment with him and your parents this afternoon."

"Yeah," Kane said. "We were on our way. We'll head over right now, I promise."

Everyone waited to see if a consequence would happen, and it did. The same officer rounded the cruiser and popped open the back door. "Miss, you head home. Kane, grab your stuff. You're coming with us."

· TWO ·
THE WITCHES

THE EAST AMITY POLICE STATION HAD THREE INTER-
view rooms. Two of them were simple boxes of concrete, contain-
ing only steel tables and steel chairs. Interrogation chic. The third,
Kane was told as he was led through the halls of the station, was
called the Soft Room. It had couches, a basket of plastic gerani-
ums flanked by tissue boxes, and a lamp.

Kane clung to these details. No one was going to torture him
in a room with upholstered couches, right? The blood would soak
into the fibers. It'd take a small pond of seltzer to scrub out.

No one had told Kane what was going to happen to him.
They weren't allowed to talk until his parents arrived, which made
him want to throw up. He wondered what would happen as he
pulled himself into a knot of shivering limbs on the couch. He
wondered if a person could shiver apart. If they could, would it

happen slowly, or all at once, like a Jenga tower flying apart after one, singular piece is oh-so-carefully removed?

Kane became sick of wondering. He held himself tighter and clutched a book—*The Witches* by Roald Dahl, a favorite he'd stashed in his backpack. He'd grabbed it from Sophia's car before he was dragged off in the police cruiser. He turned the pages every few minutes, but only pretended to read in case he was being watched.

Were the police meeting with his parents separately? Should he text Sophia? His phone had been lost in the crash, but he had her old one on loan.

Kane turned another page, though it wasn't words he saw but the shadow from the Cobalt Complex. His mind drifted over it, tentative, like approaching the memory of a dream you know will break apart if it sees you coming. Even at the edges, he knew there was something messed up about what he'd seen. Something unreal and unbelievable.

He shook off the notion. He couldn't afford *unbelievable* right now. He needed to figure out a way to explain all of this. A *real* explanation for what *really* happened. And he needed to figure it out before Detective Thistler did.

Kane tensed at the thought of Thistler, who wore a suit with a badge clipped to his belt, who smelled like cigarettes and spearmint. Thistler was always smiling when he questioned Kane, like he thought they were about to share a secret adventure. Kane had a fear of people who smiled too much, and Thistler proved why. In their first meeting at the hospital, Thistler laid out Kane's circumstances in a cheerful, rushed explanation, like someone enthusiastically describing their odd hobby. He let loose terms like "Third-Degree Arson" and "Permanent Record" with a flourish. When Kane was suitably panicked, Thistler started his strange, meandering questions about Kane's life. Did Kane have a girlfriend? *No.* A boyfriend? *Not yet.* Did he participate in any clubs at school? *No.* How did he feel about school? *Good.* And so on.

Toward the end of their two hours, Thistler began circling in on something much larger than useless details about Kane's life. He was targeting Kane's stability. The questions turned pointed. Why do you find yourself lying to avoid people? *I…I…don't.* Why would you decide to hurt yourself? *I wouldn't. I didn't.* You seem angry. Does talking about what you did make you angry? *Yes, but*—Why is that?—*but I didn't do what you think.* You seem upset. Why are you upset?

Kane awoke to the insidious craft of these questions too slowly to work his way out of them. It was as though the lights had come up on a stage he didn't know he was standing on, revealing a play he didn't realize he was performing in. The play was a tragedy. He was the lead: a gay boy, lonely, suicidal, brimming with angst. He had played his part beautifully.

Even now, Kane's whole body burned in humiliation. His parents had been there. They'd whispered with Thistler after, in the hall, and their whispering continued until the next day when they sat Kane down and told him about the psych evaluation. Kane's second chance.

"You're a Montgomery," Dad had said. "That means something in this town, you know. Your uncle is on the force."

"You're lucky," Mom had said. "They're giving you a chance to prove you're committed to helping yourself. Not everyone gets that, sweetie."

"You're screwed," Sophia had said. "They think you're nuts. You're gonna have to figure this out for yourself. Prove them all wrong."

And that's how they'd ended up at the mill.

Fear splintered through Kane's guts. If he made it through this conversation with Thistler, he promised he'd never go back to the Cobalt Complex. He'd never even wonder about it.

The door to the Soft Room opened.

Kane burst to his feet. "Detective Thistler, I can explain—"

But it wasn't Thistler at the door, or even Kane's parents. Framed in the cold light of the hallway was someone entirely new to Kane's small, disastrous world.

"Mr. Montgomery? I hope you weren't waiting long in this dim, sad place. I left as soon as I got the call."

The person said this with humor, in a voice adorned with theatric flourish that warmed the small room. They wore a fitted suit sashed at the waist and sleek pants trimmed in satin, all of their outfit rendered in a rich, golden fabric that revealed an elusive pattern beneath the lamplight. Even their skin glowed with a gold luster, shifting as they sat. Kane sat, too, a bit dazzled by the person's faultless face, which would not allow him to answer the question as to whether this person was a man, a woman, both, or neither.

They slipped a pad of paper from their bag and peered at Kane through curled lashes.

"What, you've never seen a man in mascara?" he said, answering the question on Kane's face.

"I'm sorry." Kane's cheeks burned. How often had this man caught people staring? How many times had he been asked that question? How many more times had he answered it without being asked, just for the sake of people uncomfortable with ambiguity, who ignored what this person had to say while instead wondering viciously at his identity?

"I'm sorry," Kane repeated. "I didn't mean—"

The person pinched the air, snuffing out Kane's apology. Kane sat a bit deeper in his shame. This was not a person usually found in suburban Connecticut. This was not a person Kane knew how to hide from. He found instead a need to impress them.

"You're not Detective Thistler," Kane said, even though it couldn't be more obvious.

"Ah, how astute. They told me you were a clever one." The man winked conspiratorially, making Kane grin. "Thistler is occupied with…I don't know. Whatever occupies the pathologically heterosexual. Perhaps trying to find just one more use for his three-in-one shampoo–conditioner–body wash? Maybe he ought to use it as a mouthwash, too? It might help that dingy rainbow of a smile he keeps showing everyone."

Kane outright laughed, surprising himself.

"Anyhow. It'll be just you and me today, Mr. Montgomery. You may call me Dr. Poesy."

Kane was fascinated by Dr. Poesy, especially by his conspicuous queerness. He was not naïve enough to dismiss this similarity

17

between himself and the doctor as a coincidence, because (and as a rule) Kane didn't believe in coincidences. Life so far had shown there was something awful and determined about the way the world put itself together for people like him. A seductive sort of unluckiness that repeated in infinitely small and cruel ways. And at first Kane thought Dr. Poesy was part of that wicked design. A further unluckiness, sent to trick him one more time. But how could someone so like him be bad for him? Deep in his distrust, Kane felt something long lost blink to life: hope. This meeting wasn't a coincidence, but perhaps it wasn't unlucky, either. Maybe Dr. Poesy was good. Maybe he was here to help Kane break free from the wicked designs of his life. Maybe, just maybe, Dr. Poesy was the brighter edge of fate.

The thought stung Kane's eyes. He bit down the emotion, telling himself this new hope was dangerous. He needed to stay on guard. Wiping his face clean of emotion, he asked, "You're the psychologist, aren't you? You're here to do my psych evaluation, right?"

"I'm one of many people here to help you," Dr. Poesy said. "And yes, I am here to evaluate, though today we're only talking. Your parents have been informed and have left the station for the evening."

"Do they know what happened?"

Dr. Poesy's smiled impishly. "Not quite. I told the officers to let me handle them, and I haven't yet decided what I'll say. I suppose I'll decide during this meeting."

Kane drew back a bit. Was that a threat? What did that mean?

"I see you've brought a book. What is it?"

"Oh." Kane was still clutching *The Witches.* "Nothing. A kid's book."

Dr. Poesy gazed at it. His eyes held a color that slid between black, blue, and oblivion.

"Witches interest me," Dr. Poesy said. "If you look at most female archetypes—the mother, the virgin, the whore—their power comes from their relation to men. But not the Witch. The Witch derives her power from nature. She calls forth her dreams with spells and incantations. With poetry. And I think that's why we are frightened of them. What's scarier to the world of men than a woman limited only by her imagination?"

Kane sat forward. He sensed he was supposed to respond, but how? Was this part of the evaluation? He hadn't been careful with Thistler. He would have to be with Dr. Poesy.

"It's just a book," Kane said cautiously.

Dr. Poesy flipped through a file. A golden pen appeared in his hand, and it waggled haughtily as he wrote something.

"So, in your own words, Mr. Montgomery, why are we here?"

"I was in a car accident."

"Painting in broad strokes will get you nowhere with me. Try again."

"I…" Kane flattened his voice. Steeled himself. He knew what needed saying. "I ran away a week ago today. I stole a car from my parents, and I drove it through the Cobalt Complex after a big storm. I lost control of the car near the river and crashed into a building. The car caught on fire. So did the building. I got out and the police found me in the river. I passed out and went into a brief coma, but I woke up in the hospital later. I'm in a lot of trouble. I don't remember any of it."

Dr. Poesy looked at Kane for a long time. "And, of course, you were back at the mill today. Did you remember anything?"

"No." It wasn't a lie, but should he tell Dr. Poesy about the thing that chased them? How could he even begin to describe what happened without sounding even guiltier?

But Dr. Poesy moved on. "Why does a runaway return home, just to steal a car?"

Kane's mind hiccupped. No one had asked him this yet. "I don't know. I don't remember doing it."

"How does a mostly brick building catch fire in the rain?"

"The…the car must have exploded or something."

"That's cinematic, but not usually how cars work. There were, however, traces of gasoline found all over the crash site."

Kane frowned. "Cars run on gasoline. Gasoline explodes."

Dr. Poesy tapped the gold pen against his temple. "Clever." Then he wrote something down.

"What are you writing? I didn't set that building on fire on purpose."

Dr. Poesy continued to write. "I didn't say you set it on fire at all, but that's a curious thought."

Kane slumped backward, horrified. "I wouldn't…I mean, I didn't—"

Dr. Poesy held up a quieting hand once again. "I'm going to be honest with you, Mr. Montgomery, in a way that no one else will be honest with you, because I understand you, and I understand

your misfortune. Know that I want what's best for you, and so even if my honesty is harsh, it is not cruel." He waited for Kane to give a consenting nod before continuing. "First, your story of your misadventure is clearly false. None of it quite works, does it? You attempted to vanish, but very poorly. You destroyed your cell phone, yet what little you posted online you didn't bother to delete. You stole a car from your own family, but not cash or credit cards. You drove this car, miraculously, through several security perimeters in a very direct route to the river, before swerving at the last minute into a building. A crash of this sort would kill a person, normally, but the EMTs found you conscious and mostly unharmed, sitting in the river several yards away, so you couldn't have been in the car upon impact. Do you know how they described you in the police report? 'Polite and detached.' Those are the exact words. The report says they found you sitting in the shallows, humming to yourself and picking apart flowers. And, only after you were safe, did you suddenly lapse into a coma. That's odd, too, I think."

Kane could feel the deep frown on his face, and he forced it away. It was too hard to look at the doctor, so he focused on his clenched fists instead.

"None of it works, does it?"

Kane shrugged. It was all he had.

Dr. Poesy sat back. "And here is where I will tell you the actual truth, Mr. Montgomery. My colleagues disagree with my decision to do so, but I feel it is important you understand the reality of the situation in which you find yourself. Or, at least, the reality so far."

The lighthearted act was gone, replaced by an inscrutable, clinical stare. When Dr. Poesy smiled, it was like he had just learned how; all in the mouth, nothing in the eyes.

"What do you mean?"

"I mean that your story takes place within a much larger story, an ongoing case bigger than the scope of your small town's police department. You've managed to attract the attention of some very powerful, very bad people, Mr. Montgomery, who will go to extraordinary lengths to keep you silent about what you witnessed. As fortune would have it, I reached you first. I can protect you."

Kane squirmed. "Am I in danger?"

Dr. Poesy dipped a manicured hand into his bag and placed a small square of paper on the table between them. Absurdly, it was one of the postcards Kane had been thinking of before. The ones that showed the mill painted in wistful watercolor.

"Let me introduce you to the work of Maxine Osman," Dr. Poesy said. "She was born in the year nineteen forty-six and has been a fixture of East Amity for seventy-four years. She married, but her husband died eons ago. She has no children. She used to head the East Amity Craft Guild. She is known for the watercolors she completes every year for the East Amity tourism board. In fact, she's most known for her seasonal series of the Cobalt Complex, completing twelve every year for the official East Amity calendar. Her favorite subject was the old mill, which you blew up."

Kane stared at the postcard. There was something he knew here. Something important he couldn't quite grasp.

"You think a painter is going to come after me because I burned down the mill?"

Dr. Poesy pinched the bridge of his nose. "She was set to paint the mill the morning of your crash. She was set to paint it at sunrise, about when the crash happened."

Kane tried again. "I'm really sorry. I can apologize to her."

"No," Dr. Poesy said. "You can't apologize to her, Mr. Montgomery, because she's dead."

Kane's eyes went wide, dry and unblinking. "She's…what?"

"Dead. Deceased. Departed."

"I know what dead is."

And then Kane realized what Dr. Poesy was saying, and the air went out of the room. The doctor smiled wider, now speaking with deliberate easiness. "Maxine had a small box of supplies she brought with her to her painting sites. Aluminum, with clasps and a handle. In it would have been her paints and brushes. Other artists' tools." Dr. Poesy's eyes were feline in nature. Kane felt that if the lights were to switch out, the cobalt of those eyes would turn to moony disks. "That box was found among the ashes of the mill, melted shut. What's clear is that you were present for Maxine's final painting. What is less clear is *why*."

Kane's eyes stung. He couldn't resist the compulsion to run his fingers over his burns, to hide behind his white knuckles. Dr. Poesy leaned forward, intrigued by Kane's reaction, as though he already knew Kane was guilty.

"Your parents do not know about Maxine Osman. The police do not know, either. I am not your appointed psychologist, as Thistler believes, nor do I answer to the East Amity Police Department. I answer to forces much more powerful. Those forces have an interest in Maxine's disappearance. Those forces wish to keep this investigation a secret, and your involvement risks that secret, but I do not believe you are a risk yourself, Mr. Montgomery. I believe you are an answer."

Kane thought he had known fear, but this new horror recalibrated all the bad he'd gone through so far. This was so much worse than he thought. It must have been a long time before Kane answered, or maybe he never answered at all, because the next thing he heard was a ringing, hammering laugh.

"Do not look so aghast, Mr. Montgomery. I do not think you murdered Maxine Osman. I'm not sure who did. That's why we're here, together."

Kane shook off his shock. He couldn't lose himself now.

"You need my help figuring out the murderer?" he asked.

"Ah, so you *are* smart! Yes, I have a proposition. A bit of homework for you." From their bag Dr. Poesy pulled a notebook and handed it to Kane. It was thin and had a supple red leather cover so bright Kane thought the color would stain his hands. It came with its own golden pen in a leather loop, and the pages were blank except for the first, which read *My Dream Journal.*

"You want me to keep a dream journal?"

"Of course not." Dr. Poesy laughed. "I may not be your real psychologist, but you are still under my evaluation, and as long as that's the case, the police cannot touch you. Keeping this journal, along with weekly check-ins with me, should give you the time and inspiration you need to give me the information I want about Maxine Osman and your incendiary evening together. Do this for me, and I will handle the rest."

Kane's voice was a pale-blue whisper. "But I told the police everything I know."

Dr. Poesy smiled. "You and I both know there is more to your story. Perhaps you've lied. Perhaps you haven't. Perhaps your dreams will reveal what your waking mind cannot bear. It does not matter, so long as it makes it onto those pages. No detail should be considered irrelevant. Withhold nothing, or I will know. You have three weeks."

"But…"

Kane stopped himself. What was he doing, revealing how little he knew? Dr. Poesy had just said Kane was untouchable so long as he was being evaluated. If Dr. Poesy lost faith in his ability to be useful, the evaluation ended, and Kane's freedom winked out like a light.

Dr. Poesy crossed his legs at the ankle. He draped his hands, one over the other, at the knee, and a flare of gold chain on his wrist caught the lamplight. Kane stared at it, helpless beneath the fear and panic surging through him.

"Look at me."

Kane looked. Dr. Poesy leaned over the table, daring Kane to join him in a new, hushed closeness.

"There is a dangerous truth within you, Mr. Montgomery, that not even the most competent artifice will conceal for long. And, as with all dangerous truths, the trick to surviving it is letting it out in a way you can control." Dr. Poesy leaned even closer. "People like us? We must tell our stories ourselves, you know, or else they will destroy us in their own violent making. And I assure you this truth will destroy you, too, if you're not careful. It'll crack you apart from the inside out"—Kane lurched back, Dr. Poesy's fingers snapping an inch from his face—"like an egg."

Kane's throat was raw as he sucked in a deep breath. The Soft Room pulsed. He could not believe this person was accusing him of lying *and* blackmailing him into keeping a journal. A fake *dream* journal. Absurdly, he was overcome with the urge to tell Sophia she'd been right. He was being told to figure out his testimony through arts and crafts, after all.

"I understand," Kane whispered.

"Grand," Dr. Poesy said, softening. "I thought you might. Now, when we leave this room, I want the blood back in your face. A pep in your step. We've only just been getting to know each other, haven't we?"

Kane got the hint. "Of course."

Together they left the Soft Room, walking through the station and the doors that buzzed when they were unlocked. In the lobby, Kane and Dr. Poesy exchanged goodbyes, and Kane rushed to the double doors.

"Kane."

Dr. Poesy stood back in the lobby, fiddling with the cuff of his right wrist.

"Be careful. The things we cannot outrun are the things we must fight, and you are no fighter. You will need help. You will need me, and I do not provide for liars."

26

Kane saw the shadowy monster in the clouds of dust and light. He saw it turning, slowly, its eyeless head stopping to consider him. And of course he had run. And Dr. Poesy knew.

A pair of officers walked by. Dr. Poesy smiled vacantly, handing Kane something. The postcard. "I want you to have this. A bookmark, so you will always know your place."

His face burned as he took it. He held it close as he shoved through the double doors of the police station, fleeing back into the embrace of summer and the singing of cicadas.

THREE

BEWARE OF DOG

AS SOON AS KANE WAS OUTSIDE, HIS PHONE ERUPTED
in a million messages, all of them from Sophia. They were coming
in too quickly to read, so he just called her as he hurried away from
the station.

"Kane? Where have you *been*?"

"At the police station. I'm fine. Where are Mom and Dad?"

"They're at the house. Didn't you see my texts?"

Kane walked faster. He had the urge to run, but people were
still out and about in the town center. The sun was still setting.

"I haven't read them yet. What happened?"

"You tell me. I don't get it. I got home and Mom and Dad
pulled in twenty minutes later, saying the meeting was canceled
and that you were meeting a counselor for your evaluation, or
something. I told them I'd pick you up, but that was two hours

ago! So then I told them we were grabbing Froyo. I think I bought us some time to talk."

Kane was not comforted by this. He suspected his meeting with Dr. Poesy was unofficial, somehow. No paperwork. Nothing to document what they'd talked about. A blank yawn in his life. Just like the accident.

"What happened, Kane? Where are you?"

Kane bit into the flesh of his cheek, trying to decide if he should lie or not. Sophia was already overinvolved in this.

"Nothing bad happened. I just met with a counselor, like they said. I had to write out some answers for a report and talk about my feelings. It was dumb." The lie left him feeling more alone than ever.

"Where are you? I've just been reading at Roost. I'll come get you."

"I want to walk home."

"You're not supposed to be alone. Mom said I should—"

"Lie for me again, will you?"

Kane hung up and turned off the phone. He had the urge to throw it into the rhododendron that bordered St. Agnes, the university at the heart of East Amity. He cut through the campus, speeding toward Harrow Creek.

East Amity was an ill-conceived town, a concrete canvas thrown over the sodden greenery of the Housatonic's flood lands. For that reason the fabric of the suburban grid was eaten through in places, sunken by ravines that filled with rainwater and grew fuzzy with forests. Harrow Creek ribboned through these small forests, hemmed to the land by a running path. It was the least direct route home. But it was safe. No cars could drive alongside it looking for him. No little sisters out searching for their brothers.

Kane needed time and space to think, and the path had always given him both.

He looked up through the birch trees that webbed across the dimming sky. By the time he was alongside the creek, night shaded the distance and drew a curtain of shadow right up to the path's edge. Every few yards stood a glowing lamppost wreathed by moths, neon and frantic. Down a steep bank the creek slid over its bed of worn rocks, silent and unbothered and everything Kane was not. On the path two kids scraped by on scooters, followed by their parents. They stared at Kane, which is how he realized he looked as dismal as he felt.

Kane took out the postcard Dr. Poesy had given him, his hands shaking. In the corner were the initials *MO*. Maxine Osman. Smothering dread curled in Kane's throat as he forced himself to stare into the painting's pleasant colors. The image wasn't any different now that its creator was dead, yet it somehow brimmed with new life. It was all that was left of her, and so in a way it was where she existed now. Trapped, in her own watercolor world.

Kane thought of how he had stood and looked at the mill, imagining it in the dreamy brightness of watercolor. At the time it had felt like just another daydream, but now? He itched with his usual instinct to run, to hide. To stop himself from discovering anything else.

He knew now it wasn't a daydream before—it was a memory.

Waves of anxiety bubbled up from his stomach. What had he done? Who was he? He didn't want to remember, but he also didn't have a choice. The truth was his *only* choice if he wanted to survive this story, Dr. Poesy had said.

Kane breathed steadiness into his nerves, imagining their frantic energy drifting from his hands as waves of writhing static. He shook himself out, hopping in a small circle, then hopping in the reverse direction to undo the coil. These small rituals often worked for him, and the tension eased from his body. He had made it this far, hadn't he? He wasn't going to let himself crack apart now.

"I'm not an egg," Kane told the night, pulling out the journal. Into its soft leather cover, he whispered, "I'm not an egg."

By now his only company on the path were the clots of gnats around his head, and the moths, and the occasional glimmer of moonlight on the creek's edges. When he reached a bench beneath a lamp, he slumped into it and opened the journal.

Experimentally, Kane clicked the pen twice. It made a clean, expensive sound. He clicked it six more times, then drew a few squiggles.

"What your waking mind cannot bear," Kane muttered, printing the words in careful letters. He read them over and over, until they no longer looked like words, finally turning to the postcard.

Whatever had happened to Kane, it somehow connected him to Maxine Osman. This meant he needed to learn everything he could about her. Already he had some details. He wrote down her name. Dr. Poesy had said she was born in 1946, which made her seventy-four. Kane didn't add *when she died*, because he refused to know that. Not yet. Poesy had also said she'd always lived in East Amity, but where? And she did paintings for the tourism board, a series for the town's calendar. One such calendar was hanging in Kane's kitchen right now, had hung there every year since Kane was little. In a way, he'd known Maxine Osman all his life.

Now what?

Kane thought of the frustration that boiled through him—fine and corrosive, like soda bubbles—when he stepped into the water near the mill and felt nothing. He thought of watercolors, and of what Sophia had said about how someone must have dragged him from the fire. He didn't think an old lady had rescued him, which meant someone else had to have been involved.

But who?

Hunched on the bench, Kane penned in a version of what had happened that afternoon at the mill, sanitizing it for Dr. Poesy. When he got to the part where they were running, specifically when he looked back to see what chased them, he stopped. He still didn't know what he'd seen. The more he imagined it, the more he remembered. It had not moved like a person, one leg at a time. It moved like a spider, every leg at once.

Chills spread over his body, the night turning cold on his thighs. He tapped his boots against the pavement, eight taps each side then eight taps together. He should go home. Get inside. Dr. Poesy had warned Kane about those that wanted to keep him silent. What did that mean?

And then it hit. Dr. Poesy believed Kane had been with Maxine Osman when she died but had not killed her. That meant two things: someone else had murdered Maxine Osman, and that someone knew who Kane was.

Why hadn't Dr. Poesy pointed this out? Kane's hand tightened around the pen. He was about to stand when a gleam like moonlight on a blade drew his eye across the creek. He squinted into the flat darkness.

There it was again: an edge of light floating above the creek's other bank. His heart raced as a portion of shadow shifted, and the glare vanished. Was it a wolf or maybe a bobcat? East Amity was nestled in rolling forests and sometimes the animals got curious, but something about the shadow seemed unnatural in a familiar way.

He clutched the journal as he crept to the edge of the path, his eyes never leaving the other bank. Whatever it was, he couldn't see it now, and so he listened for the sound of splashing to determine if it was coming closer. Instead, he heard a needling click, like claws on smooth stone. And it was right behind him.

Something massive scampered over the bench, knocking Kane's backpack to the ground. Dimly he registered a great many legs, long and multi-jointed like a gigantic spider, all fused together in a grotesque jumble. It skittered backward, sprawled out, and then leapt straight up into the trees.

Kane's heart jammed against the back of his ribs. Too scared to even scream, he grabbed his backpack and sprinted toward the end of the path. Around him the night filled with wind and chanting cicadas, a strange sort of laughter that filled Kane with white-hot dread. Those legs. He couldn't unsee those legs. There was no cloud of dust this time. Nothing hiding the thing that had chased him and his sister from the mill earlier that day.

It had found him, and it was going to finish him off.

Kane hit a bend in the path that sloped up toward the road. He threw a glance backward. The beast swayed from the lamppost, like a cocoon of shadow. A spindly leg separated from the main body and plucked something up. *The Witches.*

Kane tripped over himself and crashed to the ground. His hands stung, his fingernails jammed with grit. He was almost upright when he heard that clicking again, ahead of him now. He drew back a second before another mass of legs skittered over the path to block his exit.

"Leave me alone!" Kane shouted, hurling his backpack at the thing before running toward the creek. He dove into the reeds, muck sucking him down to his knees in the creek's sulfuric stink. Unblinking, his eyes ticked between the two banks, watching for movement. He waited, clutching the red journal for security.

And waited. The night waited with him, totally silent.

Then there came a voice: "Hello? Is someone down there?"

A girl appeared on the path, peering into the reeds. Crickets chirped and water slapped. "Hello?" she called again. Kane knew he should warn her, but he couldn't breathe. Shamefully silent, he waited for the darkness to grab her with its many legs, but nothing happened.

The girl jumped down the bank. "Hello? I can see you. Are you okay?" She was much bigger than Kane, dressed in running gear, and she held his muddy backpack. She stopped short when she saw him.

"There was something…" Kane began. Where did he begin? Should he even try to explain?

There was a beat of stillness as Kane and the girl realized they knew each other, and then so much dread settled on Kane he felt like he would sink right back into the mud.

"Kane?"

"No," he blurted. "It's not. I'm not."

Ursula Abernathy, another junior at Amity Regional, shifted from foot to foot. Broad and powerful, she was a star athlete on the track team. Or maybe the field hockey team? Kane just knew she did sports often, and she did them well, but that off the field she was super awkward. She'd been picked on a lot growing up. Kane knew because he'd been there for all of it. They'd gone to the same elementary school.

It was pointless trying to lie now that she'd recognized him.

"Fine, it is me," Kane said.

"Are you…okay?"

"Yes."

Ursula waited, clearly ready for an explanation, but Kane had nothing to give. He was too busy with the realization that by morning it would be town-wide news that Kane Montgomery, local gay miscreant, burner of buildings and crasher of cars, was caught nocturnally frolicking in the muddy tributaries of the Housatonic River. He could already imagine Dr. Poesy making a note of this in that stupid file.

Daintily, Kane picked himself out of the muck and padded up the bank, his boots making indecent squelches. Ursula followed at a distance.

"What were you doing down there?"

Kane glanced at her. She was dressed in a ratty, long-sleeved shirt that read in handwritten letters, BEAT PAVEMENT, NOT PEOPLE. TRIATHLON TO END DOMESTIC VIOLENCE. Sweat glazed her pink shoulders, her neck. Her copper hair was pulled into a sloppy bun that looked more like a nest than a hairstyle, and her bangs were a frizzy awning above thick-lashed, worried eyes. She wore no makeup, not even ChapStick from the looks of it.

"Are you sure you're okay?" she asked again.

"I'm fine," Kane lied. He scanned the night for those creatures and, not seeing anything, began scraping the mud from his boots. It was hopeless. He was caked up to his knees. His ass was soaked. His whole body prickled with heat. He wished he could just vanish.

Ursula kept trying to restart the conversation. "I was on a run and I heard something. I didn't know people were on the path so late, so I thought maybe it was an animal, but then I found your backpack, and then I saw you fall into the river, and…"

"I didn't fall into the river."

"Okay, well I saw you sort of stumble into the river, and—"

"I didn't stumble."

A dimple of worry bore into the flesh between Ursula's eyes. "But are you okay?"

Kane looked up at her. "Why are you asking me so many questions? Do I *look* okay to you? Can't you read context clues?"

Another person would have pushed back, but Ursula only tugged at the hem of her shorts and stared at the ground, embarrassed. In the awkward silence there was space for Kane to feel what he always felt toward Ursula Abernathy: guilt. Ursula, like Kane, was an easy target growing up. They should have been friends, but Kane was no nicer to her than anyone else. He was perhaps even meaner, to show just how different they were, or how much more she deserved their classmates' ridicule. A survival tactic of his that he was not proud of. In third grade he'd made a joke about how Ursula Abernathy was adopted from a dog shelter. He didn't remember how it turned into a rumor—only that it was a mistake—but by the next day it was a school-wide legend. He still felt bad about it, especially the part where someone put a BEWARE OF DOG sign on Ursula's desk. Whenever he saw her, he saw her as the red-faced girl facing down a room of kids woofing at her. She looked that way now.

Kane had never apologized. He wondered if she knew it was him.

"I'm sorry," Kane said. "I'm okay, really. Do you…do you want to walk me to the street? I'd appreciate it."

Ursula glanced around, possibly for an excuse not to, but relented. They walked along the path in silence, Kane doing his best not to show that he was still shaking. He played it off as shivering, though the night was warm.

"How's school?" he asked.

This surprised Ursula. "School is school. We miss you."

"We?"

"Yeah, like the teachers and everyone. People were really worried."

"But I'm fine."

Ursula gave him a once-over that told Kane she did not think he was fine. He hated how she stared, like a child at a zoo.

"Well, you know. Your whole… The whole incident with the mill."

"Incident?"

"Right, right. Sorry. Your *accident*. Everyone heard about it from Claire Harrington—her dad's a cop. There were a ton of questions, and the school called for an assembly in the gym and opened up the counselor office hours for anyone who wanted to talk."

The horror Kane felt surpassed everything from the night so far. An assembly. About him? This was his hell, manifested.

"I'm fine. And Claire Harrington makes shit up all the time."

Ursula kept pulling at the hem of her shorts. She rolled her lips together, unsure.

"Everyone was really happy to hear you woke up, even though Mrs. Keselowski said you were still pretty confused, and Mr. Adams said it was important to give you space and privacy."

"Why are the school counselors telling people things?" Kane snapped. "Isn't that like, against their privacy code or something? And I'm *not* confused. And if people really cared about me, maybe they wouldn't make shit up or pry into my business."

Ursula hugged herself. "I'm sorry, I didn't mean it that way."

"Wait." Kane stopped before they reached the road. "You talked to the school counselors? Like, you went to their office hours?"

Even in the darkness, Ursula's face glowed red. She had.

Kane felt something in him soften. He picked his words carefully. "Look. I'm sorry for…I don't know. For whatever this is. For how I am. Thank you for stopping. I know we're not really friends but I appreciate it."

Ursula gave a meek smile. "Any time."

They were at the path's entrance. He expected her to run off, but instead she leaned in as she handed him his backpack and whispered, "Is it true? About your memories? Tell me quickly. They're probably watching."

Kane pulled away. There was a hardness in Ursula's stare now that had not been there a second ago, that had never been there. Right now, there was no meekness about her whatsoever.

"Your memories. Tell me. Please," Ursula pressed. "I need to know."

"I remember everything," Kane said, defensive.

Ursula was unflinching as she assessed this for the lie that it was.

"You don't. It's true. The others were right." She glanced around until her eyes tracked upon something over his shoulder, as though she saw things in the shadows he could not. The hair on the back of his neck rose up, and his burns prickled.

Beware of dog flashed in Kane's mind.

"I remember…" Kane again felt his lost memories trying to guide him. "I remember Maxine Osman."

Ursula's eyes went wide, and Kane knew his guess had struck something. She edged even closer so that cricket song swathed them in chatter, as though she were afraid of being overheard.

"Never say that name again."

"But—"

"I can't help you. You have to find your way back to us on your own, Kane. Check the treasure chest."

And then the old Ursula returned. Meek and unsure. Rounded by anxiety. "It was nice running into you," she murmured, unable to even look him in the eye. "See you back in school."

She jogged toward the path, messy bun bouncing. Kane watched her go, watched the dark where she vanished, and only moved when he felt the dark watching him back.

· FOUR ·
FAR-FETCHED

"KANE. WAKE UP."

Toes jabbed Kane's ribs. He rolled over and pressed his cheek into the rug.

"C'mon. I have to practice."

"Go ahead." Kane yawned. "I like when you play the violin. It's nice."

"*Viola*," Sophia said, jerking open the curtains in her room. He hissed and shriveled up in the late afternoon light, but Sophia didn't laugh. She hadn't been too friendly since he hung up on her a few days ago.

Kane was pretending he didn't care. He yawned. His head hurt. He tried to remember the dream he'd been having, but all he found within himself was the usual soupy gloom. And, beneath the gloom, the same simmering dread that had kept him awake every night since he'd encountered those things on the path. And, of course, Ursula Abernathy. *Check the treasure chest*, she'd said, a riddle that wouldn't let him rest. He only slept during the day now, and only by accident, waking up at the kitchen table with a spoon in his hand, or slumped over in the sunny spot on the landing, or draped across the living room ottoman with his PlayStation still humming.

"Let me guess." She unlatched her viola case. "You've been lying here for hours, despondent."

"Yep."

"Did you eat?"

"Yep."

"What?"

"Fruit snacks."

The instrument hummed in Sophia's hands as she removed it from the velvet interior. "Fruit snacks? Sounds like cannibalism to me."

Kane propped himself up. "Was that a gay joke?"

In response, a pleasant, fat note rang out as Sophia carved the bow across the strings. She smiled at Kane vacantly the whole time, holding it extra long and finishing with a flourish.

"Why yes, it was a gay joke."

Kane frowned. Sophia's face was as blank and cold as the moon now, and she felt just as distant. Secrets were a new and uncomfortable thing between them. He wouldn't tell her about his meeting with Dr. Poesy, or being chased on the path, or Ursula Abernathy. In exchange, he sensed she was keeping her own bank of secrets locked away. And so things had been tense, and her questions had become pointed. Kane had becoming both the prison and the prisoner within their locked-up siblingship.

"You got a haircut," Sophia said.

"Mom tricked me into it to get me out of the house."

"You look like a poodle who was drafted into the military."

"Thank you."

The metronome ticked on as Sophia ran through her warm-up. Kane let his mind drift between the wobbling notes. He wished he could tell her everything, but ever since he'd learned about Maxine Osman, his pain felt fraudulent, unearned, as though Maxine's death forfeited his right to feel bad for his own near-death. The guilt didn't just disarm him; it formed a new armor around him. A heavier guard that made the very idea of asking for help, or even sympathy, impossible. Kane wasn't scared to talk about his pain; he was scared of making other people listen.

So he kept it all to himself. And, just like Dr. Poesy had said, in the absence of his own telling, his story was taken up by others. The *Hartford Courant* ran a piece on the accident, promising a follow-up as the investigation progressed. They didn't name Kane, but they didn't have to. East Amity was small, the town going silent around Kane every time he left the house. People whispered and told their own stories. It had been a very awkward haircut.

The heat of the memory spurred Kane up and out of Sophia's room. He found his mom downstairs in her office.

"Sophia says I look like a poodle that just joined the military."

His mom considered him. There was no denying this. The

barber had left Kane's curls tufted on top and done their best to clean up the hair that had gone crispy around Kane's burns, which were more prominent than ever.

"What about wearing a hat? You used to love to wear your grandmother's beret."

Kane shook his head. He couldn't afford to be any gayer.

"Hmm. I don't know, honey. I think you kind of look rock-and-roll, you know? Like, a tough guy. A tough-guy poodle." She grinned. "Or should I say…a *ruff* guy."

"That's not funny, Mom."

"Well, it certainly seemed to give you…*paws*."

Kane tried not to laugh and failed. Things had been tense with his parents, too, and this moment felt like progress. They had tried everything to get him to open up, but when he simply didn't, their warmth had cooled to firmer kind of love. Something like fear, actually. Moments of easy banter were rare, and Kane leapt at the opportunity to pretend nothing was wrong.

"You're *barking* up the wrong tree," he said.

"That's not really the right pun, Kane."

He rolled his eyes. "Throw me a *bone*?"

"Better, but your jokes are a little far-*fetched*."

"Mom, please. Do I have to go back to school looking like this?"

The question flipped her from Pun Mom into Clinical Psych Mom, which Kane was ready for; she taught psychology to freshman at St. Agnes, and these flips happened a lot more since *the incident*.

"While a haircut is not a good enough reason to *not* return to school, your father and I have been meaning to discuss the option of homeschooling with you. That is, if you feel like the pressure of returning would be a further distraction. Is that something you'd like to have a conversation about?"

Kane's usual gloom closed back over the fleeting brightness he'd just felt. Dread rose up within him like bile. Perhaps the only thing worse than returning to school was spending even more time trapped here. It creeped him out the way the house changed in the late summer's heat, with doors clicking open and rooms taking big breaths when the breezes hit. Plus, his mother wouldn't go into her job, maybe fearing he might hurt himself. Kane imagined himself as a rare bird: well loved, but still caged.

"No, I'll go back. Just…not yet. Okay?"

His mother considered him, then flipped out of psych mode.

"Perhaps going back to school will be the perfect thing for your…"

"What? Another pun?"

"I can't. I'm your mother."

Kane crossed his arms. "Say it."

"Melan-*collie.*"

"You're sadistic."

She laughed, and, because he was not entirely heartless, Kane laughed, too. Then she booted him from her office with a cheery "Dinner is at six, *bitch.*"

Kane wandered through the house. The urge to read *The Witches* came over him, but it'd been lost to whatever had chased him down the night he met Ursula. He considered going back to Sophia's room, but she'd closed her door. Doing some writing in his journal about his fear of school was always an option, but he didn't think that's what Dr. Poesy was interested in. Really, he should be searching for clues and do what he'd been avoiding since he'd gotten home from the hospital.

He should explore his own room.

Kane pressed his forehead against the door, hand hovering over the knob. He'd only entered his room for a few minutes each day, to grab clothes or a book, but then the sheer discomfort of being surrounded by all that stuff drove him out. Most of his things he recognized, but some things were entirely foreign. He hadn't told his parents this yet, or even Sophia, but it proved that much more than the summer was missing from his memory. Whatever happened to him, not all of him had made it back. Maybe not even most of him. So who did that make him, the boy against the door? The boy afraid to enter, trapped outside his own life, afraid to discover just how much he had lost.

Kane reminded himself, again and again, that he was not an egg. Whoever he was, he needed to figure out his own story. Perhaps that was the key to finally coming home.

The door creaked as he entered.

It was a large room shrunken by clutter on every surface. Kane tamped down the prickling unease and began with his desk. It was a waste of half-read books and comics. There were half-filled sketchbooks and half-finished crafts. A birdhouse, half-painted, waited in a dried pool of its own colors atop some newspaper. Kane didn't own a bird. He did own a fish, though.

"Hey Rasputin," he said to the fishbowl. The black betta regarded him nervously, then slid behind a miniature castle.

"Me, too." He pinched a few flakes into the bowl and tried to imagine what it was like to have your food magically appear above you, without warning. Then he thought about how he knew the fish's name, but not where it was from.

Kane moved on to the bookcase, a heavy mahogany beast anchored to the wall because he used to climb it. Kane poked through the knickknacks on the shelves and marveled at what was probably the early signs of a hoarding habit. There were jars of shells from the Connecticut coast, ceramic mugs crammed with bristling paintbrushes, plastic superhero figurines prized from cereal boxes, dingy stuffed animals with threadbare smiles, a milky-eyed antique camera, a handful of sea glass placed meticulously into a figure eight, and books. Countless books, spines cracked and pages spotted and covers peeling and corners rounded. The titles whispered to Kane, bidding for his attention, but he resisted the urge to open up one and close himself within. That was the old Kane. The new Kane needed to focus on the real.

He ran his shaking hands over it all, searching for the holes in his memory. There were many, and without the patina of nostalgia, everything felt like junk. Useless junk.

A few tears creeped from the corners of his eyes, but he pushed them back across his temples. It was not just sadness he felt, but homesickness. He was homesick for a place he could no longer visit, for a home that was no longer his. Then his eyes fell upon the old jewelry box on the very top shelf.

It had been his grandmother's, willed to him when she passed. It was a fitting gift. Kane had always loved to rip open the drawers when he was a toddler, taking the jewels out of their velvet coffins, until one day he managed to lose the key. His grandmother, who loved pranks, told him this meant she'd have to blow it up, jewelry and all, and start her collection over. Kane was so hysterical about it he begged his father for a hammer to crack it open. The tool was solemnly supplied and, to Kane's delight and his grandmother's amusement, just one tap did the trick. It wasn't until years later that his grandmother showed him—and only him—that applying pressure to the topmost drawer's upper-right edge opened the compartments without much fuss. The lock had never worked.

She had called the heirloom her treasure chest.

One room over, Sophia's scale shifted into a minor key. Chills swept over Kane's skin as he remembered the chatter of crickets on the path, and Ursula's words all over again: Check the treasure chest.

The viola's minor scale peaked. Kane dragged the jewelry box to the floor, his hands grazing the familiar ridges until he found the pressure point, and pushed. Something clicked and he eased open the top drawer, half expecting something horrible to crawl out. A swarm of locusts, or some Pandora-style curse. Instead what he found was…

More junk.

A pair of gold-handled sewing scissors, bunches of thread, and a small pincushion shaped like a raspberry stared up at him from a worn velvet backdrop. But in the next drawer he found a photo of two people: the first was curvy and tall, with an untidy knot of red curls and sporting a goofy smile. Her arm was flung around the other person's shoulders with chummy familiarity. Undeniably, unmistakably, it was Ursula Abernathy.

And the other person was Kane.

The flesh of Kane's inner cheek was ragged from his grinding teeth, the bite of blood hitting his tongue a second before he could rouse himself from the shock. He glanced at the old camera on the shelf, then looked at the back of the photo and saw a date: July, just two months ago.

His eyes squeezed shut on their own, unable to see what Kane's mind was already beginning to know. He could hear two things: his heartbeat, and Sophia reaching the height of a major scale.

He dove back into the drawers, pulling them all out and tipping the box upside down until dozens more photos fluttered to the carpet. He spread them out, his dread replaced by a white-hot exhilaration.

There was Ursula, blushing while a clown hugged her. In another, a cloud of electric blue cotton candy hid a person's face. In yet another, Kane straddled a waxy unicorn on a carousel, mouth open wide. A fourth showed Ursula holding Kane in her arms while a mechanical dragon glowed red and exhaled steam.

And finally: Ursula with her back to a ring-toss game; one hand was on her hip and the other proudly brandished a bag toward the camera. The bag was swollen with water, a black fish fluttering in its belly.

Sophia's scales shifted into a minor key, and with them Kane's exhilaration ebbed into a bristling fear. He looked around his room, at the clutter of a life he did not recognize.

Ursula Abernathy was not who he thought she was.

But neither was he.

FIVE

ALWAYS FEED THE BIRDS

AMITY REGIONAL HIGH WAS AN OLD BEAST, SUMMONED from bricks and concrete in 1923 and then barnacled with new additions as the town's population rose. Kane and his father sat in a rental car in the school driveway, watching the mist rise in the morning breeze. It looked suspiciously idyllic.

His dad inched them closer to the doors, killing the engine and throwing Kane a look of grim resignation before asking, "You're sure about this?"

No.

"Yes," Kane said.

"Your mother said just yesterday you were begging not to go back. She talked to the principal. You're allowed to take another week at home."

"No, I want to go back."

No one knew about the photos he'd found; therefore, no one in Kane's family understood his overnight enthusiasm for returning to school, least of all his dad. The two shared a love of avoidance that was practically hereditary in the Montgomery men. Kane hid in the lush worlds of fantasy; his father dwelled in the sparse dimension of architectural drawings. Kane used to imagine them hanging out in that dimension, perched atop translucent buildings made of frost-blue lines and panes of papery whiteness.

"Earth to kiddo."

"What?"

"Do you know him?"

His dad pointed at a boy who had just materialized on the school steps. Kane hadn't even seen him walk by.

Why do parents think their kids know every other kid? Then he realized: if he knew this person, would he even remember? He took a closer look. The boy was staring at the car. Really staring. The clean light of morning lay over a face of brown skin and sharp angles, illuminating two gray-green eyes.

Like sea foam, Kane thought.

The boy must have been deep in thought; tension lined his jaw and neck. Distance yawned in those eyes.

"Don't know him," Kane said. "Come on, let's get this over with."

Kane hurried his dad into the office, where they had to fill out a bunch of paperwork ensuring that Kane was approved to return to school. Or something. He only half listened, unable to stop looking down the hallway, his heart jumping every time someone crossed his periphery.

"Nurse's office next," his dad said, squinting at some forms.

Kane brought him there, losing himself in murky dread as he thought of the photos. He had them in his backpack, ready for when he ran into Ursula and could confront her. He was rehearsing what he'd say. *You know me. You knew me.* He was replaying their conversation on the path over and over. *You told me where to look. You knew.*

Amid a discussion with the nurses about medications, Kane found that he was absolutely furious. The joy of finding out that he had a friend was totally eclipsed by the realization that she had let him believe he was all alone, giving him only a riddle to work out for himself.

Or maybe Kane was making it up. Maybe, like him, Ursula had no idea they were friends. Maybe, like him, her memory was messed up.

Beneath his doubt, Kane knew this wasn't true. Ursula had been on that path for a reason, and that reason was Kane. So why not just tell him?

Back outside the school, his dad pulled him into a tight hug while Kane's body continued to thrum with suppressed rage.

"Kane, you're shaking."

"Nerves."

"You're going to do great, okay? And if you want to come home, just text us."

"Okay."

This was the moment for a heartfelt goodbye, but Kane had just noticed a familiar head of orange hair among the crowd of kids at the bike rack. He gave his dad a bright smile, said he'd be home later, and ran off.

Fifty feet. Twenty feet. Kane pierced through the milling students in the parking lot, rehearsing under his breath as he closed in on Ursula. Ten feet. She was barely done locking up her bike when he stopped short, the rack between them.

The instant she saw him, Kane knew he was right. Her face opened in shock, then closed in careful neutrality.

"Hey, welcome back."

The words Kane had prepared vanished in this throat. All he could think to say was: "I have some questions."

Ursula shouldered her bag and walked away from Kane, who was failing at the confrontation he had imagined dozens of times. Luckily, she turned back.

"You know the old court?"

The old courtyard. Not really a courtyard. Just a slab of concrete penned in by three windowless walls that opened to the wooded area behind the school. An optimal meeting spot for cutting class, smoking, and hooking up. Or so Kane assumed. He'd never done any of that. But he knew what it was.

"Meet me there after homeroom," she said before he could even nod, and then she walked away.

Homeroom was clearly expecting Kane. He burst in, mind buzzing, and only realized there was nervous applause when it ended and a big silence settled.

Everyone watched him, waiting for him to say something.

"Thank you for the card," he mumbled.

Viv Adams raised her hand. Ms. Cohen, who had frozen while writing *WELCOME BACK KANE!!!!* on the whiteboard, seemed hesitant to call on her but did anyways.

"I like your haircut," said Viv.

"Thanks."

"Looks like it hurts."

Someone snickered. The room went electric with cruel energy as the other students bit back laughter. Viv was always calling herself brutally honest, but she was more concerned with being brutal than with being honest. Kane was in no mood.

"No, Vivian, getting a haircut doesn't usually hurt unless, like yourself, your head is neck-deep up your own ass."

"*Mr. Montgomery!*"

And with that, Kane's triumphant return to high school ended in its own fiery crash.

Before he knew it, he was outside the school, in the back court. Alone. Finally.

The first thing he did was shake himself out. Anxiety swirled in his chest as a breeze pulled loose garbage and leaves into a small whirlpool. Dizzy, he dropped onto a flaking picnic table, and soon his journal was in his hands. He recorded the strange events of the day before and the morning, messy and meandering and full of embellishment.

There is something unreal about everything, and I have proof, he wrote, *so why do I feel like I'm making it all up? Why do I have to feel like the crazy one, when it's the world that's wrong?*

Kane tapped his boots on the bench, wondering if it was a mistake to look for answers to who he was by coming to school. He was the least of himself here, and on purpose. Kane's exclusion was one he'd cultivated over years, withdrawing from a world he'd always felt wrong in.

It wasn't due to being gay, or who he was, but instead how he came to be. Kane had been outed pretty young by his eccentricities. Maybe a more astute child would have tried harder to rein themselves in, but Kane was the last to know he was gay and therefore powerless to deny it once he was finally told. He only found out as the other boys began to evade him in elementary school. Sleepover and birthday party invitations dried up. Teachers became overkind, which secured his shame. He became marked. A curiosity placed in the limbo between the worlds of boys and girls.

The limbo yawned wider every year, and no one yet had dared to join him. Alone, Kane felt himself warping into someone who didn't trust anyone. Sometimes he would get messages through the limbo—people reaching out to him through unsigned notes or anonymous emails saying they wished they were out, too—but it was hard to tell which were real. Most of the time, they were pranks from the same sleepovers he wasn't invited to anymore. More than once the conversations got shared throughout the school. Eventually Kane stopped responding.

Statistically, Kane knew he wasn't the only gay person at Amity Regional, but he had been marked in a way that made it risky for others to associate with him. That's what curiosities do:

they draw the eye. No one else wanted to be the focus of the eyes that scrutinized Kane. No one wanted to share his limbo with only him as company. They watched from afar, and Kane made himself at home within his habit of hiding.

People left him alone, which he liked. Not anymore, though. Vivian's comments would be the first of many as Kane's classmates remembered him—and how little they liked him.

In the back court, Kane once again sensed he was being watched. This time it was worse than homeroom because it was not the eyes of a crowd, but the stare of a predator.

Kane looked up.

Twenty yards toward the forest, slashed into the brightening day, stood the shadowy figure of the boy he'd seen that morning. He did not approach. He just stared, the gaze from his eyes radiating such intensity that Kane's bones hummed with the urge to run.

Upon reflex Kane ventured a small wave, which the boy did not return. Instead, he pointed at the journal. Where nothing had been before, a photo jutted from the seams where the pages met. Plucking it out, it showed four pairs of shoes from above. Four people standing in a tight circle, their toes almost touching.

In the photo he recognized his own boots and what he remembered were Ursula's running shoes, but the two other were anonymous: a pair of white ankles in straight-boy sneakers and a pair of gray sandals on brown feet.

Something flashed in Kane's memory, like a far-off lighthouse whisking its beam across black waters, there and gone before he could tread toward it.

When Kane looked back up the boy was gone. Now—inches from where Kane sat—stood Ursula.

"Jesus!" Kane snapped the journal closed over the photo.

"You came," she grinned. She had a hat over her curls, and she wore a neon green windbreaker. Her frostiness from the morning had thawed, but timidity still rounded her posture as she rocked on her feet. Kane looked around. The boy was for sure gone. Scared off when he saw her coming, maybe? How was everyone so able to sneak up on him? Was he that oblivious?

"You wanted to talk?" Ursula asked.

"Yeah." Kane was prepared this time. "Where did I get my fish?"

Ursula stopped rocking. "Your what?"

"My fish. Where did I get him?"

There it was, the flash of deceit in Ursula's eyes as she looked away.

"I have no idea what fish you're talking about."

Kane tore open his bag, dug out the photos, and slapped them down on the table. The one of Ursula holding the fish in the pouch of water was right on top.

"You're lying."

Ursula's face went from pink to red to gray. She attempted to smooth out her expression, but there was no saving this. She'd been caught and she knew it. Her stiff posture relaxed, and a hint of a smile brushed her lips. Was she relieved?

"Okay. Fine," she said, acting defeated. "I won him at the Amity Agricultural Fair this summer in one of those ring-toss games, and I named him Peter, but my brothers kept on trying to play with him so you offered to take custody. And you renamed him Rasputin after the mystical adviser to the Tsar of Russia, which I thought was kind of gruesome because of where his body was found—the mystical adviser, not the fish—but you told me that this sort of overbearing behavior was going to cost me visitation rights, and—"

"We were friends?"

Ursula was silent for so long that her breathing blended into the simmering cicada song. Then: "We're still friends, I hope."

Simple, earnest words. They plunked into Kane one by one, like bits of sea glass. They sank into his depths and glimmered at him from his shadows, hinting and unknowable. The truth was deep within him and well beyond his reach.

He needed to know more. Everything.

"For how long?"

"Umm. I guess since third grade when I asked to borrow your comb on picture day and you told everyone I had fleas from the pound or something, which turned into this whole thing about me and dogs, and then your dad made you come over to my house and apologize. Been friends ever since. Except I guess part of seventh grade because you went through this pretty intense goth phase and started doing tarot card readings, which my dad thought was Satan worship, and we got into this big fight and you cursed me."

Painfully, Kane remembered that phase. He did not remember Ursula during it, before or after. She had been cut from his memory entirely. How was that possible?

"I cursed you? Like, with magic?"

"Yeah, I guess. That was the goal, but it wasn't the real stuff or anything."

"The real stuff?"

Ursula let out a tight laugh. "Did you find my note?"

"Your note?"

"It was with the box I dropped off at the hospital? They said no visitors except family, so I left it at the desk."

There had been many gifts and flowers. Sophia had diligently brought them all home from the hospital, and Kane had diligently shoved them all into the trash.

"I missed it. Sorry."

"Don't worry about it. It was dumb." She sounded relieved, but after a beat of silence her tone turned hesitant. "Look, Kane, I'm sorry I didn't tell you when I saw you on the path. I've replayed that night like a million times in my head, and I mess it up every time. When you didn't recognize me I just…I don't know. I panicked. I heard the rumors that your memories got messed up, but I thought maybe when you saw me…"

Her voice failed her. She swallowed.

"I shouldn't have left you like that. I just didn't want to confuse you even more."

"I'm not confused."

The air between them tensed.

"Okay. I'm sorry."

Kane sighed. In his head he watched Ursula running into the night. He replayed it again and again. The steeliness, the concealed anguish. It had seemed so odd then, but he understood it now.

Like thick mist, pity threatened to blot out Kane's determination. The familiar urge to retreat pulled at him. To sink into the limbo, where no one could find him. But he darted away from the urge like a fish sliding up from the darkness, toward sunlit waters; he needed to see this through.

"Listen," he said. "It's not just you, okay? Other stuff is foggy. I'm not sure how much I'll get back. Or when."

"Okay."

"And I might never remember our friendship fully."

"Okay."

"Or at all."

"Okay."

"Can you say something other than 'okay'?"

Ursula smiled. "This is sort of stupid, but I brought something for you." She pulled a plastic container from her bag. "Close your eyes."

Kane did. Ursula placed something cool and smooth into his hands.

"Okay, you can look."

At first he mistook them for flat dolls of some sort. One had a tuft of brown hair, the other had red hair. They smiled wanly at Kane while he tried to figure out what strange, occult talisman he'd just been handed.

"I couldn't get your boots as detailed as I would have liked," said Ursula, pointing to the brown-haired one, "But I got some tips from this baking blog, and I think I could do the laces with a finer piping tool."

"Oh!" Kane was holding cookies. Two incredibly detailed, frosted sugar cookies, made to look like him and Ursula.

"You *made* these?"

"Yeah."

"And you've just been carrying them around?"

"Ha. No. You and I are good friends with the lunch ladies. They let me keep them in the cafeteria freezer. I just grabbed them."

"But…why do this?"

Ursula's smile turned bashful. "I needed to do *something*, I guess. And I…I missed…" A sad pain rose in Ursula's voice. "We used to have this joke with my dad about how we wished we could live as cookie people in the cookie kingdom and… Actually it's hard to explain."

She didn't bother. She shook herself and said, "And I wanted to try out this new recipe. They might suck, just warning you."

"They look too good to eat."

"Oh, please. I have like, hundreds more. Here." She took one cookie, snapped off the leg, and handed it over. They both took a bite.

"It's…" Kane's eyes widened.

Ursula was the first to spit it out. "Oh, God, these are *awful*."

Willfully, Kane swallowed.

"Oh, God!" Ursula snatched it from Kane, staring at the cookie faces as though they could tell her what was wrong with them. They kept their secret.

"I knew I shouldn't have tried a new recipe on something so

important. I'm *so* sorry, Kane. Oh my God I'm so embarrassed, this is so embarrassing, you must think I'm like trying to *poison* you."

"Relax, Urs," Kane said. "It's cool. They still look good."

Her face turned wondrous. "You called me Urs. That's what you used to call me."

It hadn't been on purpose. Kane shrugged uneasily, feeling no more familiar toward her than before.

Ursula joined him on the table. Sparrows quizzically circled the fallen crumbs. Ursula snapped off bits of cookie anatomy and tossed them to the birds.

"You don't even like sugar cookies," she confessed.

Kane held very still. This was true. He thought sugar cookies were for people who had never tasted actual happiness, but he wasn't about to tell Ursula that.

"Like, the last time I made sugar cookies, you told me that sugar cookies were for people who had never tasted actual—"

"Stop." Kane couldn't take hearing his own memories repeated to him. The taut feeling in his heart threatened to snap right there, like a piano string ripping through him.

The silence eased him, but then made it worse. He needed to at least give her the chance.

"Actually, it would help if you told me about us, I think."

"Hmm, okay." Ursula handed Kane what was left of his cookie. "Well, for one we used to sit out here in the mornings, and you'd toss food to the birds. I used to hate it, to be honest. Like I was absolutely scared of birds. All birds. And I used to get so mad that you would try to get them to come *closer*, but then one day you showed up with bread crumbs and showed me how you can sort of conduct them if you throw crumbs to one side, then the other." She demonstrated this by tossing a handful of cookie bits to one side of the courtyard. The flock burst into a wheeling arc that plummeted through the bright air. She did it again, to the other side, and the birds flowed like water.

"I love that," Ursula said. "We used to do this a lot, even during summer break. Wherever we went we'd always feed the birds. I miss it."

Kane cast crumbs too close to the table, and the birds darted so close that Ursula screamed and laughed, tearing backward and dragging Kane with her.

"Jerk." She punched him playfully. "Good to see you haven't changed a bit."

It was odd to learn about himself secondhand, like reading his own biography. It helped that Ursula seemed so sincere. Right now, she seemed like a person who had never successfully lied in her life. The version of her from before—from the path, from the bike rack—seemed at once so improbable and totally expected. When Kane's world ended, so had the world they once built together. Maybe his limbo hadn't been so lonely, after all.

For the next few minutes Ursula talked about baking and their teachers and the frustrations of field hockey. Kane allowed himself a momentary peace. Slowly, somewhere within him, his own flock of sparrows was returning. He didn't dare get too close. He told himself to be patient and keep casting out crumbs to see what showed up.

The door banged open—a teacher finally coming to tell them

to get back inside. Kane's simmering nervousness returned. So did his guilt. As they entered, the first bell rang, and the halls congested with students. All the questions Kane had forgotten to ask crowded his mind.

"Urs, do we…have any friends?"

Ursula laughed. "Sure, Amity Regional isn't *that* big. Most of us have been in school together since like, forever."

Kane fought to keep his head down, not meeting the stares of students watching him. He thought of the photo of the shoes he found in his journal. His shoes, Ursula's, and two other pairs.

"No I mean like *friend* friends? Like, other bird-feeding friends?"

"Afraid it's just you and me. Sorry, bud."

"No, it's okay. I just thought…" Kane didn't know how to say what he wanted to say. "I thought I recognized someone. Do we know a boy? Tall, brown skin, freckles, greenish eyes, sort of a gaunt, model look?"

Like a cloud drifting across the sun, the light in Ursula went out.

"You mean Dean Flores."

"Dean Flores?" Kane tasted familiarity in every syllable. "Do we know him?"

"No. He's new here. Moved to East Amity late last year, I think. Never talks to anyone. The only reason I know his name is because he showed up at the athletics banquet right before school started and signed up for swim team. Evidently he's really good. A diver, I think? I don't know. I don't trust him."

"Why not?"

Ursula frowned. "Um, because you told me not to. You told me to avoid him on, like, his second day last year. I think your exact words were, 'Anyone that pretty and that gloomy has probably killed their whole family or is planning to do it during the next new moon.' And we've avoided him since."

He laughed. The second bell sounded, and Ursula jerked her thumb over her shoulder.

"I'm this way. You have my number, right?"

He'd punched it into his loaner phone, which he held up to show her. Ursula gave a double thumbs-up.

"Wait, before you go, can I ask another question?"

Tentative, Ursula nodded.

"That night, on the path, there were these…things, with many legs…like, monsters." A few freshman drifted by, making Kane aware of how strange this sounded. Ursula watched the freshman, as though keeping track of who had overheard. Kane lowered his voice.

"And after you saved me from them, and I mentioned Maxine—"

Ursula cut him off.

"I didn't save you from anything. I was out for a run. I run outside all the time. I'm very sporty." This was clearly a rehearsed explanation. Kane was right; she was a terrible liar. She went on. "We can discuss what you *think* you saw later. Not here. And if you *think* you see anything else, text me, okay? We usually have lunch together during sixth period. You'll be fine until then, I promise."

And she dashed off. Again.

Kane was alone in the hallway, baffled. Somewhere in the last few minutes a grittiness had risen up in the girl who baked cookies and feared birds. He'd glimpsed that edge again, and through it had seen another version of the world. A version that Ursula meant to guard.

His mind returned to the boy. Dean Flores. Even thinking the name brought back that eerie sensation of being watched, as though Dean's eyes had taken ahold of Kane and never put him back down. Even now, it was like Dean could peer through the bricks and metal of the school to where Kane stood, stupefied, trying to put the pieces together.

Determination spread over him, straightening his back and clenching his fists. *Dean Flores. Ursula Abernathy.* These people knew him. Or they knew about him. He was sure they stood between him and the answers he needed.

And if they weren't going to give Kane what he needed, fine. He'd take it at any cost. He had nothing left to lose.

SIX

THE OTHERS

FOR HALF THE DAY NO ONE SPOKE TO KANE, AND IT was lovely.

In Statistics and Analysis, Kane was allowed to opt out of the pop quiz. In Spanish, Señora Pennington skipped Kane as the class took turns correcting sentences on a handout. In biology, Kane got to sit out the lab and stay at his desk and "catch up on the reading he'd missed." Instead, he took out the photo and studied it.

And no one cared.

Or, if they cared, no one dared say anything. Rumor had likely spread about Kane's outburst toward Viv, and the warm welcomes of homeroom had gone cold. People gave Kane space. Kane gave Kane space. He watched over his own shoulder as he scribbled shoes into his journal. He drifted beyond himself, like a demon unsure about possessing *this* body or a ghost debating residency in *this* house.

He wondered who wore white sneakers and who wore gray flats.

The bell rang. Kane pushed the photo into his pocket as his classmates returned to their desks to pack up. Adeline Bishop passed out the homework for Mrs. Clark, and when she got to Kane's desk she lingered, curious about his journal. He slapped it shut and gave her a scornful look and, because she was Adeline Bishop, her glance back held withering amusement. To spite her, Kane left the homework on his desk.

Next up was gym. Kane wished he didn't remember this and could skip on account of his broken memory, but he was on a mission. He scanned the faces in the hallway for Ursula or Dean and saw neither. Anyone looking at him looked away quickly. It was impossible to figure out who might be hiding something from him, because in a strange reversal, everyone seemed to be hiding from him in general. Frustration threaded through him, and by the time he reached the gymnasium he was in a terrible mood.

And then, suddenly, whatever spell his homeroom outburst had cast wore off as he approached the students in the bleachers and someone whispered: "Dude, check Montgomery *out*. Looks like he slept on a grill."

All eyes turned toward his burns. There was snickering, and a bubbling rash of *Oooooooo*s from the junior boys who were in the process of peaking early in life. They manifested their fleeting superior status by taunting basically everything. Kane was a popular target when he couldn't get out of their way, like right now. They were the main reason he hated gym this year, and school every year.

Tragically, they referred to themselves as The Boys.

"I heard he drove himself to school," said one of The Boys. Zachary DuPont. "You can smell the wreck from here."

"Brooo."

"I heard he drives a unicorn now."

"I heard it runs on top of a rainbow."

"I heard the rainbow comes out of his—"

Bursting laughter cut the rest off. Kane slumped down on the far side of the bleachers. He didn't dare take out the journal—it would attract even more attention. He wished he had *The Witches*, but just then Coach O'Brien showed up and took attendance. Kane began the tedious task of turning invisible again. He was so busy doing this that he almost missed O'Brien's announcement.

"There is good and bad news. The good news is no one has to get changed for gym. The bad news is we're square dancing this week."

A sarcastic cheer went up from the students, who were mostly resigned to Connecticut's strange fixation with folksiness. This happened every year, and there was even a club that sometimes went to regionals in Waterbury.

Kane went rigid with terror. He dreaded what was next: The Coupling. Boys began to pair up with girls like drops of water joining, but no one picked Kane. In seconds, only two people were left: Kane, and—of course, because this always happened to Kane—another boy. Elliot Levi. One of *The Boys.*

Shit.

The jeering wasn't concealed this time. Elliot's friends weren't going to let him live down dancing with another guy, least of all the only openly gay guy at Amity Regional.

"Get your jazz hands ready, Elliot."

"And your leotard."

"Don't let him get too close."

"Make sure to leave room for Jesus."

"Yeah, a threesome with Jesus and Grill-Head Montgomery."

Coach O'Brien jumped in on that one, but the damage was done. Kane was being used to make fun of Elliot, so now Elliot would do whatever he could to punish Kane and save himself. It was the way straight boys worked.

"Those guys are idiots."

Kane jerked up. Elliot stood over him.

"What?"

"I'm sorry about those guys. They're idiots. Ignore them."

Kane's pulse twitched in his neck. "You're actually going to dance with me?"

Elliot shrugged. "Sure. Why not?"

"I'm a boy."

"Cool, me too. Come on."

Kane began to truly panic. This, somehow, was so much worse. Elliot was willingly dancing with him? What trap was he being led into?

Elliot put out a hand. Kane spent too long considering it. Elliot was as annoying as the rest of The Boys but perhaps a bit more remarkable because he had moved to East Amity from the west coast in seventh grade, had dirty blond hair but darker eyebrows, and wore a fine gold chain around his neck. It had a glinting Star of David on it, Kane remembered. As the class stood in rows facing each other, Kane could see the ridge of the chain beneath Elliot's thin white shirt, drawn taut against his collarbones.

Belatedly, Kane remembered an old crush he used to have on Elliot. He felt himself begin to sweat as Coach O'Brien kicked a speaker to life, shouting steps over the fiddling.

Elliot took Kane's hands. Kane continued turning as red as possible.

"I'm not…" Elliot began.

"Don't worry," Kane rushed in. "I know you're not gay. We don't have to do this. I was going to skip anyways."

Elliot shook his head. "I was going to say I'm not like those other guys."

They parted, rejoined. Elliot's hands were hot.

Kane's jaw clenched. "They're your friends."

"Yeah, I know, but I'm not like them."

"How so?"

"They're assholes. I'm different."

Coach O'Brien walked over, observed, huffed, and strode down the line. Elliot's friends were in a fit about all of this, of course. They kept trying to get Elliot's attention. Zachary DuPont kept chanting *Kiss! Kiss!* Kane's cheeks flushed.

"You're not different," Kane said, looking down. "Whatever you're trying to do, just get it over with."

A long pause.

"I'm not—"

Kane pulled away, suddenly. The people next to them stopped dancing, hyperaware as Kane left Elliot in the middle of the gym and dove into the bleachers to grab his bag. The jeering came, but Kane heard none of it as he tore open his journal. He was looking for the photo of the shoes. The white shoes.

The same shoes he'd just been looking at, on Elliot's feet.

Kane found the photo and was instantly sure he was right. The right shoe's uppermost eyelet was missing, same with Elliot's. Kane turned, triumph blazing on his face, ready to confront Elliot, but the gym was empty. The music stretched into an eerie keening.

"Hello?" Kane called into the emptiness. His voice was muffled, like yelling into thick wool.

"Give it to me."

He jumped. Elliot had simply appeared next to him.

"The photo. Give it to me," he demanded.

"Where is everyone? What happened?"

Elliot's phone buzzed. He picked it up testily. "Yeah, I know. I'm coming. Just hold on. What? Yeah, he's here. No, it's all good. I'll be down in a bit." He snatched the photo from Kane's hand, looked at it, and made an expression indicating it might not actually be *all* good. He shoved his phone in his pocket and said to Kane, "Don't tell anyone about this, okay?"

"About what?"

Then, in a whoosh of golden shimmer, Elliot vanished, and the gym snapped back to the version full of kids shuffling to a racing fiddle. Coach O'Brien was shouting, "Please stop trying to dip Erica, Mr. DuPont."

Everyone else in the gym was completely oblivious.

"Montgomery, you good?" O'Brien called over his rhythmic clapping.

Kane had no idea what had just happened. Clearly no one else did, either. Whatever space Kane and Elliot had just occupied, it had been private. And it was gone, and Elliot with it.

With that photo. With *Kane's* photo.

"I'm going to the nurse," Kane called, snatching up his bag and running after Elliot. If he suspected a connection to Elliot before, he was sure of it now. Logically, he knew he should feel fear, but all he felt was the blue electricity of adrenaline in his blood.

Kane ran into the hall in time to catch a glimpse of Elliot as he swung around a corner. A moment later Kane was there, waiting a beat before turning in case Elliot glanced back. Then he saw Elliot jogging down the south staircase, which was odd. Students weren't allowed in the basement. That's where the theater department stored stuff and where the janitorial offices were. And the boiler room.

The boiler room.

Something in Kane bristled. Something under his thoughts, not a memory, but the shell of it, like the brittle husk left behind by a cicada. He tiptoed down the stairs. Whatever the memory was, he held it in his head with a gentle grasp as though it were his only precious thing. To his surprise, it guided him through the basement tunnels, to the boiler room doors, without making one wrong turn.

The doors were ajar. The hot sigh of machinery breathed out, smelling of grease and dust, and he remembered all the legends about the monsters living in the dark guts of Amity Regional High. Flesh eating. Freshman hazing. Could they be real?

There wasn't time to wonder. He wanted his photo back.

It was easy to sneak into the noisy, dark room. Through the whirring he made out a voice, then two voices, and soon he was able to make out a whole conversation from where he hid among the pipes.

Except it wasn't a conversation. It was a debate.

"How can you be sure?" asked Elliot.

"Because I just am, okay?"

Kane clapped his hands over his mouth. That was Ursula!

"That photo is proof he's still in there," she said.

"The only thing this photo proves is that we didn't do a good job purging his room."

Kane's whole body went cold, then numb. They were talking about him. They were talking about his room. They had been inside his house.

"If anything," Elliot was saying, "it shows he's trying to figure things out himself using hints, which *somebody* is clearly leaving for him, *Ursula*. What did you tell him on the path? You wanted him to find those photos, didn't you?"

"Is that an accusation?" The level of drama in her voice told Kane, and probably Elliot, that she was definitely guilty.

"Chill out, you two," said a new voice. An icy soprano Kane didn't know. "Even if we missed a few photos *by mistake*—right, Urs?—Kane has no real idea who we are or what we do. I spent all of bio watching him write in that journal, and he didn't even look at me until the end. He's not going to remember anything on his own. He can't."

"She's right," said Elliot. "Adeline knows better than anyone about this sort of thing. We'll have to go on without him."

Kane seized on the name. Adeline, the girl who had tried to give him his homework in bio. Adeline Bishop. "Popular" didn't do her justice. It was more like Reigning Sociopath of Amity Regional High. What someone like her was doing in a boiler room, Kane didn't get. He pictured the scene he was spying on: Ursula Abernathy, alleged lesbian jock; Elliot Levi, jawline-blessed Adonis; Adeline Bishop, the gold-plated queen bee, all having a secret meeting in the basement of the high school. It was an after-school special on break.

"But what about the reveries?" said Ursula. "It's Kane's job to unravel them. And what about those things he said chased him? They sounded like they escaped from a reverie. I didn't even know things *could* escape from reveries."

"Maybe it's the next reverie," Adeline said. "Sometimes the stronger reveries formed partially at first, in bits and pieces. Kane called them visions. Maybe the next reverie will form near Harrow Creek?"

Elliot sighed. "No, the next reverie is going to be here at the school. I'm sure of it."

"Because of the lobsters that started glowing in the bio lab?"

"They're not lobsters, Adeline. They're isopods. Completely different thing."

Kane could not see Adeline, but the eye roll was clear in her voice. "Elliot. Focus. The glowing is what's important, not the taxonomy."

"But isopods are—"

"Who *cares?*" cut in Ursula. "What's important is that *Kane* is the one who usually unravels the reveries, and he's basically powerless right now."

"*Good,*" said Elliot and Adeline at the same time. Elliot picked it up: "We can't risk involving Kane, not as he is now. Not even if he regained his powers. Remember what happened to Maxine?"

Kane's stomach twisted. They knew about Maxine. They knew what happened. If there was any doubt he was involved with Maxine's death, it had just been obliterated by the horrible connection this conversation was creating.

"We can't manage another cover-up," said Elliot. "We're barely getting through this one."

"But Urs is right, Elliot. We're not the Others without Kane. We need him so we can do it right. I know I said I could probably handle erasing the reveries when they form, but it's not the same."

"If they form," said Ursula, hopefully.

"*When* they form," Adeline snapped. "And they will form. You know that. We need Kane's powers, but we can't involve Kane until we figure out a way to fix him."

Fix him.

"He's not broken," Ursula said. "He's just lost."

"Whatever," Adeline said. "Right now, he's deadweight."

"He's our leader."

"Then why did he abandon us, Ursula?"

Tension silenced the boiler room, letting the din wash back over the secret meeting.

"Kane hid a lot from us, didn't he?" asked Ursula.

"Seems like it," said Adeline. "But we can't dwell on the past. That Kane is gone. We need to move forward with whoever he is now, and he's got no idea about any of this. We've got to recruit him like he recruited each of us to the Others. Gently. Or else he might break apart all over again."

"We may not have time for gentle, Adeline," said Elliot. "The visions of the next reverie are getting more frequent. If you're sensing what I'm sensing, the reverie might even form today. We have to be there when it happens so you can do your thing to the reverie's hero."

Ursula sounded panicky. "Is that going to work, Adeline? Is it safe?"

Adeline sounded far away. "I guess we'll see."

Elliot just kept going. "Based on the visions, we've narrowed possible heroes down to someone on the senior football team or JV soccer team. Both have practice today, so we should spread out. And someone is going to have to stay on the outside to prevent Kane from getting in and to protect him in case there *is* something worse hunting him."

"Who?"

"You."

"Me?" Ursula's voice jumped an octave.

"Yes, you," said Elliot. "I can set up an illusion around the reverie to prevent most people from entering, but we need you on the outside to stop Kane."

"Why me?"

"Because you're the one who led Kane back to us, Urs. He's your fault. Plus he trusts you. It should be easy to keep tabs on him for the rest of the day, right? Just text us if he does anything else weird. Oh, and Adeline, can you get to him in the meantime and erase his memory of the photo?"

"I have Latin homework."

"Adeline."

"Fine. Urs, I'll come with you to meet him before lunch. Make sure he doesn't get away."

"Good. We've got a good plan, then?" Elliot asked.

The girls grumbled in agreement, and the meeting ended. Kane ducked low as the Others left the boiler room, his hands over his mouth. *The Others.* He was sure he had never heard that name before, yet it was more than familiar. It felt like his own, like something he had once worn with pride.

He sank farther into the corner, hands holding back small, hiccupping sobs as tears pushed down his cheeks. He could run from the Others, but he couldn't run from himself. His body was betraying him. His life was betraying him. Now, more than ever, he wished he could withdraw, but with his own mind compromised, there was nowhere left to run.

· SEVEN ·
BEWARE OF DOG II

KANE DID RUN TO THE NURSE AFTER ALL. IT SEEMED like the only safe place to go. The Others knew where he lived and had searched his room. The Others knew his class schedule, where he was supposed to be and when. Kane thought of leaving school and going someplace in town—maybe Roost, or St. Agnes—but every idea seemed too predictable. Too like him. The Others knew all about him, and therefore anything familiar was off limits.

The nurse's office was not familiar. The nurse led Kane into a back room with a small cot wrapped in paper, where he sat and watched the doorknob. Eventually he felt brave enough to take out his journal, and for the next several hours he wrote down everything that came into his head. Every theory. Every whim. It didn't matter how strange or unreal. He just needed it on paper and out of his head.

A knock came at the door, waking him up sometime later. He

didn't realize he'd fallen asleep. Politely, the nurse let him know the school day had ended and asked if he needed to use a phone to call his dad.

"I'm good. I want to walk home," he said as he collected his things.

The school was eerily empty in the rich golden light of the afternoon. There was the sound of lockers slamming and laughter, but they were distant sounds that seemed to emanate from another world. Kane blinked away his sleepiness. Unsure of where to go, he pulled into the library and slumped into his favorite spot by the back shelves. There he scanned the lists he'd made in his journal before passing out. The first was labeled THE OTHERS:

URSULA ABERNATHY—BAD LIAR, SPORTY. HATES
    BIRDS.
ADELINE BISHOP—A LITTLE MEAN BUT ALWAYS
    RIGHT
ELLIOT LEVI—STRAIGHT YET MAGICAL THIEF
DEAN FLORES—HOT RECLUSE?

The second list was labeled QUESTIONS:

AM I OTHER? DO I UNRAVEL?
WHAT DID THE OTHERS DO TO MAXINE OSMAN?
WHAT IS A REVERIE? VISION? ARE THESE MAGIC??
WHAT IS REAL??
GLOWING ISOPODS (NOT LOBSTERS)

Then, at the bottom of the page, Kane had scrawled one word over and over.

DEADWEIGHT.

Kane shoved the journal in his bag and made for the high school's front exit, but something stopped him going home and giving up. He was uncertain about so much—about this world, about these people, about what it meant to be deadweight—but he did know one thing: he was alive.

Since his grandmother's funeral, he realized that when people tell stories about the dead, they create life in reverse. What's remembered about a person becomes what was real about them after they're gone. But Kane wasn't dead yet, and his story was still his to tell. Whatever he'd been through, whatever mysterious calamity he had survived, it was up to *him* to figure out what happened next.

He texted Sophia: Tell Mom and Dad I'm staying after at school for something.

He switched directions, his boots echoing in the empty halls until he burst through the doors leading to the back of the school. The fields were where they'd always been, unchanged and unremarkable. The soccer team stood in a line and took shots on their goalie while the field hockey girls sat in a circle, stretching. Tiny figures paced in circles on the track that surround the football field; the football team ran sprints, tapping the white lines as they pivoted. Distant shouts reached his ears, and whistles cut the golden air. Coach O'Brien bellowed something. There was no folk music.

The normalcy of it all stung. What had he expected?

Kane trudged to the edge of the field. He'd slept through his chance to catch the Others doing whatever they were going to do. His determination didn't matter; this story had gone on without him. But then, through his pity party, he heard someone yell his name.

None of the kids in the parking lot were looking at him. To his left were the field hockey girls, but he didn't know anyone on the team.

False. He'd just forgotten.

As Ursula stood, her stray curls caught the afternoon light and burned a halo around her head. As she loped over, Kane registered an anger in her body that melted by the time she reached him, replaced by her usual easiness. Between them towered a ten-foot fence but it didn't matter. He'd been caught.

"Hi!" Ursula's grin was wide, like from the carnival photos. Kane scoured her face for a sign of insincerity, and he found it: a small dimple of worry embedded between her eyebrows, the same telling dimple from their conversation on the path.

"Hi."

"How are you feeling?"

"Fine." He heard how curt he sounded, so he added, "Sorry I didn't show for lunch. I was out for most of the day resting."

"But you're okay now?"

"Just tired." He began walking along the path that led to the stadium entrance. Ursula followed. It made him edgy, but the fence was ten feet tall. Ten whole feet. And it was metal.

Ursula asked, "So... Why not just go home?"

Kane forced himself to keep walking. "Had to chat with some teachers. And I need to talk to Coach O'Brien."

Kane watched Ursula for her reaction, but her eyes were trained on the stadium. Haltingly, she said, "You can't. He's busy with football practice."

"That's okay. It's quick."

"Oh, well...you can just talk to him tomorrow, can't you? And besides, they're doing a scrimmage. He's busy."

"He's expecting me. At the practice."

She raised an eyebrow. Kane wondered where he was going with this very obvious lie. He desperately tried to recall how people did football. He'd seen a few movies, and sometimes the start of the Super Bowl after the most important part ended, which was the national anthem.

"Yeah, he invited me to...bring him his coin."

"His coin?"

"For the coin part."

"Do you mean the coin toss?"

"Yes."

Kane picked up his pace. Ursula followed. They were behind the football bleachers now. The stadium had locker rooms, and Kane could use the back entrance to get through the fence.

"Oh, you know what? I have a coin in my equipment bag. I'll bring him one! Why don't you head home, okay? I'll talk to O'Brien for you. Isn't that what friends are for?"

Kane was out of excuses and out of patience. His hands were

shaking. Actually shaking. Ursula disgusted him with her desperation. He disgusted himself with his desperation to believe her. His eyes burned, a preview to tears. The fence didn't turn the corner, and he readied his escape.

"Kane, you're looking kind of pale. Why don't I just drive you home?"

"Stay *away* from my house."

Fear opened on Ursula's face. "What?"

"Don't play dumb," Kane spat. "I heard you talking in the boiler room with Elliot and Adeline."

Ursula went white.

"You were following me that night on the path, weren't you?"

"Kane, listen—"

"What's a reverie, Ursula? Why are the lobsters glowing?"

"Kane—"

"What happened to Maxine Osman?"

The dimple between Ursula's eyebrows spread into a series of disbelieving lines. Her head shook in slow horror.

"Did you guys kill her?"

"Kane, stop, you don't understand. You're confused, and if you'd just calm down—"

"I'm not confused, and don't tell me to calm down." His voice smoldered. "I thought you were my friend!"

She looked hurt, as though she actually cared. "I am! I was going to tell you, but not like this!"

His withering glare was his only response before he pivoted toward the locker rooms.

"Kane!" she called. "Just wait a second, okay? We can find a place to go. I'll explain it. I'll explain everything. Just give me a chance."

"I gave you your chance," he called back, done listening. He was going to find out for himself what Ursula was hiding. Like a cresting wave, the betrayal swept him into a jog.

"Kane!" Ursula screamed. "You can't go in there!"

He ignored her.

"*STOP!*"

It wasn't a plea. It was a command. Kane had to look back. Ursula's hands were bunched in the chain links, her face dark with sudden contempt. And then, in one swift motion, Ursula tore the fence apart like a curtain of beads.

Now Kane was sprinting. He rounded the corner at a dangerous speed, sliding on a patch of mud. In a whirl he was on the ground, hands full of muck. He threw a glance back. Ursula rocketed around the corner, closing the distance between them.

His mind screamed for him to get up. To do anything but watch as she bore down on him. And instead of terror, he felt a sensation at once familiar and foreign. An inward reaching, a crystallization of panic, anger, and determination. His body moved against his retreating mind, throwing him onto his feet, toward Ursula. His palm shot out to stop her.

"Leave me *alone!*"

A needle of pain sliced through Kane's temples as a dazzling blaze engulfed his fingertips. With a sound like the air itself ripping apart, pure iridescence rocketed from his hand. It struck

Ursula directly, surging over her like a thick jet of water, dragging her off her feet and into a brutal backward tumble.

A breathless beat passed. Ursula lay in a small crater, smoke curling off her stilled body, probably dead, and Kane's hand still crackled with the otherworldly light. The flames were faceted like gemstones but had the fluidity of fog, and they held every color imaginable in their dancing depths.

Kane waved his hand frantically, desperate to get the fire off his skin. He dug his knuckles into the soupy mud, but still the light boiled over his flesh.

"Help!" Kane screamed, though the fire did not burn him. Instead, an electric vibration pulsed through the bones of his hand, in time with the pastel flames, as though Kane clutched not fire but sound.

Then Ursula sat up. "Kane," she growled with pained restraint. Her uniform was burnt through in places. Bits of rock fell from her hair as she stood and glared at Kane with eyes that now glowed a neon pink.

She stalked toward him.

"We're friends, Kane, remember? If you'd just listen to me I can help you."

"Stay *away!*"

This time when the plume erupted from Kane's hand it did not sweep Ursula over. Instead it came within a foot of her and collided with… Kane didn't know what. The beam hit an invisible barrier and burst apart, swarming past Ursula in a million harmless embers.

She was only steps away now. She looked *pissed*.

And just like that, the fire winked from Kane's palm. He ran for his life. The locker rooms were his only option and by some maniacal grace the door was propped open. He lunged for it as Ursula lunged for him.

"*Don't!*"

But Kane was at the door, swinging himself inside and throwing his whole body into closing it behind him.

Inches away, Ursula screamed, "I'll find you!"

The door slammed shut. The lock clicked into place with a gratifying THUNK!

And Kane was safe.

EIGHT

SPOILT BLOOD

KANE GULPED IN BREATH AFTER BREATH. EVERY inhale clung in his throat like syrup. He kept his eyes on the door. Ursula had torn through a metal fence. Could a door hold her?

Somehow it did and Kane was safe. For now.

He finally let himself cry.

To some, the sudden onset of magic might be shocking, but to Kane it was owed. Ever since he was little, and ever since he knew he was different, he had woven the hope for magic into every one of the world's disappointments. Every sneer, every snuck glance, every birthday spent alone with Sophia as his only guest. Each felt like a debt.

Prove to me that it's all been worth it, he used to tell the universe. *Let me have power that they can't take from me.*

Like the X-Men. Like Sailor Moon. Like Avatar Korra. He thought that if he suffered enough, magic might find him in a moment of insurmountable peril. Telekinesis, like Carrie. Or control of water, like Sailor Mercury.

Kane had not, in any of these imaginings, envisioned his hands erupting into projectile rainbows.

But that's what had happened. He sniffed as he inspected his hands. Surprisingly, there were no burns. All that covered his skin was a layer of grime from his fall. In fact, he was covered with mud everywhere. A mixture of clay, sweat, and something both sticky and pungent.

Blood.

Kane flew into a frenzy feeling for wounds, but instead found that his cotton T-shirt was suddenly made of coarse twill. And his shorts were gone, as were his roper boots. He wore badly torn cargo pants and a pair of brown loafers that crunched on the uneven stone floor of the tunnel he now stood within, which was lit by torchlight.

Torchlight?

Cargo pants?

Kane was not in the locker rooms anymore. He wasn't even sure he was awake. A crude tunnel curved into the darkness behind him. Veins of scarlet crystals webbed through the stone, their pulsing glow dyeing the passageway a ghastly crimson. A single torch jutted from a mount where the locker room light switch had been.

Kane ran to the walls to feel if they were real. They were. His hand drifted toward the torch to see if it was hot. It was. What was happening? Where on earth did the locker room door actually lead?

In a daze, he turned back to the door in time to see its metal melt into a cobbled mosaic. Still a door, but one that matched this new world. The mosaic depicted a scene of figures bowing before their god, a gigantic, pincered thing inlaid with rubies and black-red garnets.

"Glowing lobster," Kane whispered.

This is what the Others were talking about. This was the reverie. The realization inspired more questions than it answered, but Kane forced himself to stay focused. He was done crying. For now, at least.

Then the door lurched upward, and Kane let out a cry. Voices hissed through the gap at the bottom, sending him stumbling backward. He reached for his phone but instead found a holstered revolver at his hip. He threw it away in disgust and shock.

"*URĪB!*" the voices chanted in time with the door's rise. It sounded like men, and many of them. "*URĪB!*"

Absurdly, white subtitles appeared on the bottom of Kane's vision. They read: HEAVE! HEAVE!

He blinked. The subtitles stayed. The voices grew louder, sending Kane sprinting in the opposite direction, down the sloping tunnel and out into a cavern of breathtaking space. The same crimson crystal webbed across the ceiling, clustering and breaking apart like blood vessels, and against a glowering red horizon stood an entire subterranean city. Buildings of stone, crystal, and moss thrust up through the cavern floor, each hundreds of feet tall and honeycombed with balconies. Massive stalactites hung from the cavern ceiling, carved with windows that showed through to torch-lit apartments. Rope bridges threaded between the homes, and gardens of white-leafed plants hung over the grooved avenues and cobbled walkways.

All of it was articulated in bloody red by the pulsing crystals, which summoned the elaborate city into focus and then banished it back into darkness every other breath.

Kane had never had such a realistic dream. He forced himself to keep moving through the streets as he waited to wake up. The city was empty, and he could guess where the citizens were; far in the distance he heard a massive crowd, their roar so loud it vibrated up through his boots.

Then, from behind him, came the sound of men approaching.

Kane threw himself into patches of darkness between a toppled stalagmite, ignoring the angry clicks of whatever creatures he'd startled.

What is happening? What the hell is happening? Am I dead? Can I be dead soon?

Kane tried every trick to wake up. He pinched. He bit. He slapped. He held his breath. He tried to pee. Nothing worked.

Then the men were near, and Kane could only watch. There were a dozen of them, and their uniforms were a futuristic take on barbarian-chic: armor plated in buffed metal over garments of cured flesh. Some wore masks of jawbones and teeth. They were humans, and they were *dressed* in human.

Kane swallowed back the bile and listened closely as the leader spoke, his words written in white text on Kane's eyes.

"Sounds like the other caravans arrived. Hurry up, or it'll be you on that sacrifice block!" He was massive, overgrown with thick muscles and brandishing a whip that looked to be woven from hair. Kane didn't need to know the language to understand there was something wrong with the man's tongue, which slid thickly around his words.

His men understood him just fine. They pulled forth a makeshift cage of petrified wood. It swayed atop stone wheels, filling the abandoned city with creaking. Within it huddled a gaggle of girls Kane instantly recognized from the cheerleading squad, except their uniforms had been replaced with oddly dated looks that contrasted with the rough environment. There was Veronica McMann wearing a blue blouse, her hair pushed into a bun. And Ashley Benton in a once-crisp cream-colored pantsuit. And the third might have been Heather Nguyen, but her hands were pressed to her face while she sobbed.

The girls and their outfits were a further complexity Kane couldn't make sense of. But the cheerleading squad practiced near the football field. They would have been in the stadium, too.

Slowly, it dawned on Kane: the men pulling the carts looked familiar, too. It had taken him a second of hard staring to look through the armor, but their sneering faces all looked like boys from the football team.

"Hurry or I'll sacrifice you all!" roared the leader. The boys cheered merrily and the girls whimpered.

"Sir," one called, "You know none of us to be virgins. Th'mighty Cymotherian would be furious if she tasted our spoilt blood!"

The brigade trundled on, and Kane followed in the shadows.

The next swell of red light allowed him to see a fourth girl in the cage. She was at the back and was not crying. She held her arms crossed over her chest and looked outward with an expression of annoyance. She wore a rosy dress that belled just above her knees, and the stiff magenta belt clasped around her waist matched her shiny magenta pumps. Her copper hair had been coiffed into a bulbous beehive that stayed up—huge and proud—with no deference to gravity, and on her upturned nose balanced a pair of horn-rimmed glasses. Quite clearly there was a dent of contempt between her newly sculpted eyebrows.

Kane gasped. It was Ursula.

He began to comprehend her final words before he'd slammed the door shut.

I'll find you. It wasn't a threat. It was a warning. A promise. She'd known.

This was the reverie. *This* was what Kane was not supposed to discover but was somehow supposed to unravel.

He crept to the back of the cart, where no barbarians were stationed, and was able to get right up to the cage without anyone even noticing.

"Ursula."

Ursula's foot tapped impatiently. She didn't respond.

"Uuursulaaa."

Nothing.

Kane stuck his finger through the bars and poked her side. One of Ursula's hands darted out and caught Kane's finger, then dragged him close.

"Hush," she hissed, still facing away. "You need to hide. *Now.*"

Her grip was like iron. Kane thought of the torn fence. How easily could she break his knuckles if she wanted to?

"I'm going to get you out of here," he whispered.

"Run." She squeezed so hard he was surprised his bone didn't snap.

"Just break the bars," Kane begged. "I know you can do it."

"I can't."

"You *can.*"

"I mean of course I *can*, Kane, but I *can't.*"

"Why?"

Ursula huffed. "It's not ladylike."

A crack rang out like a gunshot, and Kane's arm erupted in pain. He was dragged to the ground, the whip of braided hair burning around his wrist. It yanked hard as the leader rounded the cart, grimacing at Kane, his pupils two black pits bored into irises of cloudy white.

"Hands off the meat," he slurred.

Pain fuzzed Kane's vision as he tore uselessly at the tether, which only bit deeper into his wrist. The cage ground to a halt and the boys huddled over their new capture. The stink of them was real. This was all *real.*

"Found this one prodding around," said an underling, a sophomore Kane recognized from his lunch period last year, except in this world his cheeks were covered in bright scars. Unlike the leader, his eyes were their usual blue.

"Cut out his jaw!"

"Smother him with his own guts?"

The leader knelt over Kane. "Where's the rest of you?"

"Rest of me?"

"The other *Keologists*."

"I don't—"

The leader nodded, and two boys pinned Kane down while a leader wrenched the whip back, pulling Kane's arm. Someone handed the leader a gigantic axe and took the whip from him. He lifted Kane's chin with the serrated tip, gently, showing his exquisite control of the weapon.

"Tell me."

"I said I don't know!"

The leader backed up, raising the axe, and then took two quick steps as he brought the axe down toward Kane's limb. Kane screamed and jerked against the weight of the boys holding him, but the bite of the blade never came. When he opened his eyes, he saw shock eating away at the leader's bloodthirsty grin. One of the other barbarians had intervened, catching the ax's handle.

"Enough."

This boy was unlike the others. He wore matching harnesses of leather and bone, but his status was marked by an elaborate mask of bone shards fastened to his brow, cheeks, and nose, as though his skull lay exposed. There was a deadliness to him that the other underlings lacked. An authority that even the leader felt compelled to obey despite the boy's youth. The axe was lowered.

"You must go to the ceremony. Leave this one," commanded Kane's savior.

Thank God.

He unsheathed a blade from his harness.

"I wish to slaughter him myself."

· NINE ·
PARASITES

OH SHIT.

The brigade simmered with irresolute whispers. Kane looked from the boy to the leader to Ursula, but he didn't see any of them. He saw only the numerous ways he could—and was probably going to—die.

"Why should I leave this *Keologist* to you?" asked the leader.

"The ceremonies are starting soon. You must deliver the sacrifices."

"Why not bring him along for sacrifice?"

The brigade murmured in agreement.

"Because he's a *Tijxorn*."

No subtitle showed for that word. Just <EXPLETIVE>.

"*Tijxorn!*" the slur echoed in hushed horror.

The boy went on: "Th'Mighty Cymotherian would never host

in such spoilt blood. He is better slaughtered beyond the sanctuary. Otherwise, we risk defilement."

The brigade simmered with irresolute whispers.

"So be it." The leader shrugged, and the boy was handed the whip. "But you may not kill him. Put him in the dungeons. I will cut out his jaw after the ceremony."

The masked boy bowed. "As you command."

Deflated by the utter civility of it all, the brigade resumed their slow trek, and the cart rumbled off. Kane tried to catch Ursula's eye, but she had turned away. And now Kane was trapped. The boy was much bigger than he was. Stronger. He looked down at Kane with mild distaste.

"Come on. Let's go," he said in English, walking off. Kane trotted after him like a dog unsure of being walked. He looked for an opportunity to escape, but the whip was secure around his wrist. The boy was less hostile now, almost disinterested as he lead them through a network of walkways, into a hollowed-out stalagmite, and up a staircase of smoothly carved steps.

"Where are we going?" Kane wheezed as they reached a landing.

"Not barbarian jail, that's for sure."

"Who are you?"

"A barbarian."

"You don't sound like a barbarian."

"Well, I am."

Kane tried to recall the word that he'd been called. "What's a tiich…tiixoo…"

"*Tijxorn.* I think it means you lay with other men. The other boys were saying it, so I tried it out. Whatever it means, it worked."

"You outed me?"

The boy gave the whip a yank. "I saved your life."

"Are they actually going to cut out my jaw?"

"Ew. No."

The passage reached the tip of the stalagmite, and a sturdy bridge lead them over a dizzying drop toward a half-moon tunnel carved into the cavern's wall.

"But you said—"

The boy rounded on Kane, rocking the bridge dangerously. "I said what I had to say to get you out of there. Otherwise Ursula would have had to break character, and the reverie is much too fresh for that. It only manifested an hour ago. Now be quiet and hold on to me."

Kane held on as they advanced through a network of tunnels similar to the passage he had first appeared in. He smelled smoke, and elsewhere water dripped. It was more level here, and Kane could walk upright. He was about to start asking more questions when the boy beat him to it.

"Do you still want to run?"

Kane surprised himself by answering honestly. "If you were going to kill me, you would have. I think I'm safer with you than without you."

The boy produced his knife, slicing through the whip of braided hair. "That's right. Now tell me, what do you remember?"

Kane rubbed his wrist. "I was running away from Ursula and tried to escape into the locker rooms, but I ended up here instead."

"Before that."

"I tried to go to the football practice to…deliver a coin."

"That's a terrible lie. Here, does this mean anything to you?"

With the tip of his dagger, he traced something on the damp floor.

"It's the number eight?" Kane guessed.

The boy was unimpressed. He asked, "Okay. And what do you remember about reveries?"

"Reveries?" Kane stumbled on a loose stone, and the boy hauled him forward. They were moving quickly now. "Like, dreams?"

"Sort of."

They crept into another cave, this one marbled in bioluminescent pools the color of a cloudless June sky. Things moved in the pools, their wakes edged in phosphorescence.

"Reveries are what happens when a person's imagined world becomes real. They're like miniature realities, with their own plots and rules and perils. For instance this reverie appears to be about a subterranean civilization that worships a god called the *Cymo*. My guess is that we are in someone's rescue fantasy, made real. For instance you appear to be some sort of—what do you call the people who study bones and dirt?"

"Archaeologists?"

"Yes. *Keologist*, as they say here. The reverie's plot appears to be about archaeologists that stumbled upon these caverns and must rescue those girls."

"The cheerleading team?"

"Evidently."

"But why were they dressed like sexy secretaries?"

The boy shrugged.

"And those boys—they were the football team, right?"

"Right."

"How come no one remembers who they are?"

The boy hooked an arm around Kane's waist, helping him over a mound of mushrooms.

"Most people never know they are in a reverie. Their mind just accepts the new world they're in and the new role they're given. Think of it like a movie, full of actors, except they don't know they're acting. They think it's real. Very few people remain lucid like us and Ursula, but we still need to play along or else we'll get in trouble."

"What kind of trouble?"

"Every reverie has a plot. If you don't follow the rules of the reverie, you risk triggering a plot twist, and plot twists can be pretty deadly for people trapped inside reveries. So we have to play along, and we have to do our best to keep people safe until the reverie reaches its end."

The skin of Kane's neck prickled. Something splashed nearby, gone in a sparkling ripple.

"But if this is all just a wild fantasy, how can it be dangerous?"

The pale light pitched shadows into the boy's eye sockets. "Just because something is imagined doesn't mean it isn't danger- ous. Sometimes the things we believe in are the most dangerous things about us. That's why people build entire worlds in their minds. Because they think they're safe, but they're wrong. Dreams are like parasites. They grow up in the dark within us, and they grow deadly. Trust me when I tell you these reveries can kill you."

"I don't believe this."

"You don't have to believe it. You just have to survive it."

"How?"

The boy pulled them into a cavern with a vaulted ceiling and irregularly spaced columns.

"Reveries don't last forever. As they reach their ending, they become unstable and start to collapse. If you can last until then, you can unravel it."

Unravel, like the Others had said.

"Unravel it how?"

"I guess we'll see."

The boy enforced silence after that. The roaring crowd Kane had heard earlier was much louder now. The sounds vibrated right from the stones. When they walked out onto the remains of an ancient, truncated bridge, the roaring resolved into chanting.

No, cheering.

He stepped to the edge and then wheeled back, dizzy from the height. This cavern was a vast bowl; thousands of people swarmed the shallow slope. They chanted and stomped, giving the whole view the reeling, spacious chaos of a stadium. And as inconceivable and chaotic as the space was, it was all drawn like a gasped breath toward one single feature: a monstrous shrine at the far wall, carved to look like a face contorted with rage. The mouth, full of a golden inferno, was so big a house could sit on the tongue. The plucked-out eyes poured forth streaming white waterfalls that sizzled against the cracked lips. Steam swept into the crowd, which writhed and cried out for more.

"What on earth is this? Where did all these people come from?" Kane gasped.

"Most aren't real," said the boy. "You can tell by the eyes. The people created by the reverie have white irises."

Kane remembered the icy stare of the barbarian leading the caravan. Everyone else had been from the football team, but he had been a creation of this world.

"What are they doing?" Kane asked.

"Look closer, at the court."

The court was a platform of obsidian wreathed in magma, giving it a malevolent under-glow. In the center whirled a man in filthy robes, shouting as he wielded a gnarled staff topped with a rattle of tiny skulls.

"The High Sorcerer," said the boy.

"What is he doing?"

"Look closer."

Stabbing up through the black tile of the court was an altar of pale marble, carved in the shape of a gigantic hand and draped in chains. Things were bound to it.

Not things. People.

His eyes came to rest on Adeline Bishop, her deep brown skin glowing against the cold marble holding her.

Of course, he murmured inwardly. Adeline had been the third person in the boiler room. Within the warped logic of this world—this *reverie*—it followed that someone as powerfully beautiful as

Adeline Bishop would be cast as a damsel in distress. The main damsel, it looked like. The other girls were strung among the reaching fingers, while Adeline hung dangerously vulnerable in the palm.

"What's going to happen to her?"

"Probably she'll be sacrificed," the boy murmured. "It depends if the hero makes it to her in time. He's close."

"What if he doesn't make it?"

"Then definitely she'll be sacrificed."

Kane looked at the boy and then, perhaps by the brightness in the cavern or by the closeness they shared, recognition finally took hold. He knew this person. It was the eyes, the only thing about the boy visible beneath the thick mask of bone.

"You're Dean Flores, aren't you?"

The boy kept his eyes on the court, unblinking. Kane knew he was right.

"You're the one who gave me that photo of the Others. You wanted me to find my way here, didn't you?"

Dean turned to Kane. "Not quite, but I'm glad you're here. They need you. But for now you need to keep out of sight until Elliot shows up. He's with the hero—the person at the center of the reverie, the one creating it. They're traveling through the traps beneath the cavern. They're going to try to thwart the sacrifice, and maybe they'll be successful. Regardless, the reverie is going to start collapsing soon after."

"But—"

"And then it'll be up to you to unravel it."

"But—"

"And this last part is very important, Kane." Dean's face was a loveless mask of shadows. "You must never tell the Others about me. If you do, they will hurt you, and then they will hurt me. Do you promise?"

Dean was unflinching. Curiosity clawed at Kane to ask more, ask about the Others and their secret worlds. About his role in all this. He promised himself he would if he survived.

"I promise."

"Good. Now don't move, and try not to get in trouble. I've already spent too long here—I won't be able to return."

Another explosion blew from the mouth. Behind the blackened teeth squirmed a crimson tongue, something swollen deep in the earth's throat.

When he tore his eyes away, Dean was gone.

He spun around. Dean had slipped into the caverns without disturbing a single pebble. Kane knew it was stupid to try and catch up; the boy had moved with the smoothness of a centipede through those lightless corners.

Kane had two options: stay, or go.

He made his choice.

· TEN ·
PLOT TWISTS

KANE HAD MANY REGRETS, AND SOMEHOW THEY ALL had to do with Ursula. Sneaking into the boiler room to eavesdrop on Ursula and the Others. Confronting Ursula on the fields. Running away from Ursula and into a deadly dreamworld. Going after Ursula *again* only to get whipped by a whip of actual *hair*. Disgusting.

Kane's newest regret, however, was about Dean. Kane had of course decided against listening to the boy, sure he could find his way out of this cavernous mess, but as soon as he reentered the tunnels he was instantly lost. After ten minutes he couldn't even figure out how to get back to the perch in the arena. The tunnels, he was sure, were rearranging themselves. Dean had said the reverie would collapse. Was it happening? What would it feel like to be crushed beneath miles of rock and dirt?

"Amazing work, Kane. Really awesome, amazing choices today. You're killing it."

He was so busy scolding himself he didn't hear the barbarian guards until he waltzed right out of the passage they'd been guarding. They sat up, as surprised as he was, but soon had Kane backed against the wall at spearpoint. Their eyes were normal. People from school.

"*Keologist*," the bigger one grunted menacingly.

Kane could have sworn he was standing before Evan from the pep band, except this version had a much more flattering chin. The other—possibly Mikhail Etan, also from band—had temple acne even in this world.

"Mikhail, Evan, it's me! It's Kane, from school! We had homeroom together last year!"

They blinked at Kane, uncomprehending.

They don't know they're acting. They don't know this isn't real.

"This isn't real! This is all like…a dream or something. You guys aren't really—"

Just then a sickening shudder rolled through the tunnel, toppling the three of them. A dark electricity zipped through the fibers of the world itself, shocking him—literally. The reverie felt…angry. The texture of the air went taut and smothering, like it was twisting itself around the trio. Punishing Kane for getting caught.

The two guards lunged, but Kane was quicker. He fled, and suddenly the world around him began to twist and warp. The rock beneath his feet shifted with every step. The tunnels before him smashed together, rearranging themselves into new routes, leading him somewhere like a mouse trapped in a maze. Dean had told him that it was imperative he play along with the reverie, and Kane had just broken character in a big way. Now he sensed the reverie was deftly leading him toward something much worse. But he couldn't stop running. The guards were right behind him.

Kane's next step struck nothing, and he was falling through open darkness until he plunged into a frigid, brackish pool. He splashed and sputtered as a current dragged him along curved walls slick with grime, his hands slipping and scraping. The current quickened, and a glow pulsed ahead. From it he heard chanting. The roar of falling water. He knew what came next.

The current pulled him under, out into the crashing chaos of the waterfalls that poured into the arena. He curled into a ball as he slid down a slimy slope, jolting and bouncing between clots of moss until finally he rolled to a stop.

Water hissed to steam all around him on a floor of glittering black. He was aware of dropping into a brand-new, stunned silence, like when he'd entered homeroom that morning. He sat up and stared, and three thousand cloud-white eyes stared back. The crowd, the entire arena, was captivated by the boy who had just gushed out of their giant god's weeping grimace.

Kane felt like he should pose. Or wave. Or do something. It felt strange to make such an entrance with so little flair. He looked at Adeline, bound to the altar, and her face was the only one absent of awe. The cloud of her black curls rocked as she shook her head. She looked deeply, witheringly annoyed with Kane's arrival.

The silence ended when the other sacrificial virgins started screaming.

"We're saved!"

"Our hero!"

"We knew you'd come!"

And, just like that, the plot twist was complete. Kane went from distant spectator to sudden savior. Outrage exploded from the crowd, bathing the court in a dissonant demand for sacrifice. Sacrifice. *SACRIFICE!*

Shivers rocked his body, rattling his teeth. He had messed up so bad that the worst possible scenario was being realized, and there was nothing he could do to stop it now.

"Kane! The sorcerer!" Adeline shouted.

Up close the man was something between corpse and exoskeleton, his skin scaled in smooth burns, his teeth just rotten pebbles jammed up into gooey gums. He pulled a twisted bone dagger from his sleeve and, locking his white eyes on Kane, rushed toward Adeline. He drew the dagger back, aiming right for her stomach. She flinched, but there was nowhere to go.

Against all his instincts, Kane sprinted after the sorcerer. He was not as fast. His soaked clothes caught with every stride. There was no way he could reach the dagger as it plunged toward Adeline...but...

Kane snatched the rotting robes and yanked as hard as he could. The dagger skewed upward, caught in the hollow of Adeline's jaw, and then wheeled away as Kane pulled harder. Together they fell to the ground, entrapped in the clinging fabric.

Kane grabbed blindly at the knife, finding the sorcerer's wrist and squeezing hard. The old man spat and whined, and next came the clatter of the dagger hitting the floor. Success! With a kick Kane dislodged himself from the robes, snatched up the weapon, and ran for Adeline.

Pinpricks of blood rolled down her neck like stray jewels, but nothing more. The dagger had only nicked her jaw.

"What are you doing?" she hissed.

"Saving you!"

"Wrong move, Kane." Adeline flinched as Kane slashed at the chains. "I'm set. You should be—will you please be careful?"

"I'm trying!"

"Well try *running*!"

"What?"

"Running. Like, with your legs."

"No, I heard you."

Just then Adeline thrust her knee into Kane's stomach, doubling him over in time for the sorcerer's staff to whistle over his head. It smashed into the altar, shards of skull bouncing across the floor. Adeline had saved Kane, but the sorcerer's hands fell on him, grabbing his shirt and tossing him into the center of the stage with inhuman strength. Kane landed too hard; his neck snapped back, and his head cracked against the obsidian floor. The dagger skittered away from his twitching hand, and he saw red.

Everything slowed. The sorcerer loomed over him, eyes hard with hate, cloak churning like volcanic smoke. He knelt and dragged a filthy finger across Kane's upper lip. It came away coated in blood. He brought it to his mouth, sinking the bloody finger between his lips with relish. Then he smiled, showing Kane all his teeth. All five of them.

"Virgin," the sorcerer said, and another dark twist gathered in the reverie.

He turned to the crowd and thrust the staff into the air.

"*VIRGIN!*"

The response shook the cavern, the reverie warping to accommodate this new path. The hysterical shrillness of the cheers seemed to fortify the sorcerer. He put a bony hand to his ear and leaned toward one half of the spectators. "Sacrifice!" screamed the men. He did this again, to the other side, which also chanted: "Sacrifice! Sacrifice!" He made a show of deliberating which side had been louder, then shrugged comically and gave each side another chance to outdo the other. It was the cheesy dramatics of a halftime performance at a minor-league sporting event. Kane, in his delirium, found himself wondering if the cheerleaders would be released for the purposes of tossing T-shirts into the crowd.

The sorcerer declared the right side the winner, and the resulting cheer was earsplitting. It ran through Kane, numbing him. He barely felt the sorcerer heaving him up and carrying him a short distance. Idly he wondered if it was getting hotter.

His head rolled to the side, and he could see Adeline. She was yelling at him, but he couldn't hear her. He was being carried away, toward the other side of the arena. Toward the hearth shaped like a mouth, ready to eat him up.

Adeline did a weird thing then. She grew calm, almost stern, as though she'd made an important decision. Her fingers wrapped around her chains, like she meant to tear them off herself.

The sorcerer jostled Kane, forcing him to look into the hellish flames before him. The mouth filled his vision, and the air vibrated doubly with the shouts of the crowd, now interlaced with a deep tremor from below. Sweat stung Kane's eyes. He could smell his hair burning. Still, the sorcerer pushed forward, offering him up.

"Sacrifice!" growled the sorcerer.

"*SACRIFICE!*" roared the crowd.

And with that, Kane was tossed into the fire.

· ELEVEN ·
LIMITS

KANE LANDED ON THE GROUND, FLUNG BACKWARD instead of forward. The chanting of the crowd dissolved into confusion. Bewildered, Kane opened his eyes and saw the dagger on the stone beside him, the bloody tip flashing in the firelight. He blinked away his tears and made out the sorcerer desperately clawing toward it as a chain, fastened around his leg, dragged him back.

Kane followed the chain to its source: Adeline, now standing in the center of the arena, legs braced as she used one hand to reel in the sorcerer while the other spooled the chain into a neat coil. The sorcerer, who had been strong enough to lift Kane, was no match for Adeline's fluid, deliberate movements. He clawed and gasped, as powerless as a caught fish.

"Get away from the fire!" Adeline screamed.

There was nowhere to go. The sorcerer lurched forward, his

pupils just pinpricks in the yawning white of his blank eyes. Kane slammed his boot into the man's hands, bending the brittle fingers like straws. With another kick Kane sent the dagger skittering into the fire, and the man screamed in rage. In a blink he spun toward Adeline. Like a kite caught by the wind, he launched into the air and dove upon her, but she was ready. Maneuvering the chain as easily as one might maneuver a ribbon, Adeline twirled gracefully and whipped out the spooled length in a violent slash. It cracked against the sorcerer, cutting into him like a wire through soft cheese.

Blood splattered Kane and evaporated instantly. He stumbled out of the hearth's edge, fighting down vomit as he hopped over the crumpled body of the sorcerer to join Adeline.

"That was wild!" he panted. "How—"

"Later," Adeline snapped. "Right now we need to get the real people out of here before the next plot twist. Give me a hand."

She was wrenching lengths of chain from the hand-shaped altar. Kane couldn't figure out how she'd gotten free, but then he saw an ancient lock by her feet, popped open with a single hairpin.

"That actually works?" he gasped, helping a girl off the altar.

"The reveries love a good trope," Adeline grunted, "Get ready for the twist."

"*Another* twist?"

Adeline dragged her chains up, coiling them again, as the last girl ran off. None of what just happened pleased the crowd, but it appeared to be the virgins saving themselves that fundamentally offended the reverie, and not the sorcerer's defeat. Kane sensed another distortion boiling through the fabric of this universe.

"Here it comes. Get behind me," Adeline said, putting herself between Kane and the crowd.

"Where are the glowing lobsters?" Kane asked.

Adeline glanced at him. "How'd you know about that?"

"I was in the boiler room. I heard you talking with the Others. That's what you call yourselves, right? *The Others?*"

Adeline unraveled a length of chain. She was looking past Kane now, her face unreadable as several barbarians vaulted onto the court. They were the biggest people Kane had ever seen, each one a tower of mass and muscle, glaring with pearly, white eyes that matched the polished blades of bone they swung.

Adeline shrugged. "Okay, Nancy Drew, I hope you're ready to fight. Do you remember how to do that snappy thing with your fingers?"

"What?"

With a shriek, the closest warrior lowered into a gallop, sword held high over his head. Adeline grabbed Kane's arm and held it up, his hand aimed at the warrior's chest.

"Snap!" she commanded.

In a flash he remembered the jet of magic that had burst from his fingertips to stop Ursula. He wiggled his fingers and, when nothing happened, Adeline heaved them out of range of a slicing blade. The warrior snarled, ready for another jab, and his friends were close behind him.

"I said *snap*, not jazz hands!" Adeline screamed.

Kane snapped.

The sound was loud like thunder, sharp like a gunshot; the sight

was a vein of iridescent brilliance carving the air apart. It was hard
to see anything else as the flare slammed into the warrior with such
savage ferocity that he was blown backward, very quickly and in a
great many pieces. And then the other warriors were upon them.

Adeline didn't let them get close. She swung her chain in
elegant sweeps and slashes, flicking the metal whip with remarkable precision. She struck where the joints of armor failed. Throats,
elbows, groins. The warriors barely had time to gnash in frustration as she drove them back.

"Kane. Focus," she commanded, but Kane was transfixed by
the remnant blaze that played across his knuckles. Every color
he had ever known vibrated in the pale magic. The prints of his
fingertips glowed, as though he'd pressed his hand into liquid light.

Adeline was breathing hard. "Any day now. Just take your
freaking time."

Kane shook off his stupor, ready to attempt another snap.

"Not you." Adeline pushed his hand down, drawing them into
a retreat as her eyes searched the crowd. "Save your energy. We'll
need you fresh."

"For what?"

A chorus of cries broke out from the crowd, and Kane saw
entire bodies tossed upward in the distance. Adeline grabbed
Kane's wrist. "Get ready to run."

Whatever it was, it was getting closer with amazing speed.
Something burrowed through the crowd, and it was heading right
for the altar. Just before it reached the rim, Adeline dragged him
into a protective huddle, but he couldn't look away.

The crowd split open and admitted, by force, a dashing bolt of magenta, a girl swathed in pink. She hurtled into the air, her rosy dress splashing around her hips as she contorted into a flying kick.

Kane heard himself laughing. It was Ursula!

Her heels were the first things to land, and they struck the throat of one warrior. He went down without resistance, and Ursula leapt off without hesitation. If it wasn't for the sparkling leather of her shoes it would have been impossible to see her leg sweep out and slam sidelong into the next warrior's ribs, forcing him down. A blink later, Ursula was on him, his neck caught in a two-arm choke hold while his legs kicked wildly. Then there was a crunching noise and the man dropped. Lifeless. Ursula's punches just kept coming, each hit sending a shock wave of magenta light crackling into the super-heated air of the arena.

"We should back up." Adeline said, pulling Kane toward the hearth. He watched, transfixed by her speed. Her power. The fact she was zipped into a housewife costume and the further fact that it didn't stop her in the slightest. If anything, the costume helped. Now Ursula was atop a pile of bloodied, wriggling men, beating them in turn with one of her shiny pumps. And through all this, her hair didn't move. Not even a little. Kane thought that whatever hairspray she used deserved as much credit as Ursula herself.

Adeline's hand wrenched Kane's face away from the action. "The reverie is collapsing, which means it's about to get even worse. I don't know how you got in here, Kane, but since you're here, you're going to have to do your job."

"My job?"

"Yes. You need to unravel the reverie."

Adeline might as well have told Kane he needed to drink the Caspian Sea. There was no sense to that phrase. No action Kane could even conceive of taking.

An especially loud crunch drew them back toward the fight. Ursula had gotten hold of a spiked bludgeon and was using it to block the simultaneous attacks of two more warriors. In unison they brought their immense blades down onto her, and the stone beneath her feet—one heeled and one bare—fissured.

Adeline pulled Kane back. "Now, Kane. You've got to unravel it *now*."

"How?" Kane screamed. The cracking stone and the heat from the blaze dizzied him. More warriors were spawning from the crowd, all of them lumbering toward Ursula.

"Usually you clap your hands and—" Adeline was cut off by a sudden belch from the mouth-shaped hearth. Something within the inferno was moving. Something solid and slithering. Something worse than anything they'd encountered thus far.

The chants of the crowd suddenly synchronized. It was not the sound of a demand, like before. It was the sound of celebration as they cheered, "Bloood sacrifiiice!"

Adeline's face twisted. "Kane, where's the dagger?"

Kane searched his memory. "I kicked it into the fire!"

Adeline's eyes widened. "You threw the ceremonial dagger with my virginal blood on it into the fire?"

"But you're not a virgin."

Adeline's face twisted. "Oh, God. Oh my God. Kane, it doesn't matter in this world. You fulfilled the sacrifice!"

At the lips of the hearth, the flames shaded a deep scarlet, pulling into a smoldering mounds. Then, like a bloated tongue, a gargantuan beast slithered forth from the throat of the earth and out into the arena.

Its body was a composition of blazing plates sliding over thousands of undulating legs. From beneath it, Kane could make out serrated mandibles large enough to chew apart a bus, and beady, ancient eyes that scanned the empty altar with hunger, then outrage. Whatever it was, it was furious to find its meal escaped, and it manifested its fury through an inscrutable language of clicks and squeals.

Elliot was wrong, Kane thought. *There* is *a glowing lobster.*

A new chant cut through the din, quickly gaining momentum.

"*CY! MO! THO! AH! EX! I! GWA!*"

The fiery crustacean craned back and let out an earsplitting screech in return, then turned its laser gaze upon Kane and Adeline. Its antenna twitched, then swung away as sparks gushed forth from its glowing mandibles.

They ran, but before they'd made it halfway across the altar the creature snapped open its great jaws and let forth a neon tsunami of fire.

"I got it! I got it!" Ursula shouted. She sped between them, *toward* the fire, her arm drawn back as though she meant to punch her way through it.

And, in a way, she did. Her fist rocketed forward just as the wave of fire converged upon the three and—absurdly—the deluge split apart. It flowed around them, the heat tremendous, unbearable, all-encompassing, and like nothing Kane had ever felt, but they were alive. They were preserved upon an island of black tiles as a shimmering shield of magenta light cupped over them. Ursula stood at the front, fist thrust forward and her whole body trembling as she pitted herself against the crustacean's breath.

And still her hair would not move.

"Do it, Kane!" Adeline forced Kane to stand up. Her hair whipped wildly as the inferno began to bleed through Ursula's force field. "Unravel it!"

Kane didn't know what to do. He didn't know what she meant. But such an earnest belief shined in her eyes—belief in him. And what could he do in the face of such raw, unwavering faith? He dove into himself, searching for an answer, but all he could feel was his own stuttering heart, his own fear.

His own limits.

The fire let up, and Ursula slumped to her knees. All around them the floor was a desert of molten glass. There was nowhere left to run as the crustacean began to recharge its breath.

"This can't be real," Kane whispered.

Adeline eyes bore into his. "It's real, Kane, but only until you say so."

Sparks tumbled from the crustacean's jaw as it slid through the shimmering heat. It was right over them. Kane squeezed his eyes shut, hugging Adeline.

He had denied this world—its power and its reality—but

there was no denying what would happen if he failed. He would die. They all would. This reverie was not a dream. This reverie was not a story. There were no more twists, and there were no more chances. Just the reverie's desire to see these interlopers annihilated. And, fueling this desire was a powerful rage, as though the reverie knew what Adeline knew: that Kane had come to unravel it. Perhaps it was Kane's fear-addled imagination, or maybe it was a sense he hadn't known he possessed, but in that moment he felt as though he could commune with the reverie's core. And what beat in that core was more than desire or rage; it was fear.

The fear of being taken advantage of.

And the fear of being invaded, of being taken apart from the inside out. With new eyes Kane saw the screaming hearth and the parasite that had wound up from its molten guts. With an open mind, he understood the reverie's pattern. What lay beneath the plot. The metaphor or the thesis or the marrow that unpinned everything. Even though he did not know the mind that created this world, he at least knew the heart.

And he thought he might know what to do next.

"Remember, Kane," Adeline whispered into his ear.

He reached for the wisp of intuition, and it reached back, blooming bold and brash in his chest. The blooming sensation manifested around him, rivers of color coursing from Kane's skin and carrying him upward. Buoyed upon nebulous rainbows, he faced down the awestruck crowd, then turned to consider their god.

It considered Kane back, unimpressed, before releasing its deadly breath over him.

Kane clapped his hands.

The arching fire stopped. Time stopped.

It was an instant of unmoving.

From Kane's hands erupted a day-bright brilliance, washing the cavern in every color, as though Kane were a prism through which light split to spectrum. In this unmoving instant Kane knew the reverie for what it was: a living tapestry of memories and thoughts and dreams, sewn together with the desperation to be real, to be realized.

The reverie resisted Kane's control, searing his mind as he fought to hold it in his head all at once. But it was lethargic, its energy waning, and Kane gritted his teeth through the pain. He was able to pin its corners wide and pick at its center, which was the fearful creature frozen before him. Its hideous body sagged beneath Kane's concentration, sending out a shock wave that turned the arena to liquid. Colors and textures bubbled together. Pieces of the cavern broke apart to float unmoored in the vibrating air. Below, the floor scattered like dry leaves so that Ursula and Adeline floated in a white yawn of nothing as the reverie tore itself apart, whirling toward Kane, colliding into a knot of light gathering between his flexed palms.

The unraveling intensified, its rush growing into a thunderous riot. The pain in Kane's head was beyond even the agony from the fire, but he stayed focused on his purpose, knowing he would feel the pain later.

He held the knot of light up, a white star dragging everything toward it.

He forced himself to stay strong as the weight of the world collapsed upon his shoulders.

· TWELVE ·
THE S WORD

KANE HAD A NEW EMPATHY FOR PUNCHING BAGS.
For crushed cans kicked down the road. For the focal points of
incessant force.

His thoughts rose slow and blurry, like bruises on his brain.

He was floating. He was sinking. The aurora was dissipating,
depositing him onto stiff, plastic grass scored in white symbols. His
head hung over his streaming hands. He might have fallen asleep
there on the football field if it hadn't been for the unsure murmurs
of the many people who had just watched him fall from the sky.

"Excuse me, excuse me."

Adeline pushed through the crowd of stunned players, getting
real low and in Kane's face.

"Hey. Dream boy. You all right?"

Kane blinked at her. The cave was gone, the arena evaporated.

Behind Adeline, dusk had come to East Amity, and the stadium lights blazed white against a ruddy sunset. She helped him up, and he saw that they stood before the congregation of rapt spectators, arranged in a minimized version of the reverie's crowd. He saw the football players he'd recognized as barbarians. And farther back he spotted Mikhail and Ethan with the rest of the pep band, no longer dressed as guards. Off the side huddled the cheerleading team, as though caught mid-escape.

Kane swung around to face where the giant lobster god had been; he now looked up in the vacant smile of the empty goalposts.

"Hey! Everything okay?"

Off to the side, Ursula waved at them from the locker rooms.

"Elliot's getting his car," she called. She was dressed in her field hockey uniform (still charred). Kane saw that Adeline was transformed, too. She wore shorts and a loose mint shirt. Both girls appeared completely free of the wounds they'd sustained. Kane ran his hands over his own body.

He was unhurt and alive, and the only burns that remained were the ones around his head.

"Kane, hurry up and give it back."

Adeline motioned upward.

Hanging in the air was the knot of light, glinting like a cut-crystal ornament. Kane reached out and it floated to him with noncommittal buoyancy, stopping just above his palm. It emanated the memory of fire, of blood, of bones ground to dust. It had a sound, too. Susurrant and gentle, betraying none of the violence it held.

"Take this part easy, okay?" Adeline said. "You have to give it back slowly. Freely."

Kane looked at her, then back at the knot. "You've done this before?"

"Not personally."

Luckily for both of them, the knot knew what to do. It drifted over the confused crowd until it found was it was looking for: a player on the bench. It sank into his helmet.

"I *told* you it was Ben Cooper," Adeline called.

"What?" Ursula threw her hands up. "He seems so nice! I never took him for the misogynistic, tomb-raiding type."

"More like *womb*-raider. He's the one who tried to get with me at my birthday last year. He's a creep-o, Urs. He just hides it well."

"I thought you suspected John Heckles."

Adeline threw out a mocking laugh. "Heckles? That idiot doesn't have an imaginative bone in his body. He's a refrigerator."

"Refrigerators hold wonders!"

Kane didn't understand the joking mood. All around them people were panicking, the vanishing of the reverie having dumped them back into their home reality. Someone began an unsure chant. Others cowered, as though the summoned god still loomed.

"You better go with Urs," Adeline said. "Unless you want to lose your mind, too, no pun intended. I'll be right along as soon as I clean up these memories. Can't have that mess respawning again, can we?" She propped her hands on her hips and began counting the people around the field. Kane understood he was being dismissed and slipped through the crowd to where Ursula waited. She shushed him before he could ask her anything.

"I know," she said. "We'll explain everything. But first, are you hungry?"

Kane was incredibly hungry. He'd missed lunch, after all.

Ursula smiled. "You always are."

"So what about werewolves?" Elliot asked. "Twice for werewolves, right?"

The Gold Roc Diner was a narrow, kitschy diner on the edge of East Amity, buzzing through all hours of the night like a neon satellite. The quartet sat at the back-most booth. Ravaged plates spread across the table, covered in streaks of ketchup and grease, except for Adeline's; the crusts of her dissected sandwich had been stacked in a small tower. Kane stared at the tower. It was all he could do to keep himself from passing out from fatigue.

He had barely talked since they sat down. It was like he'd been jostled in a fundamental way, his mind falling out of alignment with his body by a fraction of an inch, and nothing was lining up. Perhaps alarmed by his silence, the Others just began telling him things. Right now, they were discussing all the past reveries they'd encountered.

Reveries, Kane thought. *Plural. These have happened before, and often.*

"Yeah I remember two werewolf reveries," Ursula said.

"Three," said Adeline, "if you count Barbara Weiss's last year, during the school play."

"Those were just giant wolves," Ursula said.

"No, she's right," said Elliot. "It was still people turning into wolves. That's three werewolf reveries."

Kane absorbed this. He was way beyond doubt, by now. He was beyond everything, spinning in some elliptical orbit around the conversation.

"This wasn't the first giant bug, right?" Ursula asked.

"Isopod," Elliot corrected, but the girls ignored him.

"There were those giant lunar spiders," said Adeline. "The ones that crawled out of the eclipse in that one reverie."

"Spiders are arachnids, Adeline."

"Elliot. I swear to God if you don't cut that out."

Ursula steered the conversation into a recounting of her favorite reverie, which was a story about rare dragons raised in ponds who were determined to make hats from lily pads. This devolved into a discussion of the merits of mermaids, a topic that deeply embarrassed Ursula for some reason. Elliot and Adeline smiled, and Adeline made as if she were telling Kane a salacious bit of gossip.

"You should have seen Ursula in a shell bra. You wouldn't know it because she's always in baggy hoodies, but Ursula has got great—"

"Adeline!" Ursula's face went as scarlet as her hair. Adeline shrugged, still grinning.

"The point is, we've seen it all," Adeline said. "And I do mean *it all*."

The orbit of Kane's mind returned to the dark star of his world, the gap in the night sky where something should have been. In their extensive debrief, the Others hadn't brought up Dean Flores once. They didn't know about him. It was as though he didn't exist to them.

"What about ghosts?" Kane asked.

The table was silent in the face of Kane's first words in an hour.

"Often," Ursula said solemnly. "Especially around the holidays."

"So what you're saying..." Kane cleared his throat. His tongue buzzed with questions now, so many he thought they might race out of him in an unruly swarm. "Is that these *reveries* just happen? They just burst out of people, every few weeks, unannounced? And you guys just deal with it?"

"Who else?" Elliot shrugged.

"The police?" Kane offered. "The FBI? The Vatican?"

Ursula scoffed. "Nah, basically everyone except us becomes useless once they get caught in a reverie. We tried to get the police to help once but they just got brainwashed, too. When you're in someone else's reverie, you're whoever they want you to be."

Kane thought about the glazed expressions of all the barbarians, the football players, the pep band, the cheerleaders. For them, the reverie was the only reality they knew.

"I remember that reverie," Elliot said. "Science fiction. Bouncy house space station. Super campy."

Adeline tapped her chin. "It was high silliness, low logic. Weren't there carnivorous bunnies?"

"Oh, that's right!" Ursula said. "I forgot about those!"

Kane's head spun with the way these three pinballed among details.

"Anyhow." Adeline folded her hands. "It's better if we handle reveries ourselves. Otherwise, things get weird."

Get weird.

Get!

Seeing Kane's face, Elliot said, "Not all of them are as intense as tonight. In fact, almost all of them are harmless at first, but it's all about how you play your cards. If something goes wrong, even the sweet reveries turn deadly. That's why it's important to play along and help the reverie reach its resolution. Otherwise it twists."

Adeline's lashes flickered in poised bitterness. "Like tonight, for instance."

She knows I messed it up. They know it was my fault for getting caught.

"Right," Elliot nodded. "Tonight's reverie came from Benny Cooper, who was supposed to save the damsels. Probably would have jumped into the arena at the last second and killed the sorcerer, avoiding the summoning. That monster looked improvised." The Others nodded. "Lots of hero fantasies coming out of the sophomore boys these days."

"But…" Kane was eager to move past his own mistakes, but he definitely didn't want to discuss the lava lobster, which, now that he thought about it, did look a little silly. "But why barbarians? And why were the girls all dressed like secretaries?"

Elliot smiled like this observation made him proud. "Every

reverie has a premise. An inspiration, right? Well, recently the football team had a party to kick off the season. The theme was 'Barbarians & Librarians.' Cooper must have gotten the idea then."

"But what about the…Cymo-whatever?"

"*Cymothoa exigua*," said Adeline. "A parasite that attaches itself to its host's tongue, replacing it. It's actually a thing. We covered them in bio while you were gone. And I know Cooper *hates* shellfish. He freaked out last year when we stayed at Claire's beach house and her dad made crawfish, and someone hid one in Cooper's cup. He only saw it after chugging the whole thing."

"That explains the glowing lobsters in Mrs. Clark's lab," said Ursula.

"Isopods."

"We know, Elliot," snapped the girls in unison. Then Adeline raised her chin at Kane. "Anyways, Kane, do you have any other questions?"

"Yeah. How come no one, like, knows about all this?"

Elliot answered again. "You know today in the gym, when we were talking and everyone else vanished?"

"Yeah. It was like we were in another dimension for a second. Was that a reverie?"

"No, that was an invisibility trick. They couldn't see us, and we couldn't see them. Pretty cool, right?"

Kane thought it was mostly manipulative, but he didn't say so.

"When the reveries started, each of us got powers," Elliot said. "All of us are stronger and faster than we used to be, although Urs is considerably stronger and faster."

Ursula blushed.

"And we each have specific abilities. For instance, I can bend perception. Manipulate what people see and create projections. I'm the master of obfuscation."

"Illusions, Elliot," Ursula teased. "Just say you can create illusions. It's not that hard."

"Fine. Illusions," Elliot said, crestfallen. "I create illusions, and I hide the reveries as they're happening."

Kane pinched the bridge of his nose. "Okay, so you can hide the reveries, but what about the people who just experienced that? Aren't they going to like, tweet about it?"

Adeline smirked. "Nah, we're good. Elliot can manipulate the present, but I've got the past. I can mess with memories. Erase them, create them. Whatever it takes so that people don't remember what they've been through. And if I don't purge the memories, people get super confused, and sometimes it causes them to create their own reveries. I guess that's what happens when you can't figure out which of your lives is real."

Earlier it had been explained to Kane that Adeline lingered in the stadium to deal with "cleanup," which meant making sure no one ever knew the reverie happened. "The trick is to erase everything, but not fill in every gap," she said. "If you leave just enough unknown, the mind lies to itself and fills it in organically. It's easy."

Adeline can manipulate memories, Kane thought. He went cold, connecting her gruesome power to his own messed-up mind.

"Adeline is the security," Elliot said. "I'm the strategy. We each can fight, but Urs is the true soldier. She channels force, taking it in through her barriers and turning into pure strength. She's our offense *and* defense. She's a beast."

Ursula smirked. "Thanks, Elliot."

Kane grew colder still. *Security, Strategy, Soldier.* He directed his icy gaze at Ursula.

"So what's my *S* word?"

The three of them froze while Kane waited, each second lasting a lifetime, for an explanation that wouldn't come. Exasperated, he just decided to be frank.

"I overheard the entire conversation in the boiler room. I know I used to be part of this group. *The Others*, right? That's what you call yourselves?"

Ursula shifted. "Yeah, we needed a name to refer to each other by in any reverie, no matter the plot. It's a code name."

"A *code name?* Whose corny idea was a *code name?*"

"Yours." Adeline's hand struck the table, silencing Kane and the tables nearby. "*Your* idea. You. Our leader."

Kane went red-hot, his hairline prickling and his clothes itching on his back.

Leader?

"Same with the term *Reverie*. And *Hero*. You said it's hard to handle a problem if you don't know how to talk about it, so you made up terms."

White heat burst at the edges of Kane's vision. Sweat dotted his lower back. How could they not feel the heat?

"You were the first to explore the reveries. The first to get powers," Elliot said. "You, then Urs. Eventually Adeline and I got dragged into a few reveries, by accident, and when our powers developed it seemed like a natural thing to form a team. So we became the Others. We're the only ones who stay lucid, and if we don't unravel them properly, they leave damage behind. People get hurt. We learned that the hard way."

It was a subtle movement, but Adeline's eyes closed a fraction longer than a blink.

Elliot continued. "And recently, the reveries have been getting worse. More…elaborate. Like whole entire worlds instead of just one story. And then around two months ago, we thought—" He swallowed. "You began talking about the *energy* of reveries. The stuff that creates them. You said there was a source of power that the heroes were tapping into, somehow, and if you could find it you could control it, too."

Adeline picked up. "We told you not to."

"Not to what?"

No one answered.

"Not to *what*?"

Adeline lowered her voice to a menacing whisper. "You went nuts, Kane." Elliot and Ursula flinched. "What? It's true. You became obsessed with finding the source of the reveries, the source of our power. You were convinced it was a weapon that you had to have, or else it was going to be used against you. It's all you talked about for weeks, and then, in the middle of a reverie, you… I don't know. Lost it? Like actually, truly lost your grip on reality? You basically tore the whole thing apart in this psychedelic explosion, and we thought you died. Like *died* died."

"What about the car crash?"

Adeline picked at the crusts on her plate. "The police saw the explosion and showed up. We needed something quick, so Ursula threw your car into the mill and Elliot created a bunch of fake evidence to make it look like a fire. I filled in the rest with some fake memories while we made sure you got to a hospital. Not our best work, but we needed to use you as a diversion."

"You threw my dad's car?"

Ursula had never looked more ashamed, not even when Adeline talked about her mermaid shell bra. "Underhand," she squeaked.

"And this was a diversion? From what?"

The chill in the booth was back, and now it wouldn't thaw. It settled resolutely onto Kane's skin, a frosted lather. He squared his shoulders toward Adeline, who was the most forthcoming, but it was Elliot who spoke up.

"The hero of that night's reverie was an old painter, and her reverie was a watercolor reimagining of East Amity. It developed as she was setting up to paint the mill, we think. It was huge and intricate, but we never got to its resolution. When you tore the reverie apart, the hero vanished. We don't know what happened to her. Her name was—"

"Maxine Osman," Kane said. He didn't see their reaction. The diner's fluorescent lights buzzed in the silence. Neither time nor feeling could reach him as the sense of betrayal he'd felt about his past earlier that day returned, filling him to the brim with a pulsing, dark truth. *You are a killer, you are a killer,* it said. He shoved it down. Kane barely knew these people, and he definitely did not trust them. What if they were creating this story, just like they'd created the crash? Just like they'd created everything else?

"How do I know you're not lying? How come I don't remember?"

No one would look at Kane. Adeline seemed miles away when she finally spoke.

"After you unraveled Maxine's reverie, we found you with this thing on your head. An artifact that was definitely not from the reverie. We think it's what set off your powers, but we don't know. It sort of looked like a crown, but it was burning you." She gestured to the burns etched in Kane's scalp.

Dread squirmed in his chest.

"I tried to remove it, but touching it did something to my powers, too. I couldn't control them. It was like my powers turned inside out or something, and the whole mill decayed. So did your car. Elliot and Ursula would have died if it wasn't for Ursula's shield. But I held on, and it worked. I got it off and it threw it away, and when we looked for it later it was gone. Vanished." She said this with the weight of a verdict. "You survived, but whatever I did destroyed some of your memories. When I checked in the hospital, everything from the summer was gone, and everything about us and the reveries with it."

The booth was as still as a graveyard. Kane waited to see how he'd react. He waited for the dread to break apart and for an emotion to crawl out. He thought it might be betrayal again. Or doubt. Instead, what hatched within Kane was none of these things. It was fear, but he was smart enough not to show it. Outrage was a handy cover, and it flowed as quick as hot oil.

"*You* erased my memory?"

Adeline thrust out her chin. "Kane, I didn't have a choice."

Kane pushed from the booth.

"*You* put me into a coma? *You* crashed my dad's car? *You* turned my family and the police against me?"

The clatter in the diner stopped, everyone focused on the boy shouting.

"She saved you, Kane," said Elliot. "She's been saving all of us ever since. Just after you went under, your family opened a police report to look into foul play, but Adeline got to them in time and made it so that they didn't remember who we were, either. She's the only one keeping us a secret."

Kane backed away, horrified. "You erased my family's memory?"

Adeline crossed her arms and glared at the dark windows. Kane's stomach turned. Elliot followed Kane as he backed away. The eyes of everyone in the diner followed them, too.

"Kane, listen to me. It's not perfect. None of it's perfect. But you're here now. You found your way back. And we need to work as a team now more than ever. You need to prove you can control your powers, or else—"

Kane lunged into a punch, catching Elliot in the cheek. His head snapped sideways and he fell, sweeping a stack of dirtied plates to the floor in a jagged crash.

In the gasp that followed, Kane addressed the other patrons.

"None of you will remember this. She's going to erase your

memories, too." He looked at the Others. "If you come near my family again, I'll kill you."

The bells clattered as Kane ran from the diner. They rang again as someone followed.

"Kane!"

It was Ursula.

Despite his rage and fear, Kane halted. "I'm going."

"You can't. Not with those things out there. At least let us give you a ride."

"I'd rather take my chances." It was true; he would rather face the horrors of the night than spend another minute with these three.

Ursula shrugged off her flannel.

"Here. It's cold."

Kane took it. The warmth that seeped into his fingers felt intrusive. It smelled like her smell of soap and deodorant, and that felt intrusive, too. A million Trojan horses, a million betrayals trotting through his senses.

"Kane, before you go—"

He stalked off, listening for the bells that meant Ursula had left him behind. They never came, which meant she was still in the cold, watching his back, watching him forget her again. Hating himself, he slipped on the flannel.

Because Ursula was right. It was cold, and it was a long walk home.

· THIRTEEN ·
THE FEMALE ANGLERFISH

WHEN KANE SLIPPED THROUGH HIS KITCHEN DOOR IT was two hours later. His feet ached from the six-mile walk. His shoulders hurt where his backpack dug in. His hand was swollen, his bruised knuckles split and seeping as though punching Elliot had curdled the bright magic hidden just beneath his skin. Now it rose through him darkly, like oil pushing up through layers of pressure and rock. Kane shook his hands again and again as he walked in tight circles in his kitchen, listening to the still house for any sound of his family. It seemed impossible that Sophia would have kept a lie going for him this long, yet he'd arrived home to peace, darkness, and quiet. Too much quiet. The way things had been, Kane was surprised the police weren't here waiting for him. Yet his phone sat sleeping in his pocket. He had vanished from this world for an entire afternoon, and it hadn't inspired so much as a text.

Kane was too relieved to question it. Being in his own room wasn't an option, so he made for the living room couch. Right before he dove onto it, a lamp snapped on, and up stood Sophia from the recliner.

"Late night at school, I see."

Kane hid his bloody knuckles behind his back while his sister studied him sleepily, pushing her glasses up her nose and adjusting her blanket. She must have nodded off waiting for him.

"I covered for you," she said finally. "Mom and Dad think you've been asleep since you got home right after school. Made me bring dinner up to your room. I dumped it out the window and brought back the plates. Make sure you clean that up."

Kane pursed his lips. He knew he should thank her, but it hadn't exactly been his choice to be abducted into a rogue nightmare. He stopped himself from saying anything at all, knowing it'd be used against him.

With a curt nod Sophia dragged herself off the recliner, her blanket sweeping behind her like a rich cape. Halfway up the stairs she stopped. "In the morning, you're going to tell me where you've been. If you lie, I will expose you to Mom and Dad. I'd rather have you in jail than lost again, Kane. Those are my conditions."

And then he was alone again. His backpack slumped to the floor, and soon he was there alongside it, just sitting in the pool of golden lamplight.

He was still there an hour later, and an hour after that, too afraid to sleep, to dream. He was too afraid that if he looked away his house might dissolve into the ether, like the arena. He felt like he did whenever he glimpsed the Cobalt Complex through the thin forest that hid it from the roads; like he was flirting with a hidden vastness folded into the fabric of reality, like if he stared for too long, he'd lose himself within it, belong to it, and he'd never find his way back out.

What the hell was he going to tell Sophia?

Oh, I put on a magical device in a dreamworld and it caused my powers to go haywire. Oh, also, I have powers.

He kept his hands decidedly clenched.

When morning arrived, it arrived in fringes, just a rosy nuisance tickling Kane's bloodshot eyes. Then the light was somehow everywhere. Soon the house would be awake.

Kane stretched his stiff legs, then flopped back onto the carpet, crushing his backpack in the process, and that's when he remembered the red journal.

It took only a second to dig it out of the bag. He eyed it like it was edible, like he was about to flay it open and devour its pages. In the rush of escaping the Others, Kane's mind had kept itself purposefully blank. Now the memories of Dean Flores burst like fireworks, one after the other. *Boom, boom!*

"'You must never tell your friends about me,'" Kane recited. "'If you do, they will hurt you, then they will hurt me.'"

Well they had already hurt Kane, which meant half of Dean's prophecy was already true. And Dean was not simply a civilian. He had been lucid, like Kane. Like the Others. Yet he was not one of the Others. He was the one constant of Kane's first day, yet he was the one thing that had yet to fit.

Drawings of shoes danced across the journal pages. What he now knew were Elliot's sneakers and Adeline's flats. Kane flipped, looking for another clue. Another photo. He was sure Dean had guided him this far. Kane was desperate to go farther.

An alarm went off somewhere in the house. His parents. Sophia rose second. She'd want answers. Kane needed to think of more lies.

Something in the pages flashed. Kane flipped back but it was gone. He shook the journal upside down, and it fluttered out.

It was a card of heavy paper, bordered in golden filigree. The font was elegant and sparkling. It said:

> **TO:** *Kane Montgomery*
> **WHAT:** *You are cordially invited to attend tea for two.*
> **WHERE:** *147 Carmel Street*

There was no signature, but scrawled at the bottom was a line of glossy black ink. When Kane brushed his thumb over it, the looping letters smudged.

It read:

When: Right now.

∞

Kane shot down Carmel Street on his bike, zipping past Victorian houses converted into boutique offices and salons. As he approached downtown, the thick foliage broke apart to admit denser developments that lost their character and melded together like braced teeth. He was sure the invitation was Dean's next clue, just like Dean had passed him the photo in the same journal. The address on the invitation was the library. He wondered if Dean liked books. Maybe they liked the same books.

Right now.

Kane had left in a rush, but not before dirtying some dishes and penning a note about some early morning tutoring. He knew Sophia would see through this, so he'd texted her. Don't worry. I'm fine. I'll tell you everything.

Then he'd turned off his phone and hoped she didn't call the police.

Kane banked through gentle curves, the pale morning rising over him and growing thick with birdsong, heat, and the chatter of insects. When the library came into view he stopped short. It was covered in construction materials. A fence lined with green canvas bordered the property, and plastic curtains had been pulled over most of the windows. Through them the library looked empty, a gutted shell of Kane's memory.

The invitation hummed in his pocket. Around him the chorus of cicadas swelled, urging him forward, except suddenly his secret investigation didn't feel like so much fun.

Still, as imperfect as this plan might be, it was *his*.

He stashed his bike in a towering mountain laurel, then snuck through the vacant construction grounds. Except for the cicadas, it was eerily quiet. Opaque curtains hung in the entryway, billowing outward in methodic exhales, and the interior beyond was impenetrably dark.

Kane pulled on Ursula's flannel. He wondered if he should at least text Ursula the address in case he vanished, but decided he couldn't risk turning on his phone. Setting his jaw, he plunged inside.

The library had been constructed around an open expanse topped with a skylight that usually saturated every inch of the space with sunlight. Kane's memory of the space was therefore a riot of oranges and yellows that burned the floating dust in the air to glitter.

The library Kane stood in now was a betrayal to that memory. The skylight had been covered with a tarp, and the sunlight that plunged through the gaps looked almost solid enough to bump into. Only a few bits of dust rocked in and out of the light, like insects. Otherwise, the air was unmoving.

There were no books. Just stripped wood and wires.

But there was noise. A distant chiming in the emptiness, somewhere above Kane. He closed his eyes to listen. When he reopened them, he was not alone.

A dog sat in a spotlight, sleek and black, with cropped ears poised like horns. A Doberman with a fine silver chain for a collar. It watched Kane with urgent eyes, whined, and then trotted toward the stairs. Kane followed obediently, climbing up two stories until he found the dog waiting at the top.

Before the construction, the library's top floor was reserved for the boring adult books. Now the top floor was a huge open room, barely lit by a grid of blacked-out skylights. Some of the skylights had shed their tarps and the effect was the underside of a pond rocking in slow motion. It lent a murky translucence to the emptiness that was, Kane noticed, not empty at all.

In the middle of the expanse was a room without walls. It glowed warmly, like a spotlighted scene on an empty, black stage. There was an ivory settee lounging across from a stiff and prim wingback chair. Between them sat a mahogany coffee table complete with a gleaming tray of porcelain teacups, saucers, and a teapot. Steam curled up from the pot's pursed lips, disappearing into a chandelier that blazed with a thousand crystal facets. Kane approached, transfixed. It wasn't until he was nearly beneath the chandelier that he sensed something about it: its light pulsed, as though alive.

Then something among the scene moved. Like an octopus unraveling from coral, an entire person shifted into focus on the settee as they stood up. The camouflage of their brocade robe against the settee was uncanny. Chills broke out across Kane's neck. He did not recognize who he saw; he recognized what he heard.

"Did you know," said Dr. Poesy, the very one who had given Kane the red journal in the Soft Room, "that the female anglerfish evolved a dark lining in its digestive system so the consumption of glowing morsels would not expose it from the inside out to its prey?"

Kane's eyes flicked up to the chandelier again.

"They live in the dark, you know," he added. "They're from the abyss."

Dr. Poesy was different from Kane's memory. Standing against the drabness, with his lustrous robe pooling around his shoulders, he radiated with pastel power. The skin of his face glowed beneath rose and peach makeup. His hair had gone from chestnut to a pearly lavender, pushed up high and backward and threaded with pearls—a wig, Kane knew. The edge of something chiffon fluttered out from where the rope fell open.

Was Dr. Poesy in drag?

"Yes, *she* is in drag," Dr. Poesy said, once again answering the questions that were plain on Kane's face. Kane controlled himself, blinking away his wonder.

"Anyways. Isn't that interesting?" she asked. "About the fish, I mean? I learned that today. It's a blessing to learn something new every day, but you'd have to inhabit a small world indeed not to. Isn't that right, Ms. Daisy?"

Dr. Poesy reached out a hand, and the dog lapped at the long fingers. She stroked the animal lovingly.

"Doesn't Ms. Daisy make a fine escort? I've always told her she could make a lot of money if she weren't so picky." She sat, crossing bare, toned legs, and motioned for Kane to do the same. Her high heels were monstrous.

"You're not a doctor, are you?" Kane blurted.

"Well, no, not in the conventional sense."

"Do you have a doctorate degree?"

"No."

"Do you have any degrees?"

Poesy—not Doctor, just Poesy then—looked affronted. "Of course."

"In what?"

"Parapsychic Architectures and what you people might call physics, but I don't see what that has to do—"

"What do you mean 'you people'?"

"Americans."

"Where are you from?"

"Not here."

"Be specific."

Poesy tapped a knifelike nail against her rosy cheek, smiling slyly. "The abyss."

Kane forced the edge out of his voice. "Well then what are you doing here?"

"Having tea. I thought I wrote that on the invitation. Would you like to join me?" Poesy slid off her robe and draped it over the settee, rendering her visible in a shimmering, beaded corset. Around one wrist she wore a bracelet laden with a dozen charms that clinked as she fussed. Kane found himself moving closer to inspect them. He spotted an opalescent skull, a copper starfish, a white wooden key.

He sat down.

There was also a small pewter pine cone. A fat porcelain bee.

"I hope you didn't have any trouble finding the place. As you can see, I have prioritized our privacy."

Kane blinked at the tea service of priceless, bone-white china beneath a dizzying lace of gold. Poesy picked up her own cup and used a little silver spoon to stir the tea into a small whirlpool.

Silver on porcelain. It was such a tiny sound. Kane wondered how he had heard it two stories below.

"You'll have some tea, won't you? We have quite a bit to discuss and not much time to do so, but there's no sense in dispensing with deportment. We aren't barbarians, are we?" Poesy chuckled knowingly as she filled Kane's cup.

"You know about the reveries?" he asked.

"I do."

"What do you know?"

"A lot."

"What are they?"

"Very dangerous."

Poesy's answers only spawned more questions, like mushrooms shedding spores. Kane shoved down his curiosity, knowing it was useless to expect a drag queen to do anything other than exactly what she wanted. From his limited knowledge, he knew drag queens often lip-synched to songs as bars full of cheering people fought to give them money. Kane didn't have any cash, and he didn't think Poesy would accept it anyway. He'd just have to let her perform her way, or no way at all, and so he shut up and sat back.

Poesy raised her teacup. Kane did the same. Together they sipped. The tea was infused with rose, and it buzzed like electricity in Kane's stomach.

"Mr. Montgomery," Poesy began. "What do you know of etherea?"

Etherea. The word was new to Kane, but it hung in his mind like a faceted gem, a feeling of familiarity emanating from its cut ridges and refracted depths. Kane whispered it to himself, feeling as though it ought to whisper back.

"Mr. Montgomery, I want you to think of reality as a cloth, lushly embroidered with everything you see in this world. Just layer upon layer of elaborate, incredible design. And if reality is a cloth, it must be woven from something, yes?"

"Like thread?"

Poesy licked her small silver spoon. "Like thread. Like etherea: the magic of creation, the magic that makes real the unreal. All things—reality around us, and the reveries you traverse, even other magics—are woven from etherea. Even this charming little town is a well-formed design. Stable and self-assured, it ought to exist for a good long time."

After another sip, Poesy's eyes darkened.

"Or it won't. That's the thing about etherea; it's a terrifically erratic magic, making and unmaking worlds in the blink of an eye. And that's what's happening in this town. A well of etherea has sprung up, and the excess magic is now everywhere, and restless. It must take shape. To do so, it has started using people with uniquely vast minds, casting its power through the prism of their imaginations and creating their interior worlds as entirely new realities." Poesy considered her own words. "Though they're not very good realities, are they? Oh, well, I suppose there's nothing to be done about other people's bad taste."

Kane fought to digest Poesy's words. It was like chewing potpourri. His mind turned to the unraveling last night, and that horrible reverie. He still felt the echoes of its anguish, its chaotic fury at having come undone. It had wanted to survive, and it would have killed to do so. Kane's teacup clattered in his saucer as he began to shiver. He didn't want to drink any more.

"So what you're saying…" Kane fumbled his way through a question that had only just begun to take shape. "Is that etherea is manifesting peoples' dreams?"

"Dreams!" Poesy grimaced around the word, like it was caked in salt. "Such deeply impractical things. I won't suffer the association. No. The phenomenon of the localized paracosm, or what you have shorthanded to *reverie*, could never originate with something as ephemeral as the *dream*. No. They come from the depth, the core, the *marrow* of the mind. The subconscious! The subcontinent, made real in phantasmagoric majesty!"

This monologue seemed very prepared. Kane let Poesy finish, gave a respectful and wide-eyed nod, and then countered with: "But this is impossible."

"Improbable," she corrected.

"I mean it's unbelievable. Like, unreal."

"So what?" Poesy snapped. "The unreality of something is no reason to dismiss it. Sometimes reveries—and dreams for that matter—are more real to a person than the reality they serve to distract from. I would expect you of all people to understand that."

Poesy's tone was cutting, such a fine blade that it was beneath

Kane's skin before he even saw it flash. But he kept his chin up, and his eyes on her. "I do understand that. What I meant is that these reveries shouldn't be here. They're wrong."

Poesy's frigid stare broke into a laugh that filled the empty library, and Kane finally took a breath.

"You're certainly right about that." She smiled, refilling his cup. "Reveries are beautiful and interesting things, but they have no place in Reality Proper. In fact, they must be unraveled at all costs or else they might punch a hole *through* Reality Proper. You can't have two realities layered one over the other for long without consequences. That's just the physics of friction, just the math of it all. And see? I told you I had a degree." Taking note of Kane's rising shock, she added, "Oh, but don't worry. With luck, you and your friends have prevented that outcome by diligently unraveling the reveries as they spawn. So, kudos."

"But why us?"

Her smile turned to awe. "Lucidity, darling. It's rare—this ability you four share to resist the hypnotizing effects of being in a different reality. I share it, too. We are all people between worlds."

"But what about the powers? Elliot can create illusions. Ursula can throw cars. Adeline can..."

He couldn't say it, even now. Poesy shrugged, like these details were as common as personality traits.

"Just like the heroes of your reveries, you each are a prism. Etherea shines through your dark depths, and it produces power. The difference is that you are awake to your power and able to regulate it. It's quite a privilege." Her eyes drifted to Kane's burns.

"Though while some power comes free, the pursuit of more power always comes at a price."

Blood burned in Kane's cheeks. The Others had told him he'd gotten those burns while hunting for some mysterious weapon.

"You already knew what happened to Maxine Osman, didn't you?"

"I did. I wanted you to find out for yourself."

"What about the police investigation? What about Detective Thistler?"

"I've dealt with them. And I will continue to deal with them and protect you, though I must ask that you help me in return."

Kane's head spun, his mind sagging in the honeyed vapor of the tea. He had to focus on Poesy's bracelet to keep himself steady.

"What do you want?"

Poesy feigned a bashful smile, as though she had not guided the conversation to this exact point.

"Haven't you wondered for yourself where etherea comes from? Haven't you found yourself dreaming of its source? Such power it must hold, to unleash all manner of dreams, delusions, nightmares, and whims into our suffering reality. Whatever and wherever this source is, I'd consider it very dangerous in the wrong hands."

Poesy sipped her tea, looking pointedly at Kane's own hands.

Kane ceased all fidgeting.

"A weapon," Kane said. He knew what came next. More accusations about what he'd done and who he'd been.

"Weapon!" Poesy laughed. "Weapons only destroy, my dear.

Instruments, however, both destroy and create. That's what makes them so powerful. The holy grail, Pandora's box, the genie's lamp; all were sources of etherea. If you look, really *look*, history is full of instruments that make the unreal real, that call forth power from nothing." She toyed with a stray pearl caught in the hair around her temple. "These instruments are called looms for their ability to weave new worlds from the imaginations of mortals. I have spent my whole existence hunting them down, one by one, to ensure they are not abused."

Poesy had said the reveries were a local phenomenon. A new one. Kane put the pieces together one by one.

"And that's why you're here? You think there's a loom hidden in East Amity?"

Pleased, Poesy dipped her cup at Kane.

"Yes. *The* loom, by the scale of its power. A crown-shaped instrument I believe you've summoned once already. Tell me about it, Mr. Montgomery."

"You think…" Kane fought the spinning vacancy spreading through his body. He vaguely remembered the Others telling him he had been searching for a source of power—a loom, maybe— and he had found a deadly crown. The actual symbol of power. But it was gone, cast away into the river or something. "I don't know where it is, if that's what you think. I don't know how to get it back."

Poesy exhaled, blowing curls of steam toward Kane. "Perhaps you don't know now, but think, Mr. Montgomery: What do you find yourself so suddenly without?"

The answer rose up through Kane like a bubble breaking calm water. "My memories."

Poesy's eyes glinted. "How inconvenient. Memories interest me, you know. In a way, you explored the very memory of this town through Maxine Osman, who spent her life perfecting its rendering." Poesy shrugged. "Her world must have been lovely. I wonder what you saw, and I wonder what you learned. But mostly, I wonder what must a person discover to make them dangerous enough to be hurt in the way you have been hurt. What power is deserving of such a thorough and vicious suppression?" She shrugged again, her downcast eyes sliding up to meet his. "A loom seems like just the inspiration for that caliber of evil, and we only know one person with the means."

Kane's breath halted as his hand traced the raised flesh of his burns. He had found the loom, and then he had been betrayed. It had to have been Adeline. Adeline was the one who had dug into his head and scooped out his memories. She said she'd done it to save him. Ursula and Elliot had agreed. Did they know, or had she brainwashed them, too?

A raw helplessness opened in Kane. It was hard to hold Poesy's gaze with tears in his eyes. "What do I do?"

Not a hint of haughtiness touched Poesy's voice now.

"You be brave, Mr. Montgomery. You face the reveries, you recover the loom, and you deliver it to me safely. Together, we will save reality from this plague of fantasy and ruin."

Kane thought again of the barbarians with their frost-white eyes. The split lips of the altar, vomiting forth unfathomable beasts.

"What happens if I don't want to?"

Poesy eyed him with unrestrained pity. "Saving the world isn't usually a matter of *want*, Mr. Montgomery. How cowardly you must be to balance the destruction of reality upon the scales of your own heart. And how selfish."

Kane sniffed. The words stung. They stung because they were true; deep beneath the swells of his fear he knew better. He nodded.

Poesy swallowed the last drops of tea, then unfastened a charm from her bracelet and tossed it to Kane.

"In my travels I have accumulated many artifacts that not only bend reality but break it in useful ways. The journal is one. This is another. Use it only in emergencies."

The charm was a tube of black metal, heavier than Kane expected and ice cold. An old-fashioned whistle. Something told Kane the sound it made would be unlike anything he'd ever heard.

"Ms. Daisy and I must be going." Poesy stood and drew her robe around herself. Kane stood unsteadily.

"And, Mr. Montgomery, if I were you I might keep our meeting a secret. There are others like me—others who hunt for the sacred looms. You cannot be too distrusting in matters like this, I find, because you never know what form darkness will take. A silver-eyed siren or a golden-haired prince, perhaps? Or even a dim-witted ogress? But do not fret. You are not alone. You never were."

A chime swelled around Kane, rolling out through the empty space, and Poesy was gone. So was Ms. Daisy, the tea, and the furniture. Then the chandelier flickered away, and Kane was again abandoned to the watery dimness of the library, a small black whistle in his palm and a chorus of unanswered questions chirping in his head.

· FOURTEEN ·
NICE AND NORMAL

KANE CALLED SOPHIA RIGHT AWAY, BUT SHE SENT HIM
to voicemail. When he texted her a simple what's up and she didn't
reply, he knew he was in trouble, but how much? What kind? Her
silence scared him more than anything. He hoped she wasn't past
trying to reason with him. Not yet. He would need her, if what
Poesy said was true.

At East Amity High School, it was as though the reverie had
never happened. Kane drifted through the sunny halls of laughing, clueless students. His eyes were glazed with the memory of a
fantasy none of them knew about. He saw familiar faces from the
reverie, now scrubbed of blood and grime and ash. He saw the
slow pulse of red light every time he closed his eyes. As though
acting as a reminder, the black whistle's cool metal bit into his

palm, assuring him it had all been real, that just because the night-mare had ended didn't mean it had never happened.

Kane skipped homeroom, instead wandering out to the athletic fields. The locker rooms were open for cleaning. They did not lead to a subterranean city. The football stadium itself did not have a moat of magma. Nothing nefarious skittered in the wavy heat rising from the track.

The mystery of the loom, and the mission Poesy had charged Kane with, followed him everywhere. Was the loom a thing you summoned, or a thing you found? If it was as powerful as Poesy said, Kane was not eager to confront the person who kept it hidden, and decided all he could do was wait and see (and hopefully not die in the meantime).

Finally Sophia texted him back: Busy. Over your shit. We'll talk when I get home.

And so Kane panicked quietly for the next few hours. Bio class came and went without a word passed between Adeline and Kane. In gym, he only got close enough to Elliot to verify the bruise on his cheek. Then Kane sat in the bleachers and watched Elliot act like an idiot with his friends. They never once made eye contact. There was no sign of Dean Flores whatsoever.

Then, at lunch, Kane had just finished loading up a tray full of food when he turned to find Ursula right behind him. She looked like she was working up the nerve to say something.

"Hi," was all she managed. Her wide, asking eyes panned over the flannel—her flannel—which he still wore, then back up.

He walked past her and ate lunch by himself, passing the

whistle between his palms like nothing had ever happened. Like everything was nice and normal.

∞

Biking home after school, Kane regretted ignoring Ursula all day. He wasn't sure why. She'd lied. She was worse than Elliot and Adeline. So why was he mad at himself for shunning her?

In part it felt like unreleased potential. All day he had silently rehearsed what he would say to the Others, entire monologues of grief and guilt and acidic words for what they'd done, but with the exception of Ursula at lunch, they'd stayed away, depriving him of the opportunity. So all that acid had nowhere to go. It burned and boiled in Kane, joining with the thousand other things that he had never had the guts to say.

Somewhere inside him he realized they had respected his wishes to be left alone. Like actual friends. And he couldn't shake the earnest heartbreak in Ursula's eyes when he'd turned his back on her. She really did care.

Let them go, Kane told himself. *Let them all go.*

The whistle sat like a rock in his pocket. Even through his jeans, the metal was cool and alive, reminding him that none of this was over. Not for him. Poesy had been right. He couldn't outrun this, which meant he had no choice but to fight.

Sophia was Kane's first battle. As soon as she got home that evening she burst into the den, turned off Kane's PlayStation, and dragged him outside before their mom could sit them down for dinner.

"You're so lucky," she seethed, pacing circles around Kane in the school playground near their house. Dusk burned around them, alive with the buzz of bugs. "You're *so* goddamn lucky you've got me as your sister."

"Look, I'm sorry, but I already told you I was just doing homework last night."

"Where?"

Kane was ready for this. "Ursula's house. Duh."

Sophia scrunched up her face. "Who?"

Shit. Kane realized that even though Ursula was his longest friendship, Sophia had no idea who she was thanks to Adeline.

"Someone from school. She's my tutor. But who cares? You've got to stop imagining I'm running away whenever you can't see me." Kane hooked his hands through the monkey bars, changing the subject. "I can't stay in that house. None of it feels familiar. My room feels like a memorial."

"You need to tell Mom and Dad. If your amnesia is so bad you can't even remember who you are, maybe you should get tested for brain damage."

"I know who I am," he shot back. "And I am being evaluated, remember?"

"By that psychoanalyst? The one who's making you keep a dream journal? That's right. I see you writing in it."

"It's not a dream journal," Kane said, offended. "It's just a journal. It's what the police want. It's what our parents want. I'm just doing what I'm told so I can stay out of jail. You know that."

Kane fled to the swings, and Sophia slumped after, a mirror to

160

his own misery as he kicked off. He hoped the momentum would wrench the conversation apart, but Sophia's voice came in bursts over the squeals from the rusted metal frame.

"Sneaking out. Is *not* doing. What you're told."

"Maybe not. According to *you*. Little Miss Anal. Retentive."

Sophia hoped off and faced Kane with her hands on her hips. His momentum fizzled out beneath her glare.

"Really, Kane? Little Miss Anal?"

"Anal-retentive. It means 'orderly.'"

"I know what anal-retentive means."

Kane smiled, trying to get her to laugh. She didn't. In the low light, her eyes churned with helpless fury, barely holding back tears.

"I can't be the only one watching out for you, Kane. Scare me again, and I'll make sure you flunk that evaluation. I'm done lying for you."

They didn't talk for days after that. A cold war opened between them, fought in glances over breakfast and silently passing one another in their shared hallway. Their parents noticed but were reluctant to add any more tension to their small, stifling house.

Kane kept telling himself he didn't care. Sophia wouldn't sabotage him, and they both knew it. She was just making this about her, and he had bigger worries than his sister's hurt feelings right now. Bigger worries, and far greater fears. He had to find the loom for Poesy. And he had to figure out what he'd done to Maxine Osman, for himself. His heart couldn't take not knowing.

His guilt turned him to the internet, where he learned everything he could about the woman. He found her address and phone number on an old committee mailing page for a banquet she'd organized. He read interviews she'd done for the paper where she talked about her love of the Cobalt Complex, which she lived near. He found a few videos, too, put together for a special about area artists on the local access channel. In them, she was a quiet speaker, but sharp and funny in a dark way. After her husband died, she'd tried any hobby that would tolerate her. Pottery, but it was too messy. Then she got into cross-country skiing, she explained, showing the camera a pair of ancient ski poles. They were pinned into the dirt of her garden as though they'd been there forever, tomato vines winding up them. "As you can see, I was very, very slow," she said dryly. Then she showed off a collection of bejeweled eggs that lay in glass cases around her living room. "We have more than one hundred. We take them out sometimes," she said, referring to herself and her friend, another lady who was somehow even older and even smaller, standing behind her. They laughed as they showed the camera a blue egg flecked in gold. "We talk about what would hatch from them," her friend said. And then the interview turned to Maxine's studio, which was the house's second bedroom. "I do most of my work in the field, but this room has the best light in winter," she said. "The light is important, for the colors. And of course my tan."

There was nothing about her being gone. To the world, she was still in her little haven, painting in her studio and surrounded by her many hobbies. Nice and normal. This broke Kane up the most. He hated himself for his role in her demise, though still he could remember none of it.

Every night—*every* night—he dreamt of her, and even though he had her face memorized, in his dreams she was always burning. Never dead, but always burning.

More than once, he found himself seated on the edge of his bed, her phone number glowing on his laptop screen. One morning after he woke up with his burns on fire and his sheets twisted around him, he actually called it.

It wasn't like he expected anyone to pick up, but then someone did.

"Hello?"

Hi would have worked, but Kane hadn't expected anyone to answer the phone in a house he thought was empty. It wasn't Maxine's voice, but it was somehow familiar. Small, questioning.

"Hello? It's very early to be calling. Hello?"

There was a long silence in which the static between the two phones whirred, and then the voice asked, "Maxine? Is that you?"

Something clicked. Through his shock, Kane recognized the voice: Maxine's friend. The one who talked about the eggs.

The one who didn't know Maxine was dead.

"Please," she said, and behind her voice rose a strange din, a whispering that swallowed her just before the line went dead. Through it, Kane could hear her pleading:

"Please, Maxine, just come home."

· FIFTEEN ·
SUSURRATIONS

KANE WAS STILL THINKING ABOUT THE CALL DAYS later. The hope in that voice was unforgettable, but so was the sorrow. And he had no idea what to make of that strange whispering.

The woman's name was Helena Quigley. She used to run a small shop downtown, and before that she was a biology teacher at the high school. Aside from appearing to be close friends, Kane had no idea why she had answered Maxine's phone so early in the morning, and he couldn't bring himself to call back.

But he was curious, and Kane usually lost all battles with his curiosity.

He kept himself busy in Roost, the bookstore downtown that had become his haven from school and his house. He'd been hiding there for the past week, burning through the mountains of homework he needed to make up. Hiding wasn't the right word, though. Sophia and his parents knew exactly where he was when he wasn't at the house or his support group. They dropped him off at Roost after school and picked him up at closing, like a day care.

Kane even went there on Saturdays, like today. Anything to escape the eerie music of Sophia practicing viola and his parents bickering in the backyard about where to put this new plant or that red mulch. The hypernormal soundtrack of a suburban hellscape, which made it impossible to imagine a drag queen sorceress watching over East Amity, and even harder to imagine just a garden-variety, standard-issue drag queen in East Amity to begin with. But here in Roost, among books about curses and adventures and cities that clung to the outermost rim of space, it was all a bit more real. A bit more reachable. Kane didn't feel so lost.

And he liked the staff. They knew all about him but never asked about any of the town-wide drama that his name represented. They saved him a seat near the outlets and brought him leftover corn muffins from the café, and they even let Kane bring in his blue Slurpees from the 7-Eleven across the street so long as he put them on a saucer, as not to mess up the wooden tables. In short, they gave him plenty of space.

Sometimes, though, Kane wished they would ask how he was doing. Or what was going on in his head. But they didn't, and so Kane poured his thoughts into the journal instead, until his hand was as tight and cramped as his heart.

"So you're a writer now?"

Kane closed the red journal quickly, unaware anyone had even sat down next to him. When he looked up, he was staring through a sweep of dirty-blond hair, into laughing, hazel eyes.

Elliot.

"Wait!" He put his hands up, trying to keep Kane from running. "I just want to talk, okay?"

Kane pushed the journal under some books. How long had Elliot been sitting there, invisible? Had he seen what Kane was writing? It was a list of places the loom might be.

"What do you want, Elliot?"

Elliot glanced around. "Can we maybe find somewhere else? I've got my car out front."

"No. We stay here. And don't use your powers again. That's not fair."

"All right. But you, too, okay?"

"I don't even know how to use my powers."

This was a lie. He had been practicing summoning the ethereal fire, then dousing it when the objects in his room began to float.

"Adeline said you did well in the Cooper reverie. Like a natural."

"Well, don't worry. I won't be doing any snapping or clapping anytime soon."

Elliot did a good job pretending this reassured him, but overall the boy still looked a bit surprised to find them actually talking. He fidgeted until Kane repeated his question.

"What do you want?"

"I guess I wanted to apologize. We were always planning on bringing you back into the Others, but not like that. Nothing went according to my plan, and it's my fault."

"You like plans a lot, don't you?" Kane bit the straw of his drink. "Plans and facts."

"I'm that obvious?"

"Yeah. I've witnessed like three conversations with you, and in every one you can't stop correcting people. I don't know how Adeline and Ursula deal with it. You're extremely patronizing."

A blush climbed up Elliot's neck. He looked like he was going to defend himself, but then he looked at his hands.

"I deserve that," he muttered.

The old words stirred in Kane, all the acid he'd saved up for Elliot and the Others, but those emotions were flat now, like old soda. He didn't know what to say to move the conversation past it, though. Thankfully, Elliot offered a path forward.

"You and I were working on this theory together, before, you know," he said. "About how our powers come from our pain or from parts of ourselves we hate. For instance, I really like facts and planning, but all I can do is create illusions. Lies and manipulation. And Ursula, right? She's like, the least confrontational person I know. She hates violence, but her power gives her that brutal strength. Seems kinda strange, right?"

"What about me? And Adeline?"

"You can ask Adeline that. And we never figured yours out." Elliot's face was still red, his shoulders tense like he was waiting to be eviscerated again, but Kane wasn't buying the hurt act.

"It's kind of weird that you hate manipulating people with illusions. You seem very good at it."

Elliot's laugh was humorless. Resigned. "Runs in the family,

I guess. My dad was a big-time liar. Super manipulative. And sometimes I don't even think he knew he was doing it. I think that's why my power freaks me out. Like, what if one day I don't know, either? I never want to be as good at lying as he was."

"Was?"

"Yeah. We moved away from him. My aunt lives in East Amity. That's why we came here. It's a lot better now, for my mom, I mean. And my sisters."

Elliot felt far away now, out to sea on the swells of huge and mysterious thoughts. Kane wanted to reel him back in.

"And what about you?"

Elliot rolled his lips together, then nodded. "It's better for me, too."

This boy who had scared Kane—who still scared Kane—had shared something precious, placing it right into Kane's poised jaws. Was this vulnerability sincere, or was it all just manipulation after all? Either way, Kane had to proceed gently.

"I'm sorry," Kane said finally. "I didn't know any of that."

Elliot seemed to remember who he was talking to and cleared the emotion out of his throat.

"Yeah, see? And that's my fault, too. You'd know everything if we didn't mess up your memories. I'm really, really sorry things happened the way they did. That's what I wanted to say." His mouth pulled into a tentative smile, showing his dimples. *Ah*. So *this* was the Elliot everyone apparently knew. Charming. Charismatic. Persuasive.

He was the Elliot that Poesy had told Kane not to trust.

"It's okay," Kane found himself saying, even though it certainly wasn't okay.

Elliot exhaled, relieved. "Can you do me a favor, then?"

When Kane shrugged in response, Elliot scooted forward. "I just want you to know that none of this was Ursula's fault. She was always for putting you first, you know that, right? I don't like that she messed with the plan, but I respect her, and I know she was just trying to be a good friend. I think you should ease up on her."

The weed of guilt that had already taken root grew even more, slowly pushing through to his heart. Elliot had named what Kane wouldn't let himself believe: Ursula was innocent. That meant Ursula deserved a better friend than Kane had ever been.

After Elliot left, Kane turned his request over in his head like inspecting a smooth stone before hurling it across smooth waters. Why had Elliot talked to him like this? What did he want? Was it possible his agenda had only been for Ursula? That made Kane question his distrust just long enough for him to grow curious, and Kane's curiosity had just about enough of being told no.

He tossed his stuff into his bag before chasing after Elliot, smacking a palm on the hood of his car as he was pulling out. Elliot jolted in the driver's seat.

"Wait," Kane said. "I need your help. And call the Others. We'll need them, too."

They drove toward the Cobalt Complex. At some point the sweltering Saturday had tipped into a stormy afternoon, and the humidity had unleashed a violent rain that lasted only six minutes.

It happened when they were on the bridge, sweeping over the river in golden and gray waves that bundled the distance into a hazy closeness. By the time they reached the complex, the rain was done, and the trees shuddered with new weight. They found the girls in a cracked lot, the pavement already drying in patchwork.

"You sure you want to do this?" Elliot asked again.

"Yeah."

Elliot waved the girls over. They piled into his back seat, and then Elliot turned out of the lot as Adeline read directions off her phone. A few minutes later they arrived. Elliot, ever cautious, parked a street over. The same caution is why they'd left the other cars at the complex. The less to hide, the better, Elliot said. And then the four of them were in front of the house, Maxine's house, which meant Kane had to explain why he'd brought them all here.

"Who else knows about Maxine Osman?" he asked.

Adeline and Elliot exchanged a look. "No one, yet," Adeline said. "We imagined she'd be reported missing by someone, eventually. But she doesn't have any family. No kids or anything."

"She has a friend named Helena Quigley," Kane said. "And I think she's in that house."

More glances were exchanged.

"And I think she's in trouble," Kane added.

"What sort of trouble?" asked Ursula.

"Reverie trouble," Kane said.

Kane expected eye rolls and anger, but what he got was direct concern from the three of them as they peppered him with a million questions. He waved them away so he could explain.

"This is going to sound so weird, but I remember hearing this whispering after I unraveled Benny Cooper's reverie, right before I gave it back to him. And then I heard that sound when I called Maxine's house and someone picked up. And I think that someone was Helena."

Adeline dialed Kane back with her index finger. "You called Maxine's house?"

"Just once," Kane said, a little ashamed. Again he waited for doubt and criticism, but the Others just nodded.

"In the past, you've been the best at figuring out where the next reverie was going to hit," Elliot explained. "Probably part of that energy you can manipulate."

"Etherea," Kane said automatically.

"Is that what we're calling it now?" Adeline asked pointedly, like she knew Kane hadn't just made up the term. He looked away from her quickly.

"Just a name," he said.

"And you feel like you can sense...*etherea* from inside that house?"

"Something like that."

The Others had a silent conversation with only their eyes, perhaps deliberating how to handle Kane's new, strange mission. Ursula was the one to step forward and say, "All right, the least we can do is take a look, right? If someone's in trouble, it's up to us to help them."

They approached Maxine's house, which was a narrow Tudor set back behind a court of hemlocks. Kane knew from the videos that if they walked to the top floor, they'd find one bedroom and one room full of light and watercolors. As they rounded the back, he knew they'd find an overgrown garden with two ski poles pinned in the dirt. And they did, though the garden was beyond neglected. Withered vines hung off the poles from twist ties. Unharvested vegetables sat in the dirt, soft with rot. No one had been back here in a while.

"Hear anything?" Adeline asked Kane.

Kane wasn't sure just yet. He heard a faint din, just beneath the warm breeze, but it could have just been his heartbeat in his own ears.

"I don't see any lights on," Ursula whispered.

"Urs, you don't have to whisper, I'm keeping us invisible," Elliot said, his eyes shining an inhuman gold.

"Part of his illusion magic," Ursula explained to Kane, still whispering.

Creeped out, Kane drifted toward the back door, but Elliot's voice stopped him.

"Come on, Kane. We can't just walk in."

"I want to check on her."

"But this isn't even *her* house."

"Then why did she answer the phone?"

Kane was acting sure, but he didn't know. All he knew was the helplessness he'd heard in the old woman's voice as she called out for her lost friend. And right now the din in his head was rising. Something was wrong.

Ursula let out a small yelp.

"I saw something! In a window! Something moved!"

They backed up to look into the stoic face of the house.

Nothing in the windows moved, but Kane was sure something was off about the house. Something about its black presence against the gray sky seemed to bend the air, like the house was a weight slowly sinking backward, pulling the world around it taut. And again he heard that shushing din. Faint and ephemeral, but there. The house whispered with dark promise, urging them to come closer.

Then, from the top floor, there was a scream. At the same time a window exploded outward, releasing a strange pressure from the house and blowing over the desiccated garden. Around them the plants came back to life, turning from gray to green. Flowers uncurled new buds that bloomed in seconds, reinvigorated by what had to be magic.

"Kane was right." Adeline sounded stricken. "It's a reverie. It's already forming!"

"We have to help her." Kane charged toward the door. Before he'd made it, just as he was passing a propped-up wheelbarrow, he collided with a person attempting to hide in the garden.

They both fell to the ground.

"Sophia?"

Sophia straightened her shirt as she stood. She picked up her phone, the screen showing it was recording a video.

The Others approached from behind.

"Great work, Elliot. *Super* invisible," Adeline said.

Kane dragged his sister away by the elbow. "What the hell are you doing here?"

Sophia shook him off. "I came to Roost to see if you wanted to get food. A peace offering, but you were with that guy. And then

I saw you race after him, so I followed. And…" Her voice trailed off as she watched the garden grow wild around them. "Kane, are you seeing this, too?"

"You were *spying* on me?"

Sophia's eyes darted between Kane, the Others, and the garden. "No, I mean, I guess. I was spying on *all* of you. Who are they? More 'tutors' of yours? What is this?"

"You need to go, Sophia. It's not safe for you here." Kane shoved her away. Golden pollen floated in the air now, and it had grown unusually sunny just over the house. The reverie was building itself all around them.

Sophia pushed past Kane and addressed Adeline. "You! I know you. You do dance at the conservatory, right?"

"Ballet," Adeline said.

"And you!" Sophia put a finger toward Ursula. "You play field hockey, right? I know I've seen you before. And you!" She had reached Elliot, but clearly had no idea who he was, and so she just squinted at him with menace.

"Kane," Elliot said gravely. "You have to get her out of here. And we can't let her remember any of this."

Kane moved between them. His anger was instant, rising in him just as a flare of etherea rose from his hand.

"If you touch my sister, I will kill you."

Elliot's eyes filled with fear as he backed away.

"Kane, we don't have time for this. Think about what you're doing."

"I *am* thinking about it. And I wouldn't have let you guys erase my sister's memory the first time if I'd been able to think about it then, but—oh wait! I was in a fucking coma, or did you forget your little plan?"

Elliot's jaw worked, his eyes never leaving the light in Kane's fist. The whispering was all around them now, a roar slowly saturating the air.

"Sophia, you need to run," Kane commanded. For once, she listened, darting out of the garden and back toward the street.

"We'll leave her," Elliot said. "We promise. But right now we need to get out of here, too."

Kane dropped the fire, letting the light burrow into the thickening grass. He took deep breaths, caught between wanting to run away with his sister and needing to follow through on his original goal. He had been right. The next reverie had come to East Amity, and it had found its home in Helena Quigley. They were the only people who knew, and they were the only people who could save her from whatever horror had just burst from her head.

"We're not leaving," Kane said, thinking of Poesy's words. Helena could not run from this, and she couldn't fight it herself, either. It was up to them, the lucid. The powerful. Kane marched toward the back door, knowing he'd find it ajar, just like the locker rooms. The mouth of the reverie left slightly agape, a tantalizing trap for anyone curious enough to enter.

Ursula caught him, her grip like concrete.

"Helena is in there," Kane shouted at her. "We can't just abandon her."

"You're not going in there," Ursula said as Adeline and Elliot joined her. "Not alone. Not without us."

· SIXTEEN ·
A BEAZLEY FAMILY AFFAIR

THIS TIME, ENTERING THE REVERIE WASN'T AS SIMPLE as running through a door. Or it was, but it didn't feel that way. Kane's vision went black the moment he entered the house, and Ursula's grip was wrenched away. His senses darkened one by one, until he couldn't feel anything at all. Then, like a computer rebooting, the world slowly came back to him. A different world than the one he had just left behind.

$$\infty$$

Music from a string quartet threaded the warm breeze, weaving together with birdsong and bursts of far off laughter. The air was perfumed with honey and wine, and though the world felt bright upon Kane's eyelids, they stayed decidedly closed as he awoke.

"The rich throw such tedious parties. It's because they only know other rich people, and money makes people boring. I don't blame you for trying to escape it all, Willard."

A hand cupped Kane's own. He tried to move, to respond, but only a croak scraped from his throat.

"You've always been such a good listener. I'm sorry we didn't talk more when you could." The voice was that of a young girl, maybe around Kane's age. "I bet you could tell me so many things about the world away from here. Maybe one day I'll get to tell you things."

Kane finally got one eye open, then the other. He sat on a bench in a ribbon of shade created by a row of poplar trees that overlooked a manicured courtyard. Through the trees loomed a shimmering château, so large that it seemed to draw up and crest over them like a great wave. In the midday glare it glowed, every window ablaze with such radiance that the garden beneath—a vast and complicated maze of hedges, fountains, and channels that wrapped around where Kane sat—was submerged in golden light.

Guests drifted through the garden—Kane knew they were guests in the same way he knew this was a party; all the women wore sweeping dresses, soft and thousand-layered, like blooming peonies. All the men wore coats with long tails and shoes glossed to match the sheen of their oiled hair. There were a great many hats.

The reverie exuded Victorian elegance, but in a way that looked costumed to Kane, like dress-up.

Beside Kane was a young girl with chubby cheeks and large

teeth. She was dressed in a satin gown the color of red roses and had on a hat piled with fake birds. She looked into the garden. Her eyes were brown, full of a dreamy hunger. She was real, and unless the reverie had drastically transformed one of the Others, Kane was sitting next to Helena herself.

"Beautiful, isn't she?"

Kane followed her gaze to a massive gazebo. Before it sat rows and rows of white chairs. Ivory ribbons trailed in the breeze and petals littered the ground. Helena was staring at a particular couple who Kane assumed had just been married, for the man wore a gorgeous black tuxedo and the woman was swathed in such an intense amount of tulle that to assume she was anything other than a bride would be absurd. As the bride turned, sunlight caught in the coronet of orange blossoms woven into her crimson ringlets, illuminating a wide and pale face.

Kane nearly scoffed. The guise was brilliant. The only unfinished bit of the costume was Ursula herself, who steamed with discomfort in her huge dress.

Kane couldn't help it. He laughed.

As soon he did, he knew it was a mistake. His throat closed, like he'd inhaled sharp smoke. He wheezed and gasped until the constriction melted away. This reverie wanted him silent.

Helena rubbed his back. "Oh Willard, you mustn't strain yourself. It's my fault. I shouldn't be talking on and on like this, as though you care at all. But, I must confess that your silence is a relief." She leaned in close, champagne and strawberries on her breath. "I have a secret for you, Cousin Willard. There is a very important man here. A Mister Johan Belanger, who everyone believes will propose to Katherine Duval tonight."

Kane wished he could push her away. Gradually, his body was awakening to his own control, and as it did he found that his hands stung with something cold.

The whistle! It was still nestled in his palms. Focusing on it brought a deluge of sensation back to Kane's body.

Helena went on. "And I know everyone gossips about my rivalry with Katherine Duval, but the truth is I know her better than anyone else. She truly believes that Johan loves her, and it makes her weak. She is distracted by this lie, as is everyone, but not me. Which is why I shall prevail."

She leaned closer to Kane, eyes darkening with determination. She placed her hands upon his.

"What's this you've got here, Cousin Willard?" She pried open his fingers.

No!

"Come on, let me see. Is it a toy? What's gotten into you?"

She got one hand open, then the other.

"Sister!"

Helena sprang back. Ursula suddenly towered over them, monstrous dress and all. She was flanked by her husband, who looked frankly surprised to find himself dragged so quickly across such a wide lawn.

"Augustine," said Helena, referring to Ursula. "You look positively lovely! I was just fetching our cousin Willard to come and say hello. You remember Willard, don't you? We used to summer together as children at the camp upstate, before Mother died."

Ursula nodded. "Why yes, of course. How do you do, Willard?" She extended a hand, which Kane knew not to take.

"Augustine, please, you must remember he prefers to keep quiet."

Ursula peered at Kane. "Yes, of course." Her face brightened. "Well, perhaps he would enjoy a tour of the gardens? I'm sure he would appreciate them, and it's been ever so long since we summered together in…" Ursula clearly did not know where she had spent her fictitious childhood summers, and so she finished awkwardly with: "The summertime."

Helena bowed dutifully. "Of course, sister." She turned to Ursula's husband and said, "Robert, come, show your new sister-in-law to a refreshment before that Katherine shows up and ruins our good time." And they left.

Ursula hooked her arm into Kane's and heaved him up. With her help they walked through the shade. Kane's other hand remained fasted around his talisman.

"So you can move, but you can't speak? Shoot. This reverie is a doozy. It wouldn't even let me loosen this freaking corset. I tried when I first woke up, but it just got tighter. And have you seen these gardens? It's like we're trapped in Versailles! Massive. At least there's no fantasy element, right? I just hope that the Others are okay. We need to find them as soon as we can and figure out what Helena is after. She's who you were sitting with, right?"

Kane nodded.

"And I'm her older sister, Augustine Beazley, although I just got married, so who knows what my last name is now. Okay, strong start so far."

They circled the gazebo's manicured courtyard and then doubled back along a glittering channel choked with lily pads. Koi slid beneath them, scaled in gold and citrine. On the walk through the elaborate hedge maze they passed hundreds of guests—some upon the small stone bridges, some raking sand in a Japanese garden, some chasing after the many bejeweled peacocks—all of them sporting the same, clear white irises. They chatted with audible deportment about things like trade, taxes, tea, and horses. Cartoon topics of wealth. On the whole it felt awfully artificial, but Ursula was right: a rigidity saturated the air—the same strictness that had choked Kane—and though he knew he could speak if he needed to, he didn't dare incite any plot twists. Not after last time.

Kane stayed silent as Ursula endured the barrage of people congratulating her, blessing her, and asking about her wedding dress.

"Where did you get it?"

"France," she'd say.

"Oh! Tell me about the material!"

"It's white," she'd say.

Kane's mind drifted from the reverie, wondering where Sophia had run to. Maybe she was at home. Maybe she was at the police station right now.

The sun set and the garden shifted to hues of pink and orange, a cue that caused the guests to drift up the wide patio steps toward the château. Ursula remained lost in thought until suddenly she clapped her hands and yelled, "I've got it!"

People turned on the steps. She rushed Kane onto the patio and into an isolated alcove behind two hydrangea.

"This is all so familiar, and I couldn't figure out why until just now. The wedding, the garden, the Beazley family. It's all from *The Devil in the Lily*! It was a big romance novel last year. Like, huge. They're making a movie."

Kane shrugged.

"Okay, well the details don't matter, but basically the book focuses on a rivalry between the main character—who I guess is Helena—and her competitor, the wicked Katherine Duval. They're after the same guy, this hot industrialist prodigy, Johan Belanger, who *totally* despises Katherine but has no choice but to marry her because of her family's investment in his business, and—what?"

Kane didn't realize he was making a face.

"Listen, don't judge me. It's a good book, okay? I know you don't read romance so I'll just tell you how it ends: Katherine is totally insane. She's like…the devil, I guess? It's a metaphor. I don't know. But this gives us everything we need to know about this reverie! Don't you see that? All we need to do is make sure we re-create the resolution in the book. Oh, it's so *easy!*"

Ursula was thoroughly convinced, and there was little Kane could do to counter any of this. She knew this story, and she knew this world. Still, Kane couldn't quite reconcile the reverie's plot with the Helena Quigley he had imagined. But, then again, he didn't know the woman at all, and it wasn't his place to speculate what worlds she harbored in her mind.

Ursula peered through the hydrangea.

"Okay, listen to me Kane. The climax of *The Devil in the Lily* happens the night of Augustine's wedding. *My* wedding, that's happening right *now*. If I'm right, Katherine is going to try to stop Helena and Johan from eloping, and Helena is going to shoot her. That happens during the fireworks in the book. My husband told me those are at midnight. That means we need to find Katherine and make sure she discovers Helena's plan, but not too soon. Only soon enough to get murdered. Oh, it's so good! I love this."

Ursula looked truly enthralled to be acting out this book, but Kane couldn't shake a churning uncertainty that something was off. Nothing was ever this easy for him.

"I'm not Elliot, but here's the plan." Ursula sat Kane down. "Stay here. You're Cousin Willard, a side character who tried to run away at the start of the book but got caught and dragged back, then put in some sort of institution. He doesn't talk and barely listens. Basically a warning of what happens to those that defy societal expectations, like Helena and Johan will by eloping. The point is that this is a Beazley family affair, and you should stay out of it, okay? Let me and the Others handles this. Just chill until we can get Helena and Johan to elope, and then we'll come find you once the reverie is ready to be unraveled. Okay? Okay."

Wait! Kane mouthed.

"What?"

Don't leave me.

Ursula took his hands.

"Don't worry, I'll take care of everything. You have nothing to worry about, okay? Just get ready for the unraveling, and promise me you'll stay here."

"I—"

"Don't say it. Just do it."

She hustled into the crowd, leaving Kane to wait with his fear.

And wait he did. Just not there. Whether it was his usual anxiety or a sharper instinct, Kane found himself edging the patio, watching the faces in the crowd. He wondered who they were. Were they completely made up by the reverie, or were the faces memories of people Helena knew? Perhaps her mind had gathered all the ghosts of her past to inhabit her imagined world, to witness her triumph over her rival, to respect Helena here in ways they'd failed her in her actual life.

It didn't feel right.

Guests pressed into couples beneath archways festooned with vines and glittering berries. Kane slipped into the ballroom, gasping at the towering pillars, glowing chandeliers, and a skylight striped with sunset. He found himself at a table heavy with fruits and pastries, where he saw the strangest thing. Topping off the lavish display was a birdcage, which was odd, but the birds within it were even odder; they were assembled from delicate feathers of porcelain, with chrome beaks and unseeing eyes made of ball bearings. Little, ornate machines.

Then they blinked. Were they windup? Clockwork? Kane

leaned close and they ruffled their feathers. It was oddly organic. Then something past the birdcage snagged Kane's eye.

It's him!

Kane rushed around the table, pushing through guests until he reached the dancing couple he'd spotted. He clapped a hand on the man's shoulder and spun him around.

Kane looked into the sea-foam eyes of Dean Flores. Recognition, then dread, masked Dean's face.

"Cousin Willard," Dean said, as lucid as Ursula.

Then the person Dean had been dancing with pushed the two boys apart.

"What in the heavens is going on?" she said, looking over Kane with unmitigated disgust. "What gives you the right?"

Kane saw her eyes, and his heart cracked clean in half. He couldn't answer even if he wanted to, for the person berating him in the middle of the reverie's ballroom was none other than his own sister.

Sophia was here. She had followed them in.

Sophia was in the reverie.

· SEVENTEEN ·
THE NEST

"*NO.*"

Kane choked the words out, the pain only a fraction of the horror he felt seeing his own sister adorned in the reverie's splendor. And the way she looked at him, without a hint of familiarity; she wasn't lucid in the least. She had no idea who he was. She had no idea who *she* was.

She belonged to this world now. She belonged to Helena.

And, by the easiness of the embrace Kane had torn apart, a moment ago she had belonged with Dean. They were *together*.

Dean shuffled them all into a dark hallway. He whispered a few placating words to Sophia before taking Kane aside.

"It's not what it looks like," he said. "I recognized her as your sister. I was keeping her safe."

"She shouldn't even *be* here, and how did you get…"

Kane had so many questions, about Dean being here, about Sophia and Elliot and Adeline and how they were all going to survive this, but before he could say another word his throat hissed shut. The sconces lining the hall flickered; a threat. Stale oxygen roiled in Kane's chest, spinning him around until he fell into Dean. Slowly his throat reopened. He exhaled unsteadily, just a few deep blue breaths, and let Dean comfort him.

"What's wrong?" Dean's hands fell over Kane, strong and knowing as they grazed Kane's ribs, his neck. "Can you speak? Why aren't you speaking?"

"Don't you know?" Sophia joined them. "This is the infamous Willard Beazley. He's...well..." she gave Dean a wide-eyed warning, hinting at some great scandal.

Dean's hands tucked into his coat as Kane stood himself up. Sophia talked about Kane like he was one of the paintings on the wall.

"You shouldn't bother with Willard Beazley. He's Eva Beazley's oldest, the one who left. He hasn't been the same since he got back from his holiday." She raised her eyebrows for *holiday*, implying it had not been a nice one. "Doesn't talk to anyone anymore. The poor thing." She looked at Kane and enunciated her words loudly. "I Am Sorry For Yelling At You, Willard. You Just Surprised Me."

Kane still couldn't reconcile seeing his sister here, like this. Her curls were woven with downy blossoms, and she wore a golden gown that matched the vest beneath Dean's coat. He gathered they were a young couple. Guests at the wedding and not main characters.

Good.

Still, Kane felt a subtle shift ripple through the fabric of this world. It was watching them.

He took Sophia's hand and pulled her away from the ballroom, farther down the hall. She let him.

"It's okay!" She flapped her hands at Dean. "He's harmless, dear! Where are we going, Willard? What do you wish to show us?" Then to Dean: "This is perfect. An opportunity to see what the Beazleys hide in all these rooms. No one can get mad at us if we're just taking care of Willard."

Kane lead the trio through the cavernous house, looking for an exit. The escape took them through room after room full of indigo shadows and chocked with furniture, but never back outside, as though the house knew better then to let them go. They kept ending up in the massive library, instead. While Sophia poked through books, Dean took Kane to an alcove to talk.

"We must go back. There is no outrunning a reverie. You'll have to unravel it when it is ready. When you are ready."

Kane felt many things. Mostly fear, but also captivation. Dean was the prettiest boy he had ever seen up close. Kane bit down on the surge of electricity that came with Dean's breath on his lips, his chin. An accent rounded his words, and it was powerful in a way Kane didn't know he was powerless against. Kane turned away. Still, they stood too close in the narrow alcove. Kane didn't know if they were enemies or friends. For now, they were simply close.

"You're more powerful than you know. Than the Others are telling you," said Dean. He fit to the curve of Kane's back, and his knuckle brushed Kane's temple where the burns began. "Never expect a world designed for someone else to show you mercy. When it's your turn, you cannot flinch."

Somewhere nearby came a click, then a yelp from Sophia. They found her at the back-most bookcase, halfway through a previously hidden passage in the wall.

"I knew it!" she whispered, pulling them in. "The Beazleys are known for two things: their sudden wealth and the secrecy it demands. I believe I just found our way toward an explanation for both."

Kane again felt that bristling dread, that subtle shift among the threads of the reverie. They had been led here for a reason. *This* reason. But were they abiding by the plot, or defying it? Was this part of Ursula's book, or an embellishment born of Helena's mind? As they entered a passage of velvet blackness he found the whistle in his pocket. He should have blown it when he had the chance, but now their sneaking demanded utter silence.

They crept down a spiraling staircase lined in spitting gaslights. When Kane stumbled, Dean caught his wrist. They held hands the rest of the way, until they entered a room that must have been deep beneath the estate.

It was a laboratory of umber wood and frosted glass. A wide desk stood in the corner, covered in brass contraptions and beakers of smoky liquid. It sat beneath an even bigger mirror. In all the cases, glittering like trapped starlight, were eggs. Hundreds of bejeweled eggs.

It was, and was not, a version of the living room Kane had seen in the videos of Maxine Osman. Kane doubted that steampunk technology or precious eggs were written into *The Devil in the Lily.* Whatever world they explored, it was not the predictable book Ursula believed she was acting out. She couldn't know all its secrets.

Sophia's eyes glistened as she surveyed the collection. "I knew it. I *knew* it. The Beazleys make their money in the trade of precious stones and metals, but no one can figure out their source. Mines, my father says. Or pirates. But this proves my theory! The Beazleys don't mine their precious stones. They *breed* them. You saw those splendid creatures in the garden, didn't you? The fish and the peacocks and that gargantuan turtle crusted in jade? Like everyone, I figured they'd simply been ornamented for the wedding, but no. Those creatures were *hatched* that way."

Kane remembered the delicate, enamel birds he'd seen upstairs. He remembered Helena, as an old woman, telling the interviewer about the ornamental egg collection that she and Maxine shared. *We talk about what would hatch from them.* This, then, was their game made real. A vein of fantasy stitched through the Victorian elegance of Helena's reverie.

Kane needed to get back to Ursula. He hovered by Sophia, unsure of how to dislodge her from her snooping. She was peering into an open case at an egg of exquisite rose gold. Ribbons of green enamel folded over the curved bottom, like new leaves, each dotted with pearls and diamonds so that the egg seemed to shiver with fresh dew.

When Sophia reached in to touch it, Dean grabbed her hand away. His eyes were distant.

"We shouldn't be here."

"This laboratory shouldn't be here, either, yet it is," said Sophia. "And besides, *Willard* led us here. On accident. Right, Willard?"

Kane resented being used as a prop, but to show it would defy Sophia's understanding of him. In both the reverie and reality, actually. He tried to catch Dean's eye, but the boy was looking at the stairs. Nervous, Kane rolled the whistle in his palms.

"Someone's coming!" Dean said. There was a commotion as the three tried to hide, all of them crushing into the space under the desk.

Nothing happened, and it seemed like Dean was mistaken. And then, sure enough, a person appeared at the bottom of the stairs.

Kane watched in the mirror.

It was Helena. She had changed from her red dress into trousers and a coat, swapped her bird hat for a sensible cap that hid her hair. She lugged a canvas suitcase to the middle of the room, set it down on the desk above them, and popped it open. Then Helena began selecting specific eggs from the showroom. She took the rose-gold egg, then the diamond and garnet one. After a long deliberation she snatched up an egg of milky opal, and finally a plain egg of simple blue stone veined in gold.

"I fear all that time in this laboratory cost Mother her perspective. She should never have created you. And Father will never see you as anything more than your precious skins and scales," she said to the eggs. "I promise I will return for the rest of you. Please be patient. Please, be good."

She kissed the blue egg and placed it in the case, then paused to pick something off the floor. The black whistle.

Shit. Kane hadn't realized he'd dropped it.

Helena held it up, looking around as she did so. Her eyes caught on the desk. She moved to block the door.

"Who's in here?" Defiance laced her voice, as hard and glinting as the cut crystals of the eggs.

Kane grabbed Dean's face and mouthed one word.

Go.

Then Kane stood up. Helena blinked, but the threat drained from her at once.

"Willard? How on earth did you find your way down here?"

Kane obediently shuffled out from behind the desk, meandering so that Helena turned away from the desk completely. It was not hard to feign bashfulness at getting caught. It was even easier to stay silent.

"I'm surprised you remembered how to get to Mother's Nest," Helena said, referring to the laboratory. Her amused tone turned sad. "I'm surprised you remember this house's secrets at all, actually, after what they did to you." She showed him the whistle. "Is this what you've been playing with?"

Behind her, Dean and Sophia crept from the desk to the stairs. Helena turned to see what Kane was looking at, but Kane grabbed at the whistle to keep her attention.

"Now, now," she laughed, snatching it out of his reach. "I'll hold on to this for now. We must be very, very quiet, Willard. Wherever did you find this? Not here, I assume. This metal is dead as can be."

Kane couldn't help himself. He frowned deeply as she strung the whistle onto a chain around her neck that also held a key. She dropped them both beneath her collar with a safe pat.

"Don't be like that. I understand. I have treasures, too. See?"

She lifted the suitcase carefully, as though the eggs within might break open.

"I wonder, do you remember our family's secret? Anyone who knows is bound to our family forever, Father says, which is why none of us are free to go into the world and make our own lives." When she said this, she said it with the flat polish of a well-worn motto, though it was cold and not her own. "Come, let's get you back to the party. I'm sure your mother is irradiating nearby guests with her worry by now."

They advanced up the stairs and into the library, then into the corridors. The sounds of merriment could be heard again, and he saw the pale glow of the ballroom deep in the distance. Helena stopped and wouldn't get closer.

"Willard, listen," she said. "I need to say something to you in case I don't get a chance after tonight." She took his hands, warming them in hers.

"I'm sorry about what our family did to you. I understand what it is like to hate the life you are given, and the form you take, and I understand the determination to find a new life and to create a new form."

Perhaps because of Kane's furrowed expression, she whispered, "I know about your piano tutor. I know you wanted to go with him. I very much understand why."

She hugged him. Kane didn't think it possible for her voice to soften further, but it did.

"Maybe no one has ever told you this, and maybe no one ever

will, and so I will be the one: I forgive you. Whatever sins they say about you, they are forgotten in my eyes. I see you not as what they made you, but as you wish to be. I hope you can forgive me, too. And I hope you can forgive Katherine."

Helena collected herself, all shaking breaths and wet cheeks. She scooped up her belongings, kissed Kane on the cheek, and she was gone.

She'd taken the whistle, Kane's only hope, but she'd also relieved him of something else. A heaviness in him that he didn't know he harbored, a layer of leaden dread that had shaped itself around his heart. Teary streaks cooled his face, and he pushed the emotion down and away.

She had given Kane something, too. The answer to the question he had been asking this reverie since he'd awoken. And the answer was: Ursula was horribly, devastatingly, and dangerously wrong about the way this reverie should end.

EIGHTEEN

BREAKING

THE BALLROOM ROCKED WITH A WALTZ.

Kane's eyes throbbed in the new brightness, searching for Sophia's golden dress in the swirling crowd. He had to find her, to protect her. He had to find Ursula, to stop her. Dean was right; he couldn't just keep running. He had to do something.

Dancers jumped out of his way as he pushed through the crowd. A hand found his and before he even realized what happened, a body was in his arms.

"Sophia is here, but don't worry. She is safe," Adeline whispered, grasping Kane's shoulder with her other hand. A convincing smile brushed her painted lips. "Don't look for her. You'll twist it again if you don't calm down."

Adeline was breathtaking in a lilac gown. In some places it clung to her like wetness, and in others it drifted from her like steam. Her hair was in dual braids, like a crown, and from the choker around her throat hung a spiked pendant. It nestled in her cleavage, its spines dimpling her skin.

"One, two, three. One, two, three," Adeline counted, guiding them in the turns of the dance. Nearby guests patronized them with bemused whispers.

Maybe if he kept his voice low, he could talk. "Helena is—"

"Don't speak. Everything is being taken care of. We know Helena is playing the part of the youngest Beazley girl. We know what she's up to. All we have to do is get Johan to meet her during the fireworks, so they can run off. Spin me on three-two-*now*."

Kane spun her. They rejoined. Adeline's eyes never left the crowd over Kane's shoulder.

"Fortunately, Elliot appears to be playing Sir Johan. Go figure. Must be the jawline. I don't know. That boy is prince-shaped all over, I bet. Anyways. Meet me in at the railing in a few minutes. Be sneaky."

The dance ended and Adeline blessed Kane with a deep curtsey. She excused herself, grabbing a flute of champagne as she exited the ballroom. Kane took the long way around the crowd and out onto the patio where he found Adeline leaning against the railing, the champagne glass already downed.

"Adeline—"

"Shut up. Take my arm. No, the other way. Good. Okay, don't rush, remember? We're just strolling. Just strolling. Don't talk. Ursula says you're mute. Don't mess this up, I swear to God if you do..."

She waved her empty glass at him menacingly. They descended into the garden, which was even more labyrinthine in the dark. Lanterns glowered, dying the lush hedges in rusty light so that the maze looked bathed in blood.

"I'm leaving you here. Don't follow me. You're not a main character; try not to change that."

Kane needed her to listen. He grabbed at her gloved hand. Adeline mistook this as fear.

"Don't worry. We know what we're doing. *I* know what I'm doing. I'm the evil heartbreaker, Katherine Duval. That's right. I'm *that* bitch, like I am in practically every one of these shit-ass reveries. Classic Bishop bad luck, my dad would say. It's whatever. My point is I know what I'm doing. Now, stay put. We'll grab you when it's safe to unravel this."

She vanished into the maze.

For the first time since entering the reverie, Kane was completely alone. He could run. He could go find Sophia. He could fight. Every option hung before him, holding him in place. He shook out his nerves. He clenched and unclenched his hands, eight times each.

What eventually drove Kane to action was not fear or even bravery. It was heartbreak.

The Others were wrong. This was not *The Devil in the Lily*. They should not be acting out the story of Helena and Johan. They should be revising it, because this was not the story of Helena and Katherine's rivalry. It was the legend of their love.

Kane thought of the small house Maxine lived in, that he

was sure Helena lived in, too. He thought of the second bedroom full of watercolor paintings doomed to fade under winter's sun. Helena and Maxine were described as friends, but was that true? Or was "friend" just a lie the world told about two elderly women who chose to live together, away from everyone else, in their own world of wonder?

Kane thought of the house's single bedroom. He thought of the gloomy, covert life so many queer people were forced to live as they found one another in a time and a world that could not adjust to them. He thought of secret meetings and secret names, and the secret sadness that grew like mold in the humidity of a life kept closed.

This reverie was not just dreams and whimsy, like Kane had thought. It was a person's psychology, rendered in vivid fantasy. They had waltzed in the ballroom of an old woman's loss and wandered the corridors of her grief. This party was her pain, this garden her purgatory, and they were just playing dress-up in it. Meddling, like it was a game.

No, it was worse than that. This reverie was Helena's last resort, and they were about to ruin it all.

Kane ran under nets of frail moonlight pushing through the trellises, hurtling over bridges and brooks and stone walkways. Nearby there was a loud bang, and acrid smoke drifted on the sweet breeze. He followed it to its source: a courtyard hidden from the château by copses of thick willows, then stopped at the edge, breathless, to take in the developing scene.

Two horses stood in the shadows, Helena fussing with the

saddles. In the center of the courtyard sat an elaborate spread of wire and tubes, like cannons. One was smoking, and small fires littered the scene. An older man lay off to the side, his mouth gagged and wrists bound.

"Helena, I'm here," shouted Elliot as he strode gallantly into the courtyard.

Panic seized Kane, but not so much panic that he couldn't notice how good Elliot looked in Regency-era formality. His coat was a deep green, and it strained over his broad chest and thick arms. Kane was paying close attention to his thighs when he remembered this was going to be a disaster.

Helena put herself between Elliot and the horses, her shock barely concealed.

"Johan, what are you doing here?"

"I heard the first firework and came to find you, my love."

Elliot's acting was very bad.

"It was an accident. Nothing more," said Helena, glancing at the bound body, which Elliot had yet to see. "You'd better hurry to the patio. The guests are all watching from there."

"You don't want to watch, too?"

"No." Helena stepped closer, keeping Elliot from advancing any farther. "I'll be watching from here. I'm making sure they go off, according to plan. And they're due to go off soon. So, please, won't you join the other guests? It's dangerous down here."

Kane had to stop himself from jumping in. He would only make things worse, like last time, but couldn't Elliot feel the electric revulsion in the air? It was sour against Kane's senses, every bit of the reverie ready to rip Elliot apart if he did not leave. But he continued to smile as though he were the best possible gift Helena could be receiving.

"I am ready to face down any danger if it means being with you," Elliot said, reaching for Helena's hand.

"Get away from him."

Adeline lurched into the scene, champagne glass hanging from her swaying form. She seemed much drunker now.

"Katherine!" Helena said, relieved.

"Get away from him, you *whore*," slurred Adeline.

Helena froze. Kane waved frantically, but Adeline's focus was tremendous. Unlike Elliot, she was a talented actor.

"That's right, I know all about what you've done," she said. "Who you really are. And to think you would try to run off, and leave your own family behind? You disgust me. You're a disgrace upon your family's name."

Helena looked small enough to come apart in the wind.

"Why are you saying these things?"

Adeline cackled. "Why, dear rival? Because Johan is *mine*. And I am *his*."

"You're lying."

"Oh? Am I?" Adeline circled her, kicking the boot of the bound man. "I see you've hijacked the fireworks and disposed of your own poor servant. I'm sure your father will come momentarily. Who do you think he'll believe? Me, or his delinquent daughter who is determined to steal off in the night, masquerading as a boy, to lay with the first man who finds her unintimidating enough to—"

It was fast. Adeline spun away, the champagne flute smashing. Helena had slapped her, hard.

Adeline righted herself and thrust out the broken stem, rushing Helena. "I'll kill you!"

And then Elliot shot Adeline. A single shot, to the stomach. It blew her back and into a tree, where she slid down in a mess of bloodied cloth.

"She won't hurt you ever again," Elliot said gallantly, believing he had successfully seen them through to the reverie's resolution. "Now, let's leave this place forever, my love."

Helena pushed him away, stumbling over her suitcase and falling. He reached for her, his face a gentle smile, but it twisted as an unseen force dragged him back.

"You—you—" Helena convulsed. Only her eyes stayed steady, locked on the corpse of Katherine. "You killed her!"

"So that we could be together, my love."

Around Kane the reverie convulsed, too, pitching so suddenly that even Elliot felt it. He looked around, unsure.

"You *ruined* it," Helena said, her voice cracking apart. She pointed at Elliot, and one of the metal tubes bent toward him. "*You ruined everything!*"

Elliot didn't even have time to put his hands up before the mortar went off. The firework was a blazing rocket, aimed at Elliot's head. The deafening explosion put wind and fire into the willows, and for ten seconds the courtyard was a riot of sparks. Then, through the smoke, a wavering pink light pulsed.

Kane wasn't sure what would be left of Elliot. Some

prince-shaped bits of body and no more. But there he stood, safe behind the curved dome of a vibrant magic shield, its source the girl at his side.

Ursula.

"Augustine," Helena seethed. "I should have known."

The flaming garden surged with heat as the energy of the reverie went from anguish to anger, and Kane felt the twist taking shape. One by one the fireworks began to shoot up into the night.

"You said you would help me, but you're just as bad as everyone else. Just as cruel. He *killed* her, Augustine."

Her words choked off as she looked where Adeline's body should have been. It was gone. So was the blood. Kane realized he had been watching one of Elliot's illusions, which had worn off at the worst time. Adeline, sneaking away, stood exposed in the flashes from above.

Helena couldn't make sense of it. "What is this? A trick? What's going on? Who are you people? *Tell me!*"

"Adeline," Elliot said through gritted teeth. "Do something."

Adeline's eyes went gray, her corrosive telepathy firing up as booms shook the ground. As though reflexive, a mortar swiveled toward her.

"Adeline! Look out!"

The words left Kane's mouth before he could stop them, but Adeline heard him. She threw herself down as the firework whistled into the trees. In the aftershock, Helena's eyes found Kane.

"Willard, you, too?"

Whatever heartbreak Kane had felt on her behalf before, she felt now as the characters of her world turned against her one by one. As her world twisted beyond even her recognition. She groaned, clutching at her head. Dark pulses of energy bustled from her, burrowing through the garden and cracking apart the tree trunks. The sky crowded with clouds illuminated from within by cotton candy explosions as the fireworks continued to go off. Dry crinkling accompanied the garden's rapid desiccation as all that had once been magnificent withered and grayed.

Elliot knelt by Adeline, dragging her back. Ursula was at Kane's side.

"This is…a trap," Helena spat. "Willard was in the nest. You're all…after the eggs. This is a trap, isn't it?"

"Eggs?" said Ursula. "There aren't any eggs."

"Katherine, too," Helena sobbed, booms overtaking her small voice. She snatched up her case. "You can't take them from me. I'll never let you hurt them."

"Them?" Ursula glanced at Elliot and Adeline. "This isn't how it's goes."

"It's too late," Adeline said, wincing. She could barely keep her eyes open. "It's ruined."

"That's right," said Helena in a hollow voice. "It's too late. It's ruined. But at least we still have each other, right, my hatchlings?"

The case popped open, and up floated the four eggs Helena had been stealing. There was the blue and gold one, and the pink and pearl one. The diamond and garnet egg flared like a match in the firelight. Besides it bobbed the egg of milky opal.

"My beauties. My darlings," cooed Helena. Her body flashed with dull light, as though she were the clouds obscuring the fireworks.

And here, Kane felt, came the twist. The remarkable maiming of Helena's wondrous world was at hand. He sensed what Helena needed from her story now was not a resolution, but a very bloody revenge.

The eggs bulged, growing in size until they crowded the courtyard and pushed into the lower boughs of the flaming willows. Embers rained down from above, landing on the eggs and warming their precious metal shells.

Helena's smoking body pressed between them, soaking the air with her malevolence toward the intruders.

There was a knock from within the blue egg, and suddenly a hole was punched open by a great and sparkling horn. Its lapis lacquer matched the crumbling eggshell. The immense insect legs that followed gleamed a metallic gold. Next the opal egg split open, a polished beak stabbing the air. An eye the size of a beach ball landed on Kane, unblinking.

The other eggs were breaking open now, too. Helena's voice dripped with animosity.

"Now, my hatchlings, it's *your* turn to feed upon the world."

· NINETEEN ·
THE RECEPTION

AUGUSTINE BEAZLEY'S WEDDING HAD BEEN LOVELY, everyone agreed. But the reception was a total nightmare.

Firstly, there was the issue with the fireworks. They scored glittering streaks through the fogging night, only a few making it high enough to pierce the low clouds. The rest landed in the garden, igniting it, and several rocketed directly into the roof, igniting that, too. The guests, who had all assembled upon the patio to gaze expectantly at the sky, watched the disaster for as long as it took one rocket to drill right through the willows and into the crowd, sending lace and limb flying in a gay blaze.

Secondly, there were the monsters: Helena's hatchlings, hewn from priceless metals and precious stones, summoned with only revenge in their minds. The great secrets of the Beazleys' wealth, unleashed against the family's assembled detractors.

The third thing was that the champagne was served warm. But no one minded that, on account of the monsters.

The one tearing apart the ballroom was a beetle. It was the size of an elephant, armed with a powerful horn and protected by a shell of faultless lapis lazuli. Its six golden legs skittered on the dance floor as two people circled it. The first was Cousin Willard, who had always been a bit odd and was known to protect bugs from the predatory swats of his mother. His intervention made sense.

The other person, however, should have run. She, of all people, deserved to pursue safety and comfort. It was her wedding, after all.

"This isn't supposed to happen!" Ursula ducked as a chair hurtled by, shattering a mirror behind her.

"Forget it!" Kane screamed back as the beetle dug through the banquet furniture. The reverie had all but forgotten about his silence. "Just forget the stupid book!"

Ursula caught the next thrown object—half of a table still swathed in linen. "It's not stupid," she groaned, pivoting in her dress and tossing the table back at the beetle. "It's my *favorite* Lorna Osorio book. Kane, *move!*"

Ursula's shield formed tightly around Kane just as the beetle charged. He expected to ricochet away like a pinball, but the beetle bounced right onto its back. Its gold legs combed the air, clicking angrily.

"Anyways," Ursula was saying. "There are hints of the occult in *Lily*, but it's just symbolism."

"Ursula, let me out!"

Ursula waved away the shield and kept explaining. Kane leapt onto a wrecked table, locked his eyes onto the chain that held up a swinging chandelier, and fired off a single ethereal flare.

The chandelier exploded into spears of crystal that plunged into the beetle. It wasn't much but it did sever an entire leg, which spun toward Kane, as big as his body and still twitching. He stopped it with his foot and looked at Ursula, proud.

"And anyways," she was saying. "The character Helena is playing would *never* betray the *real* Johan. I bet Elliot said something."

"She's a lesbian."

"What?"

"Helena is a lesbian. Or at least lesbian-ish. I don't know. But definitely not straight."

"But Katherine—"

"Her too. And so was Maxine Osman, I'm guessing."

Ursula shook her head in awe, the whole world recalibrating in her eyes. Tentatively she pointed at herself. "So, am...I...?"

Kane took her hands. "Ursula. It doesn't matter. We need to find my sister."

Resolve hardened in Ursula's eyes. Then, panic. In a blur of tulle, she grabbed Kane by his waist and hurled him backward. Then she was slashed away, the beetle ramming into her at full force. Only the flash of pink magic assured Kane she'd put a shield up in time as the beetle carried her right through the ballroom wall, then the wall beyond that, then the wall beyond that. Guests ran, screaming, as the château shook.

Kane sat up among the shattered mirrors, staring into the dust and smoke after his friend. Silence congealed around him. He closed his eyes and focused on the fabric of this reverie, feeling for the seams he'd been able to sense when he unraveled Benny Cooper's world, but his mind couldn't get a grip. This reverie was still too strong. They were trapped here, with only one choice: survive.

Kane looked at his hands and the pale glow of etherea beneath his fingertips. What power did he have? What could he do besides unravel and destroy? He looked down into the fractured depths of the glass strewn around him. He found his eyes, filled with shadows as the remaining chandeliers swung. The world around his reflection seemed to close him in a silent, deadly grasp.

Then Kane felt a sticky strand of hair loop over his ear. Swatting at it, his hand came away dotted in small orbs.

Pearls? They were clustered on a web of pinkish-gold wire, still warm from whatever had produced it.

Kane had one second to wonder: What else hatched from an egg?

He didn't let himself look up. He just shot both hands directly upward, releasing a jet of rainbow etherea that collided instantly with something that had been looming just above him. Then he launched himself sideways, glimpsing the creatures many legs as they punched after him. Massive, its abdomen sat like a bulbous egg among the nest of eight lethal legs, its entire form furred and rose-gold-colored and shivering with pearls as it rounded on Kane.

"Helena, listen to me!" Kane cried. "I know you're in there!"

The spider launched up into the spacious heights of the ballroom, nimble atop a network of wires that unspooled from its body. It gathered itself right above Kane, poised.

"Helena, please!"

It leapt downward, balling itself up and unclenching all at once, a hand meant to crush Kane. Kane didn't want to, but he had to. Right before the spider landed on him, he unleashed a burst of ethereal energy using both hands. The magic burned from his entire body, stabbing up through the spider and ripping it apart.

Kane hissed, every nerve coursing with clarity. His body pulsed, especially his temples. He felt the raised lines of his burns, and in the remains of the mirror was his reflection, winged in ethereal light. It buoyed him, pulling him upward, as though he had mastered not just light, but lightness itself.

A rumbling pulled Kane back to earth, with just enough time to duck. The far wall exploded, and in crashed the beetle with Ursula riding atop it. The gargantuan bug slid and swung, but somehow Ursula stayed put. And somehow, so did her dress. She threw a shield out ahead of the beetle's path, and the pair rocketed toward Kane.

"Kane! Jump!"

He tried to, but his new levitation was hard to control. The next thing he felt was something grab him—Ursula, he thought— and all at once he was clutching the beetle's curved horn as it flailed. He held on for dear life.

"Don't let go!" Ursula cried. The beetle screamed, and

suddenly its shell popped open like a car hood. Clear wings veined in cerulean shot out, beating in rapid motion as the beetle took to the sky.

Kane closed his eyes, fighting not to vomit as the beetle flew straight up and through the ballroom's skylight. A cloud of razored glass tore over him, but there wasn't time to feel the pain before the beetle crashed back down, tossing him onto a roof eaten through by fire. Ursula was at his side a second later.

"Kane! Your powers! Can you fly?"

"*Fly?*"

The gardens smoldered below them, an impossible escape. The beetle turned and charged, but Ursula was ready to block the guillotine slice of its horn. She stopped the attack with a shield before catching the horn in her bare hands.

Her voice came gritty and urgent. "Are you ready to jump?"

"Are you *nuts?*"

Ursula did something with her feet beneath her tremendous skirt, perhaps to brace herself, because the next thing she did was hoist the beetle straight into the air. It gave a few stunned clicks as it reached the upright point of momentary balance.

"Kane," she wheezed. "Scoot to the left, will you?"

Kane did just that. As the beetle's wings shot out again, Ursula brought it down in an epic backward bend that crushed its own wings beneath it. The château shook, the roof buckled, and Ursula dove for Kane, wrapping him in a hug as they hurtled off the edge.

"Fly, Kane!"

What right did Kane have to tell her he couldn't? He'd just

watched Ursula execute a suplex against a gigantic gemstone beetle while wearing a wedding dress, atop a flaming dream mansion. The bubble-thin partition between *can* and *cannot* had popped right then. Kane imagined she was right, that he could fly. He believed her, and she believed in him.

He twisted toward the flaming garden and let loose another ethereal blast, opening a crater in the patio right before it was too late. The blast swung them up, and suddenly gravity's grip was broken; they careened over the garden, swathed in rolling waves of ethereal light from Kane's body.

Ursula let out a whoop. "You're doing it! Oh my God! You're actually doing it!"

Kane laughed with her, but their joy was short-lived. Down from the clouds like a shaft of moonlight came a creature of silence and speed. There wasn't time to see what it was before it slammed into Kane with a haunting cry. Ursula yelled, there was a burst of pink light, and then they were falling.

Falling.

Kane's light was gone.

He hid in Ursula's embrace as the first branches swatted them. Wave after wave of magenta magic cradled them as they bounced through the trees, finally rocking to a stop on solid ground. Ursula let the shield dissipate, falling to her knees.

"You okay?" she asked.

"I'm okay. You?"

"Oh, super."

"Was that a bird?" Kane peered into the sky, but it was gone.

Ursula shook out her hand. "Yeah, but it was made of like…
quartz or something."

"You punched it?"

Ursula shrugged. "I would literally punch any bird. They all
suck."

Then she stood and began to rip away her skirts.

"Honestly, I wish I could wear one of these outfits without
having to end up fighting. I mean, how is anyone supposed to fight
anything in this many layers?"

The air around them began to quiver with what Kane recognized as indignation.

"Ursula, I think we're in trouble."

"This frickin' dress is in trouble, I'll tell you that much! And
those frickin' geode monsters are in trouble as soon as I can actually
kick—"

"No," Kane grabbed her hands before she could do more
damage. The skirt had been shredded into a singed nest circling
her feet. She now stood in just gigantic high heels, lacy white
stockings, frilly garter belts, and a tuft of charred crinoline about
her hips. There was nothing to be done about the corset, but at
least she'd peeled off the puffy sleeves.

"You'll make the reverie mad," Kane warned.

Ursula was a little out of breath. "No sense worrying about
fashion when the whole house is on fire, Kane. Pleasantries ended
when Helena tried to blow up Elliot's face." She stepped from the
ruined wedding gown and strode off. Kane trailed after.

"But what do we do?"

"We find your sister. I bet she's hiding in this garden. Then we find the Others. And then we defend ourselves until the reverie exhausts itself."

"And then what?"

"You unravel it."

Kane stopped. "But what if I can't?"

Ursula put her hands on her hips. "Trust me, you can. You just *flew*, Kane. You've never managed that before, but look. You did it. And besides, you unraveled a reverie just last week. No more *can't*-ing, all right?"

Another no was poised on Kane's lips, but then a scream tore through the night. It was shrill and distant, a soaring last resort from the far reaches of the garden. Ursula locked eyes with Kane, and he knew she was thinking the same thing. There was one beast left, and it had found Adeline.

· TWENTY ·
CLARITY

THEY RAN ALONG THE AISLE OF POPLARS BORDERING the hedge maze, tuned to Adeline's screams. Kane pushed himself to keep up, to not stumble. The screams multiplied as they passed through archways of rotten roses and barbed vines until, finally, they burst into the place where Kane first awoke: the clearing with the gazebo.

Helena lay in a crumpled heap, sobbing and reaching toward the gazebo, pleading over and over, "Not her! Leave her! Spare her!"

She meant Adeline, who clung to the top of the gazebo as it tilted sideways, slowly collapsing as something coiled through the beams. It was a serpent, as large as the other beasts, but somehow more unreal. Its entire length was bedazzled in diamonds, the frosty white interrupted only by teardrops of garnets that squirmed upon its fluid body. It spooled and flexed, powerful and unstoppable as it peeked its triangular head over the roof's edge. Its onyx tongue tasted the air between itself and Adeline, who could do nothing but shriek again.

"I'm sorry," sobbed Helena, as though Adeline were already dead. "I'm sorry, Katherine."

Yet another beast was even closer, right in front of them on the lawn. Kane recognized the luminous opal of the thing that struck them out of the air before. Its body was shapeless at first, until it ruffled its massive wings and turned its head around completely. It gazed at Ursula and Kane with bulging, porcelain eyes. An owl.

And from its beak hung intestines.

Kane and Ursula were too shocked by the sight of blood on pastel stone to move. The owl lost interest and turned back to the meal under its claws.

Elliot.

Shock dulled Kane's hearing. Elliot's blood was everywhere. Elliot was everywhere. Here an arm, there a lung. Prince-shaped parts scattered through the garden.

Ursula crumpled over her knees in defeat.

"Gruesome, isn't it?" said Adeline's voice, right next to them.

Kane jumped, turning to find not just Adeline, but also Elliot hiding off to the side of the clearing, near the bench where Kane had first awoken. Elliot's eyes glowed golden as he focused his power.

"Those…those are…" Kane stammered.

"Illusions," finished Adeline. Aside from a dried bloody nose, she looked fine. Ursula, on the other hand, still looked sick as she stood. Kane couldn't shake the gruesome sight, either, and he reached for the whistle for comfort before remembering it was gone. Taken by Helena.

Elliot's voice was laced with effort of sustaining the magic. "It didn't take long to realize we had it wrong when Helena came after us. Luckily she was pretty focused on Adeline—or Katherine—so we were able to lure her out here. We thought it'd draw you guys here, too, and not a moment too soon. This reverie is going up in flames."

Elliot grinned, but Adeline sighed and said, "Elliot, now is not the time for Dad Jokes."

"Who is Dad Jokes?" asked a meek voice behind Kane. He spun toward his sister, who hid behind a poplar tree.

Kane rushed to hug her. She stiffened in his embrace, annoyed.

"Who are you people, really? Why have you brought me here?"

"We found her hiding in the garden," Adeline said. "She's very hard to keep quiet."

Elliot chuckled. He glanced at Ursula's tattered burlesque outfit. "Having a rough wedding, Urs?"

Ursula crossed her arms over her cleavage and turned bright red. "Unravel it, Kane," she grumbled. "Let's go home."

He tensed. Unravel all this? Unravel Helena, who tore at the grass and wept with despair? Wearily he spread his arms out and tried to regain that power he'd summoned at the end of the Cymo reverie. It hadn't felt like power then—it had felt like knowing. And so he fought for focus and did the one thing he remembered. He clapped.

A lot happened in the instant his palms met. First, with bracing clarity, the reverie snapped into gruesome detail: the desiccated flowers bobbing in the ash-laced breeze, the splintering wood of the gazebo, the estate overtaken by inferno, every particle of fog, every strung pearl.

Second, all around him, he felt Helena. She blinked at him with wide, bloodshot eyes, and he was forced to embrace her fear. Her grief. Her stunning, spinning hope, which had bloomed into a world of remarkable loveliness, then turned to ruin in the blink of an eye. That same world cracked open to breed unfeeling creatures of metal, stone, and rage. Exquisite and lethal, they defended their mistress, but now they had grown beyond even her control.

Third, there was a small explosion.

Kane's whole body rang with pain. His hands, surprisingly, were still attached to his wrists, but the poplar trees had all snapped back. Sophia and the Others were strewn around him, stunned. Pale smoke rose from the ground.

Ursula crawled to him. "Kane?"

He coughed, tasting blood. "I can't…"

He couldn't unravel it. He couldn't unravel Helena. This reverie wanted to live more than he wanted to kill it.

"Guys…" Adeline whispered.

Helena stood, swaying, her eyes finding them. The owl turned, too. Elliot's illusions had been blown away, and now the viper lowered itself to the ground, as silent as snow.

Elliot turned to Ursula. "I hope you're not spent."

Ursula shook off her dizziness. "Nah," she spat to the side, cracked her gloved knuckles, and walked right at the viper.

She didn't make it very far when a cacophonous buzz shook the air and the beetle, fully re-formed, dropped atop her like a comet. In the same instant, the viper whipped forward, cutting them off from Adeline.

"Run, Adeline!" Elliot screamed, even as the owl battered the air with great, opalescent wings. Its eyes locked onto him, the meal it had lost.

With tears racing down her face, Adeline sprinted into the hedge maze. The viper slithered after.

Kane hauled up his sister, shoving her at Elliot. "Vanish! NOW!"

Elliot for once did not dispute Kane. As soon as Sophia was in his arms, they drifted behind a curtain of golden magic. Then they were gone.

There was a series of thrashes from Ursula and the beetle as she was thrown across the clearing. Kane waited for her to turn in midair, to get her legs under her and bounce back, but her body was limp as it sailed through one of the gazebo's worn supports. He hobbled after her, his legs aching, his hands throbbing, and just as he reached her, the gazebo collapsed.

"Augustine!" Helena screamed, and she was right beside Kane as he dove into the mess of wood and vines. Together they tore away the mess, digging, thinking only of Ursula.

"I'm sorry! I'm sorry!" Helena cried.

Kane's heart was a stinging, pulsing liquid in his ears. He found Ursula's knee, dug a hand behind it, and pulled. As he did, the spider—just as re-formed as the beetle—scampered into the clearing. Its pale green eyes locked on Kane. It bent, ready to spring atop them.

Helena pulled Kane close, and something cold and metal around her neck stabbed into his arm.

The spider leapt high into the air. Its legs spread a claw across the sallow moon.

Kane had only one breath between him and death. One chance. No snapping fingers, no sparkling hands. Just one move left to make. It was too late for him and the others, and maybe even for Helena, but maybe he could convince fate to spare his sister.

As the spider landed atop Kane, he grabbed the whistle from Helena's neck, pressed it to his lips, and let his last breath go.

TWENTY-ONE

FINDERS KEEPERS

THE WHISTLE MADE NO SOUND. IT MADE SILENCE. A thrilling, halting silence that pinned the reverie in a single instant.

Humid air brushed Kane's matted curls. He was looking right into the glistening space between the spider's furred fangs, two of its legs already hooked under his arms. But the spider did not bite. It was petrified. Kane sat in a cage of unmoving legs atop the ruined gazebo.

Beside him lay Helena, one such leg digging into her thigh. The reverie had halted, but her blood flowed freely around the rose-gold dagger. She touched it, gingerly, knowing it was a mortal wound.

"H-h-help me," she whispered.

Kane untangled himself from the spider, amazed that it let him. He spun around, stunned at the whistle's work. Everything was still. No wind, no drifting ash. Even the mist of the gardens hung in frozen, marbled curls around the inert beetle. And it was quiet. Faintly, Kane could make out a distant creaking, as though they existed in the hull of a great, rocking ship.

Kane couldn't remove the spider on his own.

"Help!" he called. "Somebody!"

"Here!" It was Adeline. Kane ran for her.

"Where are you?" His voice was flat in the stilled air.

"Over here!"

"Are you okay?"

"Sort of." But the long pause before her answer told him something was wrong.

He turned a corner and came upon the serpent, its body frozen in a tight knot.

"In here," Adeline called, and Kane saw her just barely among the looping, diamond body. She'd been caught, about to be consumed when the whistle froze the reverie. The viper's jaws were already unhinged, just inches from her head.

"Well," Adeline said. "Blow it up."

He tossed two bolts into the beast's body, exploding it in glittering bursts that quickly froze. Then he pulled Adeline from the levitating rubble, turning them both bone white with dust. She held on to him longer than he sensed she needed to, and then a bit longer after that.

Her voice shook. "It got me."

Kane squeezed her hand reassuringly. "But you got out."

Adeline waved her hand around at the stilled reverie. "Did you do this?"

"Kind of. Come on."

They reached the clearing with the gazebo. Elliot was there, Sophia fastened to his arm. He was breathing hard. "We were running…from the owl, and then…time stopped."

Adeline pointed at Kane. "He did it."

"It wasn't me. It was this whistle."

"Where's Ursula?" Elliot asked.

Kane pointed at the spider. Elliot, to his credit, ran toward it and not away, but before he got close an earsplitting frequency fissured the air. It practically cut through them, so harsh it forced everyone to the ground. Kane could feel it in his teeth, in his eye sockets. He fought to hold down vomit and failed.

Was this Helena's newest twist?

Across the clearing the air dimpled, bending the light into a large, upright rectangle. A swath of the scenery was peeling away, cleanly dissociating like two great doors opening into the reverie.

Kane held his breath. His tongue tasted of blood and bile.

Through the doors floated something completely alien to the rotting reverie—a woman draped in a plush fur coat that was the soft, whipped pink of sunrise on storm clouds. Her wide-brimmed hat and thick-heeled shoes matched as though spun from the same sugary atmosphere, and her octagonal glasses reflected everything in metallic clarity. She fingered the ascot around her neck. On her wrist hung the bracelet thick with charms. The only hardness about her was the muscles of her nude calves and the frown of her glossed lips.

Poesy surveyed the scene. "Oh, what a mess."

Relief poured through Kane, as thick and sweet as the color

of Poesy's costume. She was power, personified. She would save them all.

Adeline must have felt the opposite. "Who are you?" she shouted.

Poesy smiled but did not answer. She glanced over her shoulder and beckoned something. "Don't be shy. Come in, my dear."

There came a sound like the shutter of an old camera, and with a flicker of the moonlight, Poesy was no longer alone. What had joined her in the doorway was a monster unresolved between a horse and a demon. Its twisted body stood upon four elongated legs that ended in hooked hooves. It had no face, only a long, curved beak. It had no eyes or ears, only a pair of spiraling horns. Its skin was glossy obsidian, stretched over sharp bones and an exposed spine. Worst of all was the way it walked, its legs moving with their own, inelegant independence, as though Poesy stood beneath the dark sister of the rose-gold spider.

"Others," said Poesy, "meet my Dreadmare."

The Dreadmare curtsied politely.

The reverie's rage finally broke through the whistle's suspension. The world unfroze with a wrenching shutter, and the bedazzled creatures—the beetle, the owl from above, and the spider—were all charging the Dreadmare. Above it all were Helena's screams as her life flowed from the wound in her leg.

"Quickly, please," said Poesy.

The Dreadmare stormed forward in disjointed harmony, seizing upon the beetle in a black flash. A few ruthless stabs later and the beetle's shell had been pried from its back, only half a wing jutting straight up.

The Dreadmare charged the spider next. As it galloped, its wiry body melted like shadow. It sank low, its legs peeling apart and multiplying, until it matched the spider in shape. Now two arachnids wrestled, black legs braiding with pink, until the Dreadmare grew many more legs and dug them into the spider's back. It ended all at once, like a corn kernel popping open.

Like mist, the Dreadmare vanished, and then the owl's cry drew everyone's attention upward. Somehow the Dreadmare had materialized around the bird, dragging it right out of the air. The grappling pair struck the ground violently. Kane fell forward, close enough to see the Dreadmare's beak closing over the joint of the owl's wing, rending the stone flesh like it was wet clay. The owl's shrieks died off.

Among the fresh rubble, the Dreadmare stood and regarded Poesy coolly.

"I believe one still remains," Poesy said, and the Dreadmare flickered out of sight. Then she turned to Kane. "You called?"

"Excuse me—"Adeline began again, but Kane cut her off.

"Ursula!" he pointed at the pile. "Save her! Please!"

Poesy nodded. "Of course, my dear, but first things first."

The Dreadmare flickered back into sight next to Poesy. It held the serpent's head in its jaw, which sent Poesy into a gleeful clap.

"I've been looking for this color garnet! How wonderful. Is that it then? No more interruptions?"

The Dreadmare tossed the head atop the carcass of the owl, then stepped back.

"Wonderful indeed," Poesy confirmed. She picked her way over the rubble, prodding the sparkling gore like a prospector.

Kane limped to the gazebo. Was no one going to help Ursula? And what about Helena? She reached for Kane's ankle, and he knelt by her side, trying not to look at the exposed bone deep in the gash of her leg. She gripped his arms weakly.

"Willard?" She spoke as though from deep in a dream. "I was…I didn't…"

"It's okay," Kane said. "Help is here. We're gonna get you back to the real world. But I need you to help me unravel this, okay?"

"Unravel this?" She blinked at her ruined beasts. Guilt and misery shivered through her. "You speak of the real world as though it is salvation, but don't you see? People like us… Something separates us from the real world. Something makes sure we never belong." Now her eyes were older than that of a young girl's. Kane was looking into the lucid mind of the real Helena now. "I belonged here, but even this world has rejected me. Even here, I'm a…a…"

"A monster."

Poesy's heels crunched as she stood over them. Helena saw her for the first time, and, through her fear, Kane realized something. Poesy was here to help, but she was not here to help Helena.

"No, no!" Helena pleaded to Kane. "I'm sorry. I wasn't in control. It was a mistake!"

"A *Miss Stake*, you say?" asked Poesy. "I don't know a Miss Stake, but if I did, I'm sure she would resent such an accusation." Poesy winked at Kane, and he realized again how far beyond this world Poesy was to be making jokes as Helena died right in front them. "Now, come with me. We'll fix this together, yes?"

Poesy gestured for Helena to get up. When she didn't, Poesy sighed, gestured again, and this time Helena rose into the air against her will. She clutched at Kane.

"Willard, please! Help me!"

"Wait!" Kane held her hand as she drifted up. "What are you doing to her?"

Helena's hand went cold. Seismic dread rumbled under her skin. Something horrible was happening and Kane, still attuned to Helena's mind, felt her understand she would not survive whatever came next.

"Forgive me," Helena sobbed. "Please, forgive me!"

Poesy reached into her coat and, to Kane's deepening dread, produced a teacup. Unlike the ones from the library, this one was pale pink with scalloped edges brushed in gold. She flicked the porcelain with one manicured nail and, like a boat running suddenly aground, the reverie jolted.

A ringing spun outward from the porcelain like one hundred pealing church bells, flooding the reverie with a sparkling cacophony that terrified Kane. It reverberated within him as much as he heard it around him, and he knew what happened next. The gardens began to shiver apart, their colors dripping into the chiming air. Everything began to break, to spin, to unravel.

It was just like last time, except Kane was not the center. Poesy was. The whirlpool plucked at him as though sampling his taste. His feet lifted off the ground, but before he was sucked in someone wrenched him from the phantasmagoric vortex. Elliot. They huddled together, helplessly watching as Helena squirmed in whatever psychic grip Poesy exerted. Scream after scream tore from her throat as her reverie ripped itself to shreds, as her dreamt youth ripped apart, too, revealing the crumpled form of an old lady in a little yellow sweater and elastic-waist jeans. She kicked at the air with her orthopedic sneakers, the laces neatly tied. And then, as though her world wasn't enough, Helena collapsed into the teacup, too.

And it was over.

The small backyard refocused. The Tudor house watched them, stoic. They were back in Reality Proper, where the night pulsed with a blustery chill. The gazebo, the château, the beasts— they were gone. Taken.

There was the sound of crushing, and then Poesy plucked something small and glittering from the teacup's belly. She hooked it onto her bracelet with the rest of her charms, then swiped the bottom of the teacup with a finger to sample the residue.

"Sweet. Grasping. A floral whimsicality and a full-bodied escapism. Hmm. Notes of nostalgia for times she never lived, homesickness for places she'd never been. Oh! And what an after-taste. Undertones of envy and desperation, accented by *several* harsh desertions. Hints of obsession and—oh, gross—such saccharine self-pity! Smacks of mania."

It was Adeline who finally protested. "You can't do this! You can't just steal her away!"

Poesy's smile was wide and self-assured.

"Finders keepers," she said, her nails clicking against the Dreadmare's beak as it bowed to be pet.

And they flickered out of sight.

· TWENTY-TWO ·
STILL

THERE WOULD BE NO GOING TO THE DINER TONIGHT. No one even seemed comfortable looking away from where Helena had been. It was like standing over a grave, watching the dirt settle atop the space where someone had been swallowed up by the earth. Leaving felt like losing them for good.

Then, one by one, the Others looked to Kane. Where there had once been annoyance and pity, a new expression tinted their eyes. Fear. Adeline spoke in a soft, slow voice, as though to a rabid animal.

"What did you do?"

Kane moved to his sister, who sat shaking on the ground.

Adeline tried again. "Kane, leave her, I can help her. First just tell us what that was?"

"She doesn't need *your* help," he said.

"Just let me soften the memory a little. It'll ease the shock. We need to talk about this."

Kane couldn't face what had just happened, and he wasn't going to let them hurt Sophia. He hugged her to him as he guided her from the garden. They left the Others staring after, putting the small house squarely between them, as though its new emptiness was vast enough to swallow any bridge the Others might devise.

But as they reached Sophia's car and Kane took the keys from her stiff hands, he had to wonder: Was she better off with him? Was anyone?

He buckled Sophia into the back seat and drove them home, turning to check on her every couple of minutes. Her eyes were fixed on the distance as though she could see right through this world and into the next. When Kane got her in the house, she waved off the hello from their parents in the living room and climbed the stairs, stepping as light as smoke from a snuffed candle. Her door shut softly.

"Are you two fighting again?" Kane's dad asked. He wasn't mad. In fact, he sounded relieved that Kane and Sophia were talking at all.

"We'll figure it out," Kane promised.

His parents exchanged a look, then went back to their reading, though Kane knew they were waiting for him to leave so they could talk. He gave them both quick hugs, which he was sure alarmed them, and then went to his own room. But he didn't close the door. He kept it ajar, so that he could hear if Sophia needed help, so that he'd know if anyone tried to enter their home and erase her memories. Focusing on Sophia meant he didn't have to think about Helena.

Kane listened all night, until he didn't even know he was falling asleep, and in his dreams the burning form of Maxine waited. Only this time, Maxine didn't wait alone.

Helena burned, too.

It was two days later. More than that, actually. It was sixty hours later. It was twenty-three cold glances from Adeline later. It was six missed calls and five voicemails from Elliot later. It was nine notes from Ursula later, each stuffed into his locker and each left folded. Kane couldn't respond to any of it. He could only count, and keep counting, wondering how much longer it would take the world to forget about him.

And then Elliot kidnapped him.

"I'm sorry for the trap," Elliot said as he drove them toward an unspecified location. A moment ago, Kane had gotten into his mom's car, with his actual mother, to head home from Roost. And then, suddenly, his mom was gone, replaced by a teenage boy. Elliot. Kane's mom's Subaru was gone, revealing Elliot's car. It had been an illusion. "A *necessary* illusion," Elliot said. "We really, really need to talk to you."

Kane texted his mom. Grabbing food here. I'll call when I'm ready to go.

They pulled up to an unfamiliar house.

"Urs's place," Elliot said, leading them up the driveway. "And, just a quick warning before we go in, don't say anything about the mess. Urs goes on baking rampages when she's stressed."

They entered through the kitchen door.

"I got him!" Elliot called, his footsteps crunching. The floor was covered in grains of sugar. And then Kane saw what Elliot meant. By the looks of it, Ursula was *very* stressed. Baked goods covered the entire kitchen. Cupcakes, cakes, pastries, cookies; they littered every surface of her kitchen in a sugary clutter, as though they'd washed up in the low tide of some mania.

"Down here!"

Footsteps stomped up from the basement, and Ursula rushed in holding a battered muffin tin. She casually popped out its dents with her bare thumbs. When she hugged Kane he could smell the vanilla in her hair. Adeline was with her, and by the looks of it she'd been helping all evening. Flour smattered her arms like dusty bruises, and instead of hugging Kane she simply gave him a cool nod.

That counts, Kane thought. *Twenty-four cold glances from Adeline.*

"Dad and the boys are home but we should be fine in here," Ursula said.

They sat at the kitchen table, among stacks of cookies and bowls of scraped-out frosting. Elliot and Adeline seemed anxious to hear what Kane had to say but Ursula was desperate for anything else.

"I made apricot scones today," she said. "I don't even like apricot. Does anyone want to try one? Oh, wait, actually try this batch instead. Elliot, do you still keep kosher? I can pull out the ingredients if you want to look at them. I've learned it's important to ask beforehand, because one time a girl on the field hockey team said she was a celiac, which I thought was a hobby. Anyhow, I almost poisoned her. But kosher is different, right?" Elliot nodded. "Right, well then, let me find a plate. You might have to clean one yourself. Dad and Gail have been using paper ones, I think, which makes me feel bad. I guess this is a big mess, isn't it?" No one confirmed this outright, but Ursula explained anyway. "My mother and I used to bake when my father had shifts with the fire department. Always calmed me down. Probably a focus thing? I don't know. It's a habit. After she died I didn't bake for years, but this past year got me back into it. Don't know why."

Ursula had told Kane that her father was remarried, with two new kids. Toddlers. He could hear them elsewhere in the house, clapping and singing. Their mother, Gail, was a nurse, and she worked nights.

"Kane," Elliot said finally, "don't worry. We're not mad. We just have a lot of questions."

He didn't expect that. He didn't know what to expect anymore.

"I'm a little mad," Adeline said, smirking. A joke. She went on. "I had ballet at the conservatory last night and jeez, Kane. Your sister. She is persistent. She nearly did all of warm-ups with us, trying to get my attention."

Kane sat up straighter. He had totally forgotten that Adeline and Sophia both went to classes at the conservatory associated with the university.

"Don't worry," Adeline said. "I'm not messing with her head. She's smart. She knows what's real, what's not. I keep telling her to ask you all her questions, but it sounds like that's not going great for her."

It was exhausting finding new ways to evade Sophia now that she'd come out of her stupor, the reverie fully cemented in her memory. Kane shrugged. "I don't want her any more involved in this than she has to be. She never should have gotten caught in a reverie."

"Then we'll leave her out of it," Adeline said. "But we need to talk about what happened. Helena is gone. Same as Maxine. And I think we know who to blame. I think *you* can tell us all about who's to blame."

Kane took a deep breath. He was shaking. In an effort to comfort him, Ursula slid a ceramic plate of scones toward him, real slow. It reminded Kane of a detective sliding gruesome photos across a metal table toward the person they were interrogating. He took another deep breath, then two more, and then he talked for a long time.

He told them about his first conversation with Poesy, in which she promised Kane safety from the police in return for his cooperation. So far, that had been true. He told them about the invitation that had appeared in his journal, and the strange furniture that had appeared in the abandoned library, and the conversation he could barely recall beneath layers of floral vapor that curled the edges of his memory. He told them about Ms. Daisy the Doberman, and as he did he realized the dog, like everything about Poesy, shifted forms. Ms. Daisy was a dog, but she was also Poesy's pet nightmare, the Dreadmare, which he now recognized as the same many-legged shadow that guarded the old mill from him and Sophia, and then followed him on his walk home.

There were things Kane did not share. He did not tell the Others about Dean, who he could not fit into anything so far. He did not tell them the reason Poesy had come to East Amity: the loom. And he did not feel bad about it. Poesy had been miraculous for Kane, an advocate and a mentor when everyone else who loved him had treated him as a liability or a prop. Poesy had given Kane knowledge, insight, and tools to understand the reveries. She had kept her promise, and she had *saved* them all, using just a teacup and a well-manicured nail.

Kane knew power when he saw it, and Poesy was power. He also recognized Poesy's violence, but wasn't her violence used to dismantle something far more dangerous and malicious than herself? Helena's world had tried to kill them, and if Poesy had not retaliated with force, Helena's world would have succeeded. Kane didn't think he could trust the Others to understand this cost of survival. He wasn't even sure he understood it himself. What he did understand was that he had called upon Poesy for help, and she didn't deserve betrayal for showing up and saving them on her own terms.

Whatever wrong she had committed, it was on Kane to right it. But had she committed a wrong?

"I have some questions," Elliot said at the end of Kane's story.

"Same," Adeline said. The way she looked at Kane made him wonder if she could trace the outline of all the memories he had omitted. He took care not to look her in the eye.

"Same," Ursula said through a mouthful of scone. "Like, was she really tall? I saw a drag queen once who was like, eight feet tall. It was the hair."

"Nine feet at least," Elliot said. "What does she want, though? She's got to have a goal for showing up. Is she after the reveries? She turned it into a charm. She clearly had a few on her bracelet, already. Is she some kind of collector?"

Kane had thought about this. She had said she would fix what happened with Helena, implying she had a plan to undo all the twists the Others had caused. This spurred Kane's own question.

"Why do you guys give the reveries back?" Kane asked. "If they're so dangerous, wouldn't it just be easier to keep them? Or erase them completely?"

Ursula and Elliot looked to Adeline. She rolled her lips together, like she didn't want to say. "We thought that once. We didn't know better. It turns out, when a person is missing such a big piece of themselves, they're not themselves anymore. They become…hollow. Same shape, but nothing keeping them going inside. It only took us a few accidental hollowings before we figured out you have to give the reverie back, all of it, or you might as well just kill a person."

"Who did that happen to?" Kane asked.

Now Kane couldn't look away from Adeline. She stared at him, past him, and for a moment he felt like he had her power and could see a person's memories dancing deep in their depths.

"My grandmother," she said.

The room went too quiet. Ursula pushed herself up and began

pulling pans into the sink. Elliot might as well have turned himself invisible. Adeline and Kane were locked in a staring match.

"People get hurt when we mess up this bad," Adeline said.

"I'm sorry," he said. "I didn't know."

"There's a lot you don't know."

He flinched. "Yeah? And whose fault is that, Adeline?"

She snorted, then addressed the room with patronizing cheer. "So when are we going to talk about how, on his first official mission back, Kane went ahead and smuggled an entire-ass drag queen sorceress into a reverie, and it cost an old lady her life?"

"She's not dead," Kane said, heat rising to his cheeks.

"Well then what is she, dream boy?" Adeline spread her fingers toward the small kitchen. "*Where* is she?"

Hadn't they seen what Kane had seen?

"She's in her reverie. She was happy in there, before we messed it up."

"*Happy?*" Adeline shoved back her chair, standing. "You think she's living happily ever after, locked into a *fake* world on the wrist of that glittering maniac? Jesus, Kane, you're as delusional as ever, but at least you used to know the difference between right and wrong."

"I know wrong." Kane stood, too. "Unlike the three of you when you destroyed Helena's love story. If any of you stopped for a second and looked at her, I mean really took a look, you would have seen what I saw. She was a person, not a plot."

Adeline's knuckles turned tan as she grasped the back of her chair, and her voice went low. "Exactly. She *was*. She no longer is, all thanks to you and that witch."

A commotion broke the tension as two small boys raced into the kitchen, pursued closely by Ursula's father. He was a gargantuan man—like a lumbering cottage, really—but he deftly swooped the two kids over his shoulders. They screamed and reached for Ursula.

Mr. Abernathy laughed, a boisterous and booming noise. "All righty, we've had enough heroes and monsters for one night. Time to wash up and head to bed, right boys? Sorry, Urs, sorry, guys." Then he spotted Kane. His face was craggy and hard, but in that moment of recognition a sweetness shone in his eyes as tender as his grip on his children. He let the boys down and scooted them toward Ursula and Elliot, who had retreated into the hall.

"Kane," Mr. Abernathy said. "Haven't seen you around here for a little bit. I'm glad you're feeling better. Ursula and I—we've been praying for you before dinner. Mason and Joey, too, and Gail even, although she doesn't believe in that."

"Thanks," Kane said quickly. "I appreciate it."

Mr. Abernathy put his hands on his hips and surveyed the kitchen as though seeing the mess for the first time. "Ursula's been pretty busy, I guess. More for the poker club, am I right? They'll be over in a bit, if you'd like to join. I've been showing Elliot the basics, but to be honest I think he's gonna be better than all of us. You two interested in sticking around?"

"Sorry Mr. A., but we were actually just heading out," Adeline said. She grabbed her jacket. "Kane, I'll drive you home."

Mr. Abernathy went off to find Ursula and Elliot. Adeline pushed Kane from the house before he could protest.

"We need to talk. Alone," was all she said.

But instead of talking, a heavy silence fell as they pulled out. She drove with smooth turns that went on and on, never nearing Kane's house. She was waiting on him to start.

"I'm sorry about your grandmother," Kane offered.

"It's okay. That wasn't your fault. She was fading anyways. Alzheimer's. It runs on my mom's side. I like to think I gave her some peace once all her good memories left her, and the bad ones became their own kind of reverie."

"Still," Kane said.

"Still."

He wasn't sure how to ask this next thought. "You said a person needs their reverie, that they're not the same without their dreams. How are you sure this isn't better for Helena?"

Adeline thought about this at a stoplight. "Because it wasn't a choice she made for herself. We can't be sure, because she can't be sure. She doesn't know any better, and she never will. We have no idea what Poesy does with those reveries."

"She said she would help Helena fix it. Maybe she's like a reverie doctor."

"Or maybe she crushes them into bronzer? Why are you so confident she knows best, Kane? How did she win you over so quickly, when we can't get a word out of you for two whole days?"

Kane wanted so badly to respond, but he couldn't find the words. A new, burning agony brimmed behind his eyes. He didn't know why he was about to cry, or why the question felt like such an invasion.

Adeline pulled to the side of the road and parked the car.

"Kane, you need to know something, and I couldn't tell you with Ursula and Elliot there. They know what happened the night of the incident, but not everything." She turned to face him. "You asked me to do what I did. When that crown was taking over you, you grabbed me and begged me to destroy your memories. Told me to destroy everything. And I didn't know what to do, so I listened to you. And it worked. The crown let you go, and you survived."

She looked at Kane, something like hatred in her big, brown eyes.

"And it kills me that I listened. I think of the person you used to be, and I hate myself for destroying him, too."

The air thinned to nothing. To poison. Kane died upon each word, sure he couldn't take another breath of whatever Adeline was saying. This wasn't his fault.

This wasn't his fault.

"Poesy is manipulating you," Adeline went on. "Can't you see? She's setting you up and breaking us apart. Again. You need to forget about that crown. I'm sure she's the one who gave the crown to you, to trigger your blowup. And maybe she stole away Maxine Osman's reverie, too. And now she's back, to finish what she started, to finish—"

Kane grabbed his backpack and bolted. He left Adeline in her idling car, passenger door swung wide. He left her like he'd once left Ursula: running away, determined to take the long way home.

TWENTY-THREE

SEA FOAM

THE FOLLOWING DAYS WERE BRIGHT AND CRISP, announcing the official end of September with the onset of October's subtle moodiness. And October was promising everything: cool breezes, tinges of yellow brushing the trees, milky clouds dragging shadows over the suburb—they were the details Kane always looked forward to. October was the month he loved most.

But Kane was not in a loving mood.

At all.

"Honey, you've been brooding for days," his mom said. She and Sophia had convinced Kane to come shopping with them in preparation for a barbecue in honor of their dad's birthday tonight. They did it every year, even when it was too cold.

"For *years*," his sister added.

Kane ignored Sophia, which he was incredible at by now. If there were an Olympics for ignoring Sophia, Kane would be unrivaled.

"Did something happen at school?"

"Yeah, tell Mom what's up at school, Kane."

Kane twisted around and gave her a hard look. Sophia, since learning about the Others, had adjusted into an outright asshole. After that first night, she'd had so many questions—questions Kane refused to answer. Now she was making him pay. He didn't care. He'd told her he couldn't keep her safe if she knew more than she already did, and she hated that. Go figure that the moment Kane started finally acting like an older brother was the point at which Sophia went from simply resentful to outright hostile. When guilting him didn't work, she turned to threats of exposure, and when that clearly wasn't going to work, either, she went full-blown brat. Always, she leveraged their parents.

"You're a dick," he told her.

She winked.

Kane turned to look out the window, gazing at the changing trees. Their beauty made him feel worse. He reminded himself that autumn, for all its cozy brilliance, was actually a flamboyant sequence of decay. And there was more melodrama where that came from, all of it dripping through Kane with nowhere else to go.

There was one bit of brightness that Kane couldn't shake, though. Adeline had told him something amazing: Poesy may have been the true culprit behind the unraveling of Maxine Osman's reverie. If that were true, and if she'd been taken in just like Helena, then she lived.

She lived.

"What happened in school?" his mom asked.

"Nothing."

"Then what?"

Oh, you know, I fell into the path of an omnipotent, dream-harvesting drag queen, and now a pair of queer elders have been quarantined in the form of kitschy jewelry, and even though we're all a lot safer for it, my friends hate me!

"Everything is fine," he told her.

His mother sighed.

"You're not sleeping," Sophia piped in from the back seat.

"How would you know?"

"I can hear you stomping around at night."

Oh, actually I'm asleep, but I'm having such vivid nightmares that I wake up floating, because a fun new thing about my uncontrollable reality-bending magic is that I now sometimes levitate myself and objects nearby!

"I'll be quieter," he said.

Forcefully, the subject was changed to Sophia's day, which had been—as always—*particularly* eventful. She told an elaborate story about how Headmistress Smithe had announced a required fall seminar that would cut into elective hour, which Sophia reasoned was *exactly* the sort of maneuver the vindictive Headmistress Smithe had been concocting ever since Sophia managed to finagle *two* electives in a row at the beginning of the year, both of which she spent practicing viola anyways.

This is why Kane didn't want her involved. Everything about

her was a plot twist. He tuned out her story, only tuning back in when his mother threw some cash in his lap.

"Here," she said. "Buy candy while I get gas. As much sugar as it's going to take to bring you back to life."

"I'll come with you," Sophia said with a wicked grin.

All through the gas station's aisles, she served Kane theories about the sick fantasies she suspected her classmates of harboring.

"Pemberton's School for Girls," she implored, "is *full* of weirdos."

Kane went right for the Slurpee machine, per usual.

"Kane, this stuff is radioactive. How can you drink it?"

He shrugged. The bright blue mixture in the machine whirled around and around as the slush looped into Kane's cup.

Sophia bounced on her heels, clearly wanting to say something, so he finally gave her a sideways glance.

"I figured something out, Kane. I know," she said.

"Know what?"

Her voice was golden with pride. "Your accident wasn't real, was it? It was related to the reveries, wasn't it? The whole car thing—was that just a cover-up?"

Kane set his jaw and started rooting around for a lid. Sophia blocked his path.

"I'm not stupid, Kane."

"I know."

"If I knew I was in a fake world, I never would have acted that way. I'm smart."

"It's not about being smart. It's about staying lucid."

"I can stay lucid. I can help you guys. I see stuff that no one else sees." She held out a straw but whisked it away before he could grab it. "For instance! I know you're into that boy. And I get why. He's super cute."

Kane rolled his eyes. Of course she had a crush on Elliot. It must run in the family.

Sophia's prodded him with the straw. "I've met him before. It took me a long time to remember, though. But I remember seeing him at the fair with you. And I know you two would sneak out together at night. I even knew your secret signal."

Seeing Kane's surprised reaction, Sophia said, "What? You thought you were discreet? Drawing those number eights everywhere? I don't know why you didn't just text each other. Or maybe you did. I don't know. But then I'd see him outside, late at night, waving for you to come down, and it'd be hours before you got back."

Kane grabbed away the straw. "I don't know what you're talking about."

That was true.

"He seemed…different than the others," she said. "When you were with him, you seemed…happy."

Something about this sentence softened Sophia's accusations, filling her words with sad wonder. And now Kane was full of his own questions. He and Elliot, happy together?

"Elliot isn't gay, Sophia."

Sophia leaned away, as though she regretted pushing into this territory. "Not Elliot. The boy who took care of me during the reverie. I remember his eyes. They weren't green, and they weren't quite blue."

"Sea foam," he said, barely registering Sophia's nod as the world around him washed away.

Sea foam.

The Slurpee fell from Kane's hand, splaying its neon thickness across the aisle. He barely heard Sophia cuss.

Sea foam.

She was describing Dean. And, without knowing it, she was telling him exactly where to look for the rest of what he had lost.

Kane had no idea if this would work, but he had to try.

He stood in the wings of the auditorium where it was dark and cool. The empty space amplified the sounds of students going to class in the background. Shouting. Lockers slamming. Laughter. It was a period earlier than Spanish. None of the Others knew he was here. This had to be done alone.

Kane waited until the second bell to see if anyone entered the auditorium. No one did. He walked onto the stage—it was set up for *A Midsummer Night's Dream*, full of watercolor trees and papery vines. He crouched in the middle, pulling out the red journal and a thick marker.

What would he do if it worked?

Hunched in the center of the stage, Kane drew a looping number eight on a fresh page.

Nothing happened.

Kane shook out his hands and rewrote the eight, just like he'd seen Dean do in Benny Cooper's reverie, and arranged in shells on his bookshelf. All over his old belongings, he found eights.

Nothing happened. The auditorium was unchanged, its invisible crowd unimpressed. What had he thought would happen? Sparkles? A sudden, mystical wind? After the past weeks of magic and the supernatural, reality felt insufferably unengaging.

Kane tore the page from the journal, crumpled it up, and tossed it as hard as he could into the seats. This was so stupid. He rushed into the wings, already wondering if he should skip class and just go to the nurse, when he saw something in the auditorium flash.

Kane backed out onto the stage. There, standing in the center aisle, was the boy Kane had summoned, but not expected.

"Hello, Kane," Dean said.

He stepped onto the stage and handed Kane the crumpled page. He had between ten and twenty freckles across the bridge of his nose. A necklace with a pendant in the shape of a chess piece—the knight, carved in obsidian—hung around his neck.

"I was wondering when you'd figure this out. Now, don't do it again," he said.

"The signal worked? How did you see it?"

Dean's face was unreadable, his eyes as blank as a doll's. They were the color of coastal sunlight chewed to froth by the lips of the Atlantic.

Sea foam.

Kane stumbled through what he'd prepared. "You know me,

247

don't you? I mean we know each other. You were one of the Others once, weren't you? You have powers. You can see things other people can't, and you look out for me. But only me."

Finally something stirred in Dean's eyes: resentment. When Dean brushed by, Kane caught his wrist.

"I have questions for you!"

Dean spun, grabbing Kane's hand tight. "Don't you know how dangerous this is?" he hissed. "Didn't I make myself clear?"

Kane shivered. Nerves. The edges of the crumpled page poked into one palm, and Dean's nails poked into the other.

"I just want to know who you are."

"Forget about me," Dean said.

"Evidently I already did," Kane shot back.

Something shifted in those sea-foam depths. He had hit a nerve. Exposed something. Now Dean watched him with guarded eyes, as though the very sight of Kane hurt him.

Kane knew what he wanted to ask, but he also knew he would never believe a single word that came out of Dean's mouth. Everyone lied. If he had learned anything, it was that words from mouths could be beautiful and deceptive, but mouths could tell you their truths in other ways. Kane wasn't going to leave without that one truth. And so, beneath a paper moon and among the false forest of the stage, he kissed him.

And, taken by surprise, Dean forgot the strict rules that held him together, and kissed back.

There was applause from the ghostly audience, Kane imagined. When Dean tried to speak, Kane breathed the words back into his mouth, refusing their deceit, until Dean's hands climbed over Kane in sure familiarity. Kane, hungry to know, took everything he could from the kiss—Dean's truth and his pain—and when it ended, it was against Dean's will. And that's how Kane knew.

Kane stepped back, leaving Dean's hand to clutch empty air.

"You love me," Kane said. He couldn't look Dean in the face, so he looked at his hands. Brown skin, smooth palms, perfect nails. The hands of a prince.

Dean didn't deny it.

"What did you do?" Kane asked. "You were one of us once, weren't you? Why don't the Others remember? Did Adeline do this?"

"Not Adeline."

"Elliot?"

Dean clasped his hands in front of him, then unclasped them, leaving them to twitch restlessly at his sides. "You."

"I don't understand."

"You took everything from us."

Kane's throat felt straw thin, one molecule of air sliding into him at a time.

"Is this about my accident? About Maxine Osman's death?"

"Accident." Dean grimaced. "What happened to Maxine was the accident. What happened to *you* was on purpose. It was…" Dean searched for a word, his mouth working through his anger. "It was what you wanted."

"Do you mean finding the loom?"

"The loom." Dean wrapped his long arms around his narrow

frame. "I thought that if we found it, we could be free together. But I was wrong."

"Free from what?"

Dean circled Kane. Before he left the stage, he turned.

"You and the Others were never supposed to find out about me. Those were my orders. But I thought you were worth breaking every rule for, and I thought you'd do the same for me. I was wrong."

Kane didn't understand what Dean had said, but he knew enough about heartbreak to know what he meant. Kane had left him behind in a horrible way. For the loom? For power?

Dean pulled something from his jacket and tossed it to Kane. "Here, this is yours."

Kane had caught a book. *The Witches* by Roald Dahl. Hadn't he lost this, recently? Yes. But where? The path. When he was being chased by the Dreadmare.

"Where did you get this?" Kane asked.

"Found it. I've been looking for a chance to give it back."

Kane flipped through it. Nowhere had he written his name in this book, but he knew it was his by the way it fit in his hand, and the dog-eared page he'd last left off, and the worn spine from all the times he'd lost himself within it.

Dean said, "I read it. I can see why you love it. You should try a little harder to hold on to the things you love."

He left. Kane peered at the shadows that had folded over him. He didn't know what had just happened, but he knew it was important. And he knew that Dean had given him more than a book. He'd thrown Kane a key.

Kane waited to see what it would unlock within him. Waited, like he had waited in the river, among the bishop's-weed and silvery fish and swirling pollen.

Sure enough, something clicked.

· TWENTY-FOUR ·
HUNCHES

THE ST. AGNES CENTER FOR THE ARTS—OR AS SOPHIA
and Adeline called it, the conservatory—was all right angles, stone,
and glass. It was newer than the rest of the campus, and good thing.
So much discordant music filled its hallways in the late afternoon
that Kane imagined the previous building, which was probably an
old Victorian like many on the St. Agnes campus, had vibrated apart.

Elliot had driven Ursula and Kane over. They were meeting
Adeline, who refused to skip ballet unless there were, "urgent,
ethereal catastrophes afoot." An emergency meeting called by Kane
was evidently not an urgent, ethereal catastrophe, so they were here
waiting for her break. She'd only have a few minutes.

While Elliot peeked into a tap-dancing class, Ursula and
Kane sat on a bench, savoring the music from every angle. Ursula
had made homemade granola, and it was great. She and Kane

munched on it, comfortable being quiet together. Among all the tension, their friendship had become a fragile but surely growing thing, and Kane was thankful to have at least that.

"I wonder what it'd be like to walk around on your toes like that all the time," Ursula said as the girls in the studio spun on their pointe shoes.

"Very tall," Kane said.

"They look like flamingos."

"Is that a good thing? Flamingos are birds, you know."

"Yeah, but like—" Ursula tipped the last of the granola into her mouth, then crushed up the bag and tossed it toward a trash can. "They're like, funny birds. Dinosaur birds."

The bag missed. She stood to grab it off the floor.

"And dinosaur birds are somehow better?"

"No, dinosaur birds just aren't native to Connecticut."

The piano music cut off and the routine ended. Girls dressed in skirts and tights fled to the perimeter of the room to grab water and check their phones. Adeline pushed through the doors and walked right by them. After a beat, they followed her to the stairwell and out into the back parking lot.

"Welcome to my house," she said, a sarcastic hand tossed up at the conservatory and the dumpsters they hid behind. "Thanks for popping in. What can I do for you?"

Kane hadn't shaken the shivers from this morning yet. They'd rolled through him all day, fitful and jagged, and they skittered through his palms now. To steady himself, he reached into his backpack and pulled out *The Witches*.

Everyone looked at it, then at Kane.

"Who is Dean Flores?" Kane asked. "Don't lie to me this time."

Ursula, Elliot, and Adeline exchanged glances. They all looked back at the book, then Kane again. They were confused.

"He's a new student at school," Ursula said. "He's a diver on the swim team—"

"I mean who is he actually?"

More glances. Adeline took a swig from her water bottle, then twisted to stretch something in her back.

Kane grew frustrated. They weren't taking this seriously.

"Is he an Other, too? Was he?" Kane looked at Adeline. "You know, don't you? You know something about him."

If she did, Adeline betrayed nothing. She shrugged and began picking at her gossamer skirt blowing in the October breeze. "We don't know, Kane. We were going to ask you the same thing when the timing was right. We think he might have something to do with your accident."

"Why?"

"A hunch."

"Tell me what you know," Kane demanded.

"You called us all here. You first."

Adeline took another swig. They were all waiting for Kane. His resentment simmered just below the surface. He knew Adeline would be like this, insulting and petty, after he'd left her in her car the other night. He couldn't let that distract him. Kane knew Dean was part of his lost past, and therefore crucial in unlocking the mystery of how to recover the loom. This might be the answer to all the questions, the thing that would bring the reveries to an end for good.

"The last time I had this book was when I was attacked by the Dreadmare on the Harrow Creek path. Remember that, Urs?"

She nodded.

"Well, today Dean Flores gave this exact book back to me." Kane held it up high. "Ms. Daisy the Doberman isn't the Dreadmare. Dean *is*."

The reaction was slight but instant. Eyebrows raised, spines went rigid. Again all eyes fell to the book, then Kane.

"This is…" Adeline began.

"Silly," Elliot said.

Kane's jaw dropped.

Adeline continued. "You think because Dean gave you a book, he's a gigantic nightmare horse-spider?"

"No, I just—" Nervous laughter bubbled out of Kane. He shoved it down. "I mean yes, it's the book, but he also had a charm like the ones Poesy has, and also…"

Kane cut himself off, wondering again how easily Adeline could peer into his memories. He wanted to tell them everything, but in the past Kane had decided to keep whatever relationship he had with Dean a secret from the Others. He didn't think the reason was shame, because there wasn't shame in the way Dean had kissed Kane back. It was a kiss bitter with loss. It made Kane believe Dean was good. Or he wanted to be good. But something bound him to Poesy, and so whatever Dean and Kane had together had to be kept secret for Dean's sake. He had so much more to lose.

255

At least that was Kane's theory. He had to learn more, but he couldn't give more to the Others than he already had, and so Kane said, "I just think that Dean is maybe on our side. And that we should talk to him."

Adeline let out an incredulous laugh. "You've got to be kidding. If Dean is the Dreadmare, how could he be an ally? That thing literally tore through Helena's reverie."

"It saved us."

"It executed Poesy's orders. There's a difference and you know it."

Kane felt himself turning red. Of course Adeline called out this contradiction right away.

"Wait," Ursula said. "I mean it's possible, right? It's not the strangest thing we've seen."

Adeline shrugged and pulled out her phone. "I've got to get back."

Ursula gave Kane an encouraging nod. "Kane, what do you think we should do?"

Kane's knuckles were white around the edges of the book. "Talk to him. Learn more. We could get his file from school and see where he lives and…go there. And talk to him."

"That's a bad plan," Elliot said. "We don't know enough."

"Exactly," Kane said. "That's why we need to investigate, dumbass."

"He's not on Insta," Adeline said as she scrolled through her phone. "Not on Snapchat."

Kane kept his voice level. "Isn't that weird? And you said it yourself. You think he has something to do with my accident."

Adeline shrugged again. "That was just a hunch."

"Well, this is a hunch, too!"

"Both of you stop it," Elliot said. "We can't be operating off hunches. It's too dangerous. And what if you're right, Kane? What if he is the Dreadmare? Do you really plan to fight that thing?"

Kane absolutely did not want to fight the Dreadmare. He wanted to kiss the Dreadmare. Maybe. He slumped, defeated.

"Well, this has been great," Adeline said, still on her phone. "Urs, did you bring me the *you-know-what?*"

Ursula looked around furtively, then pulled another bag of granola out of her windbreaker. She passed it to Adeline with cool discretion, like it was an illicit substance. Adeline took it with just as much drama, winking at Ursula.

"These girls get grabby after hour two, and I don't share my snacks. You guys should leave soon. Kane's sister is going to show up in about twelve minutes for her string ensemble."

She left, leaving Elliot and Ursula to talk Kane down.

Elliot said, "I'm sorry Kane, but we need to focus on what we know. We know we need to unravel the reveries before Poesy does, or else she'll take them away. We know she used you to break into Helena's reverie, so unless we really mess up again, we're good." He didn't say it, but he meant Kane blowing the whistle. "We need to prioritize our security first before we go on the offense against Poesy to get back Helena's reverie, and hopefully Helena herself. People are going to start asking questions any day now, and we need to make sure we don't come up as the answers or else we can't help anyone. Does that make sense?"

"Yeah," Kane mumbled.

Elliot ducked to look Kane in the eye. "Yeah, as in you're good?"

A plan was forming in Kane's mind, a daydream he had entertained in the event the Others didn't agree. He looked at Elliot and attempted a perfectly resigned smile.

"I'm good," he lied.

· TWENTY-FIVE ·
HANDS

IT WAS A CLEAR AND BRIGHT NIGHT IN THE COBALT Complex. Moonlight drenched everything, icy and pure, so that the gutted buildings were carved from luminous ivory and encrusted in silver. The fog of Kane's breath wreathed his neck as he pedaled over bleached concrete. Frogs and loon-song told him he was nearing the river. It was one o'clock in the morning.

Kane skidded to a stop. A second later, so did Ursula.

"I can't believe we're here," she huffed. "I can't believe you tricked me into doing this."

"I didn't trick you. I just told you I was doing it one way or the other, and you're a good enough friend to recognize a request without making me beg."

"Yes, Kane, that's what we humans call a trick."

Kane gave her a wry smile. It had actually been Ursula

who called Kane after their meeting, which had left them both restless. And as soon as Kane knew Ursula also felt the need to do something, to take actual action, his mind was made up. Ursula's mind, he sensed, was made up, too, but she'd complained the whole way here. Probably to balance out the guilt she felt about sneaking behind Elliot and Adeline's backs. That, and her usual nervousness. This was not a great idea, and they both knew it.

They weren't being stupid, though. Kane had left a note for Sophia with instructions to call Adeline and Elliot if he wasn't back by sunrise. Then he'd packed a bag with his red journal, *The Witches*, some chalk, and an old aluminum baseball bat he found in the garage. Just in case. Then he and Ursula met near the bridge, dressed in all black, the reflectors on their bikes taped over as they careened toward the complex's eastern edge.

Biking through it, Kane thought about how the complex was, in some ways, its own reverie. An entire city imagined into being, then abandoned to the slow melt of neglect, then forgotten altogether as the world folded over it. Connecticut was full of these lost worlds, and the more Kane thought to look for them, the more certain he was that they slumbered everywhere. Just across this river, or beyond that hill, or behind that curtain. In many ways, the Cobalt Complex was the perfect place to bait nightmares into the light.

They reached the mill, Kane's chosen spot.

"You sure he's gonna show?"

"I'm sure," Kane said.

Kane drew a huge number eight into the tilted pavement, big enough to stand in each loop. While he did, he thought of Helena.

He owed her and Adeline for a lesson learned too late: sometimes a person's dreams are all they have and taking them away can break a heart or even stop a body. The act of crushing a dream can't be minimized. At best, it's mean. At worst, it's murder. Either way, Kane had let Poesy take what was not Kane's to give, and it was time to set things right. To get Helena back, and help her heal, if that was even possible.

And they needed Dean's help to do just that.

Kane stood back from his work. The moon winked at them from the river, and the few cicadas that remained this late in the season sang beneath the silence.

Minutes passed. Nothing happened.

"This worked before?" Ursula whispered.

"Yeah."

"Does he like, get a notification or something?"

Kane imagined Dean's phone lighting up on his nightstand. *Kane Montgomery would like to send you a direct message.*

"Dean?" Kane shouted. "Either you show up, or we call Poesy. I've got the whistle."

He brandished the charm. The few birds chirping went silent as something darker than the dark rose from the imploded roof of the mill, taking the shape of a lustrous beak and horns. Ursula got into a boxing stance. Kane tightened his grip on the bat, and an aura of etherea gathered around them in pulsing fractals, his powers at the ready.

Once, the Dreadmare had chased Kane and Sophia from this very mill, as though they were grave robbers. Now, Kane would make sure it knew he owned this particular grave. Dean couldn't chase Kane away from his own past forever, not when Kane had recruited the strongest person he knew as backup.

A flash swept over Kane from the left, then another. Twin flashlights cutting through the trees as Adeline and Elliot stumbled into the clearing.

"Shit," Adeline panted.

"Told you they'd be here," Elliot responded, out of breath.

The Dreadmare flickered away, the mill nothing but empty walls beneath Adeline and Elliot's garish flashlights. They pointed them right at Kane and Ursula, like they were criminals. Kane let out a frustrated groan and, not thinking, released his pent aura. It washed over the Others, unbalancing them, then soaked into the forest beyond. Everything was ruined.

"Whoa, Kane," Elliot said, hands up so his flashlight lit the trees. "Chill. Sophia called us. Your note sent her into a panic."

"Where is she now?"

"Your house. We told her we'd report back after we got you."

"*Got* me?"

Adeline moved between them, switching off her flashlight.

"It's not like that, Kane. She was freaking out. We had to give her something, or she was going to go out looking herself. And I'm glad she called. You both know trying to fight Dean is like, literally so dumb, right?"

Kane adjusted his grip on the bat. "So you believe me that Dean's the Dreadmare, then?"

Adeline rolled her lips together and looked over the river,

262

clearly not wanting to answer this question. Elliot shrugged and said, "Doesn't matter what we believe, to be honest. You guys are our team. If your beliefs are strong enough to bring you out here in the middle of the night, we should be right there beside you."

Kane knew this was a peace offering, but he had something to say. "So where was *our team* when I brought this up at the conservatory? Be honest, Elliot. You're only here because Ursula's in danger, right? You know you can flirt with her without also trying to get brownie points for being an awesome team captain, right?"

Adeline outright cackled at the dumbstruck expression on Elliot's face. She pulled herself into a barely contained smirk, and for a second she and Kane connected in the dark humiliation that burned between Elliot and Ursula. Kane decided he was starting to like Adeline.

"Wait," Ursula said. "Wait, what?"

Elliot, blushing, waved away the jab. "I prioritize safety. I'm just being cautious. You guys know this about me."

"And you know that we don't have the luxury of caution," said Kane. "Not when we're the only ones able to take action. My choices may have cost one woman her life. Maybe two. Worry about yourself all you want, but don't stop me from trying to get Helena back."

Ursula put a hand on Kane's shoulder. "We don't know what happened to Maxine, and what happened to Helena wasn't just your fault, Kane. You have saved many, many people from their reveries, and we should have listened to you when you spoke up for her. What happened was Poesy's fault. The blood is on her hands."

The group considered this.

"Her very well-manicured hands," Adeline added.

Kane had to admit she was right. Poesy had great nails.

Adeline's eyes were laughing at Kane. "You really thought you could take on Poesy and her Dreadmare?"

"No." Kane still wasn't sure how he felt about Poesy. Scared, sure, but he still felt her scariness was rooted in necessity. He didn't want to confront her; he wanted to investigate her. Learn more about what she meant when she said she would "fix"Helena's reverie.

"I thought Dean would help us in secret. I'm sure he's part of…"

"Part of what?"

Kane bit off his plan. He wasn't ready to tell them about his past with Dean, which he barely understood himself. He wasn't ready to remind them about the mysterious loom and its role in generating the reveries and attracting Poesy and nearly annihilating his life.

But then he saw their asking faces in the moonlight, and he saw they were the only things holding the darkness of the mill at bay. He realized that, as messy as their entrance had been, they had shown up for him after all. They each had arrived in their own way, choosing to chase the flame of his half-imagined hunches over the comfort of their own beds and the safety of their own dreaming.

Kane could almost feel his lost friendships, then, like shadows beneath the new friendships trying to form. So why was he protecting Dean, who vanished when Kane needed him the most?

"Do you remember," Kane began, breathing deep, "how you said I was obsessed with finding the true source of the reveries? Well I did, in Maxine Osman's reverie. It was that crown. It's called the loom. It's some kind of weapon that is leaking etherea like radiation, causing the reveries to mutate out of people. Poesy said that if we find it, we can stop the reveries. She thought maybe one of you had stolen it. That's why I helped her."

"No one stole your crown," Ursula said. "That thing was awful. It nearly killed us."

"And what about Dean?" Adeline asked in a clipped tone, pushing her question in front of Kane's accusations. Once again he was sure she knew more than she let on.

"I think he's here for the loom, too. I think he wants to use it, somehow."

"And where does that leave you?" Adeline asked. "If you found that kind of power again, what would you do?"

Kane clenched his hands. "Knowing what I know now? Destroy it."

Adeline lifted her chin, peering at him through the lens of this new fact. "Give me the whistle," she said, her face unreadable.

Kane sagged. Maybe telling them the truth had cost him his chance tonight. Maybe he'd chosen wrong.

"Making a deal with Dean was a bad plan," Adeline said as she took the whistle. "But it was the right idea. If what you say about Poesy is true, I'm guessing she needs our help in finding the loom, which means we've got leverage. And she clearly values your life. Let's see if she's open to negotiations."

And she blew the whistle.

Kane's mind stumbled. Bubbles of anxiety fizzed in his throat, filling him with the bright sting of excitement. Elliot and Ursula looked just as shocked.

The whistle's silence cut through the birds' chirping as though it'd cut through the birds themselves. Then a rushing, whispering discord blew through the mill and the moonlight ahead bruised, dimpled, and peeled apart. A pair of double doors towered before them, finished in a lusterless black, and starkly flat against the drifting river beyond. Kane braced himself for the Dreadmare to fly through but minute after minute passed in glassy stillness.

"It's a door," Elliot said.

"Yes, Elliot, we can all see the door," said Adeline.

"Do we knock?" Ursula asked.

"I think we already rang the bell," Elliot said.

"The whistle opened up some sort of passage into Helena's reverie," Kane said. "Maybe this leads to wherever Poesy came from?"

Adeline marched forward, grasped a massive handle, and pulled the heavy door open a few inches. Mellow light spilled out.

"No one's here," she whispered. "Kane, what do you want to do?"

Kane felt absurd relief. He considered the door and all that might be behind it. Something told him fate had dealt them a very rare chance to enter Poesy's realm when she wasn't home.

Or it was a trap. Either way, they had to enter to find out. Otherwise, manicured or not, all their hands were covered in the crime of doing nothing to bring Helena home.

"Let's go," Kane said.

· TWENTY-SIX ·
TRICK OR TREAT

KANE WASN'T SURE WHAT HE EXPECTED, BUT IT wasn't this.

They entered a room full of height and golden glow, with curving walls made from glass display cases. Turning around, Kane wasn't surprised to find that the room was actually circular. The double doors they'd just walked through stood alone and without any discernible wall to lead through. Just a door frame made of the same obsidian as the whistle, gilded with gold filigree. It stood upright like a lone domino upon a circular stage at the room's center. It almost reached the chandelier.

Elliot propped the door open with Kane's bat.

"I think we're okay," he whispered. "But no one touch anything. This place could be rigged."

They each picked a different area to explore. Kane sought

out the squat coffee table and the tea set. There were a few cups ready for use, but Poesy's specific cup was absent. He moved on to the cases. They were backed by mirrors so that at first each case appeared to hold nothing but far-flung infinity. Then he looked closer.

Curios. Artifacts. Charms. Small, strange objects that each emanated the same reality-bending aura of the reveries. They whispered to Kane of their mysterious magnitude, their stolen vastness. Some lay in pieces, crushed but then meticulously arranged, like an exotic pinned butterfly made beautiful in its unmaking.

Poesy didn't fix reveries. She collected them. Kane craned his neck, following the cases all the way up to the ceiling. There must have been thousands in this room alone. How many lay in pieces? How many people were locked away in false realms?

What little hope Kane had for Poesy finally crumbled, and it left him dizzy and drifting. He stumbled back, catching on the corner of a wide desk. The Others glared at him, but no alarms sounded. Nothing changed. They went back to inspecting the charms, Kane's same grim conclusion hanging over each of them in the silence.

Kane turned to the desk. It was covered in papers and books and odd, sharp instruments. He picked up a scroll full of diagrams and cryptic print. Buried beneath it was a book with a bright red cover. Chills prickled across Kane's neck. He knew that red.

Kane slid the journal forward and ran his hands across the supple leather. The elastic band slid off smoothly, his eyes filled with his own penmanship. Except not quite; all the words were backward.

Kane made sure no one was watching as he took out the journal Poesy had given him from his backpack. The two books were identical. Experimentally, he flipped them both open to the back-most page and scribbled across one. On the other, like a bruise rising to the skin's surface, the scribble reappeared in reverse.

Deceit slid through Kane's heart, oil-thin and burning, amplifying the humiliation he already felt. He'd dutifully recorded every lousy detail of his recovery (even his dreams!) into that journal with no intention of giving it back, but Poesy had been reading along the entire time.

He was sure this is how Poesy had sent her invitation for tea. On this hunch, he put his pen between the pages of one journal, then opened the other. The pen rolled from the spine, a bit warm from its journey.

Kane's anger gave way to wonder. He did the trick several more times, captivated by the magic. He could feel himself getting carried away, so before anyone noticed he grabbed both journals and shoved them into his backpack.

Then he saw the egg.

On a cleared corner of the desk, nestled within a satin cushion, was a bejeweled egg no bigger than an acorn. Its surface was crammed with exquisite gems of every color. There was no mistaking it: he had found Helena's reverie.

"It's here!" Kane called, and the others hurried over.

"You sure?" asked Elliot.

"I'm sure."

Several other charms were scattered around it, but Helena's felt different. From it drifted a rumbling, desperate energy, as though it verged on hatching.

"Good. No negotiations needed, then. Someone grab it," Elliot said.

"How about *you* grab it, Elliot?"

No one wanted to touch the thing. Then the lights flickered, and everyone looked up. A far-off creaking sent shivers down Kane's spine.

"Well, that's ominous," Elliot whispered.

The lights flickered again. The door vibrated in its frame.

It was Ursula who finally moved. She snatched up a small velvet pouch from the desk and swept the charms—Helena's and all—into it. Then they were following Elliot to the door, which was still propped open by the bat. The night beyond was a sliver of navy beckoning them from the room's golden warmth, promising safety, but right before Elliot slipped through Adeline wrenched him back. There was a *crack* and the door slammed shut, slicing the bat in half.

"Shit," said Elliot.

Ursula pushed open the door. It showed clearly to the other side of the room. The mill was gone. She closed it again and opened it again. Nothing. On the third try she paused.

"It's...cold?" she said.

Kane grabbed the handle. It was frigid.

The light of the room waned, and a jitter ran up Kane's arm.

Adeline pointed to the bottom of the doors. "Snow," she whispered, and sure enough a dusting of flakes seeped beneath the door on an icy draft.

"Hide!" hissed Elliot, but already they were stumbling over one another to stuff themselves behind the settee. A second later the door groaned open, and freezing air gushed into the room, kissing the nape of Kane's neck. Kane watched from beneath the settee, stifling his frantic breaths as a flurry of snow revealed first the legs of a dog, then the dip of a silver chain, and finally human legs in thigh-high boots.

The door closed, shutting out the blizzard and trapping them inside.

Elliot's eyes glowed gold as he worked up his invisibility magic, but Kane knew he couldn't hide them all for long.

"I know I say this every time, Ms. Daisy, but that is the last time we visit Saas-Fee," said Poesy as she unlatched the silver chain. "Next time I decide where we walk."

Ms. Daisy growled. Kane felt a hand squeezing his calf. Adeline's. Kane had been right. Ms. Daisy had been on a walk with Poesy this whole time, which meant the dog and the Dreadmare were not one and the same.

"Stop that. You love the loop around Belgrade."

For the next few minutes they listened to Poesy walk about the room, shuffle things here and there. Tinkering with something. Then, quite calm, Poesy called out, "Would any of you like tea?"

No one moved.

"It's no trouble, really," she said. "I'm making some for

myself—to warm up—and it'd be rude not to at least offer. I know Mr. Montgomery is inclined to decline, but I'm fairly positive Mr. Levi should like a cup. Ms. Bishop, Ms. Abernathy, one lump or several?"

Elliot stood first, dragging Kane up with him. Adeline followed and, after a stiff nudge, Ursula stumbled up, too. Poesy, dressed in a fur-fringed house coat, watched with bright eyes across the room. In her hands was a tea tray, the teapot already steaming. Ms. Daisy trotted up to them with a bone clamped in her jaw and placed it cordially at Ursula's feet.

Kane tried to sound tough. "We didn't come for tea."

Poesy gave a patronizing smile. "Yes, Mr. Montgomery, I know. You came for Ms. Helena Quigley's charm, and I see you've got it. You'd think I'd have this place alarmed but, alas, with no discernible entrance I don't get too many unsolicited guests, never mind haphazard trick-or-treaters like yourselves. If you'd given me a little more notice I'm sure I could have summoned a charcuterie board."

"We're not staying," spat Adeline. For the second time she nudged Ursula, now because Ursula was patting Ms. Daisy on the head.

"Yeah," Ursula stammered. "We're *leaving*."

Poesy lifted one eyebrow. "How?"

Confidently, Adeline brandished the whistle.

"Hmm," Poesy watched the charm without concern. "Whistles are for beckoning. You appear to be in need of a key."

Kane opened his mouth, then closed it. His eyes flickered to

Poesy's bracelet, where he remembered there was a small, white key. This was a very bad plan indeed.

"You come and go as you please," said Elliot. "You'll let us go."

"Will I? I am not so sure."

Elliot elbowed Kane. "Threaten her!"

"Oh, right." Kane stretched out a hand, producing a cloud of vaporous light. Instantaneously, the cases of charms began to whisper as they sipped the ambient magic.

The whites of Poesy's eyes glistened as she scanned the heights of the room. "That would not be a wise move, Mr. Montgomery."

"Then let us leave," Kane demanded.

"Come now, child. There is no need for savagery."

Adeline gawked. "Savagery? How about what you did to Helena Quigley? How's that for savagery?"

Poesy's eyes lowered, brimming with menace. "Don't," she seethed. "Do not call my ethics into question, *Other*. What I do and how I do it is founded in necessity."

"Necessity?" Adeline spat. "Was crushing an old lady's dreams a necessity? You might as well have murdered her."

"Murdered? Ha!" Poesy let out a throaty guffaw. "And I suppose she was safer under your dubious protection? It didn't look that way, when Mr. Montgomery invoked my intervention. But he did, and I rid reality of the fantasy you four poisoned, and now Ms. Helena Quigley is safe. She would thank me if she were awake to my mercy. You should thank me, too."

Adeline gripped the settee. "You're evil. All these charms are evil."

Poesy gave an amused smile. "And what do you think that makes you? You haven't a clue where your powers come from, do you? And to think, here you've invaded *my* sanctuary to denounce the very mechanism I used to create *you*? I have no taste for irony. Such insolence from my own children will not be suffered."

Poesy was still holding the tray and, as though nervous, the teacups atop it rattled.

Elliot's voice was firm. "What mechanism?"

Poesy dipped her chin. "The sacred process of turning a person's pain into power, of course, but I see no point in entertaining the curiosity of a few failing prototypes. I see now that the powers I have granted you have made you too bold, and we can't have that for our new world, now can we Ms. Daisy?" She looked over them appraisingly. "I suppose I could try taking you each apart and putting you back together, but that'll take some time. And it's a rather painful process. I'd have to get changed."

The light was fading in Kane's palm. He had been so wrong. This person, the only person he saw himself in, was supposed to protect and help him, but she had used him like a prop. She had isolated and manipulated him, and now they were all going to suffer.

"You're not hurting anybody," he said weakly. "You said you would protect me. You said you needed me!"

Poesy's eyes were glass marbles in her painted skull. Airily, she said, "I need no one. I need power, only, and you've brought it to me. I had envisioned a partnership with you, yes, but this newfound disloyalty will not do. You have chosen your friends. You have chosen poorly. You are my biggest disappointment."

A black blur lurched from the carpet and pounced on Adeline, dragging her and Kane to the floor. Without aim or discretion, the pent-up magic burst from Kane's grip.

Poesy dumped the tea set and snapped up the tray, deflecting the bolt into the chandelier above. Sparks and glass hailed upon them. Kane heard a dog snarl then yelp as Elliot threw Ms. Daisy to the side, and then they were all running.

"Get them out of here!" Poesy screamed as they dashed into the halls beyond the sanctuary. The corridors filled with clicking claws on marble, the Dreadmare unfolding from the shadows. Elliot cried out and vanished. Ursula vaporized a second later.

Adeline shoved Kane to the right, and a spidery leg sliced the air between them. He pivoted and ran down a new hallway, running hard through Poesy's labyrinthine lair. He opened doors at random, cutting through a room full of blazing stars, an armory plated in black blades, and finally ending in a greenhouse.

Kane slipped through aisles of ivy and ferns, whipping past flowers that looked as surreal as they did poisonous. He tore away from their nettled grasps, only slowing in the far reaches of the massive greenhouse where he found a forest of upright, woody stalks. He slid inside, panting.

Had he escaped?

The Dreadmare must have ran after Adeline instead. What had happened to the others? Their screams had cut off like clipped film.

Kane's nose burned with an incoming sob. He forced it down when he heard the door to the greenhouse open.

"Perhaps in here?" came a voice that was distinctly Poesy's, though now it simmered with the song of cicadas. Hearing this, Kane wondered how those two sounds had ever sounded different to him. He backed farther into the stalks.

Footsteps advanced upon the greenhouse floor. He heard the sniffing of a dog, and Ms. Daisy whined. Water hissed from turgid hoses. Past the opaque glass of the walls, shadows as big as whales drifted and turned.

Kane's lungs burned for air. His vision was going gray. He was so focused on the footsteps he did not notice the odd vines encircling him. Vines that were steely and black, with hooked hooves at the end. It was only when one wrapped around him that he thought to look up into the great, shining beak of the Dreadmare as it opened.

There was no chance to scream. The beak closed over Kane's shoulder, as certain and deft as a kiss, and Kane was dragged into blackness.

· TWENTY-SEVEN ·
IN THE
IN-BETWEEN

WHEN KANE WAS TWELVE, SOPHIA CONVINCED HIM to turn up their parents' treadmill all the way to see if he could run on it. Arms braced on the bars, he had hovered over that rushing track, knuckles white as he guided himself downward. For the briefest second he kept up! And then, inevitably, he tripped into that breathless moment between rising and falling—a place of reckless momentum without any movement.

That's what Kane felt as the Dreadmare closed around him. There was no gravity, no direction. Only momentum and the sick inevitability of impact. Kane had to get out. He clapped his hands and light fractured open the darkness, catapulting him outward with terrific speed.

The impact when he landed was softer than it should have been. Kane sat up on a bed in a dimly lit room. He felt for his backpack straps before remembering he'd ditched it during the escape. The thing wrapped around his shoulder was actually another person.

Kane scrambled away from the figure coated in a bodysuit of pliant leather, black like the Dreadmare's hide, with plates of obsidian armor jabbing into the whirled sheets. A pointed, full-head helmet had replaced the beak, but the horns remained. It was the same beast in a new form. It sat up, watching Kane. Waiting to see what he'd do.

"It's you, isn't it?" Kane said.

The Dreadmare slid from the bed and gave Kane its back. It flexed its shoulders, causing the armor to pull and slide on the thin leather.

This room smelled of boy, of detergent and a hint of cologne. Pine, or something close. It made Kane's instincts itch, made his head fill with fog.

"Show me your face," was all he could say.

The Dreadmare turned. As it did, its armor transformed, billowing and then unraveling into inky rivulets that flowed rapidly into the Dreadmare's palm. And then it wasn't the Dreadmare anymore. It was Dean Flores, holding a small chess piece—the knight, carved from black obsidian. A charm, like Poesy's, locking away his armor. Dean pocketed it and said, "You're bleeding."

It was true. Scrapes all along Kane's arms had dotted the sheets with blood. Dean was no better. Red rimmed a split in his lip, and a cut on his neck slowly stained the collar of his shirt.

The shock of the revelation lay furious and bare between them.

Even though Kane had been daydreaming of this exact moment, he found the sudden reality oddly surreal. What happened now?

"What just happened? Where are we?"

"We teleported. Or we were teleporting when you let out that blast. It got us both pretty good. Do you think you broke any bones?"

"I don't think so."

"Good. That could have gone much worse."

"What could have gone much worse?"

"Your rescue."

Kane laughed. "You call this a rescue? You just...abducted me into your bed."

Dean shrugged. "I needed a soft place to land you after you built up all that momentum."

"And where are my friends? What have you done with them?"

Dean looked unsure. "They're mostly safe, but—"

He's stalling.

Kane dashed from the room, expecting to find himself in some dank dungeon under Poesy's lair. He called for Ursula, for anyone. He stopped when he reached the end of a long corridor and found himself not in a dungeon, but in the middle of a sparse room of glass and steel. An apartment, clinically immaculate, with windows that leapt from floor to ceiling and overlooked a river Kane knew.

"This is..." Kane realized the lights across the river were those of East Amity.

Why do I know this place? Why does this view look so familiar?

"My house," Dean said from behind him. He emerged from the kitchen with two large bowls of water and several cloths. From the bathroom he fetched a plastic bin of bottles and bandages. He motioned for Kane to join him at the table. "You know this place as the Cobalt Complex, right? They are building condos here. I am one of the only tenants right now."

"This is where you live?"

"Yes."

"Alone?"

"For now."

"Where are your parents?"

"Visiting my grandmother."

Kane sat across from him. His panic had resolved into, of all things, triumph. He had a hunch. His hunch was right. The proof sat before him. The urge to gloat rose, fat and content in him, which reminded Kane to again ask, "Where are my friends?"

"They are safe. I teleported them to the high school. On the roof."

This thrilled and terrified Kane. Even if they knew he was here, it would take them at least twenty minutes to cut through the entire town and get over the river. He was truly alone with Dean. With the Dreadmare. With Poesy's henchman. But right now, Dean was not henchman-like. He was wringing out a washcloth and dabbing at his cut-up arms. He nodded for Kane to do the same. The bowls of water blushed to rose as they sat in silence, the plinks of dripping liquid holding their ceremony intact.

"How do you know when I draw the number eight?" Kane asked.

"I see it."

"But how?"

"It's one of my powers. I can see things in my mind."

"So like clairvoyance?"

"Something like that, yes."

Kane rung out his cloth. "You were watching us tonight?"

"I was. But I got shy when Adeline and Elliot arrived. Then I wasn't going to show up at all, but when Poesy called I had no choice. It was a mistake to go to her sanctuary. It's where she's most powerful."

"Where is it?"

Dean nodded, as though he liked that Kane had asked this. "It's unknown. An in-between space."

"Like a reverie."

Dean thought about this. "Similar, but with some key architectural deviations of Poesy's own devising."

"Such as?"

"Well, for instance, people can enter and exit it."

"Like through those doors?"

"And teleporting, like we did earlier."

Kane felt sick at the thought of that stretched oblivion. He was not eager to reenter that space between spaces that were between other in-between spaces.

"I don't get it."

Dean blotted his elbow. "Teleporting is actually very simple once you get the hang of it. Distance matters, but not as much as trajectory and momentum. You have to be able to see your entry clearly. That's why I can't teleport in and out of reveries, which warp distance in a similar—"

"No, about Poesy. She's your boss, isn't she?"

"Yes." Resentment flashed in Dean's eyes, but he stayed focused on his cuts. Kane understood that. He was angry with himself, too, for being taken in by Poesy's authority.

"But you saved us from her."

"Yes."

Dean's tenderness was gone now, replaced by a face as cold and faultless as marble. And Kane realized he wasn't resentful toward Poesy. He was resigned.

"Are you disobeying her right now?" Kane asked.

And, like the first crocus breaking winter's frost, Dean smiled. A confession. An unspoken yes. Kane was smiling, too.

"Give me your arms."

Kane put out his arms, and Dean gently washed out the scrapes, erasing the drying blood from Kane's skin. Then he applied some hydrogen peroxide to another cloth and dabbed. "This will sting," he said too late. Kane didn't mind. He watched the bubbles fizz under his skin, as though their effervescence was his excitement escaping his body. Then it was Dean's turn. They sat close, Dean tense as Kane cleaned the scrape on his neck, Kane doing his best despite the distraction of Dean up close. His jaw, the brownness of his skin, and the browner brown of his freckles.

Kane got to count them this time. There were twenty-nine, total.

"We'll need to change," Dean said. He left and then returned with two fresh shirts. He began to peel off his bloodied clothes but stopped when he saw Kane's expression. "Did you want to change in the bedroom?"

Kane blushed. "Oh, no, here's fine."

Dean turned away. Dutifully Kane removed his own shirt and thought of something Ursula once had said about Dean being on the swim team. It showed. His body looked meticulously drawn, like an anatomy diagram. It was not because he was especially bulky, nor because he was especially skinny. It was the way his muscles moved beneath his skin; there was such a beauty to them that it was hard to imagine Dean had not been designed with lovely intent.

He saw a cut he'd missed on Dean's collarbone.

"Wait, come here."

Shirt halfway on, Dean slid back onto the stool and Kane dabbed at the cut. Yesterday Kane had been trapped within the imaginings of who he and Dean had been to one another, and what they might have done. Now, he was singularly focused on pretending they were perfect strangers. Dean, half-naked, was doing the same.

Dean winced, his hand grabbing the back of Kane's thigh.

"I'm sorry," he said.

"I'm sorry, too," Kane said.

"For what?"

"For trying to blow you up."

"You were scared," Dean murmured.

Kane nodded.

"Are you scared now?" Dean asked.

Kane thought about this. He thought about the way he held the Others and Dean apart, like they could never be combined. He thought maybe part of losing his memory was letting go of the distrust that defined it. He thought about how Dean had not let go of his thigh.

The sound of Kane's phone vibrating saved him from answering. Dean slid into his shirt while Kane fumbled with the device.

"It's Ursula," Kane said.

"So, aren't you going to answer it?"

He knew he should be concerned about the Others, but here he was more concerned about ending this moment too early.

Dean took the phone and answered it on speaker. "Hallo?"

There was a great deal of shushing. Then Ursula, in an contrived tough voice, said, "Listen up, Flores, and listen good. We know you've got Kane. We don't know what you're trying to pull, but you've made a *gregarious* mistake—"

In the distance Elliot whispered, "It's *egregious*, Urs."

Ursula was back. "You've made an *egregious* mistake. If you don't return him in the next hour we are prepared to—"

"Ursula, it's me. I'm okay."

"Kane?"

After some scuffling, Adeline was on the line. "Where the hell are you?"

"Dean's apartment," Kane said. "He's...he's..."

Dean nodded.

"He's the Dreadmare. He teleported us out of Poesy's sanctuary. He saved us."

Adeline's voice did not conceal her incredulity. "He separated us. Where are you? The condos at the Cobalt Complex?"

"How did you know that?"

"We may or may not have broken into the school to get his file. Seemed as good as any other hunch you've had lately."

For all the animosity between them, Kane had to laugh along with Adeline at this. His triumph swelled further.

Elliot entered the conversation. "Tell him to bring you back."

Kane felt his defiance flare.

"No."

"Then we'll come to you."

"No. You won't."

"Kane," said Elliot, all fatherly. "We know his address. We're already on our way. Don't get any ideas."

Boop. Kane hung up the phone and noticed about a hundred texts from the Others, along with a handful from Sophia. Great. On top of everything else, she was mad at him, too. He powered down the phone before it started ringing again, then turned to Dean.

"Can you teleport us again?"

· TWENTY-EIGHT ·
DARK WATERS

POESY HAD ONCE REFERRED TO EAST AMITY AS A tapestry. From above Kane could see she was right.

From horizon to dark horizon, the cloth of the suburb whirled and sunk, kissed together and tore apart. It smoothed to an ironed grid and then bunched into soft hills against the forested mountains. Streetlights dotted the cloth like sequins, sparkling in the clear navy air, and the moon illuminated the occasional river, drawn through the dark like silver stitches. Other pricks of light moved—cars, working their way through the folds and toward the bridge, rushing beneath where Kane and Dean watched.

"Why the bridge?" Kane said, kicking his legs into the drop. Drafts from the river pushed into his sleeves and nipped at his ankles, but he was past the chill now. Dean had nestled them into the crisscrossed girders overlooking the water. He was holding Kane's hand. For "safety" reasons.

"We used to come here," said Dean. "To practice your flying."

This surprised Kane. Not the flying but the openness with which Dean mentioned their past, as though asking Kane to ask for more. And Kane found he couldn't. What if it wasn't what he wanted? What if the fiction in his head was better?

The bridge wasn't falling; the feeling of collapse was within him. Kane focused on the cold metal beneath him, and not the gathering warmth held in his hand. He grabbed for the next question he could think of.

"How does the whistle work?"

"It's a beacon. It beckons the threshold—those large doors."

"And it always leads to that place with all the charms and artifacts?"

Dean nodded. "Poesy's sanctuary."

"Are all those charms made from reveries? From people?"

"I've never had the courage to ask. I assume so."

Kane's heart clenched thinking of all those stolen lives. He veered again. "Your eyes. Are they actually that color?"

Dean laughed. "No, my eyes are brown. Like yours. They turn when I use my second sight, and I guess I use it all the time now. I've gotten so used to seeing things from every angle, it's hard to just be stuck with my own point of view."

"Ursula's eyes turn pink when she uses her powers. Elliot's turn yellow. Adeline's go all gray."

Dean shrugged, committed to letting Kane rule this conversation.

"Poesy said she made the Others by turning pain to power. What did she mean?"

Dean considered this. "Poesy is a master manipulator of etherea. Her expertise is crushing ethereal power into new forms, like when she crushes reveries into charms. Like the Dreadmare armor I wear. That was an early attempt, I think."

"At what?"

"At weaponizing etherea in a way she can control. Etherea needs to be channeled through a form, so she tried creating armor like the Dreadmare. It was once some sort of shape-shifting abyss of terror, but she basically turned it into a pelt. And now she's working on channeling etherea through people. Through us, I guess."

"But wouldn't that create a reverie?"

"With a normal person, yes. But we're lucid. It means ethereal manifestations—reveries—don't overtake us like everyone else. That's why she chose to grant us powers. To see how people who are always between worlds, and never within them, might manifest power. She's been watching you and the Others for a long time."

"Can she control us?"

Dean swallowed. "She doesn't have to," he said. "Think about it. Our powers... Don't they feel more like curses? What she said to you about pain confirmed a theory of mine. Etherea taps into our subconscious and materializes our fantasies, correct? Well, some people have bad fantasies and believe bad things about themselves. Whatever Poesy's method is, I think she filters etherea through our pain, and the result is a power that we fear. That's a pretty ingenious way of making sure none of grow too power hungry or surpass her, I would say."

Kane thought about Adeline, whose grandmother suffered from Alzheimer's. He wondered if she thought it was her fault that her grandmother's memory faded so fast. And Elliot. Pragmatic, pedantic Elliot, whose powers forced him to live in the half-light of trickery and illusion. To hide among the familiar manipulations of his father.

Ursula was the most gentle person Kane knew. Ursula was the girl who had been torn apart her entire life because of her body and her strength. Ursula was the strongest among them, her powers the most brutal.

"What about your powers?" Kane asked. "What about your pain?"

Dean was silent. He had a way of watching things without looking at them. His eyes were always on the distance, but his body was open to Kane now, considerate and patient, waiting to be held.

"I can see things I should not be able to see, and I can go to places I should not go. I can run from anything, and in my life this has always hurt me."

And he would say nothing else. Kane's thoughts selfishly turned to himself. "But my eyes don't glow."

"That's right."

He passed his free hand over his temples, his burns now turned to scars. "So I'm not like the you and the Others."

"That's right. You're the piece Poesy has yet to figure out. She didn't give you power. You just have it, like her. Actually, you are like her in many ways. She thinks of you as her protégé, you know."

Like her?

The thousands of charms spun in Kane's mind, cut into kaleidoscopic shards that shredded him with their muted agony. His mouth went acidic. If he hurled off the bridge, would the vomit just float on the updraft as a gooey net of chunks? *I'm not like her,* he told himself. *I would help those people, not keep them trapped for... for...*

Adeline was right. They had no idea why Poesy kept those charms.

Dean squeezed his hand. "Still there?"

"What does she want with all those reveries?" Kane asked. "And who is she, even? And what is she?"

"Poesy is Poesy," Dean said. "No one knows where she began, or how, but by now she is more a force of nature than she is human. This power to manipulate etherea that you both share—it's incredible. She uses it to harvest reveries, and then she experiments on them. She dissects them for their resources."

"Resources?"

"Treasure, beasts, architectures, magics. She can even take out weapons and magical artifacts—like the whistle and the door. Anything she wants, she takes. It's all just material to her."

"Material for what, though?"

Dean lowered his chin. "You really can't tell?"

Kane shrugged.

"She's building her own world," Dean said. "Her own entire

reality, bigger than just a reverie. All she needs is a source of etherea powerful enough to help her weave it all together."

Kane's eyes cut through the tapestry of East Amity, up into the wide, blank clouds. "That's why she's after the loom."

"And that's why she must never find it," Dean said. "Whatever reality Poesy creates, it's going to replace this one. I'm sure of it."

Kane reminded himself that the wavering was within him, not beneath him. He fought for focus. He wanted to ask how to stop Poesy, but he already knew the answer. He had to find the loom before she did and destroy it utterly.

"You helped me try to stop her once, didn't you?" Kane asked.

Dean nodded.

His scars prickled as he looked upon the dark waters that had once held his burned body. He was playing with a similar fire now, guessing at his past instead of just asking about it. But it felt safer to guess, like passing his hand through a wobbling candle flame whose little licks couldn't burn him.

"But whatever I did hurt you, and now you're not helping me anymore. Not in the same way at least."

"I have been helping you."

"Helping me survive is not helping me achieve."

Kane pulled his hand away, jamming his leg into the corner of two bars so he could look at Dean head-on. Dean reached for him, but stopped, seeing a new hardness in Kane's face. It was time to know the truth.

"Tell me what happened. Tell me about us, and how it all ended."

Dean's eyes skipped over Kane with the dexterity of a dragon-fly. "There is a lot to tell."

"Start from the beginning, then."

Dean's eyes settled on his own empty palm and stayed there. When he spoke, it was like each word hurt more than the last.

"Poesy recruited me last winter. My instructions were to watch over the Others as she experimented on their powers and to follow you closely. Your powers are connected to the loom, somehow, and Poesy believed that your abilities would eventually lead you right to it. She told me that looms are like wishes; they appear to those who are desperate enough to need them. In that way, you were her key to this loom, but also her competition. She needed me to watch you. And keep you safe. She gave me my powers and the Dreadmare armor as protection and told me to never interfere in the reveries unless your life was in peril. I kept to the shadows, only watching, until one day you found me out. We fought. You won. You forced me to tell you everything I knew. Somehow, we became friends."

"And the Others never knew?"

"I think they suspected something. They became very suspicious when we began..."

"Began what?"

Dean looked dizzy. His voice was strained.

"Searching. We used to sit up here and talk about what we'd do if we had the loom's power. The worlds we would create. The wrongs we would right. But then, when we did find the loom... when *you* found it, in Maxine's reverie, you..." Something shook Dean's voice, a fissure breaking open in him. "You didn't wait for me.

You took it for yourself, and the ensuing blast tore Maxine's reverie apart. It nearly tore through reality itself, but then Adeline—"

"I know," Kane cut in. "I know what Adeline did. But this doesn't make any sense. I would never take that power for myself. I would never ask Adeline to...to..."

"You gave up," Dean said, suddenly loud. "You made the choice to take that power for yourself, and when it was too much, you decided it was easier to start over than to finish what you began."

Kane was stunned. This whole time, Dean had never raised his voice. Dean stood, swaying in the wind like the fall couldn't kill him. Then he hiccupped—a strange, strangled noise. Kane realized he was trying to stop himself from crying.

"You forced Adeline's hand. *You* took yourself away. Like it was easy. Like everything was just a game to you that you could reset when you weren't winning. You ran away, like you always do."

"I'm sorry," Kane said, defensive. "But I'm not that person anymore. I'm not the one who left you."

Dean rubbed at his eyes. "Funny, you have his smile."

Kane watched cars glide beneath them. Black holes were heavy, right? He wondered how a bridge of thin metal bars could withstand the weight of the void opening within him. Dean was right. He was the same, lost person, always running, always failing.

"Here," Dean said, tossing Kane a small pouch. In it were the charms they'd tried to steal from Poesy's collection. "Maybe you can still save Helena."

He wouldn't look at Kane. The moment was over, and Dean was closed again. Kane took out his phone and turned it on.

Messages poured in. Texts, voicemails, DMs. Tons of them, so quickly Kane couldn't read them. Then his phone lit up with a call. It was Ursula again.

"Urs, don't worry. I'm fine. I have Helena's charm. We can—"

"Kane." It was Adeline. Instead of anger, her voice shook through barely managed panic: "Please. Come back."

"What's wrong? What happened?"

Kane's phone vibrated madly as more messages poured in.

"It's a reverie. Elliot and Ursula are already inside. They're looking for her. It's…"

A frequency rose in Kane's ear, needling and hysteric. "Who, Adeline? Whose reverie?"

"Sophia," Adeline cried. "Kane, it's your sister."

· TWENTY-NINE ·
THE ARCHIVIST

DEAN WRAPPED AROUND KANE, SWINGING HIM AWAY from the drop and holding him steady. And good thing; otherwise Kane was sure he would have burned apart, just a million embers scattered over East Amity as he fell.

Through the phone, Adeline's voice might as well have been cast from another world. Already Kane could hear the telltale whisper of etherea swallowing her up as she quickly tried to give him the details.

"I *told* you to let me erase her memories of the Beazley Affair. I *told* you. Her mind was vulnerable, and then you ran off tonight, and she fucking *snapped*. It's all in her messages. She felt her reverie taking over. She called all of us, and when no one answered, she drove herself to the complex to find us. I have no idea how she made it that far, but that's where it took her down. Somewhere in the complex. And now she's in there, and she's alone, and…"

Whispering static swallowed Adeline's voice.

"Where?" Kane cried. "Tell me where!"

Adeline's voice faded in and out.

"You can't let her in," Adeline hissed. "You can't allow Poesy to get her, too."

The line cut off, leaving Kane to stare down the litany of messages that had been building up while his phone was off. Sophia had called him, over and over. In her messages, her voice was barely audible against that same, horrible whispering.

Kane, I'm here at the complex. Just pick up. Please pick up. I'm here. Something bad is happening to me. The buildings are breathing. I'm lost. I feel—"

And from there her screams merged into the undulating static, the line going dead with a polite *boop*, just like Adeline.

She was gone. Lost to her reverie. All while Kane and Dean sat atop a bridge, talking, watching over the exact location where Sophia's reverie had formed: the Cobalt Complex.

Kane shoved Dean off him, nearly losing his balance on the girder. "Where is Poesy?"

"Her sanctuary. If she knew about the new reverie, she would have already summoned me, but she'll be expecting me to return soon either way."

"Can she enter without the whistle letting her in?"

"Yes, but the whistle is her shortcut."

Did Adeline still have the whistle? Kane could barely think. There was no logic to any of this. It was all unreal, but it all mattered.

"Distract her. Make sure she doesn't find out what's going on. Teleport me to the reverie's edge, but make sure you don't get too close."

Dean reached for Kane. "I can help you from the inside."

"I don't want your help *inside*," Kane snapped, remembering the violence of the Dreadmare annihilating Helena's precious creatures. He couldn't subject Sophia to that pain. "I don't want you anywhere close to my sister's reverie. Or did you forget you're still a nightmare?"

Dean pressed forward. "I'm not losing you again, Kane."

Kane's fury ignited. "This isn't about me! It's about my sister!" Kane choked on the words, on his regret. The last thing time he'd talked to Sophia was in that gas station, in front of the stupid blue Slurpee machine. "All you care about is what *you* lost."

"You're wrong," Dean shouted back.

"And you're *nothing*."

It echoed out over the river, breaking the peaceful night. Kane breathed around the knot in his throat. "You're nothing but Poesy's pet nightmare. If you want to help me, get in Poesy's way and get out of mine. I'm not running away from this."

Resolve started in Dean's eyes, smoothing him out as it passed through his long limbs, until he was back to the stoic, distant boy Kane had first met. He pulled the chess piece from his pocket and with a whisper it unwound into a silent storm of black ivy. The magic weaved over him, until the black-armored knight stood in his place.

This time, when the Dreadmare reached for Kane's hand,

Kane took it, grasping the smooth leather for half a breath before it flung him into the in-between and whatever lay beyond.

$$\infty$$

Kane walked into the reverie alone.

This time, when he came to, he was standing in a ragged breach carved into the side of ruined skyscraper. He swayed above a perilous drop of pure darkness. There was no one to keep him from falling, so he sunk down, held on tight, and faced the world Sophia had created.

It was nighttime in the reverie, but dawn glistened upon the utmost edge of a far-off sea. The scene before Kane was a futuristic city. Buzzing neon signs hovered over bladelike buildings, casting grainy colors into the low clouds so that the city lay cradled in a dreamlike, candied haze. Whirring aircraft dipped through the clouds, their spotlights sweeping the streets below, and far off in a residential district there were sirens. But that was the only noise. The city returned the echoes with silence that felt more than indifferent. It felt enforced.

There was a curfew, and someone had just broken it.

Kane drew into the breach, turning to explore the wrecked skyscraper. It was full of forgotten junk, as though abandoned midway. Graffiti covered everything. OUR SOCIETY IS A SCAM, read bloody letters. Another slogan said: KNOW THY UNHOLY HISTORIES.

The most vibrant graffiti was on the back wall: a glove, palm up, a moth alighting upon gently curled fingers. Beneath it in block letters was DAMNATIO MEMORIAE. All of it was brilliantly white against a panoply of flyers calling for the capture of a group called the Archivists. Kane grazed the graffiti with his fingers; the paint was fresh. Had his character done this?

A crash sounded in the depths of the building, and the cords in the elevator shaft whipped into a frenzy. Kane hid beneath an overturned desk, watching as the elevator lurched up to reveal, miraculously, Sophia. He stood up, not even thinking they might be enemies in this world.

"Brother!" Sophia cried. She wore a structured jacket and high-waisted slacks that made her look like a matador, and her hair was tucked up into a wide-brimmed hat. Her whole outfit was a deep, lusterless green, except for her gloves. They were so white they glowed, dazzling Kane as she clapped her hands over his face and said, "We have a *most* distinguished guest!"

In the elevator was the narrow shape of a girl. Adeline. She wore a gray shift dress and a gray headband. She was handcuffed, and the look she gave Kane meant he better not ask about it.

"You know I don't usually fancy the Nobles, but I needed a hostage," Sophia explained. "We'll ditch her here for The Society to find. Those sirens are close. I'm sure they'll be here any minute. You secured our extraction point, right? The fourth and fifth corridors are already locked down, but we can take the ninth to the bridge, then make our way to the harbor." Sophia's boots clicked as she strode to a mound of boxes in one corner. She ripped into them, pulling out cartridges of ammunition. Then she produced no fewer than five handguns from her jacket, which she began reloading with the ease of someone who held (and emptied) guns often. Kane thought one gun was an antique revolver, but then Sophia rolled several glowing orbs into the barrels. She pressed a button and the seams of the weapon glowed blue.

"I want you to see tonight's haul. It's fantastic." Sophia gestured at Adeline. "She's got it on her. I knew they wouldn't blow it up if they knew it was being transported on the body of a Committee-Man's daughter."

Kane approached Adeline. "What's your name?"

"Adeline," said Adeline.

"It's Ms. Adeline *Van Demure*," Sophia called, mockingly. "I hid it in her girdle."

Adeline grimaced as Kane fumbled under her dress, locating a small knot of burlap. In a whisper he asked, "Where's the whistle"

"Around my neck. Safe."

"Are you okay?"

"Yes," she whispered. "I appeared in whatever house she was robbing—I'm assuming it was mine. I ran into her, literally, and the alarms tripped. I let her take me hostage, and we lost the guards on the way here. She's some sort of thief, but she keeps hinting at a rebellion. She's being kind of tough and boisterous. Judging off clichés, I'd say this is a dystopian teen reverie, and she's the tough, no-nonsense female lead."

Sophia finished loading her guns, then strode into another room of more boxes.

"What about Ursula and Elliot?"

"Not sure," Adeline said. "This reverie is huge. Kane, if Poesy gets in—"

"She won't. Dean is going to stop her."

Kane wished he felt as confident as he sounded.

"What's the plot?" Adeline asked. "You always figure out the plots."

Kane opened the small bundle. He expected a jewel, or something precious, but instead he held a plastic disk the size of his palm, with pills in clear bubbles arranged in a ring.

"It's a birth control packet," Adeline provided. "How can you not know that?"

Kane shrugged. "Haven't started ovulating yet."

Adeline rolled her eyes. "Convince her to uncuff me before I do it myself."

"Relax," said Sophia as she reemerged. She swung a long cape over her shoulders. "One of your own kind can set you free after we ditch you, but mark my words: this is the freest you're ever going to get. Enjoy it, Ms. Van Demure."

There was tension between Adeline and Sophia. The privileged girl paired with the renegade rebel. The bookworm in him told him that this was a relationship that would last the plot.

Wait. For the first time, Kane perceived the blue lightning that arced between Adeline and Sophia.

Wait.

"You'll fail," Adeline said, a clever move because it launched Sophia into some much-needed monologuing.

"Denounce me if you must." Sophia's cape swept her ankles

as she closed in on Adeline. "But never forget that I am fighting for *your* freedom, Noble Girl. For *everyone's* freedom. What they teach us in schools is a lie. There are centuries of history that they've erased. History in which women gained the right to be more than just political servants. History in which there was no Underclass and no Committee controlling everything. Don't you see? The city of Everest is a lie. Holy Society is a lie, dreamed up by the Committee to control us. But you're at the top, so why would you question it? I suppose obliviousness is how the elite must tolerate themselves."

Adeline set her jaw. Kane thought she was an expert actor in this moment. Her voice dripped with incredulity. "How can you be so sure?"

Sophia chuckled, wagging her white-gloved fingers. "Look, and you will find. Those of us who follow the Bright Hand have been collecting artifacts for years. The heists never make the news, but I assure you our archives have been growing, and they reveal a history of glorious blasphemy." She leaned even closer. "You think the year is 1961, don't you? It's not. It's the year 2123. I know, because *that*"—she thrust a hand at the pill packet Kane held—"is from 2009. It's a type of pill that stops the Mothering. Did you even know that was a choice?"

Adeline feigned disbelief about the concept of birth control, and Sophia's face split into a gloating grin. She snatched the pills from Kane and kept her eyes locked with Adeline's as she stowed the artifact back in Adeline's girdle.

"Move it, rich bitch," she commanded, leading them from the tower, down into the future's city of Everest.

THIRTY

PRETTY

THE CITY OF EVEREST WAS DEAD.

It was a public death that emanated from everything. Dark windows shown straight through empty buildings to the other side of the block. Vacant streets stretched, empty under fluorescent lights that collected no moths. Strangest of all, there was no trash. Life, even its litter, had been scoured away.

Sophia demanded silence as they ran through the shadows. Kane and Adeline traded glances when they could. Mostly, they scanned for threats and kept their ears trained on the sirens, which stayed distant.

Closer was the sound of thunder. Whatever dystopian regime kept Everest clean couldn't tidy up its weather. As the trio traveled across a network of abandoned highways, the humid air buckled under a sudden, ferocious rain, forcing them beneath an overpass.

"Perfect," said Sophia, yanking down her hat. "Kane, stay here with her. I'll go secure our transport. Wait for my signal." Before Kane could protest, she ran into the downpour.

Adeline stopped Kane from following.

"Don't. You know better."

Kane glared at her. "Do I?"

"Clearly not, but let's pretend you give a shit about my life, too, for a second."

Dirty streams of rainwater carved their way between Adeline and Kane. This was the girl from school. The one who had everyone, teachers included, scared out of their minds. It was too much for Kane, and his anxiety flared to fury like kindling.

"Do you always have to be such a bitch?" Kane sneered. "Like, do you get bitch royalties or something? Is your bitch-craft a tax write-off?"

Adeline shrugged. "Doesn't matter if you hate me. You're going to work with us if you want to save your sister."

Kane laughed. "Oh, because you guys did such a great job with Helena?"

"Winning takes teamwork, but so does failure, Kane. We failed as a team."

Kane laughed harder. "What team are you talking about, Adeline? The one that lied to me? Hurt me? Hid from me?"

"Saved you!" Adeline yelled back. "Salvaged you! Protected you! And here we are again, in another *fucking* nightmare. For you. For *her*. And you're *still* acting like a child."

Adeline stalked off through the rain. Kane groaned, his exhaustion dousing his smoldering grudge. Before, when they had summoned the doors, he had felt that elusive comradery with the

Others. Adeline had inspired it, again. They could have left him to save Sophia alone, but they were all here. Except Dean. Kane had done a good job driving him off, already. He couldn't afford to do the same to Adeline. He knew she was right.

Kane found her huddled against a cracked pillar, soaking wet. Seeing him, she wiped at her cheeks and started pulling sections of her hair into a side braid.

"I'm sorry," Kane offered. She ignored it.

Kane tried again. "Don't worry, you still look pretty."

Adeline's laugh was frosty "That's what you think I care about? Looking pretty? Spare me, Kane, seriously. Pretty is the last thing I care about, but you wouldn't know that, would you? No, because you're too busy reducing everything I've done this past month to pettiness and spite. Fuck pretty."

Kane's mouth fell open.

"Don't look at me like that," she said. "When you first recruited me to the Others, Elliot and Ursula still thought I was this superficial queen bee, and it took months of backbreaking work on my part to undo that impression, to prove that I was, in fact, a person with real thoughts and real feelings and—heaven forbid—substance. But I never had to prove that shit to you, Kane, because you *used* to know what it was like to be misunderstood by everyone, avoided and discarded for the way you look or act."

Kane's knees were weak. Here it was again: the feelings people had for the person he used to be, bruised with loss and turned to anger with who he was now. Kane yearned to fold right then and there, to give up, but Adeline was still speaking.

"You think just because you've faced trauma you're excused from treating people with compassion? You think just because your sister is in trouble, you get to opt out of being a leader? Well, Kane, guess what. I've got sisters, too, and they might be next. We all stand to lose people if we don't stop Poesy."

She took a long breath. Adeline's next words were smaller. "And I care about Sophia, too."

The rain softened, and all Kane could hear was the breath they shared.

"I'm sorry," she said. "I keep forgetting that you don't know me anymore, either."

"It's okay," said Kane.

"It's not. I can do better. We can all do better."

Kane nodded. He felt real tears join the water dripping down his face. "I'm afraid of failing again," he said.

Adeline stepped toward Kane. "Then we won't fail," she said. "We'll be better than we were."

"I'm sorry," Kane said. "For all the blame."

"I know. Me, too."

When Sophia's headlights found them, Adeline and Kane were holding hands. They broke apart quickly as Sophia rolled up atop some sort of hovering motorcycle that looked like a Jet Ski. Another bobbed behind her.

She was in a hurry now.

"Rain's clearing up. They're here. We've got to boogie," she said to Kane.

"Wait! What about me?" Adeline whined. It was very convincing.

Sophia slid from her hovercycle. "What about you?"

"I've seen too much," Adeline said. "They'll hurt me."

"If you know they'll hurt you for seeing," Sophia said, "then you already know the fragility of the lie they've trapped you in. It's too late for you, no matter what. You're already waking to the truth."

Adeline set her jaw. The perfect impression of a brat.

"Or," Sophia whispered, circling Adeline, "perhaps you wake yourself up in time to save yourself."

Adeline followed Sophia with just her eyes. The next words barely fit between the two girls.

"How do I wake up?" asked Adeline.

"You pay attention," Sophia said.

"Pay attention to what?" asked Adeline.

"You pay attention to what you know, not what they say."

"I know..." Adeline faltered. She wasn't acting now. Her eyes were trapped by Sophia's imploring stare. Her lips pinched, pulled, frowned.

Had Sophia made Adeline...bashful?

An aircraft swooped down from the night sky, then another, their lights finding the trio quickly.

As the spotlights tore open the dark, they found Adeline pressed to Sophia, their lips locked. There was a force to the kiss that magnetized Sophia and sent gleeful static through the reverie's fabric. Kane gasped. Actually gasped.

Adeline broke off the kiss, saying, "Now you have to take me. If you leave me, you kill me."

Sophia uncuffed Adeline. "Then you'd better keep up. Both of you, get ready."

Kane took one hovercycle, and Adeline slid on the back of Sophia's. They maneuvered to face the ship that had just landed. From its hull slid a ramp, and out poured soldiers sporting large guns. Then came the music. A soaring string overture Kane recognized from his mom's record collection of girl group music from the fifties.

Kane didn't know how to drive a hovercycle, but he thought it might begin with the big green button in the shape of an arrow. His hand hovered over it, ready.

The soldiers fanned out, keeping in time with the beat. One opened an umbrella for their leader, who stepped down the ramp daintily. She was a woman in a tweed suit, the narrow skirt allowing her only small steps. She was perhaps in her sixties and immaculately composed. Her femininity cost her no authority, and it was clear she scared Sophia.

"Miss Smithe," Sophia whispered, her eyes locking with the woman's white glare.

Kane realized this was a projection of Sophia's real-life nemesis: Headmistress Smithe of Pemberton's School for Girls, a beacon of antiquated thinking according to Sophia. The reverie began to make sense.

"That's right," said Miss Smithe silkily. "The Bright Hand has plagued my Committee long enough with your juvenile pilfering. I thought I would personally attend your capture."

Sophia stood in the seat of her hovercycle. "The rebellion will never die! History can never die!"

"Tsk tsk," said Miss Smithe. "A little girl, playing at archivist, but if she had any talent for history she would recognize the erroneous ways of the world she wishes to resurrect. The truly liberal are the truly misguided, for there is no bastion in a world without Holy Society. You know this. You've heard of the Doom that lays beyond Everest's lights. It is the Doom that we, the Committee, hold at bay so that all citizens may thrive."

"You're wrong," Sophia screamed. "Everest isn't a bastion. It's a prison! I've been beyond the lights. I've seen—"

"Enough!" said Miss Smithe sharply. "Miss Buffy Crawford, please step forward and arrest this radical at once."

The soldiers shifted as a cluster of girls marched from the aircraft. They were dressed in brightly colored bouffant dresses that matched the satin scarves adorning their pinned-up hair. They all wore large, bug-eyed glasses. They didn't walk so much as they swayed through the rain, their pastel umbrellas breaking apart to reveal their centerpiece: Ursula, mobbed in pink, her height identifying her immediately.

"Read them their arrest bill," ordered Smithe.

Ursula clearly didn't know where to get this bill, so she very confidently put out her hand in the hopes that someone would hand it to her. Very politely, one of the other girls reached into Ursula's own purse and took out a tablet, turned it on, and put it in Ursula's hand.

"If we make it out of this, we need to make Ursula take an improv class," Adeline whispered to Kane.

Ursula shouted into the rainy yard. "It is with our most

profound regret that we, The Rectification Committee of Our Lady Miss Smithe, Obedient of Holy Society, leader of..."

While Ursula read, Kane watched Sophia pull her revolver from her back holster. "Stay out of the rain," she whispered.

Ursula moved on to the charges. "I, Miss Buffy Crawford, hereby charge you with acts of blasphemy against Holy Society, the endangerment of a Noble, and the possession of an artifact contrabanded under penalty of Corporeal Refinement."

Sophia pulled the trigger, cutting the air with an electric screech as lightning arced from the barrel. It webbed through raindrops and sunk into the puddles. The soaked soldiers seized, their weapons firing in their hands as they fell. Some of the girls fell, too, leaving Ursula exposed.

"Eat shit, socialite!" Sophia cried, cocking the revolver and firing again.

Ursula was forced to block with a shield, but she must have been holding back, for the shot carried her right off her feet and into the hull of the aircraft, lurching the upbeat music. Ursula fell to the soaked pavement, groaning. Sophia aimed again.

Kane punched the green button, lurching in front of Sophia.

"Leave her!" he cried. Ursula wouldn't fight. He couldn't let his best friend die so that his sister could live. "We need to go. *Now!*"

Sophia holstered the gun, annoyance cutting her voice.

"To the Doom we go, then," she said, and they rocketed away from the skipping music.

THIRTY-ONE

THE DOOM

KANE SHOT AFTER SOPHIA AND ADELINE, PUSHING his cycle to top speed as they plunged into the milky glow of a desolate downtown. Fumes from the cycle filled his nose, and the engine screamed with throaty solidity, almost covering the sound of the aircraft flying over them. They sped from the main road onto narrow side streets, swinging out onto a boulevard split by a placid channel. Kane slid over the water, cutting a wide wake as they shot beneath bridges.

"The lights are up ahead!" Sophia called over the splashing. "Get ready!"

They pulled up from the channel and broke through the city's edge, hitting a cobbled plaza slowly being reclaimed by wild grasses. The plaza melted into a field overgrown with weeds, which led to an abrupt and impenetrably dark forest. So tall and so thick were the trees that the forest seemed to lean over the plaza, held up by only a belt of blue and red lights. The lights formed a perimeter around the city they'd just escaped. These must be the protective "lights" of Everest.

"These won't work outside Everest's perimeter," Sophia said, halting her hovercycle and dismounting. As she helped Adeline, she explained, "But the citizens won't follow. They're too scared of the Doom, and crossing the lights means death." Kane slid from his cycle and walked beneath the lights, staring into their alternating colors. He wondered if the Doom took inspiration from the forest that surrounded the Cobalt Complex, and if the protective lights were meant to be the colors of sirens. Then the lights blackened as something cold stabbed through Kane's spine.

Sophia stepped over where Kane fell, her revolver pointed directly at his heart, another bolt of lightning ready in the barrel. Kane's mind buzzed with the aftershock, barely registering that his sister had just shot him.

"And I'm afraid you can't follow, either. A quarter charge should keep you grounded long enough for Smithe to find you, brother," Sophia said down the line of the gun. "Or should I say, betrayer."

Kane blinked, speechless. He couldn't feel his hands or feet. He could barely feel Sophia's grip on his collar as she hoisted him up. Her eyes were full of pain, but there was no conflict; in this world, she believed Kane had betrayed her.

"That's right, I've been tracking you," she said. "I know you've hidden things from me. I know every other word from you is a lie, every explanation an excuse. I defended you to the other leaders. I've *protected* you ever since we joined the revolution. And you repay me by smuggling our secrets to the Committee? I should have done this long ago."

"I'm not—" Kane squeezed out what little protest he could. "Sophia, please." He found Adeline a few steps away, watching the scene unfold with rigid concentration.

"Search him," Sophia commanded, keeping the gun trained on Kane as Adeline knelt tentatively besides him. The sounds of the airships were getting closer.

Kane tried to focus on his next move, but all he could think about was how every move he had made in real life had turned him into a villain, a betrayer, in Sophia's mind. The heartbreak was enough to stand him up, but Adeline forced him down.

"Don't," she whispered. "This is the plot. You have to let us go."

Kane shook his head. *No.*

"The other pocket," Sophia said. "Quickly."

"Adeline," Kane begged. "Please don't leave me."

"I'm sorry," she whispered. Then her eyes went wide as her hand found something in Kane's coat. Sophia noticed and pulled Adeline away, snatching the item from her. It was the small velvet pouch with the stolen charms that Dean had given him, and Sophia thrust it at Kane with heartbroken triumph.

"Don't. Don't open it," Kane managed, but Sophia was dumping the charms into her hand. Kane saw what she saw: Artifacts. History, smuggled from a lost era. And proof that her own brother had never been worth her hope.

"I wanted so badly to be wrong about you," Sophia said.

"It's not real!" Kane pushed himself onto his side, then gained a knee. Spit fell from his numb lips.

"Don't," Adeline warned.

But Kane couldn't lose his sister again. She had told him once that she was a smart girl, and that she could stay lucid if she knew she was in a fake world. Kane curled himself into his reckless desire to free her, and the selfish desire to save himself. He needed to not fail her again.

"None of this is real, Sophia. It's a reverie. You're in a reverie," he cried.

The lights flickered. The forest flinched.

"Reverie."

Sophia said the word as though trying out a new language, one with words that scalded the tongue. Kane saw the lucidity settle behind her gaze as she took in her false world, her sharp mind reorienting itself. But it didn't last. The airships had finally found them, and their hurricane breaths swept Sophia back into her fantasy.

Except now the reverie was twisting. Kane could feel it building.

"Sophia, this is your world to control," he shouted over the winds. "You can make it stop."

But Sophia was lost to reasoning. She clutched the charms in one hand. Her other hand pushed the gun between Kane and the advancing soldiers. "You lie, Kane. You're always lying!"

Shock waves rippled out of her, into the fabric of the reverie.

Kane felt the agony of his sister as her fantasy began to turn acidic in her mind. He felt, physically, the ripple pass over him, and his uniform became that of a soldier.

"Kane," Adeline murmured. "The charms."

The charms smoldered in Sophia's grip. If any of those reveries were activated...

Kane crawled toward Sophia. "You need to give those back. They're not safe. I was protecting you from them."

"What are they? A trap? Incendiaries? Nano-tech?"

She wasn't waking up, so Kane dove into his knowledge of the reverie. Of tropes. He attempted a reasonable tangent. "They're dangerous to the Committee. A secret weapon developed by Headmistress Smithe that I stole for you."

"*Headmistress?*"

Sophia blinked rapidly, seized by an inner storm that sent another ripple through the reverie. It washed over the city in fractious echoes. The airships looming over the plaza bobbed dangerously, as through magnetized. Their cannons swung toward Kane, Adeline, and Sophia, electric energy crackling in their barrels.

This was it. This was how Sophia's mind would murder her own brother. Revenge, for all the lies he'd fed her and all the mistruths he'd forced her to live within. It was a just and horrible fate, but it would kill Sophia, too, and Kane couldn't allow that.

The cannons fired. Kane fired back. He flung his hands toward the assault, releasing a pure and singular hope, a formless yet torrential explosion of energy. He felt the etherea rip from him like rocket fire, then pushed himself to give more. To give every-thing he had.

Just as the ethereal blast was set to collide with the fleet, it hit something. A shield that had been waiting there to protect him.

Ursula's shield, there all along.

She must've been close. There wasn't time to look because suddenly, Kane was facing his own attack as it reverberated back at him, crushing him in a prismatic riot that swept over Adeline and Sophia. They screamed, and the reverie screamed with them.

Then, there was only the rising, discordant whisper of the charms as they began to sing the song of their waking worlds.

· THIRTY-TWO ·
POLYCHROMATIC

WHEN THE RINGING FINALLY STOPPED, KANE LAY beneath drifts of blue steam and lemony sunlight. Dawn had surged over Everest all at once.

He sat up in the center of a scorched crater the size of a tennis court. Water gushed from snapped pipes jutting from the earth, filling the crater with hissing pools. His whole body was one giant ache, blood gathering in his eyebrows and turning his eyelashes sticky.

Find Sophia. Save Sophia.

Kane tore through the rising tide, still dizzy. A moment later Adeline punched up through a turbid pool, sputtering and gasping, her ruined dress clinging to her like a second skin. She grasped for Kane, and he heaved her up.

"Sophia!" Kane shouted. "Sophia!"

Adeline wrenched him around. "There!"

Sophia was hunched at the top of the craters' edge. Kane stumbled up the steaming walls, with no regard to the new blisters that kissed his palms. Reaching her—seeing her—he halted.

Sophia faced the city, her whole body an expression of awe.

Kane turned.

Sophia's reverie was gone. In its place was a maddening, kaleidoscopic chaos. Six reveries, combined. Everest, and the five charms Kane had awakened.

The sky was a patchwork of dawn, night, and day, shared between two suns, a moon, and a looming planet that looked like Earth. Mountains swelled on the horizon, shifting from craggy cliffs to hills ribboned in waterfalls to dunes of silky ochre. The stoic buildings of futuristic dystopia had distorted into a buffet of architectures: contemporary castles, medieval office buildings, and rococo skyscrapers plated in glass, iron, and filigree. They leaned over the plaza, over Kane, capturing his spellbound reflection a thousandfold in their crystal facades.

And the plaza… It was a scene Kane knew; a garden choked with roses and poplar trees, with a gazebo at the center. The fallen soldiers at its edge were recovering slowly, finding their uniforms now came with bow ties and coattails. The aircraft sputtered and wheezed as they attempted to regain flight that had been possible in one reverie, but not another.

Kane could feel the chaos of it all, as though he himself were a single strand coiled tight within this polychromatic knot. He could not even begin to understand how to unravel this.

"Sophia—"

Kane turned to her just in time to see Sophia pick something off the ground. Something black and shiny. She raised the whistle to her lips, her eyes dim with wonder.

"NO!"

Kane tackled her. The whistle bounced into the crater and Adeline lunged for it, but no sooner had the silent tweet emitted from the charm when, with slapping abruptness, the reverie halted, and the black doors appeared.

Nothing happened. Kane held Sophia and let himself believe Dean had been successful.

Then the doors burst open, catapulting a spiky shadow into the reverie. The Dreadmare, a mutilated mess of twisting legs, slid to a stop at Kane's feet. It was coated in a dark substance.

Blood.

No.

Poesy was in the doorway, her whole body furious with magic as she strode into the reverie. She wore a velvet leotard as black as her doors, thigh-high platform boots, and a cropped jacket thick in opalescent fringe. It flashed like armor as she lowered her hand. From her posture, it was clear she had literally just slapped the Dreadmare into this dimension.

Poesy swept a gloved hand over her bald head, as though looking for her hair.

"That wig was expensive," she seethed. Then she noticed the rest of the scene. "Oh my, another mess, I see." She beckoned with her hand, and the whistle zipped to her bracelet.

Alarms erupted in Kane's mind. He had to do something. He had to distract her.

Kane flung Sophia behind him and in the same motion burst toward Poesy. His fists swarmed with etherea, and for a moment Poesy raised an eyebrow. Then she simply sneered, and Kane felt the crack of her hand against his jaw. He spun out and collided with the gazebo, and before he'd even hit the ground, she was in front of him, her fingers around his throat. His back bristled with splinters as she ground him up against the ruined post. Poesy's painted face filled his vision.

"Such a crude way to welcome," she said, "the person who is about to save your life."

Kane tore at her sleeve. "Leave my sister alone," he choked. "Please. I am begging you."

Poesy clucked maternally. "Oh, no, I am afraid it's too late for Sophia Montgomery. Perhaps if you had summoned me sooner we could have made a deal—her world for the ones my homunculus of an assistant stole—but it's too late for that. Teasing these apart would be tedious, meticulous work, and I'm in no mood for tedium or meticulosity."

Black dots burst in his vision. He was losing consciousness. The muscles in his neck popped as the grip tightened, and Poesy moved so close Kane could pick out the flecks of black that swam in her cobalt eyes.

"And what to do with you, Mr. Montgomery? I do admit, I am quite disappointed. A power like yours comes once in a generation; I had hoped together we could conquer this reality and bring forth the next. Something better. Something beyond. But what good is a power like ours if we're too afraid to use it?"

"I'm not afraid of you," Kane spat. He tossed his weight into a punch, which she caught by the wrist.

Poesy leaned in. "Not me, Mr. Montgomery. The world. It takes a certain bravado to confront, claim, and take control of the things around you. A bravado that you have *always* lacked. The very ability to manipulate the fabric of reality—of all realities— and you choose to throw a punch? You have devastatingly bad taste. We could never work together."

Kane begged his arms to move, his feet to kick. He couldn't. Didn't. Nothing. He reached for his power but it wouldn't come to him.

Poesy smiled. Her voice gave way to a rattling, insect drone as she whispered, "Feckless child, how do you intend to save the world if you're too unimaginative to change it? Could it be that you have finally realized that yours is a world not worth saving?"

A fist collided with Poesy's right cheek, driving her off, and Kane was being dragged away. The person dragging Kane was Elliot. The person who had landed the punch was Ursula.

"Ogress," Poesy sneered, circling her.

Ursula didn't talk back. She swung into a roundhouse kick and sent Poesy flying into one of the fallen aircraft. The machine ground backward with the impact. Before it even settled, Poesy shot out—an arrow of sparkling malevolence—and thrust her bladed nails toward Ursula's throat.

Ursula got her hands up just in time, magenta energy blossoming between them as Poesy's strike pressed her back. Ursula dug her heels into the ground, leaned into her defense. Her shield strained, redoubled, strained harder, but Poesy's edge lost no momentum.

"Give...up..." Poesy hissed.

"Screw...*you*," Ursula spat back.

With a shout, Ursula drove her shield over Poesy, throwing the sorceress away in a shattering of rosy light. The shock wave burst the windows of the nearby buildings, forcing Kane and Elliot to cower in the gazebo. When he finally looked, Ursula stood upright before Poesy, but barely. In another second she would be finished.

Though her glasses were bent, Poesy put them on her nose to assess. She snapped her fingers, and the teacup appeared.

"NO!" Kane screamed, struggling against Elliot.

Ursula burst forward, accompanied by a blur of gray—Adeline. Together they danced with Poesy. Ursula's strength and Adeline's speed kept pace with the sorceress, until Poesy shot into the sky with her teacup raised.

No.

Kane could feel it—the vicious magic that hid in the perfect porcelain bowl—as it liquefied the buildings of the plaza. Kane could feel it. The pull that would swallow Sophia and take her away forever.

Then, as silent as a blade of night, the Dreadmare appeared behind Poesy. For a moment they were framed beautifully against the patchwork sky, and then the Dreadmare snapped its beak over the drag queen's arm, severing it at the elbow.

What happened next happened quickly.

First, the Dreadmare teleported away.

Second, Poesy fell and did not get up.

Third, Sophia snapped out of her stupor. "Kill them," she ordered. The cowering soldiers swarmed into the wrecked courtyard and the airships turned their cannons downward.

The rest was chaos as the soldiers quickly overwhelmed the Others. Ursula tore through the battle to get to Kane, reaching him just as a hail of bullets pitted the ground. Her rosy shield dulled their racket, but Kane knew she was exhausted.

"Go!" she commanded.

"I'm not leaving you," Kane shouted. The guns let up to reload, and Ursula backed up toward Kane. She was pushing them sideways, toward the black doors.

"Ursula, I'm not running!"

Ursula blocked another round of gunfire. "You're our only hope of unraveling this. You need to recover. Regroup, and then—"

The soldiers had reached them, and they swarmed over Ursula. Kane went to help her but found she had placed a shield right between them.

"GO!" she yelled, her voice muffled.

Kane pounded the shield. "NO! Don't do this!"

Ursula tore against the soldiers who had her arms. For a dazzling flash the shield vanished, but it was only so that Ursula could plant a sturdy kick into Kane's stomach. Like a rag doll he crashed backward, right into Poesy's sanctuary, slamming into the desk headfirst. His vision went gray, and the sight of the doors closing was the last thing he saw before unconsciousness claimed him.

· THIRTY-THREE ·
SANCTUARY

SOMETHING COLD AND WET PRODDED KANE'S eyebrow. It made a high-pitched whine.

Kane's lurched awake. He blinked at his surroundings, momentarily dazzled by golden brightness. Was it sunset? Why was everything soft and sparkly? Was this heaven? Why was there a black dog in heaven?

Ms. Daisy pawed Kane's knee impatiently and let out another whine. Like a playful sheet of ocean surf, Kane's memories pulled away, then swished over him all at once.

The merged reveries. Poesy's dramatic arrival. The crumpled Dreadmare. Shattering glass and spitting gunfire and…

Had Ursula drop-kicked him?

Wincing, Kane felt new tenderness on his stomach. His collarbone. He focused on the pain, afraid of what came after, but the horror didn't wait for him to be ready. It dragged him under itself and pressed the breath right out of his lungs.

Kane rushed to the doors and forced them open. There was nothing on the other side except the second half of an empty room. Kane was by himself. Cast out. Banished. Alone, with no way to return and nowhere left to run.

He sank back to the floor.

Ms. Daisy barked. A curious bark, aimed at the boy who had just tumbled into her house and was now hiccup-sobbing on her stoop. She nosed an empty bowl at his feet.

Kane swiped away his tears. She was hungry. How long had he been unconscious?

Ms. Daisy distracted him from crying by nudging his hand and then her bowl again, which was about the only thing not tossed about the room. The sanctuary was an utter mess. Most of the carpet had gone crunchy with glass. Charms and artifacts were everywhere. Kane's backpack was here, vomiting its contents where Kane had dropped it. The chandelier dangled from the top of the black doors like a popped-out eye.

Dean had certainly put up a fight. That much was clear.

The dog seemed a little embarrassed about the mess. She gave Kane low looks full of eyebrows as she navigated through the destruction, leading him to a closet just outside the main room. There he found many coats, canes, and leashes. Slumped at the bottom were bags of dog food, like you'd find in any store. Their normalcy felt eerie in the surreal space.

Water was easier to find. Poesy had left a carafe of water on her desk. Kane drank from it, then poured the rest out into a teacup for Ms. Daisy to share.

He dropped down beside her and wondered what to do next, though he tried not wonder too hard, not entirely sure he *wanted* to reach a conclusion. There was no way out of this place. Not without the key on Poesy's wrist or Dean's power to pass through in-between spaces.

He scooted over to the doors and pressed his head against the cool varnish like a prayer. Maybe he slept like that. The urgency had vanished, but the tears had not. Darkly, an old and familiar urge opened within him. There was no way out of this place, sure, but maybe out wasn't the way to go.

Maybe escaping didn't mean leaving this place at all.

Kane turned to the room of stolen dreams, and he recalled the library of his childhood. The feeling of thick air and soft spines, of tilting your head sideways to read the names of authors. Mostly, Kane recalled the intoxicating potential of it all. For a child like Kane, potential was his forever friend. The promise of something else—or somewhere else—where Kane could start over and actually belong. It wasn't just about finding a world that would tolerate him. It was about imagining a world that loved him back. That enjoyed him.

Kids like Kane weren't often enjoyed.

There was a charm at Kane's feet. A moon. From it emanated the caress of hemlock on a winter night, the iron smell of blood on frostbitten blades. From another charm Kane sensed a world of carnivorous flowers, dynasties, and revenge. Then there was a reverie about football and family betrayal. A reverie of black and white with smoke sifting through drawn blinds. Then a scorched planet, completely hollow, life teeming on the curved pith of its interior. A reverie loud with carnival jingling, and a reverie with no sound at all.

Kane could go anywhere. He could be anyone in these worlds. He could inherit any life, become anything, and forget everything else.

He could forget this battle. He'd forgotten once before, hadn't he?

Kane took a great breath in, held it, then let it out. He shook out his hands. No. He didn't want to forget. Not again.

He reminded himself of the few reveries he'd witnessed. They all taught him something new about the way dreams inhabit a person. Dreams can be parasites we sacrifice ourselves to. Dreams can be monstrous, beautiful things incubated in misery and hatched by spite. Or dreams can be the artifacts we excavate to discover who we really are.

Kane didn't know what his own dreams were. He only knew that if he wasn't careful in this moment, they could rise up and dethrone his rule over what was fact, what was fiction, and what was right.

Harvesting reveries wasn't right. Hoarding them away in an ethereal vault was not right.

Running away wasn't right, either.

But what could he do?

He rummaged through the debris, the desk, and the shelves,

sensing for any ethereal object that might help him. He attempted to venture into the passages beyond, but every time he did he ended up back in the room with the curios, which amused Ms. Daisy endlessly.

When it got to be too much, he took a break from searching to cry some more. He wasn't the right person for this. He wasn't brave, like Sophia. He wasn't smart, like Elliot. He wasn't cunning, like Adeline. He wasn't independent, like Dean.

And he wasn't strong, like Ursula. More than anyone else, he wanted to be like Ursula. He wondered how anything could ever touch a person who was that strong and that good. He thought about the unfairness Ursula had endured, from others, and ultimately from herself in that final moment. He made himself face his own cruelties toward her, too. He hadn't written the BEWARE OF DOG sign all those years ago in elementary school, but it was his imagination that inspired it. He was a scared kid, hurting who he needed to hurt so he could escape, and Ursula had been his friend anyways. It made him cry harder.

Beware of dog.

This memory turned a switch in Kane's head, and before he knew fully why, he was kneeling in front of Ms. Daisy. She raised her dog eyebrows at him. It was very doglike. Too doglike. Why would someone as ridiculous as Poesy own a normal dog?

"Beware of dog," Kane said. He looked between Ms. Daisy's sleek, black coat and the door's lustrous, black finish. The only time he'd seen the door work from this side was when Poesy was returning from walking Ms. Daisy. Otherwise, the whistle had to be used to call it. But whistles didn't call doors. Whistles called dogs.

Kane's hands were shaking as he scratched behind her ears.

"Find Sophia," Kane begged.

Nothing happened.

"Find Ursula."

Ms. Daisy's nubby tail wagged, but that was it.

"Dean," Kane said. "You know Dean, right?"

Ms. Daisy's ears shot up, looking around for Dean excitedly. Kane pulled her to the door and pointed.

"Can you find Dean?"

Ms. Daisy sniffed at the door, circled it twice, and then assembled her sleek frame into stoic focus. From her keened a whine like Kane had never heard from a dog, but it was an old language between her and this doorway. The locks tumbled apart, reassembled, and clicked. The doors groaned open just an inch, issuing a strange, melodic whispering. To Kane, it sounded like triumph.

"Good girl." Kane patted Ms. Daisy on the head absently. She licked his knuckles.

"Dean?" he called through the door.

Ms. Daisy bound into the hallways of the sanctuary, returning with a leash in her jaws. Gingerly, Kane took it from her, clipped it to her collar, and then fastened it to the leg of the settee.

"Stay," he commanded.

She blinked at him, betrayed.

"I'll use the whistle to call you," he promised. "I just have to find it."

Kane approached the doors like they might eat him. Again he had the urge to vanish elsewhere, to deny that he had been given this chance, but the invasive daydream only lasted an instant before he snuffed it out. Running was not the answer; it was just the thing that he wanted.

And, he reminded himself, saving the world was not usually a matter of want.

· THIRTY-FOUR ·
WONDER

KANE TOOK ONLY WHAT HE COULD CARRY IN HIS backpack, unsure what to expect from the reveries. He knew it was useless to prepare too much. Reveries had their own rules, and Kane was about to break all of them in a mad search for his friends, his sister, and the lost whistle.

The doors lead Kane into a dark copse of trees that swished gently against the tall frame, nearly hiding it. Kane shut the doors quickly—he couldn't risk anyone finding their way into Poesy's sanctuary or activating any of the remaining thousands of charms. He'd have to find another escape; hopefully, Ms. Daisy had done some of his work for him.

It was night here, wherever here was. A rain forest, maybe? The air smelled sour with the musk of rot and overripe fruit. Neon birds flitted between bulbous nests embedded in thick trunks, curious about Kane. He thumbed a wide leaf, surprised to find it was plastic. The trees sounded hollow when he knocked. Odd. Kane looked up.

Above, the night strobed with starlight as the constellations zoomed by above. Planets passed, too. As they did, small labels appeared on them, or rather appeared on the glass dome that covered the false rain forest. Outside the dome was a vast, metal wing, which is how Kane reasoned they were on some sort of spaceship. One that was flying through deep space very fast, by the looks of the stars cascading around them.

The dome flickered, and an announcement began to play.

We hope you enjoy your flight on Starship Giulietta, said a pleasant voice-over accompanied by text. The glass now showed a 3-D rendering of the spaceship. It looked like a massive cruise ship with wings and rocket blasters. *Our estimated time of arrival to resEarth is six hours and nineteen minutes. Your all-access ticket allows you to avail yourself of all amenities up to one hour before docking. Thank you for traveling with Giulietta Beyond™. We thank you for patronizing our reservation planets and hope you will continue on with us to resMars next.*

The stars returned. Whatever. No time to wonder. Kane pushed through the plants. The forest floor was carpeted in glowing moss, and Kane quickly identified a trail of blood. His heart burned. He forced himself to take calm breaths as he pushed apart fanning leaves that hid a clearing at the forest's edge. Within it lay Dean, unmoving.

Dean.

Sensing him, Dean's hand tightened around something—the

Dreadmare charm clutched in his bruised knuckles—but then Kane had him in a hug.

"It's you," Dean whispered, as though this was the last thing he expected.

"Can you move?" The question was warm against Dean's neck. As an answer, Dean's arms tightened.

"What hurts?"

"All of it," Dean whispered.

He was in and out of consciousness after that. Kane pulled him up as gently as he could, talking to him to keep him focused.

"We're in some sort of spaceship," Kane said as he dragged him through the forest. The doors had vanished. "How did you get here?"

"Teleported."

"Can you see where the Sophia is?"

"No."

"What about the Others?"

"No."

Kane already knew the answer, but he asked anyways. "Are you able to teleport?"

"Not from space." Then, as explanation, Dean added, "Space is so big. Too big. And I can't account for the velocity. It could kill us."

Kane began to wonder about the sheer size of these combined reveries, but again stopped himself. No time to wonder. They stumbled through a copse of palm trees and entered what Kane realized was the ship's pool deck. And it was quite the pool deck. Above the sheet of cerulean water, waterfalls poured into floating, oblong tubs with clear bottoms, filling the dark deck with aquamarine light from above and below.

People lay strewn across plush pool chairs, sleeping or passed out. Kane and Dean snuck into a large structure Kane hoped was a locker room. It wasn't. It was some sort of cabana equipped with a curtained bed, and the entire back room was a tiled shower. Perfect. Kane could work with this. He let Dean slide onto the floor, locked the doors, and hid away his backpack by a cracked window. Just in case.

"Hey, hey, wake up. We're safe. We need to get the blood off you, though." Kane said, nudging Dean. "Can I get you out of these clothes?"

Dean nodded sleepily but was no help whatsoever. The Dreadmare armor had done a good job protecting Dean, but Kane's fingers still grew sticky with blood trying to peel the boy's shirt off. The source was Dean's chest. Even through the Dreadmare armor, Poesy's nails had left deep gouges in Dean's flesh.

Looking for soap, Kane located a lit panel showing teardrops in different colors. There was blue, there was red, and between was pink. Kane went with pink.

Water came from every direction, soaking Kane and Dean instantly. Kane slammed the panel until it lessened, but this also activated a small light show of pink and green.

"Sorry," Kane said, blotting Dean with a soaked towel and what he hoped was soap. Dean's face scrunched up in pain, but he endured it.

Kane continued to apologize the whole time. Then he needed

to remove Dean's pants. He got the button open and then had to stop, because.

Just.

Because.

"Are you *hard?*"

Dean was grinning goofily. His eyes stayed closed. "Got you," he said.

Kane swore at him, throwing the towel in his face. "You've been fine this whole time?"

"Oh, no, my chest hurts." Dean scrubbed his face with the towel. "But I was enjoying the attention. And I do need help."

"What did Poesy do to you?"

It took Dean a long time to put his words together. "She tried to take away my sight when I refused to tell her where Sophia's reverie manifested. If it wasn't for the Dreadmare armor, she would have taken everything from me. As it is, she got me pretty good."

Dean wouldn't look at Kane. Downcast, his eyes weren't their usual shade of green. They weren't brown, either.

"Look at me," Kane said.

Dean's gaze rose. His eyes were pure white.

Kane fell backward until he was against the opposite wall. "You're not…"

Dean crossed his arms over himself, turning to give Kane his profile and closing his eyes again. "Not what?"

Real.

Kane couldn't say it. He didn't want to say it. He didn't understand what he was seeing. White eyes told you who was real in a reverie, and who was from the reverie itself. And Dean's eyes were undeniably white. He was reverie-born.

Finally, Dean spoke. "I told you, anything Poesy wants from a reverie, she takes."

A hundred moments replayed in Kane's mind. A hundred unspoken thoughts shouted through him. Kane had wondered from the start what someone like Dean was doing working for someone like Poesy, and now he understood. Dean had no choice. He was a weapon, salvaged from a world crushed by Poesy long before this battle began.

"I'm so sorry," Kane whispered.

"Don't be," Dean said, still looking away. Kane knew there was nothing he could do but wait for Dean to go on, if he wanted to, and soon enough he did.

"The world I come from is a cruel one. People like me are hunted. Slain. Eventually, I got caught looking too long at the wrong person, and that was my end. They found me, but Poesy found me, too. She offered me a choice, and I'm glad I took it. I survived and my cruel world didn't. That's it."

"What do you mean, people like you?"

"People like you and me. There is no nice word for it in my world. To name it is a crime."

Kane knew. He himself had lived a life beyond the true horrors of society's many hatreds, but the one he could glimpse easiest into was the horror that would have been his own if he'd been born into a different place, at a different time, or within a different life. Dean's life, maybe.

Kane scooted forward, unable to resist the need to touch Dean and confirm the boy was solid. Dean's hands rose automatically to rest on Kane's hip, the same place they held Kane when they'd kissed.

"It's okay," Kane said. "It wasn't—"

Dean's eyes flashed. "Don't say that. It was real. It was real to me." His hands tightened, and he pulled Kane closer, like he needed to hold on to him or risk fading away. Or apart. His shoulders shook under a weight Kane couldn't see.

"I feel real," Dean said into Kane's chest.

"You are," Kane said back. "It doesn't matter where you came from, or how you got here. You survived, and you're here now, and you're real."

Dean's breathing steadied. "That's what you told me the first time."

He held on tighter, and Kane let him. Their past was an ache between them. A knot that wound tension and tightness through the space they shared and the skin they touched. Kane had fought to untie that knot and destroy it a few times now, but he knew he had to let it live. He couldn't destroy the past Dean loved any more than he could unravel this reverie. It was real to the person who needed it, and Kane was powerless against that need.

Kane put his head against Dean's, who traced infinity symbols into Kane's temples.

"So you can't teleport us off this ship," Kane said.

"Correct."

"And we're trapped here until we land?"

"We are."

Kane had closed himself to wonder when he'd entered this reverie, but now wonder was everywhere within in. Wonder about the vast dreams around them, about the bad power within him, and about the nightmares that raced ahead of them. In every scenario, he faced what came next with the boy before him. They would figure it out together.

Dean got Kane's hint and pushed through his pain to sit up. He placed a hand on Kane's jaw to kiss him. It felt very real.

Kane closed himself to wonder once again, turning away from all the world's bad potential to face this one good thing. This was real, was right now. To Kane, it was better than real. It was fantastic.

Kane stopped wondering, and he kissed Dean back.

THIRTY-FIVE

LAST CALL

THE WALLS WERE STILL DAMP WHEN THE CABANA unlocked itself for the robotic cleaning staff, but the boys were gone long before that. They had made the bed as best they could, which the robots were programmed to appreciate for three full seconds before stripping the sheets entirely.

Many floors away, Kane and Dean sat at a bar sipping fruity drinks, dressed in the clothes they'd scavenged from the pool floor. The shirts were bold and floral, giving the appearance of resort wear, but every seam was lined in pudgy piping. To Kane, that put this version of the future deep in the imagination of the '80s. That explained all the buttons on the ship. And the synth music. And many of the haircuts.

"I can't stop thinking about those space burgers," Kane said over the din.

"I know. You've said so six times."

Kane's face burned. Since the shower he couldn't seem to shut up, which was the opposite of his usual aloofness. He got like this when he was excited. Being with Dean felt like nothing he had ever known. The newness for Kane combined with the assuredness in Dean's touch—it was exhilarating, a world within itself. Kane wasn't about to shut up anytime soon.

"Last call," said the bartender. "Docking in one hour."

"Come on," Kane said, pulling Dean from the bar and onto the crowded dance floor. Dean hugged his arm as they made their way to the side of a platform atop which a dancer twirled and flexed.

"Are you sure about this?" Dean said.

"Yeah, we blend in better here than at the bar." People were watching the dancer, not the two boys off to the side.

"No," Dean said, stiff in Kane's arms. "I mean us. Together. Isn't it...you know?"

Kane looked around. Whoever had dreamt this world had dreamt it full of the gays. In fact the variety of people on the dance floor, and on the ship in general, felt conspicuously queer. Grimly, Kane imagined the reality that required a reverie like this as an escape.

"We're perfect," he told Dean. They hugged together, trapped in the crowd's heat, until the music ebbed into a pounding ballad. Dean pulled away.

"What's wrong?" Kane asked.

Dean took a deep breath. "Before, on the bridge. Did you mean it when you said I was nothing?"

Kane was suddenly speechless.

Dean's face scrunched up. "I mean to say that I can be nothing, if nothing is what you need. I'm very good at vanishing."

Kane's first reaction was to bundle Dean into another kiss and tell him if they survived this, they'd begin wherever they left off. But he couldn't know that. He stopped himself from kissing Dean, because sometimes kisses break wounds open instead of closing them up.

"You're not nothing," Kane said. "And nothing is not what I need. What I need right now is help getting my friends and Sophia out of here, and then a way to summon the loom and end this. I don't know what comes after that, but I know I want you there with me. We can find out together, okay?"

"Are you sure?" Dean's pale gaze searched Kane's face for an answer, as though Kane hadn't just given him one. "Are you sure that I'll be here?"

"Why wouldn't you be?"

"What about Poesy? What are you going to do when you find her?"

"Kill her," Kane said automatically.

Dean backed away, the small muscles in his jaw jumping. His hands drew into a knot at his chest.

"Then I might not be here," he shouted over the music. "It's her power that's keeping me from unraveling. I don't know if I can live without her, Kane. I don't know if I'll still exist."

And Kane grasped, for the first time and with utter devastation, the price Dean was paying to help him. If Dean was truly reverie-born, if his existence was truly rooted in Poesy's power, would he unravel with the rest of her creations when Kane took her down?

"But if you summoned the loom, you could command its power," Dean offered. "You could create something. *We* could create something, and get far, far away from her. You wanted to, once, for me. You don't have to kill her. You don't have to destroy the loom."

Couples bumped into Kane, who had gone still. Lasers combed the mist as the music jumped in his blood. He saw none of it, felt none of it. He was alone in his mind as Dean's words recalibrated his entire world.

On the bridge, Dean had told Kane they used to talk about what they would create with the loom's power. Kane had found this as innocent as any of his usual daydreams. But now the nature of Dean's origin shifted the daydream into a dire focus. Derailed it completely. Dean had revealed their true motive for hunting the loom; not creation for creation's sake, but creation as a means of sanctuary. Against Poesy's remarkable power, Dean's last resort was to use her own plan against her, and Kane had wanted the same. An eternal fantasy to hide away in, forever.

Kane felt the shadow of who he used to be drifting beneath the surface of Dean's words, a faint reflection that was undeniably his. He was, as it turned out, more like Poesy than he wanted to admit. They both were.

"I don't know what to do," Kane said. "I don't even know how to unravel this mess. Only Poesy is that strong."

Dean found Kane's hand, pressing something into it. Kane recognized the bite of cold metal.

"Poesy is strong because of the weapons she wields," Dean said. "But you're strong on your own. I'm scared to imagine what you could do with an arsenal like hers. But please, don't kill her."

Kane looked at what Dean had given him: Poesy's bracelet of charms, torn from her arm by the Dreadmare's jaws. The whistle. The teacup. The white key. The opal skull. The starfish. They were all there, waiting for him to light them up. As though recognizing its new commander, the bracelet slithered around Kane's wrist and clasped itself.

The world grew loud and bright. The windows filled with sunlight as a blue ocean and a city rose toward them. The music was ending. They had arrived at their destination of resEarth. A destination that filled Kane with eerie familiarity. He had seen this same city once, from atop a ruined skyscraper.

Over the loudspeaker, a cheerful voice said, "Welcome to resEarth's capital city of Everest. Please enjoy your stay!"

· THIRTY-SIX ·
THE KEEP

THE ONCE EMPTY CITY OF EVEREST NOW OVERFLOWED
with light and life. Crowds of people in futuristic, Victorian formality surged through the open markets. They lapped against the
esplanade, waving bright handkerchiefs to the cerulean sea where
the ships landed. Like ants, the tourists flowed over themselves as
they climbed the hill at the city's center. Atop it, balancing like an
elaborate cake, was a drastically enhanced version of the château
from Helena Beazley's reverie.

The castle. The lair. The fortress. The keep.

Kane and Dean hid in its shadow.

"Sophia has been busy," Dean said. "I'm amazed she's able to
keep this much in focus, and for so long."

"I'm not," Kane said. "She's Sophia Montgomery. She's good
at everything."

"Still, this can't last. Either these reveries are going to start collapsing, or Sophia will. We better find her, quick."

"And then what?" Kane said.

Dean didn't dare say it, but Kane knew what happened then. The teacup hung from his wrist in charm form, darkly dreaming of crushing this entire world into something just as small and cute.

"If anyone is going to unravel this," Kane told Dean, "it's going to be me."

A glare of light swept over the crowd. People clapped as a bird with wings of crystal crossed the sun. The owl, from Helena's reverie, scanning for something.

Kane pulled Dean into a roofed market of barking vendors. They passed ladies in hoopskirts linking arms with other ladies in crystalline armor. A fleet of scaled children darted past their knees, chasing a small bird the color of fresh grapefruit. The air here was full of fluttering petals and the smell of frying bread. The joy of this place was palpable, but just beneath the surface Kane could still sense the remnant rage of his sister as she felt the final straw of Kane's betrayals. If this reverie held the brightness and warmth of a dancing flame, it was because of the gnarled, black wick of anger smoldering at its core.

Horns sounded, and as though choreographed, the crowds moved in a single direction. Kane and Dean moved with them. Ahead rose the pearly castle adorned in its crenellations and spires. The crowds pushed through a yawning gate, into a corridor, and up another flight of stairs, then out into the harsh brightness of the gardens Kane remembered. They were very much ripped right out of the Helena's reverie, though their original richness had been amplified into outright obscenity. Now, the garden existed as the floor of an immense arena, and flung up from each edge were rows and rows of lacy, wicker benches. Dean and Kane, along with every other character, crammed into the seats, sitting just as the light of the garden darkened. Something was starting.

"Have you found Sophia? What about the Others?" Kane asked.

Dean's eyes shimmered with green as he tried to peer through his powers.

"I can't see anything clearly, yet," he said. "But…wait. Do you feel that?"

A rumbling worked up through the arena, and the crowd cheered. Then, from the garden floor, there was a commotion.

"It's…" Kane squinted.

He saw the pink outfit before he saw anything else, and his relief at seeing Ursula alive was immediately cut off by the blade of her predicament.

Ursula and Elliot stood at the garden's center. Ursula wore her tattered wedding dress, and Elliot his shredded tuxedo. Their costumes from the original reverie. They stood back to back as two creatures circled them: the rose-gold spider and the diamond serpent.

Kane's world narrowed into the shrinking space between his friends and those precious predators.

"They're being forced to fight the hatchlings from Helena's reverie," Kane cried. Dean clamped a hand on his leg, holding him still.

"Wait. Look. Are they winning?" Dean asked.

Kane made himself watch. Even in the absurd outfit, Ursula's was uninhibited power on the battlefield. In the span of a few seconds, she'd somehow climbed atop the spider and detached a bladed leg, tossing it to Elliot. He caught it, maneuvering a sweeping slice as the serpent struck at him. It twisted away, its severed fang rolling into a bed of magnolias.

"Yes."

"Then we leave them."

"What?"

"It's a trap. Something to lure you out. We need to get into the castle and find Sophia. Those two can take care of themselves."

"Ursula maybe, but what about Elliot?"

"Ursula will protect him," Dean said.

At the head of the arena, a gate was rising to admit a new threat: the lapis-lazuli beetle.

Kane only knew he was moving because he felt Dean trailing behind him. Then, right at the railing, Kane was yanked back and pinned to the stairs.

"Kane. You *cannot* intervene."

Kane got a hand free. "We have to help them!"

Dean caught his wrist and smashed it into the steps. "We can't. *You* can't."

The white eyes of onlookers began to watch them. The clashes from the arena drove Kane halfway up before Dean pinned him again. Then, in the depths of Dean's stare, jade magic flickered. The skin where they touched prickled as black armor spread over Dean's skin.

"No!" Kane begged. "Don't send me away! I want to fight. I have to—"

"Your sister needs you, Kane," Dean said as the Dreadmare's helmet closed over his head, and with that Kane was gone.

· THIRTY-SEVEN ·
HOMECOMING

KANE ROCKETED THROUGH THE SEASICK NOTHING
until the blankness ejected him into blinding sunlight. He flailed,
reaching for anything to stop himself, and crashed over a low
bench. When he sat up, he saw he was in the castle now, high in a
tower and overlooking a city of grays, blues, and golds. Far below
he could see the arena, just a gash of green in the castle's creases,
like a smear of moss. Through the glass came garbled cheers, and
he imagined he could see the Dreadmare joining Elliot and Ursula
in battle. Fighting with them.

Without him. Again.

Kane clenched his fists to keep from punching through the
glass. He had been forced to flee. Again.

Your sister needs you, Dean had said. Kane's fists unclenched,
and he saw Dean's reasoning. Intervening would only unspool the

reverie's rage, twisting it around the coming battle and drawing Sophia out. But Dean had ejected Kane from the action—from the plot itself—and now Kane was free to maneuver while the Others held the focus. He could find his sister without being the focal point of her aggression. Maybe, just maybe, that would be enough to wake her up.

"Sophia needs me," he told himself, tightening his backpack in determination. "I am not an egg."

Focused now, he made out the distant sound of viola music and grimly put himself to the task of pursuing it. The deeper he descended through the castle, the more physical the reverie's pressure became, until he could feel this section of Sophia's world plucking curiously at his strange resort clothes.

Kane trudged through the prickling discomfort. He must be getting close. The music was everywhere now, and people dressed in fancy attire drifted through the corridors. They all wore masquerade masks, and Kane was conspicuously out of place. He took his time, knowing it would only take one mistake to give him away, and finally he reached the music's source: the ballroom.

A crowd of girls served as cover as he snuck in behind them. His fingers wrapping around the black whistle. When the time came, would he know what to do? What would happen to Sophia if he just pulled her from here into Poesy's sanctuary? Would she blink away her dreamt identity and be herself, or would her eyes go dull and dark, the black doors severing her connection to this place where her mind now lived?

The group of girls paused to discuss something, and Kane slid from their ranks. The ballroom was immense, its edges thickly clotted in shadows. Good. He snuck behind pillars as wide as redwoods and surveyed the masquerade from afar. Hundreds of guests congregated around something at the room's center, a circular platform floating in the air. A gossamer curtain concealed what lay behind it. The material rippled as the guests plucked at it playfully.

Kane edged around the pillar until he could see the front of the room, where wide steps led up to a throne of twisted iron and filigree. Atop it sat an unlikely figure. Kane's mind lurched, barely able to hold on to the image of his sister. As though smeared there by an artist's brush, Sophia was slumped over the throne in a gown of endless, crimson fabric. It pooled at her feet and slid down the stairs, thick like syrup.

Kane's mind lurched again. There was something among the folds. Gold skin. The dome of a bald head. A badly bent leg. The stump of an arm, now blackened.

Poesy, crushed.

Denial thundered in Kane's heart. Poesy was dying—or was already dead—which felt impossible given the queen's former glory. Sophia stared at the body with hollow resignation, a faint frown pulling her painted features down. Her fingers dug up into her hairline as though holding terrible thoughts away from her unblinking eyes.

Kane was already running toward her when the crowd hushed, everyone turning to watch the curtain rise. Sophia stood, her hand still pressed to her head.

The stage was a nacreous ivory, buffed and polished so that

the light bounced off it and illuminated the great hall in hoops of rainbow. One lone figure adorned the stage: Adeline, bare shouldered and shivering in a pure white tutu. She teetered atop what Kane first mistook for stilts. He stifled a gasp. Satin ribbons crisscrossed Adeline's thighs, weaving down her muscular legs and into ballet pointe shoes at her feet. But they didn't end in blunted tips like they should. Instead, they continued into elegant blades as long as swords, forcing Adeline to pitch backward for balance as their points glanced off the stage's smooth face. The crowd leaned closer, hungry to see her fall.

"You're here for a reason," Sophia called out. "Tell me the truth this time."

"Sophia, please. It's Adeline. You—" Adeline pitched sideways, catching herself barely. "You know me. We're friends, from the conservatory—"

Sophia winced, sending a ripple through the ballroom. It caught Adeline, maneuvering her body into a pirouette atop one blade. She spun slowly, perfectly balanced.

"You can't lie here," Sophia said. "You can't lie. She tried to lie, and it killed her. Just snapped her apart." She pointed at Poesy's crumpled form before turning desperate eyes to Adeline. "Please. I don't want to see you hurt. Please, don't lie to me."

Adeline turned, rigid and barely able to nod.

Her face relaxed as Sophia slumped back, relieved. "You know my brother. You need to tell me where he is. He wants to hurt my kingdom, doesn't he? That's what the witch told me. He wants to bring the Doom home to us."

Worlds overlapped, the reveries intertwined in her mind, but Kane understood. In the mess of converging story lines clawing at her identity, she hadn't lost focus of the betrayals he had inflicted on her. And even here, barely holding on to her sanity, she still understood that Kane had run away into a darkness he couldn't defeat and had brought it back with him to destroy their home.

"Kane can help you," Adeline said through her teeth. "He's not going to hurt you."

"You're lying again." Sophia clutched her head, another ripple boiling over her. Dolls of alabaster rose up from the stage in perfect imitation of Adeline, balanced atop the same lethal blades. Sophia groaned hopelessly as they spun. Like a music box, Adeline danced within their orbiting choreography, the blades flashing by her without striking. Kane understood the trap. If Adeline resisted—if she moved so much as a centimeter out of step—those blades would find her skin.

Etherea crackled in Kane's fist, but he shook it away. He couldn't fight yet. He would only have one chance.

No one noticed as he dashed behind the pillars, up toward the throne. No one heard his footfalls. The only sound was sourceless music, like in the conservatory, and the precise scrapes of knives on porcelain. The sounds of looming cruelty. Kane reached the side of the throne's stairs, doing his best not to look at Poesy's mutilated body. He focused on Sophia, who focused on Adeline with increasingly frantic terror.

"Please," Sophia begged. "Please don't do this to her!"

Kane realized she was begging the reverie to spare Adeline.

He had seen this before, but it had been Helena. The reverie was beyond Sophia's control by now, acting out what it thought best. Punishing those that threatened it.

Adeline's knees shook. Her resolve was strong, but her body was going to fail her. She leapt straight up as the dancers blended the air beneath her. Sophia cowered on her throne, her sobs punctuating the quickening music.

"Stop! Stop it!" she cried.

And then it happened. Finally—terribly—Adeline made a mistake. One tittering scuffle and suddenly one of the blades smattered the crowd with red. Adeline kept dancing, a ribbon of blood flowing down her ribs and into her tutu, dying it pink.

Adeline said nothing, but twirled, dipped, and twirled again, increasingly unsteady. More red bloomed at her shins, then at the back of her neck. The crowd applauded appreciatively.

Kane crept up the stairs, behind the throne. Everyone, including Sophia, was focused on Adeline. When Kane pulled the teacup from the bracelet it grew to its proper size, cradled in his palm. He held it out, shaking, every particle in his body begging him to think of another way to stop his sister. He squeezed his eyes shut, then risked a glance to the stage. There was, in sticky profusion, red everywhere. The image of Adeline burned bright: wobbling, achingly lovely, atop those bladed shoes. She was looking right at Sophia.

No, right at Kane. She was watching him, failing on purpose so that he could have this chance. Seeing that he understood, she smiled, but it was wiped away as she finally collapsed. The room filled with the sounds of stabbing.

Kane's choices narrowed to just one. Adeline had been wrong; they were going to lose Sophia, after all.

He flicked the teacup with his nail.

And everything.

Stopped.

The teacup swallowed Kane, taking him down into the curves of its dizzying power. He felt as though he himself was the vibration radiating from the china, as though he himself was the sonic frequency tearing through the reverie and painting itself across every particle. Kane became not a who, but a where. He was everywhere, his consciousness in every thing.

He could feel it all, from the farthest reaches of the reveries all the way inward: the clutching vacuum of deep space, the tang of the ozone atmosphere, the shimmering streets of Everest. He felt the shattered gems ground into the garden by Ursula's heel, and the leathery musk of the Dreadmare's hide as it wound over her protectively. He felt each glittering mote suspended over the awestruck crowd. He felt the stage and its stickiness. And finally he felt Adeline's slowing heart as it pushed her blood from her punctured body.

He felt every interlocking fiber of Sophia's world—and then he felt Sophia herself as she turned to face him.

She was terrified. Her memories boiled through Kane in complete color, with complete sensation. Her triumphs and her abuses, her guilt and grief. Her love. Her loss. The scorching exposure caused her to scream, and Kane screamed with her, for they had reached a point of synchronicity as their minds intertwined in the teacup's bowl. Together, they felt Sophia's soul open, peeling back so that the teacup might implode her dreams with impartial authority, crushing her down into something cute and quiet that Kane could command.

Sophia felt this, and yet she looked at Kane with relief. With love so simple and inexhaustible that it stalled even the teacup's onslaught.

"Kane…" she mouthed. "You came home."

This was not right.

This was not right.

As though sensing Kane's reluctance, the teacup's power turned upon his own mind, breaking through him with a vengeful annihilation.

Kane let the teacup go. He heard it shatter, and then he heard no more.

· THIRTY-EIGHT ·
SWEET DREAMS

KANE COULDN'T MOVE. OR HE COULD, BUT THERE WAS
no point. The teacup's shards were scattered before him, cast across
the carpet like petals. Kane looked past them, at where Adeline lay
on the frozen stage. Her eyes were dark, her chest barely rising.
Closer, Kane saw Sophia's ankle. She had collapsed on the stairs.

The reverie still stood.

He had failed.

"Harder than it looks, isn't it?"

The crushed form of Poesy sat up on the stairs, a zombie
of the queen's usual glamour. The charm bracelet snapped from
Kane's wrist and returned to her, orbiting the bloody stump of
her arm. The arm, feeding magic from the starfish charm, rebuilt
itself nerve by nerve. Poesy's other damage shed from her, too, like
a dingy husk, and when she stood up she was brand new. She

wore a sleeved dress of thick white fabric embroidered in gold, its scalloped hem brushing her toned thighs. The belt cinching her waist was a braid of thick rope ending in belled tassels that jingled merrily as she swayed. A cape peeled from the air and clasped itself around her shoulders, and a wide-brimmed hat spun down and onto her head. Her makeup shifted on her face like a Rorschach test, finally settling on a look of pure, Hollywood glamour.

Poesy was back, and she was dressed for a finale.

"We are alike in many ways, Mr. Montgomery. But that teacup takes a certain ruthlessness that you have always lacked. You should have known better than to think you had earned its power."

Kane barely heard these words. A profound fatigue had climbed up through the void in him, and it clasped lovingly at the pieces of his broken mind. It whispered for him to follow it down and away, and to leave this evil queen to do as she pleased.

But he could still see Sophia's ankle. She was crawling away from them, toward Adeline.

"I'm not completely critical, of course," Poesy went on. "I am rather impressed you made it back here, all by yourself. But then again, that was my intention. I figured your sister was good enough bait to draw you out, though I never thought you would actually attempt her unraveling. I figured you would be inclined to let go of your old reality if your own sister served as the foundation for my new one. Your cruelty toward her surprises me."

Poesy's words were the articulate edge atop the actual sound of her voice, which was the drone of cicadas.

Kane pushed himself up through pure spite. "You're not human."

Poesy curtsied. "Thank you." Then she bent over the shattered teacup, finding the curved handle and plucking it up. The rest of the pieces swung after it like a marionette, joining together so that it rested, whole and healed, in her palm.

Steam rose from it a second later, and Poesy sipped casually.

Like lightning, Kane directed a snap right into Poesy's face. The shot glanced sideways, but the deflection sent tea all over Poesy's perfect, white dress.

"That was"—she looked over Kane with unmasked disdain, her painted face dripping—"your last act of indiscretion."

Her clawed nails crushed the air, and a psychic grip closed around Kane. He slammed onto the throne, pinned there by Poesy's invisible hand.

"It's time to summon the loom," she said, dabbing her face with her cape.

"I can't," Kane said, for once proud of his ineptitude. "And even if I could, I'd destroy it before I let you use it!"

Poesy paused in her dabbing to give Kane that same dazzling smile she'd served him in the Soft Room of the police station. She was laughing at him this time.

"I suppose it was too much to hope the loss of your memories would change your fundamentals," she said, sobering herself. "I see now you haven't changed at all. Such potential, yet so little interest in the act of creation. A fascinating apathy that I hoped to manipulate into loyalty after Ms. Bishop dubiously erased your memories. That was an accident, you know, but I thought it was good fortune for me. It provided me a chance to work with you directly. Your power, my creativity. But I can't work with an instrument that's developed intention."

"I'll never work with you," Kane sneered. "Not willingly. You tricked me."

She swept a hand over the front of her dress, and the tea stain bleached away.

"Well, it *is* a tricky business, creating a reality." She gestured at the convoluted reveries around them. "But clearly I've figured that one out. What's harder is maintaining it. One can't hope to do it all alone; one must resort to delegation. And so I sought to create gods from worthy mortals. People like your friends. *The Others!*"

This last part Poesy said with mocking jazz hands.

"And that went well, too. But I needed more than a pantheon. I needed power. I needed to summon a loom, a source of infinite energy to produce my creations. And I needed to summon this loom in a form I could control. Manipulate. That's where you come in."

She dipped over Kane. Her skin glittered like cold gemstones beneath her dusted makeup. She made sure he watched as she removed the opal skull from her bracelet. It flared in the ballroom's low light, assembling a wreath of spindles. A crown, made from bone.

Kane's scars burned with recognition. *She has the loom.* She'd had it all along.

"You recognize this, don't you?"

The invisible grip holding him to the throne tightened.

"Would you like to know how to summon the loom?" Poesy twirled the crown innocently. "It's easy. First, you build an environment that can withstand an immense output of power, such as a reverie. Second, you neutralize every competing party with small feuds and love affairs, so they occupy one another completely. Third, you wait for the perfect moment, in which the very fabric of reality has grown threadbare, right before it's about to tear open. That provides you with your opportunity to destroy the old reality and begin the new."

She dragged a nail down Kane's jaw to clutch his chin.

"And finally, you reveal that this loom is not a thing, but a person. It is you, Mr. Montgomery."

Kane stopped struggling.

"You are my vessel," she continued, "my instrument, my own little DIY big bang. And to think! Ms. Abernathy nearly ruined everything by throwing you away from me. It's a good thing I had the sense to let your sister keep me captive, knowing you'd come for her. You see? I'm not just beauty. Beneath it all, I'm everything else, too."

Kane heard the words, but he did not understand them. They slid through his head like little silvery fish. Poesy's breath cooled the tears pushing down his cheeks, the sweat prickling his temples.

"I'll admit I miscalculated before." Poesy swept behind the throne. Kane couldn't look anywhere but forward, at the crowd of stilled onlookers. All of the ballroom's motion strained against Poesy's titanium will. "Teasing open the loom in a human boy always risked that he may one day turn his power against me, and so I created this device." She returned to block Kane's view of Sophia, who had finally reached Adeline. "It's a crown, yes, but it is also a prison. This crown does not give power; it takes it. It accesses a person's deepest potential, focuses it thousandfold, and allows me to use it however I please. I hear it is very painful, losing your lucidity this way. The last time I put it on you, you made quite the mess, swallowing whole the entire watercolor world of Maxine Osman, and Maxine within it. And then Ms. Bishop had the audacity to try and *remove* it! I wasn't counting on that, either. Kudos to her. But this time your friends cannot help you. So long as you wear this crown, you are mine. My Pandora's box. My grail. My muse. Mine, Mr. Montgomery, to imagine into reality anything I demand."

"I won't," Kane said. "I won't do it."

Poesy pouted. "It's a shame you won't create for me willingly. I think you'd quite like what I have in store for this sorry world."

She kissed his cheek, then sunk the crown onto his head. It fit like a charm, the pressure against his scalp tracing his scars perfectly. It felt familiar. It burned.

"Sweet dreams, my loom."

Kane's mind went a blistering white, like the heaven-hot edge of a cloud about to uncover the sun. And then he was elsewhere, cast into the crown's oblivion. His body, his mind—his every-thing—no longer his. Whatever became of him, it belonged to Poesy now.

· ∞ ·

BEYOND

KANE STOOD IN THE RIVER, BENEATH A PALE SKY awash in drifty, pastel clouds. The low sun stretched over their dimpled banks, giving them the distinct impression of watercolors on canvas. The water, too, was stippled with light as it brushed sweetly through the slashes of green reeds where Kane stood. He grazed the water with his fingertips, watching a fleet of silvery fish wreath his ankles.

Dread flashed through him, sudden and strange. He wasn't supposed to be here. His hands snapped to his temples, an urgency rising in him before melting back into the river's slow chill. Something important, something he needed to remember but couldn't, floated just out of reach.

A pine cone struck his head. It bobbed into the water, scattering the tiny fish.

He turned to the shore, spotting the old mill. It was a majestic building, framed in a lovely court of trees that bent to hide its noble face from East Amity's judgment and curiosity.

Kane's sister Sophia watched him with imploring, white eyes.

"Come on, Kane," she called. "It's time to go now."

Kane trudged toward her, then stopped. There was someone else with him in the reeds. An old woman staring at the mill, trapped in a spell of rigorous focus. She held a paintbrush in one hand, a palette in the other, and a small easel jutted up from the water a few inches to her right. From where Kane stood, he could make out the rich reds and browns of the mill on her canvas. They matched the deep color of the old woman's eyes as they slowly zoomed out from the mill and took Kane in with dawning annoyance.

"Oh, you again," said Maxine Osman.

Kane had no idea how she knew him. He had no idea how he knew her. He wanted to unknow her, because even just thinking her name brought back that sourceless, flashing dread, like he was supposed to be doing something else. He rubbed at his temples again. Why did they feel tight?

"You shouldn't be here," said Maxine as she dabbed at her canvas. "This isn't your world. Stay here too long, like me, and you'll get stuck."

"I'm sorry, we were just about to leave."

"And go where?"

Kane shrugged. East Amity glimmered like a tumble of buffed coins in the afternoon sun, all piled up on the opposite shore. The day before him felt infinite.

"See?" Maxine swiped a gnat from her ear. "You don't know,

because even though the crown wants badly for you to belong, you don't belong. I didn't, either. Got dragged in here, I think, but now I'm a lifer."

"What does that mean?"

Maxine peered at the small mill taking shape on her canvas. "It means you ought to go if you're going to go at all."

"Go where?"

"Not where. You need to wake up, dear."

"Kane!" Sophia called from the shore. "Come on! Everyone is waiting."

Kane glanced over his shoulder. She was right. Everyone he knew was waiting in the dim forests of the Cobalt Complex. A cascade of pale, white eyes asking him to step from the water and come on, come along, get going. Kane felt that once he stepped out of the river, he wouldn't come back for a long time. Maybe never.

Kane turned back to Maxine.

"I feel a little lost," he said.

"That's okay. You are. I told you, you don't belong here."

"I'm not sure where I belong, though."

"That's okay, too." Maxine swirled her brush on her palette. "That's the thing about a big imagination. It's hard to belong anywhere when you can always imagine something better. I wouldn't worry about settling just yet, though. You're very young. Lots of time to figure out what you want, and then make it happen. But not if you stay here."

Again the dread flashed in Kane, and for a split second everything about the scene looked wrong. Fake.

A pine cone struck Kane's shoulder. He turned in time to catch the next one.

"My sister—"

"That's not your sister," Maxine said.

"She—"

"She is not your sister," Maxine said firmly.

Subtly, the river began to simmer. Steam bled up into the golden air in shredded arcs.

"See?" said Maxine. "Look, now the scene's all upset. My colors are going to smudge."

Kane dropped the pine cone into the bubbling river. It floated against the current and off into the gathering mist, leaving fragrant sap on his palm. He smelled the deep forest, and it reminded him of Dean.

But who was Dean?

"I think…" Kane reached after the unfathomable depth he had just glimpsed, where the forgotten behemoth of an entire life loomed behind this world's candied veil. "I think I need to go," he said, hardly breathing.

"Yes, I know. I've already told you that." Maxine brushed smudges of steam into her depiction of the mill. This all seemed to be a big inconvenience for her.

"What about you?" Kane asked. "Are you going to go or stay?"

"Oh, I'll be here." Her pursed lips gave way to a hopeful smile. "I'm waiting for someone. I'm sure she'll find her way here, eventually."

Kane turned from Maxine and gave his back to the shore, and

his sister upon it, and all the other figments that had gathered at the reverie's edge to entrap him. He waded out into the gathering mist, off to the waking world beyond.

· THIRTY-NINE ·
UP AND ABOUT

KANE AWOKE IN A KISS. HE GASPED, BREATHING THE air right out of the other mouth as though inhaling back his life.

"There you are," said Dean. His Dreadmare armor branched and bristled on his hips and shoulders, but his arms were as gentle around Kane as they'd been on the dance floor of the *Starship Giulietta*. One of his eyes flickered sea foam.

"You woke me up with a kiss?"

"No, *you* kissed *me* while I was trying to pull the crown off your head. It was very surprising."

"Where is the crown now?"

"You're still wearing it. It's keeping us afloat."

Kane realized they were, in fact, floating. He prodded the snug grip of the crown, and his fingers brushed through the incandescent light surging from his skin. Etherea soaked the air in neon twilight and rendered the two boys weightless. Light curled around them, protecting them, blurring out the chaos of the world collapsing below. Faintly, Kane could sense it all. Past their haven, Everest was a blitz of every reverie mashing together in hurricane-force pandemonium. Six worlds brawling for dominance as they each came undone, tangling tighter and tighter in their wild unmaking.

Kane tasted the violence and withdrew back into the light. He remembered the moments before Poesy forced the crown onto him now.

"Where is she?" he asked, panicking.

"Far below. Ursula and Elliot are distracting her, for now. I was the only one who could reach you."

"I'm the loom." Kane whispered it like the confession it was. "It's all my fault. The reveries. Poesy targeting my sister so she could use me. I figured it out once, and that's why I told Adeline to destroy me. Because I am the loom."

Dean considered this, careful and loving. He exhaled, and it played in the tight hollow between them.

"And what will you do this time?"

Kane's vision blurred with tears. "I don't know. I ruined everything by coming back here. It all went according to Poesy's plan."

Dean ducked down to catch Kane's eye. Kane still had on his backpack, and Dean curled his fingers under the straps so he could give him a little shake.

"Not all of it."

"What?"

Dean traced infinity symbols through Kane's shirt, onto his

skin. "Poesy gave you a crown that focuses your power, a plan that only works if you're under her control. But you're awake now. You're still lucid."

"But Poesy said I wouldn't wake up."

Dean shrugged. "It doesn't matter what Poesy says. This isn't her reverie. At least not yet. A part of this world still belongs to your sister, and I'm sure in no way does Sophia's reverie allow the twist of your loss."

Kane's heart felt cramped yet powerful, as though a second heart beat within it. Out there, among the chaos, he could hear a solemn ringing. A hope, as clear as bells and as bright as lightning. His sister's grace and strength. She was still fused to the fibers of this collapsing world, still alive and defending him. Even after he'd tried to hurt her.

Kane gave himself fully to his tears, but then remembered one by one the strengths of the people who had fought for him. He couldn't return their sacrifices with only tears. He had to show them he had always been worth it.

"Where is Sophia?" he asked Dean.

"Below, somewhere. She and Poesy are vying for control of the reveries. Your sister must be very strong to have lasted this long."

"And Adeline?"

"With Poesy. We need to help her and the Others. Adeline is…fading."

Kane's breath caught. The last time he'd seen Adeline, her body was broken. How long could a person last like that?

"Listen," Dean said, focusing Kane. "If you have the chance to

kill Poesy, you have to take it. I have lived my lives in worlds built
by the pain and misery of other people. Poesy has a dream, and
even if it is a lovely one, it is only hers. You can't let her make it
come true for everyone. You have to stop her."

"But what about—"

"You have to stop her."

Dean held Kane in his stare. Dean, the mystery personified,
the paradox made man. Kane could see clearly how Dean might
have been his whole world once upon a time. He thought maybe
if they survived this, they could build something better after all.
Kane hugged him tight. There was the scent of ash and sweat, and
there beneath his armor, his cologne. Pine, or something close.
Kane kissed him—their lips brushing only long enough for Kane
to feel his breath pulled up from his lungs—and then it was time
to make his choice.

Evade? Or interfere?

"I have an idea."

Kane told Dean, and between the two of them, his idea formed
into a plan. Dean gave him a stoic salute, then teleported away.

Alone in his nebula, Kane had space to breathe. He observed
the unraveling world. Planets exploding and stars falling. Horizons
fracturing and oceans boiling. Earth breaking and air rending. The
city of Everest, rocked by its slow demolition, peeling apart in
drowsy chunks as big as mountains.

Kane was small within the chaos. A simple pinprick of glittering defiance, all the way at the top of a busy, senseless oblivion. It
was scary as hell, but there wasn't any room left in him for fear. All

his worst nightmares had come true, one after another, yet here was he was—exhausted and scared, yes—but alive. Hopeful. He had survived, and he would keep surviving.

Kane let his powers unfold, stretching out like great wings, and the full discord of the reveries bombarded him. It was easy to locate Poesy; the reveries were imploding toward her, like some great wound around which flesh bubbled and bone sagged.

Also, she was cackling. Because of course she was cackling.

Breathing deep, Kane let himself fall, etherea streaming after him. He found Poesy upon the pale stage, now strewn with shattered pillars, strutting through the aftermath of battle. Elliot and Ursula were still standing, but barely. Adeline, gray dust plastering her bloodied tutu, lay collapsed over Sophia in her ragged red dress. Poesy sipped from her teacup, savoring the implosion of Sophia's world.

Kane snapped his fingers, sending ethereal blazes into Poesy's billowing cape. The teacup spun from her grip and shattered on a pillar, and she turned to him with the first authentic fear he had ever seen on her beautiful face. Then it was gone, replaced by rage. She reached for her charms without a word.

Seeing him, Ursula let out a weak cheer before falling into Elliot.

"Go!" Kane called to them as readied another attack. The power of the crown was immense, so hard to control that Kane knew with certainty that even a stray thought could destroy, transform, or create. This was the power he needed to defeat Poesy, but he needed his friends as far away as possible. "Run!" he screamed, the flares from his hands amplified to glaring beams of rainbow that cut the air itself.

Poesy twirled between them like a darting fish, her cape undulating behind her. Her charms flashed open into fragments of reveries that crashed over Kane in tidal waves of texture, sound, and sight. Kane was overtaken by a misty forest, its humidity clingy in his throat, its babbling streams tickling under his ears. Kane tore it apart with a clap of his hands and entered another reverie: a colonial battlefield mobbed with zombies. Rotting teeth sunk into his shoulder, his wrist, but the power of the crown told him this world was immaterial and his to destroy. He let his glow burn bright, eating through the hordes of zombies, and punching him into the next reverie. And the one after that. And after that. Kane flashed through them, as brief as an angel falling through the film of every new world, until finally he surfaced back into the collapsing void.

Poesy was waiting to face Kane upon the stage. She wrenched a glowing palm down, dropping a deluge of acid rain out of the cracked sky. Kane let his own consciousness rise to meet the rain, unfolding each drop into a cloud of butterflies.

"Your precious *Others* have fled, and your tricks are catastrophically clichéd." Poesy sneered, and the butterflies turned to scorpions. Kane blinked and the scorpions burst into confetti.

"Look at us!" Poesy's laugh rang like a siren as she slit reality into a cloud of snakes. They ribboned toward Kane, but he turned them into arrows and fired them back. "Look at our power! We do not belong to this world. We belong to something better.

Something with integrity that only *we* can create for ourselves! That has always been our way. That is our *only* fate!" The arrows splintered into lightning, which Poesy gathered along her painted nails and whipped at Kane. He returned it with a rainbow blast, and the two were locked into a dual for life and death, for the fate of not only Kane's world, but every world hiding in every person. For the fantastic realities people lovingly created for themselves, in danger of being subjugated by the whims of a madwoman and her teacup.

"Why do you fight for a world that does not fight for you?" Poesy spoke through the maelstrom, right into Kane's mind. "Why do you fight to save a reality that fails so many, so often?"

Their dual collapsed into a sucking silence. Lightning and etherea threaded the vacuum between them as they landed back on the stage.

"I'm not fighting to save reality," Kane said. "I'm learning to change it."

"The loom is an instrument," Poesy said. "It cannot *learn*. Your righteousness is pretty poetry and nothing more. It's time to end this."

"That's right," Kane sneered. "Dean, now!"

The Dreadmare formed around Poesy, its bladed body shearing together like scissors and slicing her white cape into strips. Kane felt the thrill of success as the first spray of blood met the wind, but then the grinding halted. There was a great ripping noise, and suddenly Poesy was back. She had Dean in a headlock with one arm while the other hand clutched the Dreadmare's flailing body. She had torn the armor right off him.

"Kane," Dean whimpered through clamped teeth. Poesy squeezed, and his jaw cracked.

Kane's powers failed. Sick gravity brought him to his knees, and his backpack slid from his shoulders. He fought for the exquisite control he'd had a second ago, but it was gone.

"You know, I was wrong about this, too." Poesy smiled wickedly in Dean's ear. "I figured conscripting the brooding love interest assured me unregulated access to the loom's every desire, but you were never the agent I needed. Ms. Bishop, however, does possess the rigor I require. Would you like to live, my dear?"

Poesy flicked her hand, and like a flock of sparrows, golden magic fluttered apart to reveal a huddle group sneaking into the battle. Elliot at the lead, stumbling as Poesy easily dispersed his illusion, with Ursula at his side. Behind them, Adeline slouched with Sophia, and then suddenly Adeline was alone as another blast from Poesy's hand threw everyone else away, into the whirling unraveling.

"No!" Kane cried.

Adeline swayed as Poesy pulsed power into her. Like leaves rustled up from the ground, her wounds peeled from her body. She choked and twitched, resisting the warm glow that spread beneath the deep color of his skin, reviving her. She had freed herself of those awful pointe shoes and cradled one blade in her arms. She looked alive and powerful; she still looked ready to fall apart.

"Ms. Adeline Bishop," Poesy purred. "The smartest. The most cunning. I was careful when I curated my pantheon to only invest power in those wronged by this reality. But even so, all the others refuse to see this reality for what it is: a failure. But you can. You know. There is a position of power for someone of your caliber in the reality I envision. At my side, you would be everything."

"Why would I help you?" Adeline asked, but her voice was a faint and blue echo of her usual searing wit.

"Sophia Montgomery will die if you don't. But I can save her, like I've saved you. I can save your friends, too. I can salvage any soul you value, but only if you purge every last thought from Mr. Montgomery's head. Our world will never be safe so long as he possesses the will to undo it."

Adeline wouldn't look at Kane at first. When she did, it was with open wonder. She was thinking about this. He wanted to reach out to her, but he felt like his hand would pass through her like a ghost. They existed in two different planes. More than distance separated them now.

Poesy's voice swelled upon cicada song. "Every life you value for a life Mr. Montgomery has thrown away twice. Finish what you started. Wipe every memory from his head."

"Do it," Kane said.

Adeline's wonder turned to shock, then disgust. "What?"

"Do it, Adeline. Take my memories," Kane repeated, looking at Sophia. At everything he was fighting for.

"I can't."

"You have to," Kane said. Then, quieter: "Believe in me one last time."

By the thrust of her jaw, Adeline understood. She wobbled toward Kane, and her eyes flared their storm-cloud gray as they peeled Kane's mind open. There was no pain to Adeline's telepathy, just the whistle of memories as they faded beneath her corrosive gaze. His fingers curled around his backpack strap. It was impossible to remember what he'd just been doing, but if he kept going, kept trying, maybe there was a chance he could...

Adeline's eyes darkened, her face bright with a smile. She had found the memory Kane needed her to find. She adjusted her grip on her blade and in one, elegant dash, she crossed the stage and drove it deep into Kane's chest.

Kane got the red journal up a moment before. He had no idea if his plan would work, but he never felt Adeline's blade touch his skin. It had instead stabbed into the creases of the journal's magic pages with only a brief, jittering resistance, its lethal tip plunging through the journal's portal and far, far away from Kane's heart.

"Did it work?" Adeline whispered.

They turned to Poesy just as she began to scream. She threw Dean away from her, revealing a shock of red spreading open on her stomach. The other red journal, which Dean had been holding open behind his back, had directed Adeline's ivory blade away from Kane and right through Poesy's glittering guts. Poesy pitched and twisted, gripping her new death with clicking, breaking nails, and Adeline gave the blade one final shove.

Kane's plan had worked. Elliot would be so proud.

Poesy reached for her bracelet and the charms that could heal her, discovering too late that Dean had snatched it from her wrist while she held him.

"Impossible," Poesy screamed.

"Improbable," Kane said, and before Poesy could summon back her teacup, Kane clapped his hands. The bright tension of his full focus exploded against Poesy's ringing domination, atomizing the teacup's shattered pieces and slicing through the reverie's curdled atmosphere. The Cobalt Complex shimmered through the gaps, the edges between the two words glowing neon as they ripped over one another. Reality itself was going to be torn apart if Kane could not overcome her.

"I am your worst nightmare," Poesy promised.

"Not anymore."

The sickening, dizzying power of Poesy's control faltered, and Kane knew what to do. He curved his power around where Poesy stooped, imprisoning her bristling magic. Then he turned his mind toward the rest of the reveries. He knew that Poesy's power came from manipulation, but without the material of others there was nothing for her to bend, to break, or to borrow. This was her end.

Kane drove his consciousness up and out, into a surreal maelstrom like so many silver needles slipping through thickly knitted knots. First he found his sister and his friends, battered but alive in a pocket of Ursula's magic. Reassured, he focused on the rest. The crown he wore opened a dimension of omniscience within him that felt, for just a few seconds, fathomless. Limitless. He felt—no, *knew*—how simple it would be to destroy these worlds entirely. Instead, he set himself to the impossible task of feeling for their edges. Their breaks and seams. Every story had a beginning and an end. Every sky had a horizon. Every tale had its twists. Kane combed himself through it all without flinching. He felt first resistance, then the utter bliss of separation, and finally the relief of their lovely unraveling.

But one knot remained.

"You..." said Poesy—a buzzing in the back of Kane's mind as he began to unravel her—"and I are...not so different, you know."

"I know," Kane said.

The unraveling must have hurt Poesy greatly. The sound she emitted was unlike anything Kane had ever known. Ancient and inhuman and so much more than simple sound. It was ferocity made sonic.

Then Poesy was gone, and there was nothing left but the polyphonic roar of the reveries as they spooled, one by one, into Kane's open palm.

FORTY

RESOLVE

KANE COULD HAVE RETURNED THE REVERIES DIRECTLY to the Cobalt Complex, but there was one more thing to do before he took the crown off for good. As gently as his bruised mind could manage, he set himself down on the manicured grass of the garden, near where Dean lay huddled.

First, he needed to apologize. Gently, he knelt by the boy and did what Dean had once. He traced an infinity symbol into the boy's back, whispering, "Dean. You can open your eyes now. I'm sorry if I scared you."

Dean blinked at Kane, and at the strange recurrence of the gardens from Helena Beazley's reverie Kane had created around them. He seemed unsure of his own weight as he stood, like he expected to just float away.

"I'm...not gone?"

Kane squeezed his hand for reassurance. "Doesn't look like it."

"But you unraveled Poesy."

"You never belonged to her, Dean. You're as real as anyone. Trust me. For once, I know stuff." Kane tapped the crown and tried out a smirk. Dean gave a sly grin back.

"Kane?"

Adeline cut through the milling guests, the grime of one reverie drifting away as her costume from the Beazley Affair wrapped around her. Trailing after was Sophia, her red dress exchanged for her golden ensemble.

"It worked!" Adeline said, wrapping around Kane. "I can't believe you let me read your memory like that! I can't believe that worked!"

He hugged her back, as hard as he could.

Sophia pushed toward Kane. Her eyes were sharp. She was lucid now. And of course she had questions. Kane waved them off, just happy to see his sister, but she wouldn't let him hug her for long before asking: "Just tell me what's real. Like, did you *just* murder a magical drag queen sorceress using two dream journals and a sharpened ballet slipper?"

Kane looked at Adeline, then Dean. They both shrugged. They were going to need a lot of time to debrief all this.

Kane gave his sister a playful punch to the shoulder. "Just gay enough to work, right?"

Sophia's serious interrogation cracked into a familiar grin, the old refrain bringing relief to her confusion. Adeline let out a wry groan, and Dean looked very embarrassed about it all.

"But why are we back here, Kane? You have all this power, so why are we in Helena's reverie?" Adeline asked.

"Because they deserve a second chance."

In the fresh, white sunlight, Elliot and Ursula were easy to find. They rushed through the crowd in a mixture of celebration and confusion. Ursula reached Kane first, embracing him over the wide hoop of her grand pink dress. Elliot, because he was Elliot, immediately started scheming about how they would outsmart the reverie.

"I saw Helena. She's here. But she's not young anymore. She's just wandering around in her normal clothes."

"Relax, Elliot. It's okay. I've got this," Kane said. He closed his eyes and let his mind hover over the depths of the crown, holding himself away from its evil entrapment. Careful as he could, he coaxed out Maxine Osman.

Like a sun rising right before them, her reverie came forth as Kane ushered her from the crown's prison. The lush garden and the gazebo turned vivid in her watercolors, accepting the shift without resistance. If anything, the two reveries merged in a way that made them impossible to imagine separated.

"We're righting a wrong," Kane said. He moved them back as the crowd gathered around Maxine, murmuring about her strange clothes and the watercolor brushes she still held. Then the crowd parted, and there was Helena, in the gazebo. She wore her little yellow sweater and her orthopedic sneakers. She blinked at the bright colors, as though her vision had just been restored to her after a long time in darkness.

"Max?" Helena whispered.

Maxine clutched her brushes. Her aloof confidence from Kane's brief conversation in the river was gone. She was fully present now, shaking as she looked at the person she had been waiting for.

The painter and the heiress joined together in a kiss that spared nothing on shame, for they were in their own world now, a haven of their own making, guarded against twists by Kane's own exertion. He pushed as much perfection into the reveries as he could muster. He filled the honeyed air with weightless petals. He filled their fists with the thin necks of champagne flutes. He raised his arm and every arm raised with him, toasting Helena and Maxine as they stood in the gazebo, talking so softly that their words were lost behind swelling, joyous music.

Dean took Kane's free hand and kissed his temple, where the crown still gripped.

"Why this? Why here?" he asked.

"It's a resolution," Kane told him. "After everything we put these two through, they deserve a happily ever after."

Per usual, Dean's eyes were on the deep distance. They were back to their sea-foam green.

"But this is a reverie. It can't last forever."

"It doesn't have to. These two have real love, not imagined love. I think they're going to be just fine after all this goes away."

Helena and Maxine hugged, and the guests broke into riotous applause. The Others cheered, too, toasting the brides as they waded down the steps and into the crowd's loving embrace to receive all the blessings the world had to offer.

The applause grew louder, tripling as Kane brought the scene to a close. He found there was little for him to do to unravel this. Resolved, Helena's and Maxine's reveries simply dispersed. There was no violence in this collapse. Just relief, and a touch of homesickness as the applause echoed across the stoic walls of the Cobalt Complex re-forming around them. Everything—the garden, the great hall, the mishmash of reveries—was gone now, evaporating against the sun rising over the river. Morning, actual morning, had come to East Amity, and it found a small group of sleep-deprived teenagers standing near a burnt-out mill, clapping and cheering as two old ladies looked around in shy bafflement.

A swarm of iridescent knots danced through Kane's fingers— the reveries he'd unraveled. He urged Sophia's back toward her and, reaching her nose, it flickered into her. He did the same with Maxine and Helena, who held hands in their daze. Then Kane took off the crown, wincing as old scars reopened, and handed it to Dean. The ground glittered with the remaining charms. Ursula picked them up carefully, and Dean handed Kane the broken remnants of Poesy's bracelet, the whistle still as cold as ever. Adeline was the one to find Poesy herself.

"You turned her into a cricket?" she asked, showing Kane the small metal bug. The pearlescent wings twitched, like it might take off.

Elliot cleared his throat. "A cicada, I believe?"

"He's right," Kane said before anyone started with the eye rolling. He didn't dare touch the bug, in case it pulled upon the magic hiding in his skin. Instead, he closed Adeline's hands over it.

"Keep her safe, okay?"

Adeline had no love for Poesy, but she trusted Kane. She nodded.

Elliot had his phone out. His eyebrows jumped. "It's the same day as when we left. It's only just past seven o'clock. We can still make it before first bell."

Everyone groaned. There was no way they were going to school, not when Maxine and Helena were going to need help getting their lives back together. Not when Sophia would snap out of her daze any second and begin asking a million questions. They needed to be present for all of that. School was simply not a reality they could belong to right now.

Elliot grumbled. Ursula strode up to Dean, pulling him and Kane into a rough huddle.

"So. Dean," she grinned, looking between them. "You like diner food? 'Cuz we've got a little tradition, and I'm thinking you're a part of it now."

EPILOGUE

HALLOWEEN FOUND KANE SEATED IN URSULA'S kitchen, watching Elliot stare down a set of handwritten instructions splattered in grease.

"Is it asking me to sift four cups of flour? Or is it asking for four cups of sifted flour?"

"What's it say?" Kane asked.

Elliot put his hands on his hips. Kane thought he looked very dashing in an apron, and he had said so multiple times. He had also suggested Elliot remove his shirt but there was only so much teasing Elliot would endure before he tricked you into thinking you were covered in leaches.

"It says four cups of flour, sifted."

Kane smiled and shrugged. Elliot's phone rang on the table, and Kane held it to his ear so he didn't get it covered in flour.

"Hey, Urs."

He listened, then glanced at the instructions. "It doesn't say." He listened again. "I don't know, why? Is there a difference between ground and minced ginger?"

This must have been an outrageous thing to ask, because Ursula didn't even answer before hanging up. Elliot looked even more confused, and Kane hoped he would start complaining again. Watching Elliot's ceaseless attempts to impress Ursula was Kane's most recent and favorite hobby.

Elliot rolled his shoulders and cracked his neck. "I will sift the flour, just in case."

"Attaboy," Kane said.

The next minute was filled with screams as Ursula's two little brothers rumbled into the kitchen in full costume. Adeline and Sophia trailed behind them.

"*Bang bang!*"

"*Vroom vrooom!*"

Adeline made slow grabs at them and they ducked her, overcome with joy at the game of tag. "Run from the cootie queen!" Sophia bellowed. "Her cooties will eat right through your dreams! You'll never sleep again!"

"Too soon," grumbled Elliot.

One of the boys threw himself at Sophia, his hands thrust out bravely.

"You can't!" he yelled. "My armor is magic! Kane said so!"

He was wearing a firefighter suit. They both were. They wanted to be their dad for Halloween.

Adeline lunged for them but sprang back, clutching her hand. "Ghastly little trolls!" she wailed. The boys screamed and ran from the room. The girls ran after them.

"I thought Sophia was helping them with their costumes?" Elliot said.

Kane laughed. "I'd say she's doing a splendid job."

The kitchen was thrown into shades of jade as Ursula and Dean appeared in the middle of it, toting paper shopping bags.

"Crisis averted," Ursula said. She produced several canisters of bright Halloween decorations from one bag.

"We had to go to three separate stores," Dean said wearily. "I said we should just go one town over, to the craft store, but Ursula said that would be extravagant."

She ignored him. "Are Joey and Mason dressed? It's almost time to get going."

"Adeline and Sophia got them into their costumes but now they're chasing them around the house threatening to give them cooties that will eat their dreams," Elliot said.

Ursula grimaced. "Too soon." Then she set her attention on the small sugary catastrophe Elliot had produced in her absence. He rushed in front of her. "Do you sift the flour before measuring it, or do you measure it after it's sifted?"

A long pause followed Elliot's question. Finally, Ursula said, "That's the same thing."

They began to discuss. Kane watched, all smiles. They had all been preoccupied with Kane's drama for so long, and rightly so, but in the time since they'd defeated Poesy there was room and peace enough for new things to grow. Ursula and Elliot now did homework together after practice. They went on runs together before school. They always invited Kane, and he always said no. He watched them from afar, preferring to observe their growing affection from a safe distance. It was the weirdest, best thing.

Adeline and Sophia had been spending time together, too. Last Kane heard, they were working on a book together about a wealthy girl meeting a scrappy rebel. Kane heard them talking late into the night.

That was a weird, best thing, too, and Kane kept out of it. These stories surrounded him but were not his to explore. You didn't have to feed every single bird, as Ursula said. Sometimes it was better to trust people to figure it out for themselves and to be there just in case they didn't. That was their newest approach to unraveling the reveries, and so far it was working well.

Dean took a seat across from Kane. They held hands under the table, even though nothing about them was a secret anymore, and they didn't say a word. Since they had escaped the multireverie, their interactions had been full of these silent, pensive moments. Dean seemed to thrive in them, and Kane did enjoy the way Dean flexed beneath the self-control. The quiet between them never felt empty, though. To Kane, it always felt full of a music only they could hear, and these small gestures were his favorite dance. It was the most comfortable Kane had ever been with another person, and sometimes he had to remind himself to say so. Like right now.

"I'm glad you're here," Kane said. "Like, really glad."

Dean grinned.

"I didn't think I'd make it back. Ursula is unstoppable," he said. "I've never met someone with such a knowledge of sweets. Did you know they make sugar that is all big? It's called 'coarse sugar' and for some reason it's more expensive."

Ursula interjected, "It's for decorating. Finer crystals don't look as good on drizzled caramel."

Elliot's face brightened into a stupid smile. "We're making caramel?"

"No, we are not making caramel." Ursula was all business in her kitchen. "*I* am making caramel. Do you know how easy it is to burn sugar? Here, grab me that candy thermometer. I'll show you."

They got back to work.

"See?" Dean whispered. "It's odd."

"Oh, be nice," Kane said. "This is odd? Of all things?"

This made Dean smile his rare, sheepish smile, an expression Kane went through great efforts to uncover. Dean's voice grew more serious. "Speaking of which, where is your crown?"

"Your house," Kane said. "On the bookshelf."

Dean's irises glowed a translucent emerald as he followed each step.

"Where?"

"On top."

"It's not there."

"Check the middle shelf. Near *The Witches*."

Dean shook his head, scanning. They kept the crown just in case they needed it again, but so far the reveries had been much easier with Dean helping them out. Still, sometimes Kane sensed something rippling the veil of reality outside the reveries. Things that spoke in chattering drone, like Poesy. Her sisters, maybe. Whoever or whatever they were, if they did come to town, Kane was ready.

After a pause, Dean nodded. "Found it. Ms. Daisy is cuddling with it again in her bed."

Kane smiled. "Let her."

Outside, the neighborhood swarmed with trick-or-treaters celebrating beneath October's final sunset. Two miniature firefighters scampered down the sidewalk. The Others followed, stepping to the side as parades of children ambled past in unwieldy costumes. There were dragons and fairies and princesses and robots. There were ninjas and archers and martial artists. There was the requisite gaggle of vampires, cats, and superheroes, but some children had opted for more cryptic costuming. One such child was wrapped in a cardboard cylinder painted like a can of soup, with nothing but a small window cut out for eyeholes.

"I love your costume!" Adeline said to this particular child as they waddled by. "What are you supposed to be?"

"A can of soup."

Adeline frowned. The can waddled off, unbothered.

Kane and Ursula hung back a bit, walking with her little brother Mason, who couldn't receive a single piece of candy without trying to eat it. Ursula's stepmom had made Ursula promise she'd budget their sugar intake but, so far, this just meant Ursula was eating half the candy herself. Kane was helping, too.

"Maxine and Helena seem to be adjusting okay to being alive

and like…back in reality, all things considered," she was saying. "Maxine is working on a new series: Mythical creatures made out of gems. She and Helena keep asking Adeline to let them remember a little bit more. She's mostly just been telling them stories. It's so cute, the way they listen. They say they want to go back, but I told them they had to convince you."

"I don't think there's much I can do. Those reveries resolved. There's not much left."

"What about the charms in Poesy's sanctuary? Do you think all those reveries are safe there?"

Kane didn't know. "I hope so. We have the only key."

"That we know of," Ursula added.

"Wow, you're already sounding like Elliot," Kane teased.

Ursula shoved him playfully. He threw a piece of candy at her, but it struck a small barrier and fell away.

"Cheater!"

Ursula laughed and strode ahead with her little brother, reaching into his bag for something else.

Kane watched her go. He watched Adeline and Dean chatting while Sophia and Elliot read the ingredients of a candy bar. He felt that strange, new feeling he was only just learning to embrace: contentment. It was immediately accompanied by melancholy, as Kane's happiness often was. Moments like this were fleeting; they came together in graceful concert, like schools of silvery fish, and drifted apart just as quick. He always had the urge to capture them, to keep them replaying over and over—his own little reverie. His dream, arrested. But sealed off things that steep too long in the human mind are doomed to grow bitter. If the reveries had taught Kane anything, it was the worth of escaping outward, and how to unstitch the seam where fantasies met the wider world. For Kane, it was all about creating something new, something better.

Poesy was right. They were alike in their goal. Still, they were separated by their methods. And of course, taste. Poesy wanted a clean canvas for her masterpiece. Kane was content to work with what he had.

Increasingly, he realized he had a lot to work with already.

A hard candy struck Kane's shoulder.

"Hey, Montgomery, get your head out of the clouds," called Ursula. "Dad called to say the cookies are done. By the time we get back they'll be cool enough to decorate."

Kane blinked away the daydream and ran to catch up with his friends.

ACKNOWLEDGMENTS

The fact of this book's publication, in all its eccentric indulgence and conspicuous queerness, will never *not* amaze me. And I have many people to thank. If my gratitude could create a world, we could all live within the loop of my infinite appreciation forever. But, you see, reveries are something I made up, so some acknowledgments will have to do.

First, I need to thank the LGBTQIAP+ community, both past and present, the countless queer people who boldly exist any way they can, who *had* to exist in order for someone like me to write a book like this. I am hyperaware that I write at the edge of a legacy created by people with far less than me, who had so much more to lose, and who fought anyway. I am incredibly proud and thankful to be part of this community. And it's no mistake that Kane's expression of salvation takes the form of a drag queen.

Many might see Poesy as just a showy villain, but I see her as Kane does: power personified. I can't thank the queens of my life enough for creating a world to which I could belong, being the wildly flamboyant child that I was (and still am). What I do, I do for us.

And, of course, my family, who I adore, and who have always surrounded me with grace, love, and humor. Dad, your sense of eccentricity and exploration (and the compulsion to bring back small souvenirs from each place) runs deep in this book. Mom and Larry, your choice to let me confront drag queens in the streets of Provincetown has had lasting ramifications. Blase, David, Julia, Shoko, and Colin, thanks for putting up with all my antics. I love you all!

To my agent, Veronica Park, for her endless humor, savviness, and smarts. I can't imagine any of this without you at the start of it. And to Beth Phelan and the whole #DVpit crew. Best origin story ever.

To Annie Berger, my dauntless and amazing editor, and to the entire Sourcebooks Fire team, including Sarah Kasman, Cassie Gutman, Todd Stocke, Beth Oleniczak, and Heather Moore. And, of course, a special thank-you to Nicole Hower, who designed a cover so magnificent that I cannot wait to have it embroidered upon a floor-length cape, and to the super-talented cover artist, Leo Nickolls, and to Danielle McNaughton, who made the inside of this book feel like home. And thank you to my publisher, Dominique Raccah. Working with the entire Sourcebooks Fire team has been, pun fully intended, a dream come true.

I have been lucky enough to make some fantastic friends in the book world, too. To my darling cherubs: Phil Stamper, Claribel

Ortega, Kosoko Jackson, Shannon Doleski, Adam Sass, Caleb Roehrig, Kevin Savoie, Zoraida Córdova, Jackson MacKenzie, Mark O'Brien, Gabe Jae, and so many others. THANK YOU for all the support, advice, and well-earned shade. And to Brandon Taylor, who snapped me out of some bad doubt. I owe you.

And, of course, to my dear friends; Candice Montgomery, who is also an insightful sensitivity reader; and Tehlor Kay Mejia, whose editing services shaped *Reverie* early on. You were both integral in helping me tell the story I wanted to tell. TJ Ohler and Taylor Brooke, your notes were invaluable, too. Amy Rose Capetta, Cori McCarthy, and Queer Pete (who is not a person, but a group of people) and the Writing Barn fam, you lifted me up when I needed it most.

Kat Enright, Rachel Stark, and Michael Strother, your early support of *Reverie* made a world of difference. Sarah Enni, your work on First Draft gave me focus, drive, inspiration, and laughs that totally changed how I wrote (for the better).

And to my glorious, absurd, usually screaming family of friends. It's a wonder this book ever got written with people as hilarious and captivating as you in my life. In no particular order whatsoever, I want to thank: Ryan and Ryan, Jess, Daniel, Tamani, Shams, Leah, Justine, Aurora, David, Tom, Jossica, Will, Fernando, Jess + Cody, Ben, Pam, Emily, Rachel, and, of course, Sal.

Lastly, I want to express gratitude to my readers and the people who find a home in this story. To all the other *Others* out there, I hope you create the world you need, or even the one you want. So chase your dreams, but beware the dreams that chase you back.

ABOUT
THE AUTHOR

Ryan La Sala grew up in Connecticut, but only physically. Mentally, he spent most of his childhood in the worlds of *Sailor Moon* and *Xena: Warrior Princess*, which perhaps explains all the twirling. He studied anthropology and neuroscience at Northeastern University before becoming a project manager specializing in digital tools. He technically lives in New York City, but has actually transcended material reality and only takes up a human shell for special occasions, like brunch, and to watch anime (which is banned on the astral plane). *Reverie* is Ryan's debut novel. You can find him on Twitter @Ryality or visit him at ryanlasala.com.

FIREreads

#getbooklit

Your hub for the hottest young adult books!

Visit us online and sign up for our
newsletter at FIREreads.com

 @sourcebooksfire

 sourcebooksfire

firereads.tumblr.com